Praise for *New York Times* bestselling author
KATHRYN LYNN DAVIS

Somewhere Lies the Moon

"Beautifully written . . . poetic."
—*Under the Covers Romance Reviews*

"Wise and wonderful . . . *Somewhere Lies the Moon* will touch you in many ways."
—*Romantic Times*

All We Hold Dear

"*All We Hold Dear* is beautiful, passionate and wild like the rugged Scottish Highlands."
—*Rendezvous*

Sing to Me of Dreams

"A graceful, lushly romantic portrait of a woman's odyssey.
—*Publishers Weekly*

Too Deep for Tears

"Stunning . . . It will remind you of *The Far Pavilions* or *The Thorn Birds* . . . Davis's story is as richly textured as a fine old tapestry . . . The emotions and conflicts are ageless."
—*Chicago Tribune*

"Get out your handkerchiefs . . ."
—*Dallas News*

"Captivating . . . a major novel."
—*San Bernardino Sun*

Books by Kathryn Lynn Davis

AT THE WIND'S EDGE

ENDLESS SKY
(coming soon)

Published by Zebra Books

Kathryn Lynn Davis

At the Wind's Edge

ZEBRA BOOKS
Kensington Publishing Corp.
http://www.zebrabooks.com

Many of the characters in this book are historical figures and many of the events actually occurred; however, other characters and incidents are the creation of the author and have no basis in historical fact.

ZEBRA BOOKS are published by

Kensington Publishing Corp.
850 Third Avenue
New York, NY 10022

Copyright © 1983 by Medora Enterprises and Kathryn Davis

All rights reserved. No part of this book may be reproduced in any form or by any means without the prior written consent of the Publisher, excepting brief quotes used in reviews.

All Kensington titles, imprints and distributed lines are available at special quantity discounts for bulk purchases for sales promotion, premiums, fund raising, educational or institutional use.

Special book excerpts or customized printings can also be created to fit specific needs. For details, write or phone the office of the Kensington Special Sales Manager: Kensington Publishing Corp., 850 Third Avenue, New York, NY 10022, Attn. Special Sales Department. Phone: 1-800-221-2647.

If you purchased this book without a cover you should be aware that this book is stolen property. It was reported as "unsold and destroyed" to the Publisher and neither the Author nor the Publisher has received any payment for this "stripped book."

Zebra and the Z logo Reg. U.S. Pat. & TM Off.

Second Pinnacle Printing: March, 1990
First Zebra Printing: November, 2000
10 9 8 7 6 5 4 3 2 1

Printed in the United States of America

To Brenda Trent, in gratitude for the big ideas.

ACKNOWLEDGMENTS

I wish to thank the several people (who asked to remain nameless) in Medora, North Dakota—particularly the tour guide at the de Mores's Chateau—who helped make this book possible. Their assistance was invaluable, and they expended a great deal of energy in order to make my job both easier and more challenging.

My gratitude also extends to Dorris Halsey, my mother, Anna Davis, and to Esther Gobrecht, who came to my aid in my hour of need. Finally, I want to express my deep appreciation to Sue Bendix, whose beautiful dance, choreographed and first performed in 1978, was the inspiration for my title.

PART I

THE BADLANDS, SPRING OF 1883

ONE

The icy wind rose with the shriek of a madman, howling across the steep, sculpted cliffs and endless painted buttes of the Dakota Badlands, and shaking the leaves of the cottonwoods into a frenzied dance. The antelope and elk, along with a few buffalo, took refuge in the shadows of the numerous outcroppings of rock or at the feet of the layered walls, which towered above the desolate land like stiff and formidable sentinels bent on keeping adventurous men away.

But to the man poised on horseback, high on a bluff at the heart of the valley, these stone guards were not intimidating. His buckskin jacket open, his white hat clutched in his hand, Antoine de Vallombrosa, Marquis de Mores, sat easily in the saddle. Undismayed by the unbridled power of the wind, the man seemed to have become part of the magnificent landscape. With his tall, well-built frame and the perfectly straight line of his back and shoulders, he might have been just another of the stark, rugged pillars that ringed the canyons below him.

Despite his impressive stature, the Marquis was the picture of relaxed elegance at that moment in late afternoon when the sun threw his elongated shadow at his feet. He was at home among the rolling rock hills and bleak, windswept deserts; the imperious tilt of his head betrayed his aristocratic heritage, from the fine sculpted lines of his forehead, nose, and cheekbones to the slight cleft in his chin. His black eyes sparkled with pleasure at the strange, magnetic power of the scene before him—a scene that was no more compelling than the man himself.

When the wind screamed by—rifling through his curly dark hair and creeping beneath his shirt to touch his chest with frozen fingers, like a thief who was unafraid of the consequences of his offense—the Marquis de Mores did not shiver. Instead, he laughed until the waxed ends of his moustache began to quiver. His laughter, deep and strong, rose from his lips, entangling itself in the lusty gales of the wind until the two were indistinguishable.

Yet the wind was clearly master of the intricately patterned chasms, canyons, cliffs, and tablelands that spread without interruption as far as the eye could see. The constant wailing gusts found their way easily through the multicolored maze of layered rock, sandstone, and clay, which seemed to have lost a ceaseless battle against the relentless forces of wind and water. At the center of the maze, the lazy Little Missouri River flowed along at a sluggish pace, an inoffensive-looking stream that had, nevertheless, in former moments of raging madness carved the broad valley through which it flowed.

The cottonwoods that crowded the banks of the river were the only trees in sight. It was as if the savage hand of the wind had swept the grim rocks free of vegetation, leaving only the growth along the river to remind the onlooker of the barrenness all around. Except for an occasional patch of dull green sagebrush, the land was stark and somehow forbidding.

Mores, however, remained undaunted. This land had issued him a challenge, and he intended to meet it head-on. What was more, he intended to win.

"Mores!"

The Marquis turned to peer along the bluff when the voice of his secretary-valet reached him through the crying of the wind. Spotting the man down to the left, the Marquis called, "William! Come up. The view is breathtaking."

William Van Driesche guided his horse up the rise until he sat beside his employer. Although he was nearly as tall as the other man, Van Driesche was no match for the Marquis. The tiny creases across his forehead and the serious expression in his brown eyes proclaimed his patient and steady character—a sharp contrast to the Marquis's vibrant spirit.

"I've seen the view," Van Driesche replied, drawing his leather jacket tighter, "and so have you. Don't you think you've spent enough time up in this wind for one afternoon?" He could not control a shiver that ran down his neck and across his shoulders.

The Marquis shook his head. "The wind does not bother me and, besides, I like to look at this," he waved his hand to indicate the rugged landscape and immeasurable deep blue sky, "and think that it belongs to me now."

"That it does," William murmured, "but it doesn't make it any less chilly up here. Even you can't control the weather."

"No, but that makes it more of a challenge, don't you think? After all, it's not very entertaining to conquer a land that is already docile."

Van Driesche shivered again as a new gust threatened to steal his hat from his head, and the Marquis, recognizing his discomfort, leaned toward him. "Don't worry, William, we'll soon be back at the tent, and the wind will not be so strong down by the river." Noting the furrowed line of his friend's brow, he continued, "You said you thought this area beautiful last month, didn't you? Now that we hold the deeds for it in our hands, has it changed somehow?"

"It doesn't take much of this late afternoon light and the long shadow it creates to change the land from beautiful to desolate." Shifting his weight, he looked away so he would not have to meet Mores's penetrating gaze. It was odd, but he had been enchanted by the Badlands a month ago when the two men had come to choose some land for the Marquis's new cattle-raising scheme. Then he had felt the land, though barren in most places, had a wild beauty that was compelling in its own right. He had welcomed the Marquis's decision to buy up the green acreage along the river, and William had been pleased with the idea of making this isolated valley his home.

But now, suddenly, with the wind keening endlessly in his ears, the land had been transformed from a fascinating, un-

tamed refuge to a treacherous series of twisting gullies; it had
become an enemy to be conquered.

Mores was surprised by his secretary's unease. It was precisely the moodiness and unpredictability of this scene that
so enthralled him. He knew this land could never bore him.
"Desolate because there are no people?" he asked, knowing
that Van Driesche had not meant that at all, but aware, at the
same time, that the man could not explain what he did mean.
"But that's exactly what we want. Here there is room to turn
around without stepping on the feet of others."

"Perhaps," William grunted, bracing himself against another flurry of wind, "but it's all so uncivilized."

"What you mean is that it's so unlike France," the Marquis
accused.

"You may be right," Van Driesche admitted. "We *are* a
long way from Paris."

Mores shook his head and, for the first time, a shadow
passed across his face. At thirty, the handsome French aristocrat, descended from a long line of titled luminaries, had
decided he had had enough of the structured elegance that
had characterized his world since childhood. For years, he
had attempted to fit himself into the mold of French life in
the 1880s by attending all the social functions and performing
all the polite courtesies that his mother had taught him. But
he had always been somehow a little too unsettled, a little
too dashing for his peers to accept him without reservation.

Several terms in the best French military schools had not
put a rein on his restless energy; not even his place in the
nation's cavalry had done that. Finally, giving in to his life-
long impatience with what he considered the drudgery of his
tame existence, he began to look to America for the adventure
he craved. He had left his parent's villa in Cannes less than
a year ago, in 1882, and come to the vast Dakota wilderness
in order to escape the ties that had bound him so tightly. But,
more than that, he had left France in order to forget. . . .

* * *

"Do you remember the first time, cherie?" the Marquis asked as he traced the outline of Nicole Beaumont's left ear.

Nicole lay back on the brocade couch, her blond curls spilling over the arm like an elegant golden fan. "Of course I do. I remember because you were only a boy, just sixteen, and you were so ardent, so very passionate." She smiled fondly at him, running her fingers through the dark curls on his forehead.

"And you, of course, were so much more mature," he teased, "all of eighteen and already a doddering matron." Then he leaned over her, noting with appreciation that her silk dressing gown had fallen open. Her smooth, pale skin made a delightfully uncomplicated landscape, from the rise of her breasts to the small round island of her belly. "I can't imagine what I saw in you."

"I really believed that was how you felt. It was so long before I saw you again. A whole year. You were cruel in those days, my love."

"I couldn't help it that my family decided to travel overseas for a while." He wound a strand of her hair around his finger and his eyes became thoughtful. "But I certainly got a surprise when I returned—there you were with a child, hidden away in the country with your husband."

Nicole looked away for an instant, brushing her hand before her eyes as if to discourage a persistent insect. She did not want to talk about the past just now. It was the present that mattered. Turning back to him, she reached out and drew him toward her until their lips were barely touching. Then, while her hands painted rhythmical patterns on his back, her tongue circled his sensuous mouth until his arms closed tightly around her.

When he finally pulled away, his eyes seemed to ignite with an inner fire and her pulse raced madly when he whispered, "I love you, Nicole."

"And I you," she responded, the familiar flush coloring her cheeks.

All at once, he stood and turned away, his hands buried deep in his pants pockets. When he turned to face her again, his brow was furrowed with thought. "Then why don't you come away with me? We'll go to America. Do you know how much land they have, just waiting for someone like me to take it and put it to use? It would be far enough away from here, and—"

"No," she interrupted, "I can't." She had known this mood was coming on; she had seen the danger signals. It had been both the joy and heartache of her life that she could never quite quench that fire that often lit up his eyes when one of his wild plans for the future had taken hold of him. She knew he would never think about the problems that might result from his schemes. He refused to recognize what she saw so clearly.

"I could do so much for you," he continued, as if she had not spoken. "I would build you a house the like of which even France has never seen."

Drawing her dressing gown closed, she crossed the room and came to stand before him. "You are so foolish," she murmured affectionately.

"Have I ever denied it?" He put his hands on her shoulders and pulled her toward him. "Besides, would you really wish me to be as staid and proper as 'The Rock'?"

Nicole smiled at the Marquis's use of her husband's nickname. Mores had coined it himself, but she had never denied its appropriateness. "A rock is good to lean upon, my heart," she said quietly. "It will hold you up even when your own strength fails."

The Marquis's eyes narrowed as a new thought occurred to him. "And you need that, don't you, Nicole? You need Charles's stability for yourself *and* your son."

Turning away in order to conceal the flash of pain that touched her eyes, she twined her hands together and stared fixedly at the rug. It was almost as if she could not look him in the face. She found that for once she could not lie to him. "Yes I do." But then, putting one long, slender finger to his lips, she added, "But you are wrong if you think that I want it from you. I would not have you change, my love. Life would be empty and cold if you did."

As she said the words, she realized how true they were. Mores had been her lover for many years, ever since she had been eighteen and newly married. She loved him wildly, with every fiber of her being, and yet her love was not quite blind. She knew, although he did not, that even if she had met him before Charles Beaumont, she would not have married the Marquis. He was too restless, and she felt that she would never understand him entirely.

But somehow, in all those years together, they had never tired of each other. And now, all at once, she was very much afraid of losing him. It was as if, by voicing the possibility that he might change, she had unleashed her own secret well of fear.

When she saw that he was smiling tenderly at her, she reached for him blindly. "Antoine," she whispered, burying her hands in his hair.

"Holy Christ!"

The exclamation exploded into the room, forcing the lovers apart. Both turned at once to stare in horrified disbelief at the man who stood in the doorway. *Tall and broad, his face mottled with fury, Charles Beaumont stood there, an implacable mountain, his shadow darkening the pale blue rug like an ugly stain. . . .*

The sun had begun to sink in the west, draining the far cliffs of their color and using it to paint the clouds with a deep orange glow. The Marquis glanced at his companion briefly and murmured, "I am weary of civilization, my friend."

Van Driesche saw that Mores's thoughts had left the Badlands for a time, and that his enthusiasm had dimmed. The pensive expression on his face was an unnatural one, and it made the secretary uneasy. "It's time we started down now, don't you think? We still have to get supper, and I don't relish doing that in the dark."

The Marquis looked up and shook his head, as if to clear it of the troublesome memories. "I can't say I'm looking forward to another meal of dried meat and toasted bread," he replied. Then he tilted his head back in an attitude of listening as he detected a high squawking from somewhere to his left. Tensing momentarily, he nodded at William and reached for his gun. "But perhaps, after all, I don't have to."

Without a backward glance, he wheeled his horse and took off in pursuit of a group of prairie chickens.

Van Driesche half-smiled to himself. He came from a family nearly as old as the Marquis's and he had worked for Mores all his life, just as William's father had served the duke, the Marquis's father. The secretary had long ago become accustomed to these swift changes in mood. Mores had simply brushed away the previous moment's frame of mind like an annoying insect, and allowed his habitual exhilaration and delight in the hunt to take over. It was not unusual; he often found release from disagreeable reflection through purposeful physical action that required finely honed instincts but no thought. Perhaps, after all, the Marquis had been right—this land and he had been made for each other.

Within minutes, Mores reappeared, a fat prairie chicken slung across his saddle. His tanned cheeks had been reddened by the wind, and his eyes glistened with pleasure. Apparently, the exertion had eradicated any disturbing thoughts from his mind.

"You see," he called, "we shall eat well tonight. I shall pluck her myself while you build the fire."

Van Driesche agreed willingly. The thought of fresh game, cooked over an open fire, was extremely appetizing. "Well, then, shall we go?"

William pulled the reins to the right and his horse started downward. But before the Marquis followed, he turned to look out once more over the glorious panorama before him. By now, the sun had set all the clouds afire, and the sandy brown and gray cliffs had turned red, gold, and orange in less than an instant. The layers of rock were no longer quite so evident except where, here and there, a vein of burning lignite lit up the stone with an eerie radiance. The trees down by the river had subsided into stillness as the wind disappeared into the fast-darkening sky.

Drawing in a long breath, Mores said quietly, "Medora will love it, won't she?"

"Yes," William concurred, "I believe she will." He paused for a last look over the canyon and was grateful for the approaching darkness, which hid his expression from the Marquis's gaze. Now, with the vision of Mores's wife standing here, her waist-length red hair flying like one more fiery cloud in the untamed wind, Van Driesche saw that suddenly the land was a little less bleak.

By the time William awoke the next morning, the Marquis had already taken a long ride along the river to survey his land more carefully. When Van Driesche folded back the tent flap, he found his employer crouched beneath a cottonwood, drawing with a stick in the soft earth of the riverbank. The eerie wail of the wind, which had kept the secretary awake much of the night, had died away; now a soft breeze set the leaves trembling and traced a nearly intangible caress through Mores's tousled hair.

"Come and see," the Marquis urged him. "I am drawing a map of the town we shall build."

As William squatted beside him, Mores used his stick to point out the various buildings he had planned. "Here, just beyond the west bank of the river, we will build the slaughterhouse," he explained. "The land is flat and the railway line is easily accessible from there. Then, west of that will be the town. I think we will begin by building an office for the company—then perhaps a general store, maybe even a hotel."

As he pictured the growing town in his mind, Van Driesche began to share the Marquis's excitement. His employer had grand plans, that was certain, and perhaps this time he also had the strength and courage to carry them out. One thing William knew for certain, though—the Marquis was a stranger to fear, and that just might be the most essential quality of all.

The man had come west with no more than a fistful of dreams and a daring new scheme that he hoped would revolutionize the meat-packing industry. Mores intended to raise cattle in the ideal conditions that the Dakota Badlands offered, and then slaughter the animals right off the range. In this way, he hoped to eliminate the costs of transporting cattle on the hoof all the way to Chicago and to initiate a whole new phase in the beef industry. The introduction of refrigerated railroad cars earlier that year—cars in which the Marquis intended to transport the cut beef—had seemed like a godsend to him.

Often, in the past, Mores had acted impetuously and even unwisely, but this time he had planned well. In spite of the experimental nature of his project and the skepticism he had encountered in trying to convince others, the Marquis had received a promise of his father-in-law's financial support. Now, on the first day of April, 1883, he had left his wife in New York expecting their first child and come to Dakota to buy the land on which to build his wife a home and himself a business empire. His dream was to establish a far-reaching, all-encompassing string of packing plants and other related businesses that would eventually swallow the Badlands and remake them into a new world—one in which the Marquis would not have to remember the old.

After he had studied the map for a moment in silence, Van Driesche asked, "And your house? Where will you build that?"

Mores abandoned his drawing and stood up. Turning with a dramatic sweep of his arm, he pointed far to his right, toward the east bank of the river. "There," he said, "on that bluff. From that height we will be able to overlook the whole town—the packing plant, everything. It will be magnificent. I shall see to it. But for now," he allowed his hand to fall to his side and turned back to the river, "we must christen the town."

"With what?" Van Driesche inquired skeptically.

The Marquis gave him a triumphant look and plunged through the grass at the edge of the river. Leaning over, he reached into the water and withdrew two bottles. "Why, with these, of course."

At his secretary's perplexed expression, he explained, "French champagne. I brought it along especially for this. It must all be official, you see. This is the beginning of a great many things."

True enough, thought William, delighted by the Marquis's foresight. With a man like Mores, one was eternally surprised.

"We have one bottle with which to christen our first structure," Mores continued, indicating the tent in which they had been sleeping for two nights, "and another from which to share a drink in celebration." He rifled through the few tin pots and cooking utensils until he found two battered drinking cups. Handing one to William, he apologized, "Not the best crystal, I'll admit, but that will come in time."

"What will you call your town? You must have a name before you christen it, you know."

Black eyes flashing, Mores assured him, "I have chosen a name." Then, without further preliminaries, he raised a bottle high in the air and brought it crashing down upon the tent post. "I hereby christen this town 'Medora,' in honor of Medora Von Hoffman de Vallombrosa, my wife . . ."

"She'll never marry, I've heard it said," William told the Marquis.

Mores, whose attention had become fixed upon a petite, red-haired woman across the ornate French room, glanced up at his secretary. "Why not?"

William shifted his weight uncomfortably; he was not enjoying this discussion. He had brought his employer to this private party at a neighboring villa in order to distract him from the problems that had been troubling the Marquis lately, but he had not known that Medora would be here. He had seen her often in the past few weeks, during which he had been keeping the Marquis's social engagements while the man himself remained at home. From the first time he had set eyes upon her, William had been impressed by her beauty and the strength he saw reflected in her eyes.

Medora Von Hoffman was difficult to overlook, despite her slight five feet. With her long, red hair that always hung down her back in heavy waves, and her piercing green eyes that saw a great deal more than most, she was a woman to remember. She was not beautiful in the ordinary sense; her nose was a little too thin and her cheekbones a little too wide. But her face was nevertheless oddly compelling. This was due partly to her exceptional intelligence and distinctive maturity. Unlike the French girls her age, she never giggled or whispered, though her smile was easy and enchanting. Even her tasteful silk and satin gowns were free of the frills and bustles that were so popular among her peers.

And now the Marquis had noticed her too. Aware, all at once, that he had not answered Mores's question, William said, "Perhaps she has not found a man who is her equal." Too late, he realized he should not have said it. Even in his present state of depression, Mores could never resist a challenge.

"And her name is Medora?" the Marquis persisted, a new light of interest in his eyes.

"Medora Von Hoffman, the daughter of a wealthy German banker in New York. Her parents have a villa nearby."

"She is American?"

Another error. Mores had always been fascinated with the United States.

"So," the Marquis murmured thoughtfully. "I think I will go and ask her to dance."

Van Driesche could offer no objection, but as he watched the Marquis make his way through the crowd, his dark head high, he knew he had made a dreadful mistake. Mores, handsome, dashing, out-of-the-ordinary, might just be the man to make Medora fall.

The Marquis approached the corner where she stood and, before she could protest, was bowing over her hand. "Permit me to introduce myself. I am Antoine de Vallombrosa."

Medora looked up expectantly. She had heard the name

before, she thought, and not entirely in a positive light. She saw when he straightened that he towered above her, but she was undismayed by his commanding height and even by his exceptional good looks. What captured her attention was the strange glowing light in his eyes; it was as if his face was lit with an inner excitement that he could not conceal. She knew instinctively that she had not been the cause of the glow.

Mores saw that she was not intimidated by him, and he found the knowledge pleasing. "May I?" he asked, leading her toward the tiny dance floor where several other couples whirled in multicolored circles.

As soon as they began to dance, their steps seemed to fall naturally into an easy rhythm. Medora thought him surprisingly graceful for his great stature and, for a man, surprisingly sensitive to the nuances of the music.

Bending his head so that he could speak quietly, Mores asked, "Do you enjoy staying in France?"

She gazed up at him, wondering if she should tell him the truth, and found that she did not want to lie. "It's pleasant for a while."

"And then?" he prompted.

"And then I begin to feel that your country is too old. It has had too long to become 'civilized.' Sometimes I find the elegance confining."

The Marquis threw back his head and laughed, and Medora saw how his laughter spread across his slightly olive skin and even touched his eyes. She felt herself drawing a little nearer to him, and she was surprised at her own response. She was not a woman who was easily swayed by a handsome face.

"You prefer America?" he said, interrupting her thoughts.

"Yes. It's not quite so civilized."

"But New York is a big city. Surely it is not so different from Paris?"

"You're right, of course. Mostly, the difference rests in the fact that Americans in New York are always trying to prove that their city is just as civilized, even though it's not as old. I'm afraid the results are not always the most pleasant." She could not understand why she was telling him these things, except that he seemed to be enjoying her recital. "But it wasn't New York I was thinking of when I said I preferred America. I was thinking of the lands to the west, many of which haven't yet become states." She paused to see if he was still listening and realized that he was waiting anxiously for her to continue.

"Tell me about them," he urged.

"Well, to begin with, the land goes on for miles and miles, sometimes without the presence of a single man. And everything seems bigger there; the hills and rivers are magnificent."

Her mind had clearly left the room where they danced and carried her back across the ocean. As the Marquis's arm tightened around her waist, she came back to the present with a jolt.

She looked up at him for a long moment, and her green eyes seemed to pierce his outer shell and recognize the longings underneath. She smiled deeply for the first time.

"How do the men who go west survive?"

Responding to the tension in his voice, she told him, "They raise cattle by the thousands, and they grow wheat and oats, even sheep. But, of course, they get most of their food from hunting. You can hardly imagine the number of buffalo, deer, and elk running wild."

Mores considered her angular face in the muted light of the kerosene lamps. Her lips were moist and slightly parted, and her eyes were somewhere far in the distance. He could see that she was as caught up in her story as he was. "Do you hunt?" he asked suddenly, amazed at his own temerity. Most women of her social station deplored hunting.

"Yes, whenever I can."

"And the west is where you would truly like to be—if you could choose, I mean?"

Her eyes suddenly blazed like stolen emeralds. "Yes," she said, "it is."

From where he stood in the doorway, William could see the two heads bent together, and he had to admit that they made a handsome couple. Dark next to light, great next to small, the two seemed to move as one. Either would stand out in a crowd, but together they were dazzling.

When the Marquis made his way back across the room, William stood waiting. At his secretary's questioning look, Mores nodded and whispered, "She is more than I hoped."

William's blood froze. "Better than Nicole?" he asked, unable to stop himself.

Mores tensed, and the muscles in his neck stood out with pulsing regularity. "Nicole made her own choice," he hissed, "as I shall make mine."

Aware that he was treading on dangerous waters, Van Driesche nevertheless asked the next question. "Do you think you can afford another scandal just now? Perhaps it would be wiser if you—"

The Marquis raised his hand to his head, and William abruptly fell silent. He should not have said it, he knew.

Mores started to turn away, remembering Medora's parting observation. "I have heard that you're leaving the country for good." The question that nagged at him now was, did she know why? *"There will be no scandal with Medora,"* he insisted, *"because I intend to marry her. . . ."*

William took up his dented tin cup, overflowing now with expensive French champagne, and raising it in the air, cried, "To Medora!"

"To Medora!" Mores answered, stepping carefully back away from the puddle of bubbles that had dripped off the tent canvas and congregated at his feet. Neither he nor Van Driesche heard the men approaching. Only the threatening click of a trigger brought them to their senses.

"What the hell do you think you're doing?" a gruff voice demanded.

The Marquis's hand was on his gun in less than an instant, and he whirled to face two strangers, seated on the backs of two dark, restive horses. The older man, who held the gun, had gray hair and a weathered face, turned reddish-brown by constant exposure to the sun. His piercing blue eyes never stayed still, even for a moment; instead, they seemed to be everywhere at once, like the eyes of a lizard. Despite his obvious age, which was at least sixty, there was a certain restrained energy about him that gave the impression of well-preserved youth. The gnarled hand that held the gun was perfectly steady.

Mores recognized immediately that this was no outlaw intending to rob him. The buckskin jacket and leather chaps were far too fine. Making a quick decision, he removed his hand from his own revolver. Throwing his cup aside, Mores drew himself up to his full height, which was considerable. "I am celebrating the christening of the town I plan to build here," he informed the strangers. "And I would like to know what *you* are doing riding across my land and pointing a gun at me?"

The old man's companion grunted. "I heard some foreign fool had bought this land. I guess that's you."

The Marquis turned his attention away from the gun in order to observe the other man. This one was much younger than the first and, from the glint of his steel-gray eyes to the angular line of his jaw, appeared to be a great deal harder. His brown hair had been pushed carelessly back behind his ears, but a few strands fell across his forehead, shading his thick, dark brows. From the length of his legs in the stirrups, it looked as if he might be as tall as the Marquis when he was standing on the ground.

After a moment of strained silence, the younger man said, "We thought you were rustlers. We've had a lot of trouble from them lately." There was no apology in his tone, but rather a tinge of accusation. It was a full minute before the old man put his gun away.

The Marquis nodded, sensing William's unease in the face of this veiled hostility. "I am Antoine de Vallombrosa," he offered, "and this is William Van Driesche."

The two strangers exchanged glances and a grim signal passed between them. "Bryce Pendleton," the older man finally answered, "and my son, Greg."

Ah, Mores thought, the Pendletons. That explained a great deal. On his last trip out here to inspect the land, he had learned that they were the most powerful family in the territory. They were cattle ranchers in a big way; they had brought their herd from Texas and now, not only did they own most of the land south along the Little Missouri; but also they owned a large percentage of the present town of Little Missouri as well. No doubt they viewed him as a competitor—which explained their hostility.

"So you plan to build a town here," Bryce Pendleton observed, a dangerous glint in his eye.

"I do."

"We already have a town." He turned in his saddle and pointed to the south, where the tiny town of Little Missouri—known as Little Misery—rose like a scar from the barren rock.

"And now you shall have another. Also, a meat-packing plant and a great deal more." He refused to acknowledge the threat that he thought he recognized in Pendleton's eyes.

"Meat packing?" Greg Pendleton gave the Marquis a superior smile. "I thought they did all that in Chicago."

"They do, now. But soon they will be doing it here as well. I intend to put Swift and Armour out of business within three years."

Greg met his father's glance, then shook his head. "You certainly have big plans. But what on earth made you choose this godforsaken place in the middle of nowhere? It's hardly the popular garden spot of the west."

"My cousin, Count Fitz-James, was here hunting last year," Mores replied. "He recommended it to me."

Suddenly, it was as though a dark cloud had covered the sun, shrouding the Pendletons' faces in grim shadows. Bryce clenched his teeth and stared fixedly down at his hands while Greg continued to glare at the Marquis. That name—Count Fitz-James—had struck the two men like a flaming arrow that set their eyes ablaze. For a long moment, neither dared to look at the other. A tense, expectant hush fell among the four men and the air fairly crackled with the vibrant electric-ity of the Pendletons' mysterious fury. It would not have taken more than a spark to set the sky blazing in that instant.

Finally, Bryce managed to find his voice and when he spoke, it was with a certain restrained violence that puzzled the Marquis with its intensity. "You'd best remember, mister, that this isn't always a friendly place. You know what I mean? All kinds of outlaws wherever you look, and they seem to take a particular dislike to foreign strangers, especially in this valley." His words were charged with a hidden meaning, and the threat to Mores was clearly apparent.

At that precise moment, the wind chose to rise again with a rush of pure, cold air that touched the skin with cruel fingers. The green valley echoed with its pained cry.

"You see," Greg Pendleton added stiffly, "even the wind doesn't care for strangers. And the wind has more power here than any man. You'd best beware." Then, without another word, the Pendletons wheeled their horses and disappeared into the canyon.

TWO

"I heard the Markee wants to fence his land," Riley Luffsey declared, pounding viciously on a nail in the half-finished wall he was working on. Luffsey was a taciturn man with long black hair that flowed out from under his sweaty hat, and today he was angry enough to speak up. For the month and a half he had been employed by the Marquis to help build the town of Medora, he had watched curiously but kept his mouth wisely closed.

Glancing around, he saw that the carpenters and bricklayers were still busily at work while dozens of other men hauled lumber or bricks or mud back and forth from the train yard to the center of the town that was springing up all around. The cool afternoon air was punctuated by the clatter of hammers and the shouts of men anxious to get their work done quickly.

"Fences!" Luffsey repeated. "Christ! As if the bastard hasn't caused enough trouble already. First he steals our land, then he threatens to put up fences to keep us out." He spit a stream of tobacco juice over the beam at his feet, peering up at his companion out of the corner of his eye. "Goddamn uppity Frenchman," he added for good measure.

"He didn't steal the land, Riley," Jake Maunders assured him. Luffsey's friend—an unkempt man with pale, shifty eyes and a slack jaw—seemed to be perpetually scowling. "The Markee bought it fair and square through Valentine Scrip. That's probably somethin' you never heard of," he continued at Riley's perplexed expression, "but that don't mean it ain't true. Fact is, you could've bought the land just as easy as he did, and real cheap besides. You just didn't know it."

Luffsey eyed him suspiciously. "I could've? Then why didn't anybody tell me? And how'd that damned Frenchman find out?"

Jake shrugged noncommittally. "I guess he's just smarter than you, and he moves a hell of a lot quicker."

Luffsey's temper was boiling beneath the surface and it showed in his hazel eyes. "Well, let me tell you, Jake, that sonofabitch better not try putting up any fences or there'll be trouble. He thinks he can come in here all high and mighty with his piles of money and his foreign accent and we'll just fall down and worship the ground he walks on. But me and the others, like Frank O'Donnell, we don't aim to take too much more of his cheatin'."

"If you hate him so much, why don't you go work for Pendleton?"

Grinning sheepishly, Riley replied, "Pendleton ain't payin' these days, and you damned well know it. He don't have the cash to compete with the Markee. Besides, the whole damned town of Little Missouri is movin' over here, one man at a time. Naw," he sent another stream of juice into the dirt, "Pendleton ain't payin' and that's one thing you can say for Moree; he pays all right."

"There you go then," Maunders said philosophically.

"Just the same," Luffsey continued, apparently not quite finished with his complaining, "the Markee better be careful, that's all I can say. He's stirrin' up a hornet's nest and don't even know it."

The Marquis sat back in his comfortable stuffed chair, puffing languidly on a thin cigar. For the past two weeks he and William had been living in the rented railway carriage 'The Montana,' surrounded by elegance and luxury. The six rooms of the car were furnished with carved oak sofas and chairs, red velvet curtains, and thick Persian carpets. The walls were suitably covered with paintings by the masters and even the tiny details, such as the cut-glass ashtrays and Chinese vases, were pleasantly appropriate. The atmosphere was a striking contrast to the chaos of dust and wood shavings outside the door of the carriage.

Things had been going well for Mores recently. He had finally completed the purchase of 220 acres of land through Valentine Scrip that gave him access to the river, the railroad, and the land around the townsite. When he added to that the 9,000 acres purchased from the railroad, he realized he now had plenty of land for grazing, plenty of water, and room enough to fill the plains with cattle for miles around.

"Look what arrived on the afternoon train," William called as he entered the drawing room, followed closely by Johnny Goodall, the man whom the Marquis had hired as foreman of the cattle ranch.

Taking the papers Van Driesche offered him, Mores saw that he held the charter agreement for their company—The Northern Pacific Refrigerator Car Company. The Marquis smiled. "This is it, William, Johnny. We're hereby chartered to conduct business in thirteen states and territories from the Pacific to the Atlantic. It's actually begun."

Goodall sank into a velvet-seated chair, running his hand through his light brown hair. "Yes, sir," he muttered. "It's begun all right."

Both William and Mores glanced at him in surprise. "What do you mean?" the secretary asked, dismayed by the note of gloom in the foreman's voice.

"I've been hearin' things in town that I don't like," Goodall explained vaguely.

"You mean the men have been complaining?" Mores asked.

Johnny nodded and William shook his head. "I'll bet Jake Maunders is doing most of the talking."

"He's one of 'em," Goodall agreed.

"I don't know why you hired the man anyway," Van Driesche said, turning to the Marquis. "I've never trusted him. The way his eyes follow you all the time, it makes me think he's planning something."

"Precisely the kind of man you want to have always within view," Mores answered. "I'd rather have him trying to steal me blind in front of my face instead of waiting for him to stab me in the back."

"There're others besides Maunders," Goodall interrupted. "Those men out there are gettin' scared at the grand scale of your plans. The way they figure it, you came here for only one purpose—to destroy the Pendletons and everyone else with a flick of your father-in-law's little finger. . . ."

"He can ruin us, you know. After all, he is a Von Hoffman."

Medora squeezed her husband's arm and murmured, "You forget that I am, too. I know how my father's mind works, believe me."

Mores refused to be reassured. "He probably hates all Frenchmen."

"As a matter of fact, he does. Ever since the Franco-Prussian War. But you have an advantage over most Frenchmen."

"And what, pray tell, is that?"

"You're my husband."

Before Mores could respond to that, his in-laws entered the drawing room with a flourish. He saw with a sinking feeling that although Louis Von Hoffman was of normal height, his bearing made him appear taller. Everything about him, from his heavy brown muttonchop sideburns and moustache to his meticulously tailored gray suit, combined to give the impression of refined overconfidence.

When he finally deigned to speak, after scrutinizing his new son-in-law from head to toe, his voice was loud and imperious. "I am Louis Von Hoffman and this is my wife, Gretta. I assume you are the Marquis." He enunciated the title with just a trace of disdain.

In spite of this veiled hostility, Mores bowed and kissed Gretta's hand. He found her much more pleasant than her husband, and he could see that she was a meek woman who probably spent a great deal of her time attempting to keep her flyaway gray curls in order and her expensive gowns un-wrinkled.

When everyone had seated themselves stiffly on the edges of their chairs, Von Hoffman lost no time in plunging to the heart of his doubts. "May I ask why you decided to leave France so suddenly?"

Mores frowned. "The decision was hardly sudden. Medora and I discussed the possibility of coming here to live long before we were married."

Leaning back in his chair, Von Hoffman lit a cigar and took a long puff before he spoke again. "I was given to un-derstand that you intended to leave even before you met my daughter."

Swallowing his unreasonable anger, the Marquis found himself wondering how much this man really knew. Was he aware of what had happened in Paris, or was this inquisition just so much hot air? "As a matter of fact, I was bored with French society," he answered carefully, avoiding Medora's eyes. "I had long been thinking of making a change, and as my cousin had gone to America recently, returning to France with glowing accounts, I was seriously considering making the trip myself."

"I suppose it had nothing to do with your huge losses on the stockmarket last year?"

Mores heard his wife draw in a sharp breath, but he did not turn to look at her. His eyes were locked with Von Hoff-man's and his voice was perfectly steady when he replied. "It's true that I lost a good deal of money in poor invest-ments. My family, however, is far from destitute. We are very old members of the French aristocracy, Mr. Von Hoffman, but, unlike most of the others, we have quite a large fortune still intact."

"Oh, dear," Gretta blustered as a deep flush crept up her cheeks, "I'm sure my husband didn't mean that. I'm quite sure he didn't."

No one paid her any mind. Von Hoffman himself held his cigar aside and leaned forward, his eyes narrowed with distaste. "I really only want to know one thing, Mores. Did you marry my daughter, or her family?"

The Marquis rose gracefully from his chair and stood facing his father-in-law. "If you mean to imply—and I must assume you do—that I have designs on your fortune, I'm sorry to disappoint you. I married Medora because I love her, and I don't intend to let you—or your money—come between us."

Von Hoffman considered Mores in silence for a long moment. Then, abruptly, he smiled. "I see," he said. "Well." He had been more than a little taken aback by his son-in-law's response and at the moment was intensely aware of Medora's angry gaze. It struck him all at once that he might have pushed her too far. Clearing his throat, he rubbed his chin thoughtfully, and said, "I understand you have developed a scheme for changing our approach to the meat-packing business."

Mores eyed him suspiciously, but Von Hoffman was clearly determined to force the conversation into safer channels. "I should like to invest in this enterprise," the older man declared.

The Marquis snorted, shaking his head. "I don't want your money."

"If you're thinking it's charity, or even guilt money, you're wrong. I like the sound of this cattle-raising/meat-packing scheme of yours, and I think it has a great deal of financial promise. I'd very much like to be in on it from the beginning"—Mores opened his mouth to object, but Von Hoffman cut him off—"as an investor, nothing more. I believe we all can get very wealthy on this thing."

At the Marquis's continued stiff silence, his father-in-law drew a deep breath and murmured, "Please. I am asking you to accept my money and my apology."

As Mores hesitated, Medora came forward, linking her arm with her husband's. "Please, Mores," she urged.

The Marquis looked down and saw from her expression how important this was to her. He sighed. "All right," he said, "I'll accept your offer, but as an investment, not a gift."

Von Hoffman's eyes gleamed with some unreadable emotion and he drew himself up to his full height, smiling with pleased self-assurance. . . .

Johnny sank further into his chair, his face creased in a thoughtful frown.

"The discontent will blow over," the Marquis assured his foreman. "As long as I continue to pay the men well, their full bellies will keep them happy."

Goodall shook his head, but before he could object, all three men were distracted by a determined pounding on the door.

"I'm sorry to disturb you, sir," the newcomer said, stumbling into the room.

The Marquis recognized Dick Moore, one of the men he had hired to help Johnny with the cattle ranch.

"But I thought you should know that I spotted several Indians up near the north border," Moore continued.

"How many?" Van Driesche asked.

"Maybe four, possibly five. I got close enough to see they had guns, then I got the hell out."

Mores considered this news without apparent distress. "Do you think they're looking for trouble?"

Moore shrugged eloquently. "Whenever you see more than one Indian with guns, you'd better assume they're lookin' for some kind of trouble. If you ask me, they were eyein' the cattle we've got grazing up there. I guess they figured they were far enough away from the town to make a little rustlin' safe."

Twirling his moustache absently, the Marquis pondered the best course of action. "All right, Dick. Thank you for the information. I'll handle it from here."

"Not alone!" William protested.

"I'll go with him," Goodall interjected. "I speak the Dakota Language and they might just tell me what they're really up to."

Mores glanced at Johnny in surprise. Clearly, the man had

talents the Marquis had not even suspected. Nodding briskly, he motioned for Goodall to follow and started toward the door.

They saw the Indians from a long distance away—five dark forms huddled beneath a cottonwood. As they approached, four of the five rose abruptly from the ground, holding their rifles threateningly, hatred and suspicion burning like glowing lignite in their eyes. Mores realized with a shock that the fifth Indian was a woman. He had only a momentary glimpse of dark hair tightly braided around a delicate, golden-brown face before she turned away, retreating further into the shadows beneath the leaves.

The Marquis reached for his revolver, but changed his mind when he saw Goodall's warning nod. Johnny kept his hands in full sight, resting comfortably on the reins, and Mores did likewise. He hoped Goodall knew what he was about.

There was a full minute of electric silence while the Indians stood with fingers frozen on the triggers of their rifles and glared at the two intruders. Then one man looked into Goodall's face. For an instant, his features betrayed astonishment and a brief flash of recognition, then he let his rifle slide to the ground. Speaking sharply to the others in Sioux, he shook his head and stepped forward until he stood a few feet from the two horsemen.

He was tall and well built, dressed in cloth pants, a white flannel shirt, and black vest. But despite his white man's clothes, his dark brown skin and rough cut features revealed his background. They would have done so even without his flowing black hair, a small section of which had been woven into a braid and decorated with feathers.

For a moment, all three men maintained a rigid silence. Then the Indian turned to Goodall, speaking rapidly in Sioux. When he had finished, Johnny looked over at the Marquis and said, "He speaks English. Tell him what you want to know."

"I am Antoine de Vallombrosa, Marquis de Mores," he

explained, trusting Goodall's instincts. By now he had recognized a certain pinched look of extreme hunger beneath the wary expressions on the faces of the men who stood before him. He was careful not to remove his hands from the reins and to keep his body relaxed, just as Johnny was doing. "One of my men saw you up here and came to warn me. Apparently, he thought you were considering making a feast out of some of my cattle."

The Indian looked from Goodall to Mores and back again, as if attempting to read their intentions from their faces. Apparently satisfied with what he saw, he said, "We stopped here because we were weary and the trees offered shade. We do not mean to steal your cattle."

"But you *are* hungry?"

Mores could not read the expression that flitted across the Indian's face. The man did not speak for a long time, and when he finally did, it was with reluctance. "Yes. When you came, we were counting our money to see if we could buy some food in town, but there is not enough."

Nodding solemnly, the Marquis cast a sidelong glance at Goodall. He knew he must go carefully now. "If you'll allow me," he said, "I have some parts of prairie chicken, some bread, and cheese in my saddlebags." He had brought the food along at Johnny's suggestion. "I'd like for you to take it."

"No." The Indian shook his head violently. "We have not enough to pay and we will not take your charity."

"Then perhaps we can work out some kind of deal," Mores suggested, noticing for the first time the proud tilt of the Indian's head. "You may have heard that I'm building a town near here. I have a great deal of construction to get done in a short time, and I'm always in need of more workers. You and your companions could pay for your food through labor if you wished."

As the Indian considered this suggestion in silence, a frown gathered across his brow. "I do not think you are aware of what that would mean," he offered at last.

"I am aware. I need your help, you need my food. It seems like a fair enough exchange."

Narrowing his eyes in thought, the Indian said something to Johnny in Sioux. Goodall turned to scrutinize his employer for a long moment, then nodded.

"Then it is agreed," the Indian declared in English. "We will come."

In the end, however, only the spokesman accompanied the two men back to town. The others had chosen to take Mores's bag of food, but they had not been willing to stay. They had started back toward their reservation to the south, taking the one girl with them.

"I will pay for their food as well," the Indian told Mores firmly.

"As you wish, though I can certainly afford to make it a gift." When the other man shook his head, the Marquis was wise enough to drop the matter. "Tell me your name," he said.

"I am Anpao Luta, but they call me simply Anpao."

"What does it mean?" the Marquis asked.

Anpao considered Mores's expression carefully before he answered. He seemed to have trouble believing the man was really interested. Nevertheless, he explained, "To you I think it would be Red Dawn."

"Tell me some others, please," Mores requested. "I'm fascinated by the sound of your Indian words."

"My brother and sister, who we left behind, are called Ginginka Magazu and Ileya—Quicksilver Rain and the Shining One."

"You speak English quite well. Where did you learn it?" To his own surprise, the Marquis realized he was really interested in this apparently cultured young Indian man.

"My brother and I were forced to attend the school the whites have built for us at Carlyle. Since we were not allowed to speak the Dakota tongue there, it was necessary to learn English quickly."

"Are you sorry you had to attend a white school?"

Anpao considered the question thoughtfully before he answered. "I am glad because of the things I learned, but sorry because of the things I lost."

The Marquis smiled wistfully. He, of all men, could certainly understand such an ambivalent attitude. As the three men approached the town, Mores began to see that Anpao had been right when he said, *I do not think you are aware of what that would mean.* Most of the men stopped their work to stare boldly at the Indian and, within minutes, the air was heavy with mistrust and shock. In the silence left by the hammers that had ceased their pounding, a chorus of speculation broke out among the workmen.

"Now what do you s'pose the Markee is doin' escortin' that Indian through town this way?"

"All I can say is, I hope he's escortin' him to jail." This last was said in a voice intended to carry a long distance.

The Marquis ignored the muttering all around him, continuing placidly on his way. He could not have known that since he had ridden away just an hour ago, the rumor that he planned to fence his land had spread like wildfire. Everyone knew he owned most of the land along the river, and they feared they would be denied water rights. Then again, many of the men were nesters who believed they owned their land, and they had been told that Mores meant to take it away from them. The sight of their employer riding companionably along with an Indian—who the workmen equated with thief and rustler—did nothing to assuage their doubts.

By the time the three men reached the Montana, not a single man was working. All eyes were fixed on the riders and hostility hung over the crowd like a gloomy pall. As he dismounted, Mores heard someone say clearly, "Should have known the damned foreigners would stick together. Frenchmen, Indians, they're all the same."

The Marquis glanced at Anpao and saw that he was breathing heavily, as if he were attempting to hold back a great wash of fury. His lips were pressed together in a thin line, but he did not speak. "Johnny," Mores said quietly, "would you take Anpao inside, introduce him to William, and see that he gets something to eat. I have something to take care of out here."

When Goodall and Anpao had disappeared inside, the Marquis turned to face the men who had not yet taken up their tasks again. They stood, as if incapable of action, staring at their employer. Mores blinked, straightening his shoulders. He did not intend to be intimidated by this group. They must see that he did not care for their insinuations and their hostility, and that he would not change his plans for their sakes. He had offered Anpao work and work he would. It was that simple.

He began to move across the crude street and in among the buildings, his imperious gaze falling with equal surprise on each pair of idle hands. Finally, he announced in a voice of steel, "I don't pay you to stand here like statues. I pay you to build. If you don't care to do so, that's your choice. But in that case, your pay will, of course, be stopped. You must decide." His eyes fell on Maunders and Luffsey. "Jake? Riley? Are you working for me or not?"

Maunders shrugged and turned back to the boards he had been nailing. It was a long, tense moment before Luffsey joined him; then, one by one, the others followed suit. When the air was again cluttered with the din of hammers and saws, the Marquis turned toward the Montana, oblivious to the glares full of smoldering hatred that never left his back.

The flames leapt and crackled wildly, sending waves of heat through the already stuffy room. Ignoring his own sweaty discomfort, Bryce Pendleton dropped another stack of papers into the fire.

"It's terribly hot in here," his granddaughter exclaimed, dragging the back of her hand across her forehead. "Why are you building a fire when it's so warm out?" Katherine Pendleton was a fourteen-year-old girl of medium height with wide brown eyes and thick dark hair. At the moment, her usually attractive face was twisted into an unpleasant scowl and her eyes were fixed accusingly on her grandfather.

Greg glanced at his daughter briefly. "We're burning our bridges," he explained in annoyance. "We don't need these papers anymore. They're our numerous requests to the railroad to sell us the land north of here."

"You mean you've given up?" Cory, his wife, asked stupidly, lifting her pale blond hair from her neck in an attempt to find relief from the heat.

"You haven't been paying attention, Mama," Katherine interjected before her father could respond. "The railroad officials sold that land to the Marquis de Mores a month ago." She heard her grandfather's sharp intake of breath and the girl hid a smile. She knew both Bryce and Greg were furious that the Marquis had so easily obtained possession of the land that the railroad had steadfastly refused to sell to the Pendletons for the past three years. "Not that it matters now," the girl added. "The men are all leaving our ranch for his anyway."

"That's enough, Katherine," Greg warned.

"But it's true."

Her father took a threatening step toward her, but Bryce stopped him with a heavy hand on his son's shoulder. "Our investments *are* in danger, Greg. You know that as well as I do. And they won't be out of danger until Mores stops moving ahead recklessly without considering the damage he causes for others."

"He doesn't care," Katherine cried, unintimidated by her father's anger. "He's a French aristocrat, after all. And that means he's arrogant, self-centered, and deadly, just like his cousin, Count Fitz-James. They're all the same."

Greg turned away from her abruptly, only partially aware of his wife's shocked gasp. Swallowing a rush of damp, hot air, he stared blindly into the heart of the pulsing orange flames until they blocked all else from his sight. . . .

All Greg could see was the smoky glare of the torch; it blinded him momentarily. But then, slowly, his eyes adjusted to the light and he moved forward carefully, guiding his horse through the narrow ravine with as much skill as he could muster. Far in the distance, he could hear the retreating laughter of the hunt, the endless thundering clatter of hooves on stone.

He had not wanted to follow the Frenchmen tonight, but Bryce had discovered his wife missing. He believed she had gone to join the hunting party; she could never resist a challenge or the promise of excitement, no matter how dangerous. So Greg had come to find her and convince her to return home with him. He did not trust Count Fitz-James and his cronies. Not for a moment.

Suddenly his horse stopped in the middle of the path, whinnying in distress. With his heart pounding a warning in his ears, Greg leaned down, holding the torch before him like a beacon. The sinister shadows of the night did not flee at the approach of the guttering flame; rather, they clung even more tenaciously to the huddled form, half-hidden by an overhang of rock. The reaching fingers of light crawled over the body, creating grotesque patterns of quivering darkness on the motionless back.

Sliding from the saddle, he approached cautiously, then his breath escaped in a horrified groan when he saw that his fears had somehow become real. Surely that bright red scarf was his mother's, and the blood-soaked skirt as well. "Mother?" he breathed, kneeling beside her.

She raised her head then, her mouth contorted in pain, and gazed up into his shadowed face. "Greg." Her voice was a hoarse ragged whisper without substance or warmth.

"What happened?" he asked, forcing his voice to remain steady.

"My horse reared and I fell," she rasped. "He didn't see me. His horse ran me down." Closing her eyes, she drew several painful breaths, exhausted by the effort of speaking.

"Who?"

"Fitz-James. I cried out, but he didn't stop."

Greg reached out gingerly and raised her head into his lap. "How badly are you hurt?" Somehow, he guessed the answer even before she gave it, and the rage began burning its slow path through his body, leaving no part of him untouched.

She was silent for a moment, as if gathering her strength; then, finally, she murmured, "I'm dying, Greg. It's the one thing I've been certain of in all my life." She attempted a smile, but her lips refused to relinquish themselves to her will. "Except for this—this promise I want you to make. Tell me that after I'm buried you'll—find that man and make him—pay. That one desire I'm certain of. Promise me." In the faltering light, her skin was ghostly gray and her eyes burned like two unnatural embers, draining her face of the last of its color.

"I'll do it," he whispered.

"Swear!"

Her fingers closed around his with desperate strength just as he became aware of the blood seeping through her blouse and onto his legs. Her energy was slipping away, but she would not give in until she had received his solemn promise. She might be dying, but she meant to be the victor in this battle just the same.

"I swear."

His mother nodded, grimacing with a last flash of agony, and then her grip on his fingers grew slack until her hand fell away. "Good," she just managed to choke out. "It will be done." Then her eyes grew wider, her skin more sallow, and the glow crept slowly from her brilliant gaze.

Greg shuddered, realizing at last that the torch had burned itself out, leaving him enwrapped in suffocating darkness. . . .

The flames had died away, and now nothing but smoldering ashes filled the gaping hole of the fireplace.

"Mores can't get away with it," Bryce declared.

"Why not? You couldn't stop Fitz-James and he was a murderer," Katherine pointed out.

"Katherine!" Greg bellowed, releasing a little of the helpless frustration that had come close to overwhelming him in the past few minutes.

"Oh, my!" Cory cried, linking her arm in her daughter's. "I forgot the bread. I need your help in the kitchen, dear." Before her husband could protest, she dragged the girl from the room, shaking her head as she went. "I don't know why you insist on provoking your father like that," Cory scolded as they disappeared into the hall. Katherine's response was inaudible.

When they had gone, Bryce turned to his son. "The girl is right, you know. We let Fitz-James get away without paying for his sins." His face was beaded with sweat and his eyes blazed with his inner torment. "But I promise your mother's memory," he added, "that his cousin the Marquis will not be so lucky."

THREE

As he stood beside his horse in the shadow of the cliff, examining the trampled grass at his feet, the Marquis heard the faraway explosion of a rifle. Then a bullet whistled by his head. He did not wait to see where it landed, but, taking his revolver from its holster, he swung himself into the saddle, heading for a distant cluster of bushes. He knew that was the only spot offering a would-be attacker enough shelter to fire from in safety, but he also knew what he would find there.

He was right. As always, there was nothing. Nothing but the limp strings of barbed wire that had been cut across quickly and efficiently, the place where the grass had been crushed under the weight of a crouching man, and the empty cartridges. There was no sign of whoever had fired the gun. Mores's fingers tightened painfully on his revolver as he guided his horse forward, searching the area for some sign, although he knew there was no hope of discovering his attacker.

This was the third time he had been shot at in the last week, and he had come to realize by now that these men knew the land much better than he did. They knew how to slip up when he was unaware, fire quickly, then disappear. He did not even bother to get down and examine the cut wires; the destruction of his fences had become another common occurrence recently. He would have to send Dick Moore out to repair it tomorrow, for all the good it would do. Whoever his secret enemies were, they would only cut it again. Various threats had begun to circulate concerning the unfor-

tunate results should the Marquis not remove the offending
barbed wire. And now stray bullets had begun to plague him.
He had been appalled at the furor his fences had caused, but
he refused to be frightened into backing down.

With a weary sigh, he turned the horse back toward the
house that rose from the bluff. After several weeks in the
Montana, he and William had decided to move into the still
unfinished house The structure was high above the ferment
that had been brewing in the town, and more easily defensible
than the railroad car. Somehow they had guessed that that
would be important. Now, as the horse picked its way across
the ridged field, Mores wondered how long it would be before
the stray bullets began to reach their target.

Frank O'Donnell propped himself against the smooth face
of a rock and grinned at his companions. He was tall and
gangly, with a shock of unruly sandy hair and pale hazel eyes
that revealed his thoughts like signboards. Chewing loudly on
his tobacco, he patted his rifle and grunted, "Guess that son-
of-a-bitch of a Markee will learn pretty soon that he can't
treat us this way and expect to stay here, unharmed."

"He'd better learn," Riley Luffsey added sharply, "or we
might have to find a new method of teachin'."

Dutch Wannegan, who had just crept back from the bushes
where he had lain waiting for Mores to pass, nodded his
agreement. The three men had gathered in a deep ravine, sheltered by two cottonwoods and a cluster of thick bushes, which
effectively hid them from sight.

"Hell, I wouldn't worry. We got him nervous already and
we ain't hardly started yet."

"Yeah, but I heard today he plans to round up all us nesters
and throw us off our land, just cause it happens to fall inside
his fences," Wannegan pointed out.

"They were sayin' that two weeks ago, and I ain't seen
him make a move yet. That's just a rumor, Dutch. You relax
and let me handle this. I got my own plans, you know—big
ones."

"Well, you'd better put them into effect soon."

All three men leapt up, rifles in their hands, to gape at the newcomer who had crept up without making a sound—as silent and stealthy as a poisonous snake. Jake Maunders laughed, pushing a rifle barrel aside nonchalantly. "You wouldn't want to shoot me, boys," he admonished, "or you might lose your source of information—and then you might just make a fatal mistake."

O'Donnell lowered his rifle but continued to eye Maunders suspiciously. "How'd you find us?"

Jake shrugged. "I know this land as well as you do. Hid out here once or twice myself."

"What're you doin' here now?"

"I came to warn you."

" 'Bout what?"

Maunders smiled enigmatically. "Dutch is right about the Marquis's plans for the nesters. In two days, he's goin' to send out his men, armed to the teeth, and toss you off your land. All three of you. He figures the nesters are the ones causin' the trouble, and gettin' rid of them is the best way to stop it."

There was a momentary silence while the three men took in what Maunders was saying. Then Luffsey exploded, "The bastard! I call that—" He paused, searching for a word.

"Claim jumpin' is a good name for it," Jake suggested.

O'Donnell's skin paled and he clutched his rifle with incredible strength. "I'm tellin' you, it ain't gonna happen," he hissed. "Ever jump us, and the Markee'll jump right into his grave!"

"It happened again," the Marquis announced, entering the drawing room after dinner. Darkness had fallen long since and William, Anpao, Dick Moore, and Johnny Goodall had gathered where the lantern light was brightest. "These attacks are becoming annoying," Mores added.

"They are likely to become more than that," Anpao said. "I have been listening in town and I believe the fence-cutting and wild shots are only the beginning." The Indian had long ago paid his debt to the Marquis, but he had chosen to stay in Medora when he realized that the man might need him. Mores needed every friend he could find just now, and Anpao was pleased to consider himself one of them.

Goodall grunted his assent, but just now he was more concerned with the notes he was coaxing from his fiddle. Johnny often said that a good tune helped him think more clearly, and clear-thinking was certainly needed now.

"It's true," Moore agreed. "The men seem to get more hostile every day. It's almost like someone was eggin' 'em on."

Mores shook his head. Puffing thoughtfully on his thin cigar, he half-listened to Johnny's fiddle music in the background. There was something about this mushrooming hatred that disturbed him deeply. It seemed that not only his dreams, but also his very life was threatened and he could not understand why. He was weary of being left in the dark. Weary of misunderstandings and lies and deceit. He thought he had left them behind when he turned his back on his past, but now he recognized that it was not so.

When the luminous ember in his hand finally consumed itself, he reached down to open what he thought was a cigar box—but, to his surprise, a soft, tinkling song escaped into the stuffy room. . . .

He slammed the lid of the music box shut when he heard Nicole come into the room behind him. She was more beautiful than ever in her dark gray gown, her blond hair loose upon her shoulders. He started toward her, but she backed away.

"Nicole," he said, "I've come to a decision. I'm going to America and you and your son are coming with me."

She looked away, shaking her head dumbly, as if she could not trust herself to speak. Mores saw that she was struggling to maintain control.

"Please," he said.

"No. I have told you before, I belong here." Her voice was cool and it seemed to come from somewhere outside her. "Besides, did you really think I would go with you, after what you have done?"

He was taken aback by her aloofness and accusatory tone. "I had no choice; you know that."

"I wonder." She turned away and wandered over to the bureau where the music box lay. Idly, she lifted the lid, inclining her head as the tinny notes spilled out.

"I love you, Nicole."

"Yes," she agreed without turning to face him, "I believe you do. But I will not leave here, just the same."

He heard the finality in her tone and sought wildly for some excuse that would change her mind. "What about Phillipe? Do you think you can handle a boy of twelve? I could help you with him."

Nicole closed her eyes as she felt herself begin to sway. It was as well that Antoine could not see her face, she thought. "My son," she told him, "is quite mature for his age, and he has already been educated well beyond his years. He will survive. Besides," she swung around sharply to meet his eyes, "you don't really want him, do you?"

"I want anything that would bring you to me."

She knew he meant it with all his heart, but it was not what she wanted to hear just now. "I'm sorry. That's just not good enough."

Mores did not understand. This woman before him seemed to be a stranger, yet he had known her most of his life. All at once he realized she was serious; she would not go with him. "If only you hadn't married Charles Beaumont," he murmured.

"But I did." Her answer was sharp and final and she saw how it perplexed him. "Antoine, I have thought carefully about this, and I have made my choice. You are still young and handsome and you have romance in your blood. I should think that would make you very desirable. You go to America; you've always wanted to. And maybe you'll find what you really want there."

He reached out blindly to touch her shoulders, aware all
the time of the tinkling notes of the music box somewhere
in the background. When his lips brushed hers, she drew back
precipitously, knocking his hands away. Mores drew a deep
breath, his gaze fixed on her flushed cheeks and shining gray
eyes. "You can't forgive me, can you?" he asked in a whisper.

There was an instant of expectant silence, then she murmured, "No, I can't."

The air was suddenly chokingly heavy as he turned away.
Had he waited a moment longer, he might have seen the tears
that gathered in her eyes; he might even have recognized her
struggle to keep from calling him back. But he did not wait.
*With a strangely painful numbness in his chest, he crossed
the room toward the door, just as the last notes of the me-
chanical song faded into stillness. . . .*

The Marquis let the lid of the music box slip from his
fingers, but he did not welcome the silence that followed.
Even Johnny's fiddle had ceased its song. With an effort,
Mores forced the memories from his mind, giving his attention to problems of the present.

"The point is," Goodall murmured finally, "that we have
to do somethin' now. We can't just wait to see what they've
got planned for us."

"Perhaps we should find out who is behind all this," Anpao
suggested.

"I know who it is."

Everyone turned to stare at Maunders as he came forward
out of the shadows where he had been listening for some
time. They had not known he was in the house.

"The man's name is Frank O'Donnell," he continued.
"He's a hunter and general troublemaker who's been around
the Badlands for years. He's used to roamin' all over the prai-
ries just as he likes, and he's real upset about those fences.
The man's out to get you, Markee, and he ain't gonna stop
till one of you is dead."

Mores exhaled, contemplating the way the light played

across Maunders's face, distorting the scowling features into a grotesque mask that reminded him of the treacherous landscape outside the door.

"If I was you, sir, I'd go lookin' for him before he comes lookin' for you. Why, just today, O'Donnell said to me, as bold as you please, that he'd shoot you the minute he saw you."

"Was he drunk?" the Marquis asked, the expression in his eyes veiled.

"Sure. He most always is, but—"

"A man will say anything when he's drunk. No doubt he was just bragging in front of his friends. I'm sure if I try to talk to the man, he'll come around."

"If you do try, you're crazy. O'Donnell's not the kind to say what he don't mean. Last time I saw him, he was on the way to the saloon to gather some men together, and I don't think he was plannin' to get up a poker game."

Mores walked to the window where he stopped to stare out into the darkness that surrounded the house like a wall, cutting it off from the rest of the world. "By now O'Donnell is probably sound asleep with his head in a puddle of whiskey on the bar," he said with unconcern.

His confidence proved ill-founded. A moment later, he heard the report of a rifle and the glass from the window shattered at his feet. For an instant, he stared at the glittering pile of fragments in disbelief, but when a second bullet followed the first, missing his left arm by a matter of inches, he leapt into action.

With his gun in his hand, he reached behind him to douse the lantern that he knew had betrayed his position. "Turn out all the lamps," he ordered as he heard the men scattering behind him. "I hope to God you all know where your guns are."

Soon the room was in total darkness, and five men were poised at the windows, firing blindly at men they could not see and whose numbers they could not guess. The men outside seemed momentarily surprised by the quick, efficient return of their fire, and their guns were silent for the briefest of moments. But then, aware that they had the advantage over the group trapped inside the house, they began firing with renewed vengeance. Both sides huddled awkwardly in their positions, unwilling to move for fear they would betray themselves, holding their breath back in their dry throats as the bullets struck all around them.

As the Marquis's eyes adjusted to the gloom, he saw that there were not enough men out there to storm the house successfully. They would have to expose themselves to certain death in order to approach across the flat grassy area between the bushes that hid them and the porch. But how long would they stay out there, he wondered, firing wildly at nothing but the vast bulk of the house? How long could this standoff last?

His question was answered almost before the thought was finished. All at once the rifles outside were still. Mores called for his own men to cease their fire while he listened, every muscle and nerve in his body tensed and waiting. Outside, there was nothing but the occasional rustling of the bushes as the attackers crept away into the protection of the night.

As a lantern flamed into life, filling the room with grim shadows, someone called, "Where's Maunders?"

"I heard him slip out the back way the minute the bullets started flying," Anpao said, his voice echoing hollowly in the unnatural silence.

"I *knew* we couldn't trust that man!" William muttered, tossing his rifle onto a chair.

The Marquis had not yet turned away from the window. "Damn!" he whispered under his breath. They had escaped him, every one of them, and he had not even seen their faces. He realized with a sinking feeling of doom that he had no defense against an enemy he could not even identify.

"Are you certain you're feeling all right?" Gretta Von Hoffman panted at her daughter's retreating back.

Medora paused momentarily to glance at her mother, who was hiding from the bright afternoon sun beneath an embroidered parasol. Gretta's cheeks were flushed from the mild heat and brisk walk through the park, and Medora suspected her high color had nothing to do with pleasure. "I'm fine," she said, linking her arm through her mother's. "In fact, I feel much better now that I've breathed some fresh air. It *is* a lovely day for a walk."

"I can't imagine why I let you talk me into this. A walk indeed! In *your* condition." Eyeing her daughter critically, Gretta had to admit that the cut of her olive green silk dress very nearly disguised Medora's advanced state of pregnancy. And despite the heat and exertion, her daughter was looking perfectly cool and unruffled. There was not even a single drop of sweat on her forehead. But still, it had been madness to agree to Medora's desire for some exercise. "You should be safely at home," Gretta continued. "I don't know *what* your father would say if he knew."

Medora smiled. "Papa gave up long ago trying to make me do as he wished. I'm too much his daughter to let anyone else control me. And you may as well give up, too."

"I'm here, aren't I?" Gretta could not conceal a little smile. Brushing a damp curl away from her forehead, she followed her daughter toward the sparkling green lake just visible among the distant trees.

Medora paused on the shore, delighting in the gently ruffled expanse of water at her feet. She had been wise to escape the stuffy house on such a fine afternoon; the walls had become far too confining of late. Despite her mother's protests, Medora did not believe the exercise would hurt the child she carried. The clean air might even do it good. It had certainly improved her own sagging spirits.

Out here, with the sun on her face and the water lapping softly on the sand, she felt closer to her husband somehow. It had been so long since she had seen him. Too long. Drawing in a deep breath, she recognized the nearby murmur of water on stones where the tiny stream merged with the lake. She closed her eyes, listening, letting the sound wash over her in soothing waves. . . .

* * *

*The pulsing thrum of the waterfall drowned out their voices
as the Marquis led Medora along the riverbank.* Hand in hand
they wandered barefoot over the moss-covered bank, but when
they reached the rocks at the foot of the waterfall, Mores
paused. He smiled secretly, his black eyes dancing, and whispered, "Come. I know a place where we won't be disturbed.
But we'll have to get wet."

Medora glanced down at her chemise and drawers. She
had left her gown on the bank near the remains of their lunch,
and she knew a little water would not hurt her. "All right,"
she agreed, following slowly as he began to climb over the
shiny flat rocks.

The Marquis himself wore nothing, having discarded his
pants, coat, vest, shirt, and tie beside his wife's gown. Now,
suddenly, he felt as if he were a child again and, grasping
Medora's hand more tightly, he drew her with him through
the heart of the raging waterfall to the cool stone hollow
behind.

Laughing, the water running off them in rivulets, they
clung together in their shadowed cocoon. Mores kissed her
lingeringly, burying his fingers in the dripping strands of her
hair. Then his hands began to stray down across her shoulders
and toward the gentle rise of her breasts beneath the wet chemise.

"No," Medora whispered against his warm lips. "Not here
in the middle of the afternoon."

The Marquis laughed softly. "My dear, no one can see us.
That wall of water separates us from the world as effectively
as a velvet curtain. Except that it's even more romantic." His
hands stopped at her waist while his fingers pressed against
her chilled skin, creating their own little circle of warmth.

"Mores," she began to protest, but he shook his head.

"Quiet," he warned, "they'll hear you."

Medora smiled in spite of herself. She knew as well as
her husband did that the sound of the rushing water would
drown out any noise they might make. This time, when he
reached for the buttons on her chemise, she did not stop him.

Slowly, sensuously, he released the buttons one at a time

while his tongue caressed her ear, her chin, her long white throat. And when the thin fabric fell away, she leaned back, shaking her head as his hands moved over her naked skin. Several drops of water landed on her shoulders and Mores followed each one, tracing its path with the tip of his tongue down across her shoulders, the satin swell of her breasts, and the hollow that led to her smooth, soft belly.

"Dory," he murmured huskily, pulling her body close to him until their hips were pressed together and their arms locked around each other in an unbreakable chain.

And as they melted one into the other, skin to skin and breath to breath, Medora allowed herself to drift, lost in the heat of her body's fire and the hypnotic song of the water at her side. . . .

A sparrow rose, chattering, and broke the spell that held Medora in its grasp. Opening her eyes, she gazed around her, bewildered by the reality of the crowded park and the calm emerald lake.

"Whatever were you thinking of?" Gretta fluttered beside her. "Your face was so strange and distant."

"I was wondering," her daughter said slowly, choosing her words with care, "how long it will be before my husband sends for me. I want to be there with him, Mother. Now, this very moment."

* * *

Mores smoothed the yellow page across his knee before he read the telegram from Van Driesche for the third time.

Trouble in spades. Outlaws shot up town last night, threatened to stop work on the plant. Say they will kill you on sight.

—William

Shaking his head, the Marquis crumpled the wire in his hand. He had left town the morning after the shoot-out and gone to Bismarck to buy a shipment of cattle, but only after Goodall had assured him that the men left behind would not be in danger. *"Hell,"* Johnny had said, *"it's you they want, not us."* Yet he had found this telegram waiting for him in Mandan, describing further disasters. It was time to take action, he had decided.

As soon as he read the wire, he went to find the sheriff to ask his advice, only to learn that the lawman was out of town. Nonplussed, he had finally located the justice-of-the-peace. Stepping up on the porch, he pushed open the door. "Mr. Bateman?" he called.

A rotund, dark little man came forward with a welcoming smile. "Can I help you?"

"It's a long story, but I'm badly in need of advice. I had hoped to see the sheriff and get him to swear out a warrant for the arrest of some men who have threatened my life, but he's out of town."

"Sure is," Bateman agreed. "What can *I* do for you?"

Mores breathed deeply before he answered, "Tell me what legal action I should take."

"You'd better give me the details," the justice suggested.

The Marquis complied, outlining the recent events in Medora with as few words as possible. When he had finished, Bateman merely gaped at him. "And you want to know. . . ." He paused, waiting for Mores to finish the sentence.

"What I should do in the eyes of the law."

The justice blinked at him several times as if he were perplexed by the question. "Well, as far as I know, there's only one thing you *can* do."

"What's that?" the Marquis asked.

Bateman sniffed, his expression implying that the answer was obvious. "Why, shoot, of course."

FOUR

O'Donnell, Luffsey, and Wannegan sat stiffly in their saddles, waiting for the train to come in. They knew the Marquis had left for Mandan three days ago, and they had been waiting for his return ever since. Their Winchester rifles were trained on the spot where Mores would disembark, and this time they were determined to finish the job they had begun. If the Marquis were on the train they could see snaking its way through the distant ravines, he was a dead man.

As the train clattered into the rickety old station, Bryce and Greg Pendleton turned down the main street and saw O'Donnell and his cohorts poised like petrified rock, their rifles in their hands. Greg glanced uneasily at his father. In the same instant, both had become aware of the unnatural hush all around them. Only the wind dared to disturb the stillness. Its mournful wail rose and fell as the disorderly gusts played a game of hide-and-seek, whooshing past the hunters' rigid shoulders, then disappearing into the cloudless sky.

Greg took in the situation at a glance and, for a moment, he too seemed to be incapable of action. Then Bryce spoke, his voice like the crack of a rifle. "They can't do it," he said.

It was enough to break the spell that held his son immobile. He dug his heels into his horse's sides and the animal shot forward. Greg called out, "O'Donnell!" But the man did not respond; he only raised his rifle a little higher. Dragging on the reins, Pendleton pulled his horse to a halt between the hunters and the station platform. He was now directly in the line of fire, but he had to stop this before it got started.

"Frank, you can't do it this way," he insisted. "They call it murder."

"*I* call it justice," O'Donnell replied.

Pendleton shook his head. "It's damned foolishness, that's what it is. You shoot him now and you've committed murder, with half the town as witnesses." He had to talk faster. If anyone had gotten off the train, he must have done so on the far side, but as soon as the cars pulled away, he'd be exposed to the waiting barrels of these three rifles—a perfect target.

O'Donnell's stony expression had not changed. "No one in this town is gonna testify against me now, are they, Pendleton? You ain't talkin' sense."

"Maybe not, but the Marquis's in-laws have a lot of money and a lot of influence. They're not going to let something like this go by without finding the man who did it." It galled him to be put in the position of protecting Mores and he suspected it would gall the Marquis even more if he knew. "I'm telling you, you can't do it this way. Besides, you'll have to shoot me too—I'm between you and your target—and you know damned good and well that my father won't let you get away with that."

The train was spitting and grinding behind him, preparing to pull away, and still O'Donnell's face had not changed. "Dutch, Riley, you know I'm right, don't you?" Greg saw a glimmer of a nod from the other two. Turning in his saddle, he looked Frank O'Donnell in the eye. "Frank?"

As the last car clattered over the tracks, Pendleton shifted slightly so he could see through the smoke and dust left behind. With one eye on the hunters, he peered across the tracks and his hands tightened on the reins. Mores was there. He stood facing them, his .45 in his hand. The Marquis held his ground for a moment, then turned his back and started toward the horse that was waiting nearby.

"Let him go," Greg warned, refusing to budge.

For a long moment, O'Donnell stared down the barrel of his gun at the man who blocked his way. His nostrils flared and the lines of his face whitened with fury, but he did not fire. Finally, when the suppressed energy of his anger threatened to explode into an action that he knew would destroy his plans—perhaps even his life—O'Donnell let the rifle fall to his side.

As he swung himself up into the saddle, Mores glanced back once at the unnatural tableau across the railroad tracks. His four greatest enemies seemed to be frozen in their places, as unyielding and drab as the stone cliffs all around them. The stillness was unnerving, almost unreal. Why didn't they shoot? Then, abruptly, the three hunters turned and rode away, leaving Pendleton to guard an empty platform as the wind rose, howling, shaking the very rocks with its laughter.

Medora loosened the pleated batiste collar of her striped silk gown in an attempt to gain some relief from the sweltering New York heat. She had long ago escaped to the dark study—the coolest room in the Von Hoffman house—to read her letter in peace, but even here the heat had penetrated through the heavily draped windows. Brow furrowed, Medora considered William's smooth, neat writing once more, attempting to see beyond what he had said to what he had not.

Madame la Marquise,

I have no right to do what I am doing, except that I believe it might help the Marquis, who has long been my major concern. I know he writes you that all is well, but he is not entirely correct. The populace is restless and they frankly do not like him. There have been problems.

I think, regardless of what Mores says, that you should come soon. I feel your presence might somehow allay some of the local fears. Not only would it impress upon the people that your husband is indeed a family man, but also I believe your influence can only be beneficial to the Marquis himself.

I realize your condition is delicate, but I understand the
event is several months away. Since you planned to bring
your own doctor anyway, I have no doubt that we are
sufficiently capable of seeing to your comfort and good
health.

It is your decision. Forgive me for presuming.
                                        —William Van Driesche

When she had finished reading it for the third time, Medora leaned back against the brocade coach and ran her hand
gently across her belly, waiting for the slightest movement
from her unborn child. The child's safety was paramount, of
course, but would that safety really be threatened by the move
to the Dakotas? Medora knew she was physically strong and
healthy, but would that be enough? One thing was certain;
the situation must be serious, for William would never have
taken it upon himself to write such a letter without due cause.
That he had done so at all made her uneasy. William was
neither imaginative nor forward and he did nothing without
good reason.

Glancing again at the date, she saw that the letter had been
written on the third day of June, over two weeks ago. Oddly,
she had not heard from her husband in that time, yet he usually wrote twice a week. Something was amiss. She sat up
abruptly, a smoldering glow in her eyes. She would not sit
here, 2,000 miles away, unaware of what was happening to
the Marquis and unable to help. If there was one thing Medora could not bear to be, it was helpless.

She had risen and started for the door when she heard her
father bellowing through the hallway. With great care, she
folded the letter into a tiny square and slipped it into her
pocket. Then she waited, forcing her breath to come evenly.

"Have you seen this?" Louis Von Hoffman exploded before
he had even crossed the threshold. Waving a newspaper in
front of his daughter's face, he added breathlessly, "That husband of yours can't seem to keep out of trouble!" His fleshy

cheeks were redder than usual and his muttonchop sideburns trembled from his agitation.

Medora took the paper with a steady hand, glancing at the tiny article her father had indicated.

ARMED DESPERADOES ARE MAKING MATTERS UNPLEASANTLY LIVELY AT LITTLE MISSOURI

From information received at an early hour this morning, it is very evident that a deplorable state of affairs exists at Little Missouri. On Sunday night, the desperadoes inaugurated a reign of terror in the town to express their dislike for the plans of the Marquis de Mores. Threats against the Marquis's life were voiced without fear. . . .

Medora stopped without reading to the end of the story and tried to suppress a flash of cold fear. Struggling to keep her face impassive, she handed the paper back to her father and said crisply, "Please ask Doctor Richards if he can be ready to leave by tomorrow morning, Papa. If not, ask him to follow me as soon as he can. I'm going to find Nell; she can help me pack."

"Where the devil do you think you're going?"

Medora raised her chin, declaring, "To join my husband, of course."

"You're madder than he is. Didn't you read this?" He shoved the folded newspaper toward her.

"I read it and I'm going."

Von Hoffman closed his eyes as if in pain. The tiny blue vein in his forehead pulsed regularly, but it took him several moments to gather enough strength to reply. "You're not. I forbid it."

Medora stared at him calmly while he glared back in helpless fury. She stood, stiff and unbending, her wide green eyes tranquil. She did not so much as blink, and her father recognized the obstinate look on her face. He knew she would not back down, but he had to try to convince her, just the same.

"Medora," he said, his voice heavy with concern, "please—"

"I'm going, Papa," she said simply, "and unless you bind and gag me, you won't stop me."

Von Hoffman considered her speculatively as he ran his hand along his chin. "Think what Mores will say about this, my dear. He wouldn't want you to subject yourself to the danger he faces."

"I'm sorry," she told him, "but if you wanted me to make a rational decision, you shouldn't have shown me the article. You could have kept it from me, you know, but you didn't. Why not?" She waited to see if he would respond, but he merely stood there in silence, a stricken look on his face. He could not answer her question; he did not know how. She touched his shoulder briefly, then swept past him, calling, "Nell! I need you."

The next morning, as Medora sorted quickly through the last pile of chemises, petticoats, corsets, and gloves, there was a timid knock on her door. She sighed impatiently and called, "Come in." She hoped it was not one of her parents. She had listened for hours the night before to an endless string of reasons why she should not go, but the arguments had left her unmoved. Now she was weary of the struggle; she only wanted to get away.

It was not her father who pushed the door open and stood there trembling; it was the servant girl, Nell. "A telegram," she murmured shakily, "from Little Missouri."

Medora reached for the wire and tore it open, her heart pounding erratically in her ears.

Madame la Marquise. I was wrong. Do not come. Too dangerous just now. Absolutely do not come. Letter to follow. Van Driesche.

She stared blindly at the yellow page for a moment before she said, "Does my father know this has arrived?"

"No, ma'am. I brought it straight to you."

Medora nodded briskly. "Good." She read the telegram through once more; then, lighting a candle beside her bed, she set the paper aflame and tossed it into the fireplace.

When the train chugged to a stop in Little Missouri one week later, Greg Pendleton abandoned his carriage and sauntered toward the station. Cory was waiting for the supplies he had picked up this morning, but another five minutes would make no difference. Besides, he needed to keep his finger on the pulse of things. He was well aware that the mood in town had been even more dangerous since the Marquis's return last week.

Greg watched curiously as the station master slid open the carriage door and peered into the dark interior. His gasp as he backed away was overly loud in the expectant hush that greeted this newest visitor.

Medora stepped down onto the warped wooden platform, brushing vainly at the dust that seemed to have settled permanently on her clothing. But even the dust was as nothing compared to the shocked silence that fell upon her like a pall as she took a few steps forward. Her eyes flicked quickly over the people within her sight. She knew without being told that the knowledge of her identity would make them her enemies. The long train ride had not been wasted; she had spent the time reading all the newspaper accounts she could find on the conflict that was consuming this town. She now knew how deep the antipathy toward her husband had grown, but the knowledge had not shaken her resolve in the slightest.

When she heard the station master bring her trunk, she turned to thank him and the onlookers exhaled in a collective gasp. They had not been able to see from the front what now became abundantly clear; the diminutive woman who had just stepped off the train was pregnant, and apparently well-advanced. It was then that Greg Pendleton finally moved.

With his hat in his hand, he approached Medora, his eyes running appreciatively over her tailored suit of checked brown cloth whose folds had been cleverly arranged to partly conceal her condition. The style alone proclaimed the wearer's wealth, even without the aid of the velvet collar and cuffs. The woman's face was a little pale beneath her soft felt hat, he noticed. But what struck him most was the grace and assurance he read in every line of her body. Despite her obvious pregnancy, she moved without awkwardness, and every action spoke of smooth self-reliance.

"Excuse me," he said, "but there must be some mistake."

She looked up at him, absorbing all in an instant his expensive leather jacket, gray-blue eyes, and heavy dark brows. The angular line of his jaw was unsoftened by a beard or moustache, and the twist of his lips betrayed his unyielding character. "I don't think so," she assured him. "I was told this is the town of Medora. That's right, isn't it?"

Pendleton's jawline tensed. That name had begun to haunt him ever since the Frenchman had first spoken it aloud. With the money he had to back him, the Marquis was slowly bleeding the Pendletons' town dry. Their only advantage was that they knew a few things Mores didn't, and Greg was depending on that knowledge to make the difference. "You were told wrong," he snapped. "This is Little Missouri."

Medora saw the change in him and it made her curious. "And who might you be?"

He surveyed her in silence for a long moment before he answered, "Greg Pendleton."

The name was familiar. Mores had mentioned it in his letters and she had seen it again in the newspaper accounts. The Pendletons were the only family in the area wealthy enough to be serious competitors to her husband. "I'm Medora de Vallombrosa, wife of the Marquis de Mores."

This time he actually took a step backward without trying to hide his hostility. "In that case," he said, "I suggest you get right back on the train and go back where you came from. This is no place for the wife of a man like that."

"I'm staying."

Pendleton closed his eyes briefly, attempting to control his temper. "I don't think you understand the situation here."

"I understand perfectly. A group of ruffians who have

clearly either misunderstood or been misinformed about my husband's motives here have begun a campaign to frighten him out of the Badlands or, failing that, to kill him. Isn't that correct?"

Pendleton faced her in stony silence. This had not been part of his plan, and the woman's presence annoyed him. Besides, he sensed already that she might be a formidable enemy. "I think you should go," he said, "at least for the sake of your baby."

"I *want* my child to be born here."

Clenching his teeth to keep his anger from escaping, Greg stood unmoving. This woman was a fool. She had stepped into the center of a steaming cauldron of trouble and, despite her tenacity, she could not really know what she was facing. The town was in an explosive frame of mind and Medora was another threat to them, whether she knew it or not, so he would have to see that she remained unharmed. He smiled bitterly. Some ironic god had cast him in the role of protector of Mores and his family, and it should not be that way. They were his enemies, one and all. But the Pendleton family seemed to be the only ones capable of keeping their heads, and keep them they must. At least for the moment.

"If you really mean to stay, I'll have to give you a ride to the house," he offered grimly.

"I can find my own way."

"No doubt. But, aside from the possibility that you'll have that baby on the way, there is also the chance that you might be struck by a stray bullet. It would be wiser to come with me. No one would dare fire at a Pendleton carriage."

Medora could feel the hostility like a palpable force all around her and she suspected that Greg was right. When an entire town was in this frame of mind, accidents were inevitable. Picking up her two light bags, she murmured, "As you wish."

Nodding briefly, Pendleton led her toward the carriage. When he had stowed her bags in among the supplies, he helped her up onto the seat, then climbed up beside her. As the carriage made its way through the streets, it was the prime focus of attention, but Medora seemed uninterested in the long, speculative looks she received. Yet she could not help but be aware of the ominous stillness that followed them like a hungry wolf.

When the silence began to eat away at her courage, she turned to her unpleasant companion. "What would you suggest my husband do in order to avert further trouble?"

He answered before she had even finished speaking. "Get the hell out of the Badlands and never come back."

"But I understand he will be shot if he steps outside. How is he to get to the train alive?"

"I can guarantee his safety if I have to." *And I could hardly be held accountable if something went wrong,* he added silently.

Smiling secretly at the admission he did not realize he had made, Medora remained silent.

"Well?" he asked finally.

"Stop!" she cried unexpectedly. She had just spotted what could only be the Marquis's house up ahead. It was a long walk up the hill, but she did not intend for her husband to see that she had arrived in Greg Pendleton's carriage. He would be angry enough at her mere presence. "I'll get out here."

"You don't mean to tell me you're going to climb that hill?" he asked incredulously.

"I am." She swung herself from the high seat before he could stop her and reached for her baggage.

Shaking his head at this further proof of her foolishness, Greg dragged the bags out and put them down beside her. This woman had made her own choice, after all. It was not his concern.

Medora read the derision in his eyes. "Don't underrate me, Mr. Pendleton," she warned. "I'm very well aware of my own limitations—which is why neither my husband nor I will be leaving the Badlands."

His face hardened into a stone mask and he found himself wondering if she would be quite so confident when she was a widow.

"And if you think killing my husband will frighten me away, you're wrong again," she added. "I'm staying for as long as it takes."

Disturbed at how close she had come to reading his mind, Greg watched as she made her way up the hill. She was not quite beautiful, like Cory was, he thought irrelevantly. But, nevertheless, there was something about Medora de Vallombrosa that commanded attention. The sun was obligingly setting her hair aflame against the cloudless blue sky, touching her with radiant fingers. But a profound sense of doom fell upon him as she disappeared. Suddenly, the game had moved outside his reach. He was no longer in complete control.

Katherine Pendleton slipped into the study, closing the door carefully behind her. Glancing surreptitiously over her shoulder, although she knew there was no one else in the room, the girl made her way to her father's cluttered desk. She hoped he had left it unlocked, or her curiosity would have to go unsatisfied again. But she had sworn that eventually she would find out exactly what was going on. Katherine could not bear to be left in the dark, especially when her father and grandfather had become so secretive of late.

Seating herself in the heavy oak chair, she reached for the top drawer—the one that she knew held Greg's most important papers—and was relieved to discover that for once he had forgotten to lock it. She bit her lip, casting one more furtive glance at the door before removing a handful of papers from the drawer.

Katherine had trouble making out the inky scrawls through the shadows that fell across the page, but was afraid to take the time to light a lamp. As her eyes ran quickly over the top two letters, her pulse began to pound rhythmically in her ears. She had been right about the sudden alarming quantity of her father's correspondence. She had guessed that he was involved in a particularly complex plan to insure the Pendletons' dominance of the Badlands, but she had not realized how far it had gone. The occasional names that leapt off the page at her forced her breath to lodge painfully in her throat. She had wanted to know everything, but now that she did, what was she going to do about it?

"Katherine!" Cory's high-pitched voice pierced her daughter's morbid thoughts as effectively as a slap across the face. The girl froze for an instant, then began stuffing the letters haphazardly into the drawer. She finished just as her mother threw the door open.

"*There* you are! I've been looking everywhere," Cory said peevishly. "I need you to help me with my hair." Then her gaze narrowed suspiciously as she noted her daughter's flushed cheeks and overly bright eyes. "What *are* you doing in here, anyway?"

Katherine swallowed once before she spoke. "I was looking for some paper to write a letter on," she lied adeptly. "You know I'm always running out. Now," she continued briskly, "let me look at your hair and I'll fix it for you."

Cory observed the girl in silence for several moments before she nodded, allowing Katherine to lead her into the sunny drawing room. She sat in a stiff-backed chair while the girl stood behind her, looping her pale blond curls into an artful design.

"Greg's late again," Cory fumed, having already forgotten the incident in the study. "Oh, dear, he does worry me so. I wish he'd be more considerate, especially when it so dangerous in town." Her forehead puckered into a frown and she drummed her fingers restlessly on the arm of the chair. "He might have been shot, you know. Or even killed."

Katherine smiled above her mother's head. "Not my father," she said. "They're not likely to shoot the man who paid for their guns."

"Whatever do you mean by that? You're talking riddles again, Katherine, and this isn't a joke. I'm frightened for him."

"I know," her daughter sighed, just managing to conceal her annoyance. Her mother was so dreadfully blind. "But no one's going to get hurt, Mama." Then, with a knowing look that would have frightened Cory even further, had she seen it, Katherine added, "At least, not one of us."

"Listen to me, William," Medora insisted, stopping the secretary in the doorway to the drawing room. "I promise you, everything will be all right and I shall be properly taken care of. The doctor is on his way right now. He should be here in a couple of days."

Van Driesche shook his head, his lips compressed into a thin line. He did not believe what he was hearing, any more than he had believed it when he saw Medora walking up the hill. He had seen the Marquis's blank astonishment, which had turned quickly to anger that his wife would take such a risk. That single moment in which Mores had revealed his feelings so clearly had shaken the secretary to the very core. For he knew, although the Marquis did not, that he, William, was to blame. He and he alone had brought her here. He knew there had been a bitter quarrel between Mores and his wife—it had raged through the house all afternoon—but he did not know what the outcome had been.

"I want you to know why I did it," Medora continued, despite his stiff silence. "I had to come. And once I saw that newspaper story, nothing would have kept me away. Do you hear me, William? Nothing."

The secretary looked away, unable to meet her eyes. "You don't realize how dangerous it is," he told her.

"I do realize. But I've made my choice, and not without a great deal of thought."

"The baby—" he began.

"Is not due for another month. And by then all this will have long been settled." At his sigh, which was laden with despair, she put her hands on his arm. "Don't worry, my friend, it will all work out for the best. Because, you see, my husband bears a charmed life."

He stared at her, incredulous, and she forced a smile to her lips. "I'm surprised you weren't aware of it. But I'm sure

Charles Beaumont would agree"—she paused, met his gaze squarely, and added—"if he were still alive."

Van Driesche took a single step backward as his breath escaped in a rush. "Beaumont?" he repeated.

"Yes," she assured him. "Surely you remember the man. I believe you wouldn't be here now if it weren't for him."

He stood frozen, unable to form a single syllable. If she knew about Beaumont, then perhaps she also knew about Nicole. Was that possible? Was it even possible that she had discovered the truth about—everything? He thought he had seen to it that the story would never come out. He had been so certain.

Before he could respond, she touched his arm briefly, then turned and left the room, closing the door silently behind her. William stood perfectly still for a long time, staring with mingled dread and admiration at the spot where she had been a moment before.

FIVE

Medora looked around the table, contemplating the faces of those who had gathered there for dinner. The expressions were grim, from William's pinched lips to Dick Moore's wooden jawline. Only the Marquis was smiling, and even his smile was tainted with unease.

Every evening for the past three days they had sat around this table, eating off the mismatched plates and saucers—the fine china had not yet arrived—a stiff, silent group. Goodall, Moore, William, and Anpao did not contribute much to the desultory conversation. Instead, they kept their gazes fixed on their plates and their voices still. Medora glanced covertly at Anpao, hoping that Mores had not seen the look. At first, she had been disturbed by the idea of an Indian eating at her table, but the Marquis had insisted Anpao stay. She had agreed reluctantly because she did not want to argue with her husband just now, when she knew that he was still not reconciled to her own presence.

Now, as they sat in the dining room, the wavering light from the lantern casting somber shadows across their faces, the men refused to meet one another's eyes. There was a deadly silence everywhere, and for three days it had hung like a harbinger of doom over the residents of the house on the hill. For hours at a time, the only sound was the whistling cry of the wind across the cliffs, and sometimes the cry became a moan of agony that the men inside swore had come from a human throat. It was as if everyone moved and breathed in suspended animation, waiting for the blow to fall.

Where it would hit and what form it would take, no one knew, but that it would come eventually was a certainty. And the longer O'Donnell and his men held back, doing nothing, the worse the feeling of dread became. Everyone was aware that there were too few of them to hold off a concerted attack indefinitely, but they also knew that such an attack was inevitable.

All at once the kitchen door swung open, surprising the men out of their rigid silence.

"Thought you might want coffee," the new cook said, holding up the battered pot.

Medora had hired Cassie to take care of the cooking and some of the cleaning in the hopelessly disordered house. Most of the women in town had refused point blank to associate themselves with the hated Marquis, but Cassie was a tough, seasoned woman who had worked on the roundups, and she had not been intimidated by local hostility.

As she poured the coffee, Cassie pushed a thick strand of wiry gray hair back from her broad, weathered face. Eyeing the chipped plates, which were still half-covered with prairie chicken and boiled potatoes, she shook her head in disgust. "Seems to me," she observed, "that you're all gonna fade away to nothin' if you don't start eatin' soon."

"Perhaps no one's hungry," William suggested, holding up his cup so Cassie could fill it.

"Hummph!" she snorted. "Even if you're scared out of your minds, it ain't gonna do you no good to starve to death while you wait for O'Donnell to make his move."

This time no one bothered to contradict her and, when the last cup was full, she planted her hands on her hips, muttering, "You're all just askin' for more trouble, it seems to me." As she passed the end of the table, she gave Medora's swollen belly a long, hard look. "Have to be ready for anything," she maintained grimly. "Don't never let 'em catch you by surprise." With this obscure warning, she gave a last violent shake of her head, took the coffeepot, and retreated to the haven of her kitchen.

Medora found herself smiling as she met her husband's

gaze across the table. Cassie was a prize all right—just the kind of person they needed to take the house and its occupants in hand. When the fragrance of the strong, bitter coffee touched her nose, Medora reached for her cup. Just as she lifted it from the saucer, she heard the noise—the sharp clink of metal against metal from somewhere outside. It was followed by several other sounds that she could not identify, but they made the hairs on her neck rise stiffly. It had come then. The waiting was finally over. She drew in her breath as Mores leapt from the table and her hand shook slightly, spilling the steaming black liquid into a dark brown puddle on the cloth.

Louis Von Hoffman leaned back in his brocade chair, sipping coffee laced with brandy from a delicate china cup. Smiling benignly at his guests, he let the coffee slide smoothly down his throat. It had been a pleasant dinner this evening, with only a few close friends to share it, and the pheasant and wild rice had been exceptionally good, he thought. Every one of the sculpted china plates was empty and the crystal glasses had been filled and refilled with sparkling wine.

Yes, Von Hoffman told himself, noting that even Gretta seemed relaxed this evening, things were going well. With the wine and good food warming his insides and the light from the glittering chandeliers destroying all shadows, he was extremely contented with his lot. Except, of course, when thoughts of Medora and her foolishness intruded.

"Louis," one of the guests said, wrinkling the blanket of comfortable silence that hung over them, "you look rather pleased with yourself for a man whose future rests in a handful of rifle barrels in the Dakota Badlands."

Von Hoffman waved a hand in casual dismissal. "That's my son-in-law's concern, and I'm certain he'll handle the situation." He suppressed a momentary vision of his daughter, heavy with child.

"You aren't worried, then?"

"Mores is the one taking all the risks. I just sit here drinking my claret and write the checks."

The guest rubbed his chin thoughtfully. "But surely you're taking a *financial* risk at the very least."

"Bah," his host declared, "it's only money. And I have plenty of that to spare."

Gretta stifled a gasp and nearly choked on her coffee. Glancing suspiciously at her husband, she swallowed the steaming liquid with difficulty and shook her head. *It's only money.* What a terribly odd thing for Louis to say, especially when she knew very well that to him, money had long been everything—his life, his breath, his only God.

"Besides," Von Hoffman said, watching his wife with disapproval, "we are not here to worry about danger that may never touch us. We are here to enjoy ourselves."

The Marquis crouched before the window, the feel of his rifle barrel smooth and cold in his hands, listening to the muffled noises from outside. The house was surrounded, he was certain, although the night was too dark to reveal the forms of the men sliding like snakes through the grass and sheltering bushes. Inside, there were only five men, scattered now through the various rooms, tensed and waiting. Mores knew that five were not enough. Not with Medora and her unborn child waiting upstairs.

All at once, the night exploded and the glass from the window shattered and fell to his feet. An instant later, he heard the reverberating boom of a second rifle, then a third. The Marquis stiffened as a bullet whizzed past his shoulder; then he fired, repeatedly, but he knew his shots went wild. He could not even see the men out there. They were crawling inexorably forward, their rifles spitting hot, angry fire, and he could not stop them.

Then, abruptly, the gunfire stopped. Mores stared out at the starless sky and, for a long stretch of time that seemed to him interminable, the wind was the only sound to disturb the deadly hush. He listened for the sound of whispering voices perhaps plotting the next move, but there was nothing. Nothing but the prickly hairs on the back of his neck and the knowledge that they were out there, waiting.

"What are they doing?" William called from the next room.

"I don't know, but I think we should send for help. Is there any way to get a telegram out?" the Marquis asked.

"I could do it," Anpao replied, leaving his post at the dining room window. "There is a gully out there that runs below a dip in the land. You can follow it almost to the bottom of the hill. With the darkness to hide me, I should be able to get past the guns."

"All right, then," Mores agreed, reaching for paper and ink. "Deliver this message to the office, then come back as soon as you can. We need you here."

"I will be back," Anpao assured him solemnly as he took the scrap of paper.

The Marquis put his hand on the Indian's arm. "Take care."

Anpao nodded, disappearing before Mores could speak again.

"Are you sure it's wise to send him?" William asked.

"I don't know. But at the moment, it's our only chance."

He was interrupted by a spate of screaming bullets that tore the last piece of glass from the window, crushing it to fragments with the force of their entry. William knelt like a rock sculpture, his body stiff with fear. He had thought he would get used to the gunfire, but the horror was always the same—the deafening noise that jarred his body every time he pulled the trigger, the smoke, the acrid smell, and the promise of the deadly bullets. Swallowing awkwardly, he crouched without moving, aware that the men out there had the advantage.

The rapid gunfire ceased again, abruptly, and a painful silence descended, pressing upon William's chest until he thought he would suffocate. The attackers neither moved, nor spoke, nor cocked their rifles, and the secretary closed his eyes for a moment. What the hell were they doing out there? The sporadic gunfire was beginning to eat away at his stamina; he could not bear the uncertainty. Why didn't they just make a wild run for the house? They must know there were not enough men inside to stop them. What was holding them back? He had no answer, and the blood began to pound in his ears, fiercely, until the pulse of his fear was the only sound he could distinguish.

Up in the bedroom, Medora paced the floor, rubbing her arms as if she were chilled, despite the warmth of the summer night. Her lips moved in a regular pattern, but no sounds came out, and her cheeks were pinched and pale. Her wide green eyes were glowing with a kind of fearful madness, and her fingers were spread like claws, rubbing furrows in the soft skin of her upper arms. Now and then she paused abruptly, clutching her hands before her, the fingers weaving and unweaving a senseless pattern. The color flooded her face momentarily, then crept away, leaving her cheeks as yellow as parchment.

She had not known the waiting would be like this. She had thought she was in control, that nothing could frighten her into inaction, but she had been wrong. With the first crack of a rifle, her heart had begun to beat erratically, and the sound of shattering glass below had brought a lump to her throat. Her husband was down there, the bullets falling all around him, and she could do nothing to help. The wrenching thought that he might be killed tonight surfaced again and again, although she fought wildly to suppress it. She must not think at all, she told herself. But it was hopeless; she was afraid. Medora Von Hoffman de Vallombrosa was frightened half out of her mind. . . .

The terror lay like a coiled serpent around her heart, its hot tongue flicking like a deadly warning through her veins. Medora clutched her worn stuffed teddy bear more tightly and began to run as fast as her awkward feet would carry her—away from the hungry flames at her back, from the smoke and the clatter and the shrieks of the maid who had not left the burning house in time. The child knew she had to escape, to shake herself free of the acrid smoke that clung in her nostrils and throat like a stubborn disease. The living, breathing fear of the people all around her brought a scream from the bottom of Medora's belly, and she closed her eyes, fleeing blindly, oblivious to everything but her desire to escape.

Then, abruptly, a heavy hand descended on her shoulder, holding her immobile.

"Medora," her father's voice boomed out somewhere far above her, "where are you going?"

She whirled to stare up into his flushed face and the two narrow slits of his eyes. "Away!" she choked, twisting to free herself of his relentless grip.

"No." His expression was impassive as he gazed down at her, but his voice was as rigid as cold, glittering steel. "You will not run in fear. Not *my* daughter." Grasping her hand in his, he led her back toward the house that had already been half-devoured by the fire. He was aware that she hung back and that her fingers had turned to ice, but he knew she would not dare disobey him.

When he could hear the flames crackling and hissing, he dragged her forward until she stood, trembling, in front of him. "You must learn to face your fears, Medora, and to conquer them. Otherwise you will be weak, like the others. And that I will not allow. You will stand here until I tell you to go. Do you understand?"

She nodded dumbly, too terrified to form the words that sprang into her mouth. The pulsing heat of the flames reached out to touch her skin with cruel fingers and she thought her heart had ceased its beating. She gasped when her father moved away, leaving her to stand alone with the fire reflected in her wide, blind eyes. Cold as it had been, at least his presence had given her a brief sense of safety.

Medora stood unmoving, knowing that her father was watching and that his gaze bound her as surely as a rope of iron. The serpent of fear had long since poisoned her blood from the top of her head to the soles of her feet, but she struggled to force the terror into silence. Before her, the flames leapt and reeled, mesmerizing her with their goldenrod dance, until her eyes and her ears and her small, shivering body were filled with nightmarish visions of death. But she dared not move, nor could she, for her body had ceased to answer her will. The fire held her in her place like a sinister force whose spell she had no power to break.

And then the house collapsed upon itself in a shower of malevolent sparks that threatened to set her clothing aflame. *A wordless scream was wrenched from Medora's insides, just as an awed silence fell upon the crowd that stood like lifeless mannequins gaping at the ruin, their mouths a series of burnt, barren holes in the cold black night. . .*

Medora dragged in a painful breath as another of the long silences lengthened into a strained and taut half hour of expectation. Her gown whispered with monotonous regularity as she moved, but when she paused, her breathing heavy and her eyes closed, the reassuring whisper stopped. Clenching her fists to stop herself from crying out, she wondered how long it would be now. How long until she could not bear this anymore and she cracked like a delicate china doll?

Mores's nerves were stretched to the breaking point. The gunfire had continued at irregular intervals for three hours now, and still nothing important had occurred. Anpao had long since returned safely, having delivered the telegram, and now they could only wait. The Marquis had come to dread the pauses between gunfire; at least the sound of the bullets was something he could understand. As he stared out into the impenetrable darkness, hoping for an inspiration, he heard William gasp. The Marquis turned abruptly to peer in the secretary's direction, then stopped with the rifle still in his hands.

Medora stood framed in the doorway, her long red hair tumbled about her shoulders in wild disarray, her eyes dark and wide. She was grasping the doorframe with both hands and her knuckles were bleached white.

Her husband crossed the room in three long strides, disposing of his gun on the way. "What is it?" he asked, when he came close and saw that there was not a trace of color in her cheeks.

She swallowed several times before she was able to whisper, "I can't—"

"Medora, tell me." His brow furrowed with dismay, he touched her cheek, but the pressure of his fingers on her face seemed to increase her discomfort.

"I'm sorry," she said. Then she clutched his hand unexpectedly, squeezing it until her own fingers refused to move anymore.

Just as he saw that she had bitten down so hard on her lip that the blood had begun to flow, Medora collapsed against him, mumbling, "The baby."

"Dear God!" the Marquis cried, lifting his wife in his arms. As he carried her from the room, he called to William, "Go get Cassie. Maybe she can help. I just don't know what else to do." Then, without a backward glance, he found the narrow staircase and started upward.

When they reached the bedroom, Mores lowered his wife gently onto the bed. By now, the color had come flooding back into her cheeks, giving her skin an unnatural glow. She opened her eyes and started to speak, but he shook his head. A moment later, another contraction contorted her face into an ugly grimace of pain and tiny drops of sweat broke out across her forehead.

He sat beside her, holding both her hands in his, and wished there was something he could do for her. As she lay there with her hair spread like a web upon the pillow, trying to conceal the strength of the pains that wracked her, he saw that suddenly she was tiny and fragile and very, very vulnerable. She clung to him as if she could not bear to let him go, and he realized in that instant how infinitely precious she had become to him.

* * *

Van Driesche found the cook perched wrong way around on a kitchen chair, firing a rifle through the window. When she heard William behind her, she swung around, her gun pointed at his chest. "What the hell? Oh, it's you. You startled me, Mr. Van Driesche, and that ain't wise. Next time I might blow your head off before I see my mistake." But when she noticed the unnatural pallor of his skin, she dropped the rifle on a chair and took a step toward him.

"What is it? Somebody get shot out there?"

With difficulty, William forced himself to answer her. "The baby is coming."

Cassie nodded sagely. "I thought so," she muttered, more to herself than to William. "I've seen me one or two mothers in labor before, and there's a glitter in their eyes and a flush on their cheeks that you just can't miss."

"But do you know what to do?"

Responding to the fear in his voice, the cook squeezed his arm. "Sure I do. Don't you worry, I'll take care of it." The woman had traveled with the roundups for many years, and since there had never been a doctor within miles, the task had often fallen to her. She had even delivered a child or two during the long, cold winters. "Perfectly natural thing, you know," she told him. "Though I admit, I ain't never done it with a hail of bullets comin' down around my head." She winked, grinning in an attempt to make the secretary smile. "Adds a little spice, don't you think?"

William merely glowered at her, but some of the color had begun to return to his cheeks.

"Listen to me now," Cassie instructed, wiping the smile from her face. "I'm gonna go right up to see how she's doin', but I need you to find me a pile of clean sheets. You should also heat a couple of big pots of water for washin' everything up and keeping it clean. Bring those up to the bedroom as soon as you can." Then, leaning down, she drew a small dagger from the top of her worn work boot. "And sterilize this for me. I'll need it later for cuttin' the cord."

When William did not move immediately, she punched his arm lightly. "You'd better get goin', Mr. Van Driesche, or the baby'll be sittin' up there holdin' court by the time you arrive." With that, she moved past him and lumbered through the swinging door, leaving William to gape after her in awed silence.

Mores looked up when the door swung open behind him. He was relieved to see Cassie enter the room confidently, rolling her sleeves up above her elbows. "I'll see to your wife now, sir," she announced. "You'd best go back on downstairs."

The Marquis shook his head. "I'm staying."

Rolling her eyes toward the ceiling, the cook moved closer to the bed. "Lord!" she hooted, "just what we need." She seated herself on the edge of the mattress and, ignoring Mores, focused her attention on Medora.

"Listen to me, honey," Cassie murmured in a surprisingly gentle voice. "Do you know how far apart the pains are?"

"About fifteen minutes, I think," Medora told her.

The cook nodded, puckering her lips in thought. "That's it then. All we can do now is wait 'til the child decides to come. You holdin' up all right?"

When Medora nodded, Cassie rose awkwardly and turned to face her employer. "I think you should go," she repeated firmly. "I'll stay with her now."

"Isn't there something I can do?" the Marquis asked, his voice hoarse with concern.

"Why sure. You can go back down there and keep those men from blowin' the house up around our ears." When he continued to hesitate, her lips narrowed into a thin line. "Besides," she added, "things is gonna get kinda messy in here, and I ain't sure you'd like that much. Hell, I've seen it before, so it won't bother me."

"Mores," Medora said, finding her voice at last, "please do as she says. They need you down there. And I'll be all right."

Reluctantly, he bowed to their combined assault, leaving them to return to his hopeless vigil with his rifle.

* * *

For several hours now there had been no change, either in the movements of the men outside or in the bedroom upstairs. The Marquis had been crouched by the window so long that his legs had grown numb and his hands on the rifle had begun to tingle and ache. And he still could not decide what O'Donnell's intentions were. Perhaps this would be a siege, he reasoned—a battle of wills in which the winner would be the side that could bear the uncertainty the longest.

Exhausted from the constant tension and his own lack of sleep, Mores propped himself against the windowsill, closing his eyes for a moment. At least no one had been killed, he thought. And thank God for Cassie and her makeshift medical talents. He only hoped she could really care for Medora, who lay just above him now, struggling with a kind of pain that he could not even begin to comprehend.

It was near dawn, and the Marquis was shaken from his thoughts by the hiss of several bullets that flew past their target, losing themselves in the shadowed room behind him. He heard furtive movements from outside and he tensed, trying to penetrate the dregs of darkness with his weary eyes. But by the time the murky light of dawn had begun to creep across the damp, trampled grass, there was not a single man to be seen. Only a few piles of empty shotgun shells revealed the places where his enemies had been an hour before. "Damn!" he muttered, infuriated by his own helplessness. But before he could move a muscle, he heard the high-pitched wail from upstairs; it rang through the house like a clear, piercing bell. The Marquis was on his feet in an instant, making his way to the room from which he had been barred for so long—the room that now held his wife and child.

Medora lay unmoving in the center of the bed, fighting to keep the persistent cobwebs of sleep from her mind. She was so weary that it was as if the world no longer existed, despite the fact that she could hear Cassie muttering to herself in the background as she gathered together the soiled sheets. Medora was vaguely aware of a sense of peaceful triumph, and when the child moved slightly in the circle of her arm, the feeling became, for an instant, sharp and intense.

She had borne a daughter, Medora thought, running a finger lovingly across the baby's soft cheek. A thrill of pleasure penetrated the mists that clouded her thoughts, even though she knew that it should have been a son, at least for Mores's sake. But that would come in time. For herself, she was deeply satisfied, now that the battle was finally over.

It was then that her husband opened the door and stood as if transfixed on the threshold. By now most of the blood had been cleaned away, though the room still smelled of sweat and struggle. Medora lay in bed, cradling the baby in her arms and Mores had to force his breath through his dry, parched throat. She was there, alive and apparently unhurt, although her skin was nearly transparent and the circles under her eyes were dark and broad. He could not help but shiver at the picture she made. The matted, wet strands of her hair fell in disarray across the pillow, her gown clung to her chest in damp patches, even her eyelids were dark and drooping with their own cumbersome weight.

"Come and see your daughter," she murmured huskily.

As her husband approached the bed, Medora smiled, still struggling to keep her exhaustion from overcoming her. "I want to name her Athenais Margaretta after my mother and in honor of Athena, Goddess of War."

Her voice faded out and Cassie grunted behind Mores's shoulder. "The poor thing was born in the middle of a shower of bullets, after all," she observed. Then, with her arms full of blood-soaked sheets, she left the room.

The Marquis bent down to look into the dark, wrinkled face of his first child. He had just reached out to touch her forehead when Goodall appeared in the doorway.

"We got the answer to our wire, sir. I think you should see this right away."

Drawing away reluctantly, Mores brushed his lips across Medora's cheek and realized that she had finally lost the battle against her weariness; she was sound asleep. He left her to step out into the hall, where he took the yellow form Johnny offered, reading the message with a sigh of relief.

Have dispatched deputy, posse for O'Donnell's arrest. Arriving 3:00 train tomorrow. Sheriff Allen.

So help was finally on the way. When he tried to hand the wire back, Goodall said, "Turn it over."

Mores did so, surprised to find another message scrawled in heavy black across the page.

You can put the help from thc posse in your eye, Markee. My men and me will meet them at the train and I guarantee they'll never make it up the hill alive. O'Donnell.

SIX

By two o'clock the following afternoon, Mores and Dick Moore had left the house behind, stationing themselves behind tall rocks along the trail that O'Donnell and his men were most likely to take out of town. The Marquis was determined to stop the hunter if he were really so foolish as to attack the posse. Anpao had suggested this particular position because although it was out of sight of the train station, the rocks and pillars that bordered it provided excellent protection for the two men, as well as a good chance of backing O'Donnell's gang against a stone wall that even they would have trouble scaling.

Mores was not foolish enough to believe the hunter incapable of luring the men away from the house in just this manner and then attacking the building, so the Marquis had left Johnny Goodall, William, and Anpao behind to guard Medora and the baby. He would have liked to have the Indian along—he knew him to be an excellent shot—but Mores had decided that if there should be trouble, it would be best if Anpao were not involved.

So now the two men waited in the expectant hush that had fallen like a shroud on the desolate landscape. Even the wind lay silent and impatient, awaiting the outcome. And then the high-pitched shriek of the train whistle exploded into the air, shaking the men free of the spell cast by their own sense of doom.

As the train came to a shuddering halt, O'Donnell, Riley Luffsey, and Dutch Wannegan exchanged a long look. Lifting their rifles, they aimed at the platform where the first members of the posse had begun to appear. One by one, the strangers followed the deputy from the train until they stood in a long, uneven line along the platform.

The hunter turned his attention to Harmon, whom he had met before and knew to be the deputy from Mandan. "Harmon," he called, shifting his weight slightly in the saddle, "I suggest you tell your men that if they so much as flick a bug off their guns, I'll shoot them where they stand."

Harmon cleared his throat uneasily and stepped forward. "Listen, O'Donnell," he began in a small voice, "I've got a warrant here for the arrest of yourself, Luffsey, and Wannegan, and I mean to take you back to Mandan for trial."

He had barely managed to get the words out before O'Donnell started laughing. "I'll never be taken alive by any lawman and you should know it. But if you care to try to arrest me and my friends, go right ahead," the hunter suggested, accompanying his words with a thrust of his rifle.

Harmon glanced at the three rifle barrels and swallowed noisily. He did not move; there was nowhere to go, and he did not fancy finding himself on the station platform with three bullet holes through his chest.

O'Donnell's lips stretched into a long, slow smile when the deputy did not respond. "Well, now," he sneered, "I guess you ain't plannin' to arrest us after all, are you?" He raised a hand to run it through his tangled hair and chewed his lip thoughtfully. "I'll tell you, though, I don't know as I trust you just yet, and I think you'd best prove your good intentions. Don't you think he should, Riley? Dutch?"

The other two agreed with curt nods of their heads and Harmon struggled to keep his breathing regular.

"I think, if you really want us to believe you, Deputy, you'll run across the street to the nearest saloon and bring us three whiskeys, just as a sign of your reformed attitude."

When Harmon did not move immediately, the hunter reached for the trigger and squeezed it, watching in amusement as the bullet ricocheted off the boards at the deputy's feet. Harmon glowered up at him, opening his mouth to speak, but when O'Donnell moved to repeat the performance, the deputy jumped from the platform and ran for the saloon that he had already located just behind the three gunmen.

He came out within a minute, walking with great care and holding three glasses in his unsteady hands. Luffsey grinned and called out, "Now don't you spill any of our whiskey, you hear? We're awful thirsty."

Harmon carried the glasses to them, but he refused to look up and meet O'Donnell's mocking gaze. Already he could feel the disdain of his companions crawling down his neck like a slippery snake.

The three men downed their whiskey quickly, then tossed the glasses over their shoulders. Then, while Harmon and his men stood by in stiff silence, the gunmen began to back away, keeping their guns trained on the posse and their eyes wide and alert. When they were fifty yards from the platform, O'Donnell suddenly dug his spurs into his horse's sides and Luffsey and Wannegan followed suit. Yelling obscenities and laughing, they fired several shots into the air; they knew they were home free. Even if Harmon had the nerve to follow them, he wouldn't be able to get six horses in time. The three gunmen turned their horses to the right as they left the town behind, raising a choking cloud of dust that defiled the still afternoon air like an insidious disease.

Cassie stood with the baby in her arms, staring out the window at the barren summer landscape. The heat hung over everything—a heavy shimmering force that distorted the carved stone into bizarre, quivering shapes along the horizon. Athenais whimpered and the cook glanced down, clucking reassuringly. "Your mama's asleep, child, and I ain't of a mind to wake her just now. She needs her rest, you know. Besides, it's better if she ain't aware of what's goin' on out there. What she don't know won't hurt her, I always say."

Cassie had developed a habit of talking aloud to herself in the long years she had spent working around preoccupied men. But she found that she was gratified to have an audience in little Athenais, even though the child could not understand.

"Athenais!" she snorted, rocking the restless baby soothingly. "Silly kinda name for a child, but then, there's no accountin' for taste."

The woman stared gloomily out the window, cursing the distant rocks that blocked her vision. She wanted to be out there in the center of things, taking care of those outlaws in her own way. The only things that had kept her here were the wriggling baby—who looked as if she were about to squall—and her sleeping mother. From what Cassie had seen, Medora was prone to unwise acts and it was better that the older woman be here to keep the Marquis's wife from involving herself in a struggle she could not possibly win.

Just then, the cook heard a noise behind her and she swung around to find Medora standing in the doorway. She had not bothered to brush her tangled hair and her face was flushed and furious.

"My husband is gone!" she cried wildly, clutching at the doorframe to hold herself upright. "Where is he?"

Cassie observed her in silence, searching for some harmless lie that would calm her excited mistress, but before she could speak, Medora closed her eyes, leaning heavily against the wall.

"He's gone to meet O'Donnell, hasn't he?"

Her only the answer was the sudden, explosive wailing of her discontented child.

In the long shadows where they waited, the Marquis and Moore heard the silence that followed the train's arrival. They waited, their muscles tense, straining their eyes in an attempt to see what was hopelessly beyond their vision. Then they heard a single shot, another long hush, then a salvo of rifle fire.

Mores signaled to Dick as the blood began to race through his veins. When the pounding of hooves approached their hiding place, he leaned out to see if Moore was ready. He was crouched with his shoulders resting on the rocks that protected him, holding his rifle cradled against his chest with the barrel pointing at the curve in the trail. The dust rose just before the horses came in sight, clouding the men's vision and drying out their throats, but neither moved to make himself more comfortable.

Then the Marquis stood up so that his head was visible above his stone shield. He saw the three gunmen, but there was no posse behind them. O'Donnell must have carried out his threat after all. Raising his hand in the air, he called out, "Halt!" as Wannegan, then O'Donnell and Luffsey, approached.

O'Donnell answered the command with a shot from his revolver, and as his companions raised their guns also, Mores flattened himself against the stone. When a second shot flew past the Marquis's shoulder, he aimed for one of the horses, squeezing the trigger just as one of the other animals fell. In the confusion of shots that followed, all three horses were downed, and O'Donnell and the others took refuge behind the inert forms, firing shot after shot as the bullets buried themselves one after another in the fallen animals.

Mores came up to his knees, aimed deliberately and fired, determined, this time, to bring this long and useless struggle to an end. These men had pushed him too far and he would not let them win. The flapping buckskin sleeves of his jacket were soon pierced with two bullet holes and one shot hit the rock beside him, knocking loose a piece that cut his cheek. The cut was not deep, but it began to bleed heavily until he had the taste of blood in his mouth. He closed his eyes momentarily as every muscle in his body grew taut and ready. Then, all at once, he was aware of the fleeting stillness—that brief instant when sound and sight seemed to stop altogether. . . .

The mist was blinding, and thick enough to keep away the normal sounds that he knew must be all around him. The Marquis glanced uneasily over his shoulder, waiting for Wil-

liam to come with his sword, but, for the moment, there was
nothing—no sound, no movement, nothing but his own suspended breathing. Then Van Driesche appeared like a wary
specter, his lined forehead betraying his own distress.

The Marquis reached for his sword as they came out of
the mist unexpectedly and found themselves on a familiar
sweep of land just outside the Paris city limits. There was
the oak tree, its upper branches still wrapped in mist, its trunk
heavy and solid with the gnarled roots coiled at the base like
fingers frozen in the act of reaching outward. Beyond the
tree, he could make out the two other men—the tall, heavyset
one with the sword and his inconspicuous companion.

Mores closed his eyes for a moment, nodding curtly when
William touched his shoulder in a false gesture of reassurance. I should not be here, the Marquis thought. It is not
right that this should happen. Nicole, he murmured without
making a sound. Dear God, Nicole!

Then the man began to move toward him and he could
see how his jaw was set in an ugly line. The man's heavy
shoulders were taut with anger barely kept under control, and
the spotless white ruffle at his throat quivered slightly, but
Mores was wise enough to know that it was not with fear.
He raised his own sword, still half-blind with wonder that
this should be happening at all, and, before he had let his
breath escape, the man was upon him, thrusting his cold silver
blade with deadly accuracy.

Mores did not want to kill him, yet he did. His mind was
a web of conflicting emotions—anger, sorrow, horror, and despair—but he did not want the man to die. As the blade cut
through his sleeve, however, tracing a deep red line in his
upper arm, the Marquis tensed, drew in his breath, and took
a step backward. His bones were frozen from his night of
restless pacing along the garden walks, but he had to force
them into action, and quickly. His sword, which had been
moving with irregular strokes, began to respond to his determination. Now it flicked through the air in a silver arc, dip-
ping and thrusting in graceful curves.

Then he saw it; the blade was coming for him, straight for

his heart, and he could not move away in time. The air stood
still for an instant, then rushed about his ears in a hissing
wave of realization. The man thrust wildly, sure that he had
reached his target, and drew away triumphant. But then, incredibly, the Marquis turned, his sword arm free, and, despite
the slight stain of red seeping out beneath his left arm, came
forward again.

He did not know what had happened. He only knew he
should be dead; the thrust had been perfectly timed, perfectly
centered, and yet, here he was with only a scratch beneath
his arm. Now he became aware of the bemused look on his
opponent's face and he lunged, suddenly wild with fury because he had almost died at this man's hand.

Three more quick strokes and the other man had fallen
awkwardly onto the wet morning grass. But before Mores
could move, a shrieking, flailing animal came out of nowhere
and flung himself on the Marquis, forcing him to the ground.
In a moment, he saw that it was the boy, and he recognized
the blade the boy held poised above his head.

"You killed my father," the child hissed. Then he brought
the knife quickly downward.

Mores almost smiled. He would die after all, but not by a
man's hand. No, it would be this boy who brought him down.
But then the weight was lifted from his chest and he saw as
if through a haze that William had grasped the boy and
dragged him away, relieving him of his knife as he did so.
The child struggled wildly for a moment, his eyes never once
leaving the Marquis's face, but when he heard a strangled
gasp from behind him, he wrenched himself free and went
to kneel at the other man's side.

Mores rose slowly, aware of the flurry of activity a few
feet away. They had propped the man up on his own jacket
and now they were attempting to staunch the flow of blood.
The Marquis felt his breath catch in his throat and then, suddenly, the fury was gone, evaporated, to be replaced with tearing pity and despair so deep it left him shaking. Despite the
efforts of the others to keep him away, he went down on one
knee beside the fallen man. He perceived at once that the

care of the man's friends had been ineffective. *Then he saw, as if in a single instant, the tear-streaked cheeks of the boy, the hand still gripping the now useless sword, the deep creeping red stain across the man's shirt, and the expression of horrified surprise frozen permanently onto Charles Beaumont's lifeless face. . . .*

"He's dead, sir, you can see that," Moore shouted, pointing to the motionless form behind one of the fallen horses.

For just an instant, the Marquis did not move. Then, aware at last that he could not let the others get away, he trained his gun on O'Donnell, who had leapt up and begun running. Mores recognized that the hunter was limping badly, and he ordered him to stop. At the same moment, Wannegan surrendered to Dick Moore, who held him at gunpoint.

O'Donnell glanced back once, clutched his wounded leg, and realized his position was hopeless. With a last ugly look at the Marquis, he threw down his gun and collapsed against a rock.

Only then did Mores climb across the horse's body and stoop to examine the grim, blood-stained bundle of rags that had once been Riley Luffsey. And no one even noticed the man who abandoned his hiding place behind a distant rock, creeping away silently, head low and shoulders hunched.

SEVEN

"He's done it now," Jake Maunders crowed. "I saw it with my own eyes. The Markee killed Luffsey in cold blood."

Aware of the dangerous undercurrent of excitement in Maunders's voice, Bryce Pendleton put a restraining hand on the man's arm. "Sit down now, Jake, and catch your breath while I think about what we should do."

Maunders shook his head, turning to appeal to Greg, who stood hidden in the shadows. "There's no thinkin' to be done. We have to *move!* Now that he's a murderer, we could hang him in ten minutes flat with nary a peep of protest."

"You forget that he still has friends, Jake, and I guarantee you they would protest loud and clear," Greg said. "No, my father's right. We have to go carefully."

Snorting in disgust, Maunders collapsed into a wing-backed chair. "Yeah, just like the other night. We could've stormed the damned house and killed him right then. But no, you order us to wait. Well, it could just be," he said, punctuating his remark with a stab of his finger on the arm of the chair, "that we're gettin' *tired* of waitin'. You ever think of that?"

Bryce's lips twitched into a brief smile. "I thought of everything, Jake. And I know how anxious the men are to get this thing over with. But I have other obligations to consider at the moment. You'll just have to trust me a little longer." At Maunders's growl of displeasure, he added, "We can do this legally now; there's simply no need for immediate violence that might get out of hand. No one can guarantee that the Marquis's men will be the only ones to get hurt."

He paused for a moment, pacing restlessly before the window. "All we have to do for the time being is see that Mores is arrested. Once that's done, he'll suffer for his crime, I promise you that."

"I wasn't thinkin' of sendin' him to jail," Jake muttered, his scowling face darkened by the shadow of the chair wing.

Greg smiled broadly. "Neither were we, Jake." He took a heavy roll of bills from his pocket, tossing several into Maunders's lap. "You've been a big help, and you can see that we appreciate it. But from here on in, you leave this to us, understand?"

Leaning down to pick up his money, Maunders grunted his agreement, but clearly he was not yet satisfied.

"Don't stew on it," Bryce advised. "This time we can't fail. We just let the people's hatred take over and finish the job for us. The Marquis has delivered himself into our hands, and we don't even have to dig him a grave; he's already dug his own, and it's so deep that even *he* won't be able to climb out." He took a deep breath, adding under his breath, "And now, finally, my wife's debt will be paid in full."

The Marquis crossed the tiny room for the hundredth time, his boots slapping hollowly against the packed dirt floor. The little bit of light that had pierced the occasional empty spaces between the logs had long since disappeared and the barred window had faded into a blur. There was nothing to see now but the shadowy form of Dick Moore in the far corner, stretched out in uneasy sleep. He himself was kept awake by his own restless nature and an increasing sense that this long night was far from over.

That he should be here at all, he thought, confined in the log cabin jail at Mandan, was absurd. He had not been the one who had threatened another man's life repeatedly, attacked his home, and attempted to destroy his town. He had merely been protecting himself and his family against the insanity of

others. Yet here he was, being held along with Moore pending
a trial for the murder of Riley Luffsey.

But from the noises coming from the people grouped outside the jail, he guessed that such a trial was becoming more
and more unlikely as the minutes passed. The crowd of townspeople milled around just beyond the single window, oblivious to the stuffy heat that made their clothes cling damply
to their bodies. Their very presence left Mores wary. He
sensed that they were not willing to wait until the hearing;
they had other plans.

Moore stirred in his sleep and the Marquis watched him
through the murky light. He knew that this man should not
be here; he had done nothing but follow orders. No one even
knew which of them had fired the shot that killed Luffsey
and besides, Mores sensed that it was *he* they were after, not
Moore. Yet somehow he had dragged the man into the center
of the conflagration with him and he no longer had the power
to protect Moore. What frustrated him most was that he could
do nothing to stop this. He was completely powerless. The
men outside were the ones who had control.

As the volume of protest began to increase, Mores crossed
to the window and peered out, being careful to keep himself
out of sight. The darkness was settling in a thick, enveloping
blanket and, under its protection, men had begun to creep
forward to voice their anger more loudly. Several torches had
been lit and in their eerie light, the Marquis saw that every
single man held a weapon of some kind. Knife blades and
gun barrels gleamed dully in the flickering light and several
men held long, heavy ropes coiled around their arms. Ropes
were for hangings, Mores realized.

The muttering had turned to cries of "Lynch the bastard!"
and "We want justice!" Behind him, Moore awoke with a
start. The Marquis motioned him to silence. Although he
could not see the man clearly, he knew the sweat had broken
out across Dick's forehead. There was a guttural chorus of
protest and then the crowd surged forward, only to fall back
unexpectedly at the last moment. Mores recognized that their
antipathy was not yet strong enough to force them into taking

an irrevocable step, but he also sensed that the hatred would grow and swell, like an all-consuming disease, until they were ready to kill. It would not be long; he could see it in the haggard, bearded faces that the flickering torches exposed now and then. The eyes were all the same color by now—slate gray and icy with hatred.

Turning away from the window, he leaned against the rough log wall and attempted to ignore the rising clamor from outside. But as the minutes passed, the chanting continued and grew into an outpouring of religious fervor with pagan death as its god. Moore shrank back onto the packed dirt floor, swallowing noisily, and the Marquis knew Dick was afraid. To be attacked in the house and face twenty or even thirty hostile guns was one thing, but to face this crowd—which had transformed itself from several angry men into a single, determined machine—was quite another.

Irrelevantly, Mores found himself thinking of Medora and the child he had seen only twice. Thank God he had left William behind. Thank God they were not alone and unprotected. Medora, he thought, with her long, luxurious hair woven around her like a cape, holding little Athenais in her arms. Medora—

As if in answer to his thoughts, a sudden hush fell on the crowd outside the window. Moore sat up abruptly, disconcerted by the unexpected silence. The Marquis swung around to peer out into the breathing darkness and for a full minute, all he could see were anonymous faces lit grotesquely by torches that had been raised high in the air. Then the crowd parted, as if upon command, and Mores saw what had drawn their attention and held it in an iron grip.

There, at the end of the crude dirt path, not thirty yards away from the window, stood Medora with the baby in her arms. The Marquis closed his eyes in disbelief and horror, but not before he saw the way the light fell with quivering irregularity upon her long, dark cape, giving it the appearance of an undulating wave of water as she walked. Her skin was ghostly white, but her eyes blazed green fire.

She was mad, he thought. Hopelessly mad. And she had

dropped into the middle of a battle that she could not even begin to understand. Once again, she had put her life, and that of her child, in danger. What could she possibly hope to accomplish with these savages who had worked themselves into a frenzied state that he very much feared would only be appeased by the taste of blood?

He opened his eyes to find that she was still coming toward him and that the men had cleared the way for her, holding their torches like royal standards above her head. The crowd was confused; they did not understand who this woman was or what she was doing here. They only knew that her presence could well mean the destruction of their plans.

When she stood directly beneath the window, Medora turned to face them without once looking up to where she knew her husband was watching. "I am Medora de Vallombrosa," she said, her voice carrying easily through the expectant silence, "and I've come to stay here tonight, where I can be near my husband." She heard a sharp gasp above her head, but she did not intend to turn her back on the crowd.

The men before her were stunned. This woman, this lunatic, had come here, knowing the danger that awaited her, to ensure that the Marquis remained unhurt. There she stood, the baby resting quietly in her arms, without a trace of doubt or fear to mar her smooth white face. The flickering light of the torches threw her expression into sharp relief and the people realized that, incredible as it might seem, she was not afraid of them. This tiny woman, who was no more than five feet tall, would defy them all, despite their fury and their weapons. And they recognized, with a sinking feeling of despair, that she would win. They sensed a kind of strength in her that put them all to shame.

For what seemed like an eternity, no one moved or spoke. Then, cursing and spitting, their frustration pulsing in their glittering eyes, the group began to back away. They drifted with unerring accuracy toward the nearest saloon. It was a long time before they had all gone, because they were reluctant to concede defeat so easily—but, unless the woman went away, they had no choice. And Medora showed every intention of spending the entire night in her present position near the door of the jail house. By now she had spread her cloak on the ground and arranged herself upon it, soothing the child when she whimpered. Medora was staying; that much was very clear.

Eventually, the last agitator disappeared into the welcome light of the saloon and the men inside the tiny jail heaved a joint sigh of relief.

"My God," Dick exploded, when he finally dared to turn away from the window, "that's a hell of a wife you got there, Marquis."

Mores nodded and moved across the room to stare moodily through the heavy bars that held him inside. The men had gone away and he and Moore were safe, it was true, but she had taken a risk of which he could never approve. They might have raped her, or even killed her, and he could imagine what they would have done to the baby girl. But they hadn't. They had crept quietly away, their anger dissipated and their lust for blood unsatisfied. Medora had succeeded where himself had failed. He now owed her his life.

He could not think straight just now. His mind was a tangle of relief, anger, respect, fear, and resentment, all for the woman who sat now beneath the window, crooning simple lullabies to her daughter. But somewhere, hidden beneath the confusion and anger, there was an intense stirring of gratitude and a surge of love that threatened to leave him blind with its unbridled force.

The next morning, the Marquis and Moore were allowed to move to a hotel where they could more easily ensure their personal safety until the trial was over. But neither Medora nor her father's money and influence could stop the trial itself. It began two days later and dragged on week after week in the debilitating summer heat. Even Medora could not prevent the town from breaking into two hostile armed camps that awaited the outcome with knives sharpened and rifles raised.

Finally, it was William who, despairing of a fair judgment,

went to see the attorney general of the territory. Van Driesche pointed out that Mores had done his utmost to act legally, and that, in fact, he had only been protecting what O'Donnell and his men had threatened time and again. The secretary also reminded the official—wisely—that the Marquis's business interests were suffering while he was forced to await the outcome of this farce.

Aware of the huge investment Mores had made in the territory and the extensive revenues he was likely to bring to the area in the future, and reluctant to allow the witless mob to manipulate the law as they had done, the attorney general heeded William's plea. The official had a long, private talk with the local judge and two days later, the judge brought in a verdict of "innocent" and the trial finally came to an end.

Then, and only then, thirty days from the time they first entered the jail in Mandan, the Marquis and Dick Moore were released. The two men left the jail and started for home, free at last—or so they thought—from the accusation of murder that had haunted them for so long.

EIGHT

"It's actually chilly!" Medora exclaimed in surprise as she stepped out into the sunlight.

Closing the door of the newly completed company office behind him, William smiled. "Summer is over and fall is on its way. Haven't you noticed that the cottonwoods are beginning to turn?"

Medora drew her light shawl more tightly around her shoulders. "No, I haven't. But then, it's difficult to notice the color of the leaves from the inside of an office."

The secretary nodded. It was true that they had not had much time for observing nature since their return from Mandan nearly two months ago. He and Mores had been much too busy with building, organizing, and buying for the business, while Medora had spent most of her time with the accounting books. But all the work was about to pay off. The packing plant was finished now and nearly ready to open its doors. The butchers had been hired and the entire operation would be ready for the upcoming fall roundup. They had indeed accomplished a great deal in a very short time.

Medora glanced around her for the first time in many weeks, taking in the impressive Dakota scenery. Even the bite of the clean, cold air was refreshing; she hoped it would clear some of the cobwebs from her mind. She found, all at once, that she was looking forward to an evening of relaxation at the house; she had not really relaxed since the day she had first arrived in the Badlands. The house, which the townspeople had taken to calling the Chateau, had finally begun to feel finished as the trainloads of furniture and other belongings arrived from New York. Now, with her favorite Persian rugs and brocade chairs to soften the barren rooms, it had at last begun to feel like home.

As they passed by one newly finished building after another, Medora realized that the town itself had sprung up with remarkable rapidity after the trial last July. And, surprisingly, there had been no further trouble from the locals. Apparently, their rage had burned itself out in the short but vicious summer campaign. It seemed that now the people were happy to do their work and collect their pay regularly.

Yes, Medora thought, considering their achievements with contentment, things were just as they should be. Mores had won, as she had always known he would.

"Good afternoon, ma'am, Mr. Van Driesche."

She looked up to find herself staring into Greg Pendleton's disturbing silver-gray eyes. For a moment, Medora had an unaccountable desire to take a step backward, but she forced herself to hold her ground. "Mr. Pendleton," she murmured stiffly, noticing out of the corner of her eye that William's expression had become decidedly hostile.

"How is everyone at the Chateau?" Pendleton asked, apparently unaware of the disconcerting effect he had on his companions. "We rarely see you in public these days."

"We've been busy," William said. "And now, if you'll excuse us—"

"But I want to know how the Marquis is," Greg pressed.

With a warning glance at Van Driesche, Medora told Pendleton, "My husband is doing excellently, of course. Why should he not be? All his plans are succeeding admirably."

There was a brief flame of some unreadable emotion in Greg's eyes, but it disappeared as quickly as it had come. "Are they? I thought he might be having trouble. After all, a man who owes his life to a woman—" he let the sentence go unfinished, but his meaning was quite clear.

Swallowing her anger before it betrayed her, Medora raised her chin and replied, "Perhaps he owes his life to the fact that he inspires such intense loyalty in others. Not *every* man has that ability. In fact, I would guess that Mores is one of very few who possess it. Good afternoon, Mr. Pendleton."

Greg was taken aback by her sharp response and he did not miss the hostile implication in her words. As she walked away with William at her side, he considered her with new interest. A remarkable woman, he found himself thinking, and a difficult woman to break. But he would find a way, somehow. He had to.

"Are you going to the Marquis's dinner party, Mr. Roosevelt?" Cory Pendleton asked her guest.

Theodore Roosevelt took a sip of his lukewarm coffee and replaced the cup on the saucer. "I've been invited, but I'm not certain I'll attend."

"Oh, but you must," Cory insisted.

"Of course you must," Katherine observed, turning away from the window that had held her attention for some time. "You'll never make yourself one of us if you don't come to all the social occasions."

Roosevelt blinked, regarding the girl curiously. In the several times he had seen her and her family since his arrival in the Badlands, he had come to learn that a Pendleton almost always had a hidden motive for his or her actions. But then, he found that knowledge exhilarating; with Katherine, Greg, and Bryce, one was always left guessing. "I don't know," he said at last. "I'm not sure I *want* to become one of you."

Bryce gazed down into his coffee cup, smiling to himself. That was the first observant remark he had heard Roosevelt make. The man had supposedly come west for the hunting in the area, and he did throw himself into the sport with a great deal of enthusiasm. Surprisingly, he was even a fairly good horseman. But Pendleton had never quite felt that Roosevelt belonged here. He was short and pale and his thick, round glasses gave him a studious look that didn't quite fit with the image of a western hunter.

Still, Bryce mused, eyeing his guest surreptitiously, Roosevelt was a rich man and he seemed likely to buy up a great deal of land in the area. For that reason alone, Pendleton intended to make him an ally. Where his struggle with the Marquis was concerned, he had to take what he could find and make the best use of it. "I'm not at all sure *we'll* be going to the party," Bryce announced.

"Oh, but of course we will," Cory cried. "I know you don't like the Marquis, but if we stayed away from all his parties, we'd never leave the house. You know very well he's the only one willing to enjoy himself around here. Why, the man brings in guests from all over the country. It's the first time I've seen the Badlands so festive in *years*." When she saw how Bryce's face clouded over, Cory bit her lip; then, regaining her courage momentarily, she added, "I'm *glad* Mores came here."

Pendleton glowered at his daughter-in-law, thinking again that she was a hopeless fool. And possibly a dangerous one. "Even you will be sorry someday, Cory. We *all* will."

Katherine saw the sympathetic look Roosevelt gave her mother, but her mind was preoccupied with her own thoughts. She had seen how her grandfather's expression grew daily more morose and his tone increasingly bitter. Something had to be done to remedy the situation—and soon. "We'll go to the party, of course," she stated firmly. "Mama's right. We can't afford to miss it."

But then, Katherine had her own reasons for wanting to be there. She wanted to meet the Marquis and his wife, to watch them and discover what motivated them, to learn how they acted and thought. Because she alone, of all the Pendletons, recognized how difficult it would be for her family to conquer an enemy they did not even understand.

The Marquis turned his horse toward the river as he made his way home from the packing plant. He was pleased with the progress the business was making and anxious for the plant to open its doors. He smiled to himself. He had said once that the Northern Pacific Refrigerator Car Company would be successful enough to make Swift and Armour nervous and he meant to see that it happened that way.

Mores let the horse find its own path along the river until he was sheltered overhead by the leaves of the cottonwoods and at his side by the rising bluff. There was a more direct route up to the house, but he preferred this one; here the sound of the water was soothing and the trees offered shade from the blinding brightness of the sun. Today he found the silence particularly welcome. But then, suddenly, he stopped, listening. It struck him that something was amiss, and when he saw the broken branches and trampled grass that twisted in an uneven path away from the water, he knew he had been right. Someone had been through here recently, and it looked as if they might have been crawling. Upright footsteps would not have left such an obvious trail behind.

Swinging his leg silently over the saddle horn, he dismounted warily, his revolver in his hand. Before he moved, he checked to see if his knife was still secure at his waist. He knew there was another in his boot top; he could feel the leather case against his leg. Secure in the knowledge that he was well armed, he bent down to make his way across the marshy ground, creeping forward an inch at a time. He did not want whoever was there to know he was coming.

It was not long before he pushed a heavy branch aside and found what he had been seeking. A girl lay face down on the ground, her hand stretched out before her as if she were reaching for something that was no longer there. Her long, black hair fell in matted tangles across her face, hiding it from view, and there was nothing about her plain gray cloth skirt to give any hint to her identity.

He guessed that she was unconscious and noted that her feet were bare and her right ankle severely bruised and swollen. Moving cautiously, he slid his revolver back into the holster and knelt beside the girl. She was obviously hurt; at the very least, her ankle was badly sprained. Mores reached out to slide one arm carefully beneath her back, then turned her over, lifting her hair away from her face. He realized with a shock that she was an Indian and he knew all at once that he had seen her before. She was Ileya, Anpao's sister. He had caught just a glimpse of her that first day when he had hired the Indian, but he knew it was the same girl; her face was a younger, softer version of Anpao's. But what was she doing here, hiding among the trees?

Whatever the reason, he knew that he must help her, not only for her brother's sake, but also for her own. He began to run his hands lightly down her body, checking for other wounds or breaks, but her ankle seemed to be the only serious problem. He discovered a lump on the side of her head; she must have hit the tree when she fell. The Marquis sat back for a minute, considering his next step. He could take her back to the Chateau, but some instinct told him she would not be welcome. He still remembered his astonishment when he had returned from Mandan to find that Medora had sent Anpao away. He made her uneasy, she had said. Mores had been deeply disturbed and had gone looking for his friend, but had never found him.

Well, then, where could he take Ileya? He certainly couldn't leave her here. Suddenly the answer struck him. He would take her to a hut farther down the river that one of the hunters had abandoned last spring. Having made his decision, he lifted her gingerly in his arms and carried her to the empty hut, where he left her lying on the dilapidated straw mattress while he went in search of his horse. He retrieved a small whiskey bottle and a ragged shirt from his saddlebags; then, while his horse drank contentedly from the river, Mores ducked back inside the hut.

Ileya did not appear to have moved since he left her, and he sat down cross-legged on the floor to cut the shirt into wide strips with his knife. But when he reached for her swollen ankle, her body jerked back in a spasm of pain. Looking up, he saw that her eyes were open; she was staring at him with a combination of pain and fear on her face. Her deep brown eyes were shadowed with her inner torment and, before he could stop her, she propped herself up on her arm and started to rise.

Placing a hand on her shoulder, he shook his head. "I

won't hurt you," he murmured, wondering as he did so if she even spoke English.

At the sound of his voice she paused, her dark eyes thoughtful, and, for a moment, some of the suspicion seemed to leave her face. Encouraged by her response, Mores took her shoulders gently and pushed her back down onto the straw. She struggled weakly, but he continued to speak to her in a soothing voice, explaining what he had to do. Then, finally, she lay still.

He worked quickly and, as the mists cleared from her mind, her mistrust faded slowly, then disappeared altogether. He thought she might have begun to remember where she had seen him before, so he told her, "Ileya, your brother Anpao is my friend." She was still wary of him, quite aside from the pain; he could feel it in the way she tensed each time he reached out to touch her leg. She did not trust him completely, but she knew that she must. He had given her little choice in the matter.

She watched him for a long time; then, her brow furrowed in thought, she seemed to come to a decision. "You are Mores, are you not?" she asked.

Her voice, which broke the silence between them so unexpectedly, surprised him into pausing at his task. "I am."

Regarding him with interest, she studied his every movement, but, oddly, her intent appraisal did not disturb him. "My brother has spoken of you," she said at last.

"Is that why you came here?"

She turned her head away, but not before he saw the flash of pain in her eyes. "I came because there was nowhere else." Then, realizing that she might already have said too much, Ileya added, "But it does not matter why I came. Only that I go."

"You can't leave for several days at the very least. You have to give your ankle time to heal."

Ileya closed her eyes, brushing her hand before her face as if to ward off a grim, persistent shadow. The Marquis was troubled by the bleak expression he had glimpsed in her eyes, but he was wise enough to refrain from asking any more questions. He sensed that she was wrapped up in her own disturbing reflections and that she would not welcome his intrusion.

When he had bound her ankle thoroughly, he handed her the whiskey bottle and she swallowed a goodly amount. By now her cheeks were pinched and gray and her lip was swollen where she had bitten it to keep from making any sound. His heart ached for her and he reached out impulsively to touch her cheek.

She drew back instinctively and he let his hand fall to his side. Perhaps this girl did not wish to be comforted, at least not yet. So he sat beside her in silence until the whiskey began to take effect and her eyelids slid down over the eyes that had never ceased to watch him. He waited for a long time because he wanted to be certain she was asleep before he left her. He would have to come back later, of course, to bring her some food and clean clothing, but for now, he knew it would be best if she slept.

When her breathing had become deep and regular, he leaned over, whispering, "Ileya?" He thought the name sounded lovely as he spoke it—so different from the names he was used to. When she did not respond, he rose soundlessly, in one smooth motion, and went to the door. Mores stopped there to take one last look and make certain he had not awakened her.

She lay with one arm flung outward, her fingers curled into a ball. The other hand was resting against her cheek, the fingers tangled in her heavy black hair. And that hair—it fell all around her body in thick, matted strands, but the tangles could not disguise the blue-black shimmer that made her face seem even paler. And somewhere along the way, some stray leaves had woven themselves among the strands and they clung there like living ornaments scattered in a deep black sky. . . .

The flowers he had picked in the garden were strewn through Nicole's hair and across her body, where he had dropped them. They reminded him of the purple and white stones she had worn the first time he met her. She lay with her hands pressed together under her cheek, her body curved into a graceful arc, her hair spread out in disheveled glory around her head. The silky swirl of her soft blue dressing gown enfolded her in voluminous comfort and she looked like a child, innocent of any transgression.

The Marquis smiled fondly and leaned against the door-jamb, watching her sleep. She was so vulnerable, so very fragile and easily broken. She had not even awakened when he spread the flowers over her; perhaps she was not afraid of intrusion.

Nicole stirred sleepily, dislodging some of the daisies that had rested in the curve of her arm. She stretched her legs out slowly, luxuriously, as if she had forever, and then she saw him.

"Antoine?" Her smile was deep and when she saw the flowers, she rose, crossing the room to place her hand upon his cheek. "Where have you been, Tony dearest?"

She was the only woman who would dare use that name, but he did not rebuke her. "Watching you."

Tossing her hair back over her shoulders, she leaned toward him until their lips met. Her mouth was warm and he closed his arms around her, drawing her against him until she was so close that he really believed for an instant, regardless of the existence of Charles Beaumont, that she was his—every fragrant, lovely inch of her.

She backed away, reaching up to remove a daisy from her hair. "I love you very much, Antoine," she said, her voice still husky with sleep. "So very much."

He lifted her from the floor, so that her curls brushed against his neck, and carried her to the bed. Then he removed his arms, letting her tumble the last few feet, and she smiled and stretched out her arms. He answered her invitation with his willing hands. *God, but she was lovely and warm, he thought, and precious to him beyond words. . . .*

* * *

Ileya, he repeated silently—The Shining One, Anpao had called her. She was very vulnerable just now. She needed him, and he knew he was the only one who could help her. Somehow, he was grateful for that.

When he returned to the Chateau, he found Medora sitting in her tiny study, a pencil behind one ear. The ledgers were spread out before her, and her gaze was fixed with severe intensity on a page crowded with numbers.

"I'm back, my dear," he announced, although he suspected she would not hear him. The furrow across her forehead was deeply etched and he had come to know that look.

She surprised him when she looked up, giving him a half-smile. "Did you know," she said, "that the last load of wine has arrived and the cellar is full? Of course, the bill is staggering, but I suppose we must entertain properly, mustn't we? I think we should open some of the French champagne for the dinner party in two weeks, don't you? After all, it will be a major celebration. It's too bad Papa and Mama couldn't come." Before he could respond, she turned back to her books.

He noticed that a few strands of hair had come loose from their tight confinement on top of her head, but they didn't detract in the least from her air of efficiency. He wondered if this could really be the same woman who had come to the jail in Mandan and risked her life for his sake. Her well-made cloth suit with its stiff collar of dark velvet did not seem to fit the image he remembered of Medora walking with her baby among the flickering torches.

"Any new business ideas today?" she asked without looking up.

Mores leaned against the doorjamb comfortably. "Actually, I've been considering the possibility of investing in a stagecoach line for the area. We need one badly for all our freight."

Medora pursed her lips, considering his suggestion carefully before she spoke. "I don't think it's a good idea, Mores.

It's such a large expense when you're so uncertain of the results."

Shaking his head, he reached out for her, but she caught his hand in midair. "I simply mean I don't want you to risk so much just now. We're still only starting and we must take care."

"It isn't in my nature to take care, my dear. You should know that by now." He took a step forward and put his hands on her shoulders, raising her deftly from the chair. Then, without allowing her time to object, he began to run his fingers lightly across the fabric of her jacket. "Let's forget the business for a moment," he murmured. He thought she was going to back away, but then, all at once, she leaned toward him, sliding her arms around his neck.

Medora gasped when his lips touched hers and his tongue slid knowingly into her mouth. Her blood began to race wildly in her veins as his hands caressed her lower back and she almost drew away from him. Sometimes she was terrified at the response his magic fingers drew from her with so little effort. Each time he locked his arms around her, pressing his body close to hers, she found that she lost track of everything but the warm, pulsing feel of him. Then, and only then, her books and ledgers, fears and worries fled with the swiftness of a brief summer storm, leaving nothing behind but her soft, hungry body.

Never once, since the day she had agreed to marry him, had Medora allowed herself to give in to him completely. Except when she was in his arms. And then the choice was taken from her.

NINE

The Marquis contemplated the blue sky that seemed to go on forever, interrupted here and there by puffs of cloud that softened the intensity of the vast azure background. Smiling to himself, he guided his horse down the hill toward the river. Today the packing plant was to open and, if the weather was any indication, the business was charmed. He could not have asked for a more perfect day.

Now, in the stillness of late morning, he was on his way to the plant to see that all was ready for the celebration later. But first, he wanted to stop and see Ileya. It had been two weeks since he found her unconscious; by now she was able to walk with the aid of a heavy walking stick he had given her. He had been to see the girl often while her ankle healed, and he believed she had come to like him, little by little. They rarely spoke when he was with her. Instead, they sat together in companionable silence, listening to the sound of the river.

It was partly Ileya's choice that they spoke so little, but there was a tenuous bond between them that Mores did not want to destroy with awkward questions. Still, he often wondered why, although she was clearly recovered from her accident, she showed no inclination to leave. He was fairly certain she was running from something, but he hadn't yet discovered what it was.

If anyone had told him these meetings were wrong, he would have laughed aloud. He had not once touched the girl since he had bound her ankle. He did not even think of her as a woman. He only knew that he enjoyed the silences they shared, just as Ileya did. Nevertheless, for some reason, he had not told Medora about the Indian girl.

When he had tied his horse to a branch outside the hut, he knocked quietly on the door, then pushed it open. Peering into the dark interior, he saw that Ileya was gone. Her walking stick was nowhere in sight, and he decided she might have gone to the river. He followed the track down to the water, where he found her footprints and the regular holes in the ground that the stick had made. Moving carefully, he made his way through the clinging grasses and ferns and ducked under the low-hanging branches until he came upon a spot where the river widened and the water was deeper.

Ileya's simple buckskin dress lay beside her walking stick at the water's edge. When he found her the first time, she had been wearing a plain skirt and blouse over the buckskin to make herself less conspicuous, but she had discarded the white woman's clothes the day after her arrival. Mores drew in his breath silently as his eyes moved across the water and he saw her. She was swimming far out in the center of the pool, moving her arms languidly in a sensuous pattern, her fingers spread as if in benediction. She had tossed her head back so that the sun touched her face, heightening the dark softness of her cheeks and forehead. Her eyes were closed, her lips slightly open, and her expression had an ethereal quality of inner peace. Her long, black hair flowed out behind her, floating like a leaf upon the water, rising and falling with the rhythm of the river as she rotated in ever-widening circles.

As he watched, her head began to sway slowly back and forth and she started to sing.

> *In the North by streams that run,*
> *There my bed is.*

She sang the words in the Indian tongue and the odd, chanting lilt of her voice seemed to rise and blend with the whisper of the water all around her.

I have roamed;
But I come again
To the arms of the river.

He thought that if the wind should rise suddenly, its shrill cry would be drowned by the sound of Ileya's voice.

All at once, her singing stopped and, unaware of his presence, she swam to a spot where the water was shallow and stood up, running her fingers through her hair. It was then, for the first time, that he saw her back uncovered by the shield of her hair, and he had to stifle an exclamation of horror. The brown skin was crisscrossed with a series of livid welts and scars, one of which ran from her shoulder to her hip. Most of the wounds had long since healed, but there were several fresh swellings, still red and ugly and obviously painful.

Mores retreated further into the trees, aware that she would not want him to see her like this. With fury at some unnamed person building in his chest, he waited until she had dried herself and slipped her dress over her head before he came out to sit beside her.

She smiled when she saw him but did not speak, and Mores himself knew he was not yet ready to break the silence. So he sat there watching in fascination while she drew a comb through her hair. But the memory of the way her back had looked a few moments before would not leave him.

Reaching out gingerly, he ran one hand gently down her back until he felt the ridges the scars had made. "Who?" he asked.

She stiffened and pulled away as he shifted his position so that he could see her face. The shine had left her eyes and her lips were a thin rigid line; clearly she did not want to talk about it. But now that he had seen the scars, he had to know. "Who?" he repeated stubbornly.

Ileya looked down at her hands. "My husband," she said, so quietly that he had to lean forward to hear her. "It was his way. So I divorced him."

Mores gazed at her, a perplexed question between his brows.

"With the Dakota—what you call the Sioux—it is right that I should do this," she explained. "If the man is afraid to go into to battle, if he seeks other women, or if he beats his wife, it is right to divorce him."

"Then why did you run away?"

"On the reservation, the Indian agent is all-powerful. He insisted we be married by a priest. That is not our way, but we agreed so there would be no trouble. Now, when I divorce my husband, who is cruel to me, the agent says, 'You were married by the Church. There is no divorce.' And he sends me back to the house of my husband."

She paused, dragging her fingers absently through the dark, soft earth. "My husband was angry because I had shamed him in the eyes of the others, so he beat me again." Her eyes grew opaque so that he could no longer read her thoughts. "I waited until he slept that night, then crept away. I ran, because I knew the agent would not understand and that he would send me back. Then I remembered you had helped Anpao, so I came here."

It had not been an accident, then, that he had found her.

"And still at night I dream that they will come and take me back." She scrutinized his face, as if looking for reassurance.

He gave it to her willingly. "Don't worry, Ileya. As long as you are here, you will be safe. I promise you."

When the champagne had been opened and Mores was circulating among the crowd that had gathered outside the packing plant to celebrate its opening, Medora slipped unobtrusively to the edge of the throng of excited townspeople. On the way, she recognized the faces of every single man she had met since she had come to the Badlands. Even Bryce Pendleton was there with his son and daughter-in-law on either side of him. Just beyond them stood Katherine, her face clouded with anger and perhaps a little envy. Everyone had come today, although some of them had probably hoped to be able to gloat when the plant refused to operate properly. If so, they had been disappointed. The first two steers had already fallen under the butchers' knives and the beef had been sent on to the cooling room in neat packages. From there it would go to cold storage and, after the plant had been operating for a few days, there would be enough beef to begin loading the waiting refrigerated railroad cars.

Medora smiled secretly. If anyone had arrived hostile, the Marquis was doing his best to see that they left in a more pleasant frame of mind. He was making a slow progress through the crowd now, a bottle in his hand, seeing that every person present received a glass of French champagne. It would cost him a fortune, of course, she thought ruefully, but it might just be worth it. Anyway, she had more important things on her mind just now than the high price of champagne.

She had seen a man hovering near the edge of the crowd, his face hidden by the shifting mass of people before him, and the very attitude of his body had drawn her attention. He seemed to be poised for some kind of action, waiting for just the right moment. She had spent the long minutes of speech-making working her way toward the man, hoping he would make his move while she was watching. Now, at last, she had been rewarded. The man had finally broken away from the crowd and, with several wary glances over his shoulder, mounted a horse waiting nearby.

Medora looked around for William, but he seemed to have gone inside the building, and she decided she didn't have time to find him. Besides, now was her chance to get away; everyone was occupied and no one had noticed her at all. As the man and his horse faded into a blur on the horizon, Medora found her own animal and led him behind a nearby stand of trees. There she mounted and started after the man, her face set in grim lines of determination.

Keeping just out of sight, she followed him to the Chateau, where she left her horse just under the brow of the hill and began to creep upward. When she reached the porch, she looped her skirt over one arm and took out the gun fastened below her waist. Pushing the front door open, she stepped into the house and listened until she heard quick rustling noises at the far end. Whoever was there, she guessed he was in the room where the safe was kept.

She moved through the house quietly, hardly daring to breathe. But when she saw who was crouched before the open safe, a sheaf of papers in his hand, she nodded to herself, calling, "Good afternoon, Mr. Maunders. If you're at all wise, you'll stand up, turn around, and drop your gun on the floor between us."

He leapt at the sound of her voice, dropping the papers as he whirled to face her. For a moment, the color drained from his craggy face, but when he saw who stood before him, he began to relax. "Why ma'am," he began, a small grin twisting his mouth, "you frightened me for a minute there. I thought you was gonna shoot me on the spot."

"I am," she informed him, "if you don't tell me what you're doing here and who sent you. But first, take your gun out of the holster and lay it on the desk."

"Well, sure, if you want," he replied calmly, "but I ain't doin' any harm. The Marquis just sent me up here to get some papers for him. There's no need to get excited." Nevertheless, he did as she had instructed him.

Medora took the gun, putting it down where he could not reach it. "My husband has not spoken to you all afternoon. I know that because I was either at his side or watching you. You never got within ten feet of the Marquis."

Maunders eyed her with new interest. Had she really been watching him? And what did the woman know, anyway? Maybe he'd better find out. "I guess you're right about that, now that I come to remember. But I'll tell you—"

"I don't want you to tell me anything but the truth. Who sent you here to go through my husband's papers?"

"No one. I came on my own. Just curious."

"I'll bet." When she saw that his obstinate expression had not changed, she decided to try a new approach. "I suppose it was Greg Pendleton," she murmured. "You've been in his pay often enough in the past."

A muscle in Maunders's jaw began to twitch and he seemed momentarily disconcerted, but he did not answer her challenge. He must be more afraid of Pendleton than of her bullets. "You may not be aware, Mr. Maunders, that Frank O'Donnell now works for my husband. And that he tends to talk when he's drunk—a lot." For an instant, he let his guard down and Medora saw that she had been right; he had not known.

Jake had just had a sudden disturbing inkling of what he might be up against. He didn't know why he had never thought of her as an enemy before. But he masked his thoughts, shrugging in apparent unconcern. "Why should I care what O'Donnell says? The man's a drunkard who can't tell lies from truth."

"*I* believe him, especially when he talks about you. He hasn't yet come right out and said you engineered the whole episode last June, but I have my suspicions just the same."

"What do you know about it?"

Medora paused, as if considering how to answer him. "Nothing concrete. If I had evidence, you wouldn't still be here. But I want you to know that I intend to get that evidence. And I'll be watching you in the future just as I did today. Eventually, I'll catch you making a mistake. It'll be your last, I promise you that."

He considered her in silence while he filed this new threat in his mind. *He'd* be watching her in the future, too, that much was certain. She was far too inquisitive for her own good—or his. "If you'll pardon me, ma'am, I have things to do."

"Report your failure to Pendleton?" she inquired. Then she motioned toward the door. "Go ahead, get out."

He edged past her without even a furtive glance at her revolver. He knew now that she wouldn't use it because somehow he sensed that she planned to use *him* instead.

When his hollow footsteps had ceased to echo on the wooden porch, she knelt to gather the papers he had dropped on the floor. Glancing quickly over the complicated documents, she saw that they were the partnership agreements with all Mores's major backers. What would Pendleton want with those? Whatever the answer she realized that there was something going on here that had not ended with the trial, and she knew that it would do her husband no good. And despite Maunders's stubborn silence, she was certain the Pendletons were pulling the strings. Which made the game that much more dangerous.

"How many beeves did they slaughter today?" Bryce Pendleton asked, brushing a breadcrumb from his shirt.

"Twenty," Mores replied. "Of course, that's nothing to what we'll be doing when the operation really gets going. By December we should be doing seventy-five head a day." He smiled comfortably as he glanced around the dinner table at his guests. Cory Pendleton sat at his right hand and her pale beauty tended to fade unobtrusively into the background, despite her gown of shaded turquoise lampas trimmed with turquoise satin. At his left, Katherine made a much more striking picture. Her heavy brown hair had been looped and curled skillfully so that it complemented her ivory satin gown. The girl's wide brown eyes moved constantly over the group, as if she could absorb all their thoughts and weaknesses just by looking.

Greg Pendleton sat beside his daughter, with Bryce next to Cory. Both sat rigid in their seats, clearly less than pleased to find themselves eating at the Marquis's table. Then, of course, Medora sat at the far end. For the celebration, she had styled her usually tightly braided hair in a soft chignon that softened the harsh planes of her face. Besides her husband, only Medora was entirely at ease. William, who sat at her right hand, looked decidedly uncomfortable, while Theodore Roosevelt, on Medora's left, squinted through his thick glasses with a slightly resentful air.

But Mores was not overly concerned with the somber moods of his guests. He was pleased with the way things had gone today, and he hoped the liberal portions of expensive French wine he was dispensing would mellow out the others eventually.

Suddenly, Roosevelt spoke up for the first time. "Even with the refrigerated cars, won't the ice melt by the time the train gets to Chicago?"

Mores shook his head. "No, because I've set up ice houses all along the route, staffed with men who put in a fresh supply whenever it's needed." The Marquis took a sip of wine, gazing benignly at his guests.

"Well," Roosevelt observed, "I guess you've picked a good spot for this business venture. I understand this area is an excellent spot for raising cattle."

"Absolutely. Thick grass, lots of water, even cliffs that offer the animals protection from the weather. The Badlands might as well have been made for cattle-raising. They're ideal."

With a sly glance at her host, Katherine said, "They're especially ideal for madmen and foreigners, who come in here—"

"But really, Mr. Roosevelt," Medora interrupted firmly, "the Badlands are best known for the excellent hunting. You may already have realized the animals are so numerous that a hunter never fails to return with a wagonful of meat."

"I don't know," Katherine mused, running her finger around the rim of her cup. "It depends on the kind of game, after all. Some are more difficult to stalk than others." She was speaking to Roosevelt, but her gaze flicked often toward the Marquis and there was a curious gleam in her eyes. "For example, the antelope is easy, because his curiosity often leads him to disaster."

"A fact," Greg interjected, "that some of us would do well to remember."

Katherine ignored him. "But the wildcat is too clever to get caught—most of the time. *He* can really lead the hunter on a wild chase. And then there are the Indians," she said, glancing around to make certain her audience was listening. "They're the most dangerous and exciting prey of all, *and* the most difficult to catch."

There was a moment of uneasy silence before Roosevelt cleared his throat. "I'd heard there were Indians in the area, but I haven't seen any. Are they still a problem?" Clearly, he had chosen to ignore the implications of Katherine's observations.

"Not anymore," Greg Pendleton answered. "The Sioux were the troublemakers in the Badlands, but they're almost all settled now at the Standing Rock Reservation. They don't cause us any worry these days." He leaned back in his chair, running his hand thoughtfully across his chin. "Of course," he continued, "now and then one or two of them gets the Indian agent to give them passes or they sneak out on their own. In fact, I was riding down south just yesterday and I ran into the agent for Standing Rock. He told me he was going to Mandan, and on the way, keeping an eye out for an Indian girl who ran away from her husband. He says it gives the government a bad name if they just let them run free like that. I told him I hadn't see the girl. I don't suppose any of you have?"

The Marquis met Pendleton's probing gaze steadily, and he did not like what he saw there. He suspected the man knew something—he and his daughter both. They were certainly looking smug enough. Mores's pulse quickened just a little. Perhaps it would be wise to warn Ileya. Greg Pendleton was just the sort of man who, if he found her, would send her back without a thought. And this time her husband might just be angry enough to kill her.

After dinner, Johnny Goodall came up from the bunkhouse with his fiddle and began to play a lively tune. Everyone was anxious for some distraction from their troubled thoughts, and it was not long before the porch was a whirl of flying satins and velvets. The hollow ring of the footsteps on the wood combined with the sound of the fiddle to disturb the languor of the night.

Mores wrapped his arm tightly around Medora's waist, breathing in the fresh scent of her hair. She was smiling, clinging to him as she rarely did, her face tilted back to catch the moonlight that caressed her now and then as they revolved to the wailing cry of the fiddle. He caught occasional glimpses of the other dancers as they passed, but his eyes never left Medora's face.

When the song came to an end, they stopped, breathless, leaning against the nearest porch railing. In the sudden silence, he looked down at her flushed cheeks and brilliant green eyes and his heart paused in its normal rhythm. Unaware of the others, he leaned forward to touch her lips with his own, just for an instant.

Greg Pendleton paused on his way to the door and stood watching his host and hostess. There was something about the couple that drew his attention, regardless of his distaste—some aura that separated them from the rest of the world, wrapping them in their own little cocoon of mutual affection. As they hung together in the moonlight, they might as well have been one person. Pendleton shook his head. The Marquis was a hopeless romantic who had chosen an unfortunate place to try to make his dream come true. The Badlands were not romantic; they were brutally real, and he knew with certainty that they would destroy the man before him. Greg meant to see that they did. For his mother's sake—and his own.

"May I dance with your wife?" As Goodall struck up a new tune, Pendleton came forward, his hand extended.

"By all means." Relinquishing Medora to his guest, the Marquis went in search of Cory.

Greg slid his arm around Medora's waist, surprised at how small it was. She certainly looked different now than she had the first time he met her. Now her figure was so slight that he felt he could crush her with his bare hands, except that he knew she would never allow it. That was partly what interested him so much. She was no fool; he had already learned that. And now he found he could not quite draw his gaze away from the light in her eyes.

As they circled near the end of the porch, where he had guided her without her being aware, she paused for a moment, listening to the sounds of the night. Her brow knitted in con-

centration, she tilted back her head, as if waiting for an unusual noise to reach her waiting ears. "I thought I heard some
rustling in the bushes," she explained absently.

Pendleton nodded knowingly. "You'd best take care," he
said, leaning down to speak in her ear. "Your husband has
many enemies."

She backed away, contemplating his face in the dim light.
"I'm well aware of that."

"But perhaps the Marquis is *not* so aware?"

"Unfortunately, my husband is of a trusting nature. He
likes to believe there is good in all men."

Greg smiled crookedly.

"I, however," she continued, "am less trusting." She peered
at him boldly, her eyes piercing and hostile.

"You don't like me, do you?" he asked.

Shivering at a sudden gust of wind, Medora replied, "No,
I don't."

He stood perfectly still, watching her face, but he did not
move toward her. "No?" he said at last. "I imagine we shall
see about that."

Theodore Roosevelt stood gazing out the upstairs window,
trying to hear the sounds of the night above the moaning
wind. Like the other guests, he had been invited to stay the
night at the Chateau and he had decided to do so, albeit
reluctantly. For some reason, which he had not yet expressed
to himself, he resented the Marquis and his elegant home.
Elegance, he thought, leaning his forehead against the cold
glass of the window—that was the problem. Despite its unfinished state, this house was utterly civilized and increasingly
elegant, as more furniture arrived from France and New York.
This was supposed to be the frontier, Roosevelt mused, yet
he was constantly reminded here of things he would rather
forget. He might as well be back East, surrounded by the
stiff elegance of his childhood. And the inevitable memories
of Alice.

Alice—the name still had the power to shake him to the

marrow. He had come out West to forget her, to be a cowboy who lost himself in violent physical labor that gave him no time to think. He did not want to remember the day when she had died in childbirth, her skin nearly transparent despite the painful flush across her cheeks. Then he had lost his mother that day, too. It had been too much. He had had to escape.

Yet now, here he was, peering out the heavy glass window, the fine oak bed behind him, with its expensive red canopy and clinging curtain. It was too much like his own home. He wanted to be riding, stiff and uncomfortable on the back of a horse—roughing it. That was why he had come. But the Marquis had somehow managed to bring the East with him when he came West.

Roosevelt frowned when he thought he saw a movement outside. He could have sworn he had seen someone creeping off the porch, but the darkness seemed to have swallowed whoever it was. Then, just when he began to shrug and turn away, a door opened downstairs, allowing the light from inside to spill out onto the porch and across the grass. Then he recognized Medora moving quietly away from the house with a gun in her hand. She did not turn her head when the light hit her; her attention was focused somewhere outside the house. She seemed to be looking for something or someone, and Roosevelt sensed that the gun she held was not a prop; she meant to use it.

As she faded out of the light and into the shadow, Greg Pendleton stepped out onto the porch and leaned on the railing, staring after her. For a long moment, he simply stood there, watching, and then he tossed aside the cigar he had been smoking and leapt down onto the grass, following the path Medora had taken.

Before he had gone far, his wife came out, her dressing gown trailing open behind her like a filmy shadow. She spoke, but her words were shielded by the glass and Roosevelt could not understand them. But her husband stopped, hesitated, then turned back to join her. They stood there, framed in the light from the doorway, Cory with her eyes wild and her hair in disarray, Greg with a mask of indifference over his face. He put his hands on her shoulders, then brushed a stray blond hair from her forehead, and Cory collapsed against him, burying her face in his chest.

Roosevelt drew the curtains closed, turning away from the window with a heavy sigh. He no longer wished to intrude on the bitter personal secrets of his neighbors.

The next morning, after he had bid good-bye to his guests, the Marquis took his horse and made his way down to the river. Pendleton's questions about the Indian girl had been troubling him since last night, and Mores had decided he must warn Ileya.

He left his horse standing docilely in the clearing and crossed to the hut, pushing open the door. For a moment, he could not see anything, but as his eyes adjusted to the gloom, he realized the room was empty. He knew then, without even looking outside, that Ileya was gone. She had disappeared as if she had never been, as if she were a fantasy he had created. His hand closed brutally on the doorframe, and he was surprised by the depth of his feeling of loss.

In the instant of pained silence that followed, the wind rushed in to fill the gap, lacing itself with a whisper of longing through the dry, yellow leaves of the cottonwoods.

PART II

NEW YORK, WINTER OF 1884

TEN

"Are you enjoying your winter in New York?"

Medora looked up at her partner's face as they revolved slowly in the brilliant light of the chandeliers. She had long ago given up trying to remember the names of the many men with whom she had danced in the past few days. It was a hopeless task anyway. She inclined her head politely in answer to his question.

"You must find it relaxing here, after all the trouble you had in the Badlands," the man continued hopefully.

Smiling to herself, Medora told him, "This is the third party we have attended in as many days, and I believe the string of callers at my father's house does not dwindle away until long after supper. I hardly call that relaxing." Despite her protestation, however, Medora was looking perfectly comfortable, without any visible trace of weariness to mar her still slightly tanned skin. Her green satin gown, with its cream lace trim, only emphasized the verdant sparkle in her eyes, which had been set burning by the light of a hundred candles.

"Oh, but you and the Marquis are very much in demand, you know. We have all been waiting for so long to hear about the Dakotas firsthand." His gaze became vague and unfocused. "All that danger and excitement. What was it really like?"

She recognized the same glistening light in this man's eyes that she had seen so often since they had come to stay in her father's New York house for the winter. Apparently, eve-

ryone had followed the events in the Badlands through newspaper accounts over the long and dramatic summer, and the
Vallombrosas had discovered, upon arriving in the city, that
they had become celebrities. The New Yorkers, fixed permanently in their drab and crowded city, had become enchanted
with what they considered the exciting and romantic wilderness of the Dakotas. Medora found herself telling and retell-
ing the same stories time and again.

This sudden display of interest did not distress her unduly,
however, because she knew that all the publicity could only
help the Marquis's business plans. At that moment, she caught
sight of her husband leaning casually against a gilt and silver
wall with a circle of avid listeners surrounding him. As she
swung by, Medora heard him exclaim, "We are now handling
eighty head a day—two full carloads—and we hope to expand
the plant to handle up to 150—" The rest of his statement
was lost to her as the crowd forced her away.

Glancing up at her partner, she realized that she had not
yet answered his last question. "There is too much to tell,"
she informed him. "I couldn't possibly describe our life there
so that you would understand. Except to say that you're
right—it is exciting and challenging, and one is never bored,
not even for a moment."

"Don't you miss it?" he asked, still unsatisfied.

Medora threw back her head, causing her hair to swing
free for a moment. Suddenly she realized how warm the
crowded room had become, despite the heavy snow and biting
cold beyond the windows. The glittering crystal chandeliers,
with their many candles, only added to the warmth, and the
press of satin and velvet-clad bodies seemed to give rise to
a single, heavy escape of heated breath that clouded the room
with a dull, stifling odor. The musicians coaxed the lilting
music out of their violins and the notes propelled the dancers
into ceaseless motion. The dark-suited men held firmly to
their partners, aflame with diamonds and rubies and emeralds,
and the stones caught the candlelight, scattering it across the
shining wood floor in brilliant, multicolored patterns.

Oddly, Medora found herself thinking longingly of the

stark, desolate landscape she had left behind. She thought the jewels of the guests were as nothing compared to the strange inner light that glowed from the stratified cliffs during the deep night. And the dancers themselves faded into insignificance when she remembered the rock and sandstone that stood in bleak relief, sculpted into bizarre spires and pinnacles by the relentless forces of the past. Even her memories had the power to transport her back to the Dakota wilderness; there was something compelling about the Badlands—some force that seemed to rise like morning mist from the chasms in the rock until the wind caught it up, blowing it across the sky so that nothing was left untouched by its power. "Yes," she mused, "I miss it very much."

"Indeed! The meat-packing business is going very well."

Medora was shaken from her revery by the sound of her father's confident voice. It boomed out, crossing the heads of the dancers, so that several couples turned to stare.

"So well, in fact," Von Hoffman continued, "that we're beginning to think about selling the meat retail. Of course, just now most of our sales are in local areas—Montana and the Dakotas—but there's no question that we'll be expanding into Chicago and New York soon."

The combination of her father and the meat-packing business had the result of dragging her mind abruptly back to the present. But then, Von Hoffman often had that effect on her.

"May I steal your partner away?"

Medora whirled in surprise at the sound of a familiar voice just behind her. "Why, Mr. Roosevelt," she exclaimed, "what a pleasure to see you." She knew that, like them, he was spending the winter in the city. He had been invited to all the recent parties, but someone had told her that he didn't like to attend these social gatherings. He preferred sitting at home with his sister. "Would you excuse me?" she said, turning back to her partner. "Mr. Roosevelt and I haven't seen each other for some months."

The man grunted an unintelligible response and bowed stiffly, clearly displeased with the interruption. Nevertheless, he did not have the courage to argue with the tone of Medora's voice. With an unnaturally bright smile, he backed away.

Theodore Roosevelt took Medora in his arms, pleased to note that for once his partner was shorter than himself. Tonight he had abandoned his flannel shirt, chaps, and cowboy hat for a dark suit and tails. His light, curly hair was brushed carefully back from his forehead and his thick, round glasses were, for once, unsplattered with mud.

"I didn't know you danced," Medora said. She could not help but be aware of the slight pressure of his fingers against her waist that betrayed an unusual inner tension. Behind his glasses, his eyes were smoky and unreadable.

"My curiosity finally got the better of me," he explained, as if choosing his words with the utmost care.

"Curiosity about what?" As they circled at the edge of the dance floor, Medora matched her steps to his and waited expectantly for him to continue.

"Well," he paused, considering how best to ask the question that had troubled him for so long. "I've meant to bring it up a number of times, but somehow——" His voice faded out and he glanced uneasily into her perplexed face. "I suppose it's none of my business, really, but I was wondering what you were doing outside the night of your last dinner party in the Badlands."

Medora blinked at him. "I don't understand."

"I mean later that night, of course, after the others had gone to bed. Well, at least some of them had. I happened to be standing at the window, looking at the stars, when I saw you leave the house with a gun in your hand. It was very curious; I couldn't understand what you were doing. I thought perhaps you were looking for Indians, the way you were moving so cautiously. I've wondered ever since that is, I thought——" His words came out in a rush, as if he had been trying to hold them back, but, once released, had lost control of them. Finally, he paused to take a long breath and judge how his question had affected Medora.

She was looking beyond him and her eyes were veiled, but he could not decide whether she was consciously trying to hide her thoughts or not. Yet he could see from the tiny lines that marred the smooth skin of her forehead that he had somehow disturbed her.

"Actually," she said, after a long, thoughtful pause, "I was looking for an intruder. I had heard some strange sounds earlier in the evening, and then, just when I was thinking of going to bed, I heard noises outside the window, as if someone were creeping toward the house. So naturally, I went out to investigate."

He did not mention that it would have been more natural, from his point of view, to have called for her husband and sent him instead. "Did you find anyone?"

Her brows came together, causing the skin over her nose to pucker. "No. I rather think I frightened him away. I looked for a good twenty minutes, but it was too dark to see much. I did find something interesting though." She spoke as if she were unaware of his presence. "It appeared to be a walking stick, carved from the branch of a cottonwood. It was lying just beyond the bushes at the end of the porch." She shook her head and focused her wandering eyes on his face to see if he was satisfied.

She knew that if he had seen her, he had also seen Greg Pendleton come out behind her, and she wondered what Roosevelt had made of that. For some reason, she did not want to discuss Pendleton's presence because she did not entirely understand it herself. She was only aware that he had been watching her, and had followed her from more than simply idle curiosity. Perhaps Pendleton knew who the intruder had been. She clamped her lips closed and tried to banish the thoughts from her mind. It would do her no good to speculate; she would certainly never find the answer here in New York. But she felt an unaccountable shiver run down her back at the thought of Greg Pendleton's eyes upon her that night.

Roosevelt sensed Medora's reluctance to mention Pendleton, so he let the subject drop. At least he knew now what *she* had been doing that night. As for Pendleton's motives, well, they would have to remain a mystery for the time being.

When the guests had gone home and silence had finally descended on the house, Medora slid beneath the heavy covers on her bed and lay there in the darkness. Her mind was not occupied with memories of the party, but rather, with thoughts of her husband. She was waiting to see if he would come to her tonight. She was homesick and she needed his company to make her forget. She had discovered, only since their arrival in New York, that he had an extraordinary ability to comfort her, to soothe her mind and body so that the thoughts that troubled her seemed to dissolve into unimportant memories.

She did not know why they should be closer here than they had been in the Badlands, but she did know that somehow she had changed. Never before in her life had she felt the need for reassurance and now, suddenly, she had lost her inner sense of deep-rooted strength. Perhaps it was because she could not rid herself of the constant forebodings of disaster that had plagued her since the trial last July. At first only vague twinges of premonition, the feelings had become stronger and more frequent in the past couple of months. And now, as she lay alone each night, with only the unfriendly darkness as a companion, she found herself creating grim fantasies that might fulfill the distressing promises of her mind. Something was coming; she knew it, but she did not know what it would be.

"Medora?"

She sat up as the light from the hall lamp spilled across her floor for a brief second, then crept away as the door swung slowly closed. Mores, who had stopped for a moment, the light at his back, now came forward, whispering, "Are you awake?"

Drawing her breath in slowly, she felt a surge of pleasure as she listened to his light footsteps across the carpeted floor. For the moment, his form was obscured by the thin blanket of darkness that covered him, but she could hear his breathing—a reassuringly regular sound. Then, as her eyes adjusted again, she saw his shadowy figure pause to loosen the belt of his robe. He moved as if he were carrying out the graceful motions of a dance, his tall body lithe and elegant.

Finally, he reached over and let the robe slip from his fingers so that it was lost among the shadows that hugged the floor. He did not speak because he knew it was not necessary, and he was savoring the air of expectancy that hung in the room like the scent of a rare wine asking to be tasted. He could see Medora leaning against the headboard, her eyes fixed on his face, and he realized that the covers had fallen away, leaving uncovered her smooth white shoulders and the swell of her breasts.

He swung himself up onto the mattress and then, reaching across the cool, empty sheets until his hands met her shoulders, he said, "You are lovely, my dear."

She moved toward him until their bodies came together in the center of the bed and she felt the pulsing warmth of his hands sliding gently from her neck to her breasts. His fingers traced intimate patterns in the soft hollows of her skin, and his breath touched her cheek with an insubstantial caress. The blood began to race through her veins, and she stretched out her body with a long, deep sigh as his lips brushed lightly against her nipples, one at a time. "Mores," she whispered, but his mouth closed over hers, stopping the words in her throat.

He tangled one hand in her hair, which she had left loose for him, while his legs seemed to weave themselves with hers until she could no longer tell which body was hers and which his. By now she had forgotten the thoughts that had troubled her just a few minutes before. Now she was aware only of the trails of tingling fire that his hand ignited as it found its way down across her belly and thighs.

Mores breathed deeply as Medora clasped her arms around him, locking them together. He raised his head for an instant, staring down into her radiant eyes as her fingers began to trace their patterns on his back. Her lips were open, so that the pink tip of her tongue could make its slow, sensuous circle and her cheeks were slightly flushed. He knew these things, in spite of the darkness, in spite of the shadows that tried to hide them from each other. He knew the feel of her warm breath and the pulsing softness of her breasts and belly almost as well as he knew his own body.

His heart pounded erratically as she came up to meet him, dragging her fingers through his hair when he found the rhythmic beat of the pulse in her neck. And when he entered her, she gasped briefly, then touched his lips hungrily with her own. And, in that moment, he was blind to everything but the wild impulses of his body and the deep, perfumed scent of her hair.

Later, when she had fallen asleep beside him, he tightened his arm around her shoulders, drawing her closer, so that her relaxed body lay against his and her hand fell lightly across his chest. With his chin resting on the top of her head, he listened to the minute sounds of the night and smiled to himself. His eyes slid closed and a pleasant drowsiness began to cloud his mind. Just before he fell asleep he thought, gratefully, that all was well with him now.

With one hand curled around the stem of his crystal wineglass, Louis Von Hoffman viewed with approval the small family circle seated at strategic intervals along the formal dining table. For the first time in many nights, there were no guests to provide for, and Von Hoffman was pleased by the unhurried pace of the meal. Tonight his family seemed strangely subdued, and the conversation was no more than desultory. It was almost as if they were waiting for something to shake them out of their lethargy.

His wife, Gretta, in her stiffly correct high-necked gown, sat slightly forward on her chair, holding her elbows carefully away from the edge of the table. Her attempt to appear "just so" was marred, however, by one stray curl that had escaped from her elaborate hairdo and now fell forward into her face, despite her several attempts to push it back. Von Hoffman saw that Gretta's hands were fluttering, as usual. He sometimes wondered if she would be able to function at all if some part of her body were not forever in motion.

Brushing the curl back for the third time, Gretta smiled uncertainly at her husband and tried to keep her busy hands still, but she knew it was hopeless. Lifting her dessert spoon, she glanced covertly at her daughter, who sat in stately silence across the table. Medora, she knew, had no trouble keeping still; her every movement was graceful, yet determined. And her auburn curls would not dare escape from their confinement, nor was there a single wrinkle in her blue silk gown. Shaking her head, Gretta marveled again that this elegant woman should have been her own daughter.

Medora sensed her mother's distress and reached across the table to press Gretta's hand momentarily, but the young woman's thoughts were really far away. She had grown bored with eating the fancy dishes that the Von Hoffman cook prepared each night, and Medora had conceived an unreasonable longing to hunt down a prairie chicken and shoot it for dinner as she used to do in the Badlands. She knew that her husband was also ill at ease with the unusual silence tonight. She could see from the glint in his eyes that he was restless, although his manner was perfectly correct. Nevertheless, she thought him particularly handsome tonight in his dark gray suit and maroon tie. His curly hair was brushed carefully back from his face, and the ends of his moustache were heavily waxed. Catching her admiring glance, Mores smiled broadly for the first time in the interminable meal and threw her a kiss.

When the front doorbell chimed unexpectedly, everyone sat up to listen for a moment. Perhaps this was a guest and the evening would not be quite so dull after all. The Marquis had already half-risen in his chair when Gretta leapt up, dropping her linen napkin in her haste. Before Von Hoffman could stop her, she had reached the doorway. As she disappeared into the hall, she called over her shoulder, "I'll just see who it is, dear. I'll be back in a moment."

Mores and Medora exchanged amused glances. Evidently, Gretta was as restless as they were, and so she had welcomed the interruption. Really, she need not have gone at all; the maid would certainly answer the door.

Von Hoffman sniffed in disapproval at his wife's unseemly

behavior and Medora laughed. "Come, Papa," she admonished him, "she is only being polite, you know."

At her father's skeptical look, Medora turned back to her dessert and silence fell again.

Several minutes later, Gretta appeared in the doorway and stood there for a moment, as if she were surprised that she had found her way back to the dining room unassisted. Her cheeks were flushed, her hands trembling, and she seemed to be out of breath. "There is a young man out there," she began, while her hands fluttered before her, "well, really only a boy, and he told me the most extraordinary thing. He said—right to my face, mind you—that he is a—a—" she paused, blushing furiously, and glanced at her husband, hoping that, through some miracle, he could provide her with the proper word. "He said that he is *illegitimate!*" Her voice fell an octave on the last word and then she cried, "Imagine!"

Phillipe Beaumont stood in the hallway listening to the surprised silence that greeted Mrs. Von Hoffman's confused announcement. He was waiting stiffly, with every ounce of his consciousness focused on the inevitable response of the other diners. He had to admit that his entrance had been rather dramatic, but then, he had meant it to be. He wanted to see exactly how the Marquis reacted.

"Well, after all," a man's unmistakably French voice bellowed, shattering the uncomfortable silence, "what do we care if he's a bastard . . . ?"

"The bastard!" Phillipe threw down the newspaper in disgust, watching it settle against the deep blue carpet at his feet.

"Phillipe!" Abandoning her flowers for the moment, Nicole Beaumont looked over her shoulder at her fourteen-year-old son, who was sprawled across a gilt brocade chair, his booted foot swinging over one arm. "I have told you, polite people don't speak that way."

"I don't care if they do or not. He *is* a bastard." His deep
blue eyes fixed themselves on his mother's carefully powdered
cheeks. "He's done it again, you know. And they set him
free. *I* think they should have hung him."

Nicole shook her blond curls away from her face and returned to her flower arranging. "Who, dear?"

"The Marquis de Mores," Phillipe snorted. Caught up in
his own thoughts, he did not notice that Nicole stiffened and
that her busy hands fell still against her satin skirt.

"What do you mean?" she whispered.

Scooping up the discarded newspaper, Phillipe threw it in
his mother's direction. "It's all there," he explained impatiently. "He's killed a man again, and the court let him go.
He probably bribed them."

Nicole smoothed the rumpled page and read the story under the headline: DAKOTA CATTLE KING ACQUITTED
OF MURDER FOR SECOND TIME.

When she had finished, her hands were trembling slightly,
but she forced them to be still.

"You see?" her son sneered. "They had him this time, but
it didn't do them much good. Now, if I had been there"—he
rose from the chair, clenching his hands at his sides, and
approached his mother—"*I* should have seen that he never
even made it to trial. I would have drawn my sword and
killed the bastard before the lawmen came. I would have—"

"Stop it!" Nicole stood facing him, her pleasant face made
unrecognizable by her fury. "Stop it! Do you hear?"

Phillipe, who was now as tall as she, drew himself up in
surprise. He had never heard his mother speak in that tone
before, and certainly never to him. "Why should I?" he asked
bitterly, attempting to hide his hurt. "Why can't I say what
I think about the Marquis? He does not deserve to be spoken
of politely, does he? *He killed my father,* or have you forgotten?"

Nicole drew in her breath and gripped the fabric of her
skirt in order to keep from striking her son. "I have not forgotten. But that does not give you the right—"

"The *right?* Who gives a damn about rights? Did Mores

have the right to stab my father and then stand over him, watching while he bled to death?"

Closing her eyes, Nicole turned away from him and crossed the room until she stood looking out over the sloping lawn and well-manicured garden. This shock had come upon her too suddenly; she did not know what to tell the boy who waited expectantly behind her. His hostility was so intense, his hatred so fervent. Right, she thought wistfully; did she have the right to tell him the truth? And would he understand it?

"Well, Mother?" His voice held her immobile for a moment. "Haven't I the right to curse that man to hell for what he did to us?" He was breathing heavily now, surprised by his mother's prolonged silence and the ramrod-straight line of her back.

"No," she answered finally, "you haven't. The Marquis de Mores did not kill your father." She heard him gasp, perhaps in horror. He must think I am losing my mind, she told herself. After all, Phillipe had, with his own eyes, seen Mores kill Charles Beaumont. "Because," she continued stiffly, "the Marquis *is* your father."

For several moments there was an absolute silence so profound that Nicole thought even her heart had stopped its beating. Then, suddenly, Phillipe rasped, "That's not funny."

"No, it isn't," she agreed, "but neither is it a joke. My husband, Charles Beaumont, was not your father. Antoine de Vallombrosa is."

Phillipe stood frozen with his hand held out before him as if in supplication. The image of his mother in front of the long glass windows, which a moment before had been so clear, blurred, then disappeared in a sea of blind fury. "You're lying," he finally managed to hiss.

"No." Nicole turned slowly, her heavy skirt swirling about her legs in an amber wave.

Her son heard the whisper of her skirts as she moved toward him, and then his vision began to return. Through his own bewildered senses, he saw, as if for the first time, the woman he had worshiped all his life. His eyes flicked over the ornate blond curls, arranged so carefully around her face and neck, the gray eyes, slightly wet now and full of some unfathomable pain. He saw her slim, milk-white neck, which flowed so smoothly into the swell of her breasts just above her lacy bodice, and her hands, long slender fingers heavy with rings. His eyes paused there, fastened on those hands, which had so often smoothed down his hair or straightened his collar.

Closing his eyes briefly, he forced his breathing to remain steady. "The bastard," he repeated. "I wonder why we didn't hear from him all these years? Perhaps he was too busy with his new rich wife."

Nicole winced as her son's barbed arrow hit home. "He doesn't know. I never told him."

All at once, her pinched face came into sharp focus. "Why not? Don't you think it would have given him a good laugh?"

She turned her back on him so that he could not see how hard she had to struggle to keep her voice normal. "I didn't tell him because I thought it would be best if we just went on as we were. He was only sixteen, not much older than you. And Charles wanted a son so badly. I really thought it would be better for everyone if I just kept silent."

"Did my father—excuse me, I mean Charles—know?" His voice was utterly controlled and utterly humorless.

Nicole's eyes filled with unshed tears. She knew she had just destroyed his childhood, cutting the security from under his feet. But no, Charles Beaumont's death had done that. Losing the man he believed to be his father had forced Phillipe to grow up too quickly. He had become a man before he was finished being a child. Yet, despite his maturity and advanced education, despite his strength of character and the wisdom he had learned through bleak necessity, despite the pain that had turned his heart to stone at the age of twelve, Phillipe was still a child in many ways. And Nicole knew that he had always drawn a certain comfort from his hatred of the Marquis, who had been a convenient outlet for all of the boy's childish hostility and bitter sorrow. He should be shouting now, weeping, anything but asking these cold and indifferent questions. "No," she told him simply, "Charles never knew."

"So you made a fool of him, too, did you? No wonder Mores had to kill him. He might have discovered the truth."

"I told you," she repeated patiently. "Antoine didn't know either."

There was a momentary pause during which Nicole heard her son take several deep breaths "Then who did?" he asked at last.

"Just me and one other person, but that's no threat to you." She waved a hand in the air with assumed nonchalance, then whirled abruptly. "I did what I thought was best for you, Phillipe, and that meant keeping this a secret." She could no longer bear the stilted, artificial sound of their voices. With her hands held out before her, she moved toward her son, but, before she had taken more than two steps, he backed away.

"Then why did you tell me now?" he demanded.

Nicole's heart sank. She should not have done it. She had been wrong after all. "Because I could not bear to hear you speak of him that way, as if you hated him."

"But I *do* hate him. I always have, and even more so now!" he swore vehemently.

Phillipe was surprised by the look of hurt and fear that flitted across his mother's face. "Don't you feel that way, too?" he pleaded. "Look what he's done to you—to us. He doesn't give a damn about us and he never did. Don't *you* hate him, Mother?"

Antoine's face rose, unbidden, before Nicole's eyes: he was smiling, his dark eyes merry, his moustache waxed and turned up at a rakish angle—so handsome and so foolish. "No," she whispered, "I don't."

Phillipe's last flash of hope died, leaving his insides raw and painful. He had never seen his mother look so young and tender as she had in that moment, and he knew she had been thinking about the Marquis. Not only did she not hate the man who should have been her worst enemy; she loved him. Still.

Suddenly, the room began to sway and Phillipe felt disgust and nausea rising in his throat. He thought he was going to be ill, and he lurched toward the glass doors, dragging them open so the outside air could strike him in the face. Then, with the memory of his mother's tender expression floating before him, he began to run.

He did not know where he was going, nor did he care. He simply had to get away. "It's a lie," he told himself again and again, "a damned filthy lie!" *But he knew in his heart that what his mother had told him was true. . . .*

"But if it's true," Gretta gasped, horrified by her son-in-law's response, "we ought to—"

"Do nothing," Mores interrupted. "I repeat, what does it matter to us?"

"Perhaps it doesn't," Phillipe said stiffly as he swept past Gretta and planted himself a few feet away from the Marquis, "although I must confess, most men would find some interest in the fact that—"

"Young man!" Von Hoffman rose from his chair like an angry bull. "You have no right to come in here, uninvited, and disrupt our meal this way. And, as for your—er—legal status, that's hardly our concern."

Phillipe drew himself up to his full height and, ignoring Von Hoffman, addressed himself to Mores. "Oh, but it is," he said, noting with pleasure the Marquis's knitted brow, "because, you see," he took a few steps forward, his blue eyes locked with Mores's black ones, "I am *your* bastard."

ELEVEN

The Marquis sat at the desk in the study staring blankly before him. In this tiny, dark room, with the flickering lamplight that could not really penetrate the gloom, Mores felt that he was absolutely alone and safe from outside observation. The fire, which gave the room its cloying warmth, only increased his feeling of isolation, and the light of the flames danced across his face, heightening the dark circles under his eyes and the hollows in his cheeks.

With his chin resting on his hand, he closed his eyes, trying to erase the events of the recent past from his mind. It had been three days since Phillipe Beaumont's dramatic arrival had shattered the calm in this household. Three days of watching while Mores's relatives avoided him or spoke unnaturally of common things. Three days of intense silence between himself and Medora, which neither seemed willing to break. Three days of waiting for an inspiration to tell him what he must do, for he could not decide on his own.

He had agreed to let the boy stay here, though why he should have done so, he could not imagine. Von Hoffman was furious, and Phillipe himself was always there, just outside the study door, as if waiting to pounce. For three days the Marquis had not been allowed to forget the boy. He knew he should have sent Phillipe away. But Mores wanted to know why the boy had come here like this. Why, with his intense hostility for the man, had Phillipe chosen to throw himself on the Marquis's mercy? But Mores knew why. The boy had made himself very clear; he was saying, "Take me—I am your son and your responsibility."

For three days, Mores had cut himself off from his family and told himself again and again that he did not believe it. It was all a lie, a ploy that Phillipe had planned in order to gain revenge for the death of his real father. Or so Mores told himself. And then the letter had come.

He stared at it now, his dark eyes hooded by blue-veined lids. The paper lay in a yellow pool of lamplight, the dark ink making erratic patterns across the page. He had known the handwriting the instant he saw it—Nicole's. With his pulse pounding dully in his ears, he had brought the letter here to read it in private, closing the door and barring it against intrusion. But he could not bring himself to look at it, now that he sat behind the huge desk that dominated the room. He did not want to know what Nicole had to tell him—not if it confirmed what Phillipe had said.

The Marquis shook his head in despair. He had thought Nicole was gone from his life forever and he had been happy with Medora and their daughter. He had even begun to realize that Medora, and not Nicole, was best suited to be his life partner. But now the boy had come, dredging up the past with the violence of an unexpected hurricane. It was not that he did not want a son. He had waited half his life to have a boy to share his secrets with. But Phillipe must not be the one, because, if he were, it meant that Nicole had lied to Mores. Not once, but many times—so many that he could not even count them. And he could not accept that. To do so would be to deny everything he had believed in for fourteen long years of his life. He simply could not do it. Nicole had loved him and could not have deceived him so cruelly.

With fingers that trembled only slightly, he lifted the letter and sniffed it, foolishly, to see if it still retained any of her scent. But it had traveled across an ocean since it left her and, somewhere along the way, the smell of sweaty hands had replaced the fragrance of lilac and roses. Mores breathed deeply once, and then, finally, he laid the several sheets of paper on the desk and began to read.

My dear Antoine,

It is strange to write your name again after so long, and sad that I should do so, not out of love or the warmth of fond memories, but in penitence for a sin for which I can never be absolved. Twice I have betrayed you—if you do not count my weakness in ever letting you touch me at all—and I cannot hope that you will understand my reasons. But I ask you to try, for the sake of a single moment in time when you meant so much to me, and, more importantly, for the sake of our son.

It's true: Phillipe Beaumont is your son, conceived during those terribly brief few days when we had just met. Perhaps you will not believe me now, after so long. I did not tell you before because I believed it best for all of us that no one knew. I carried my secret all those years, keeping my silence while I made you think that I could never deceive you. That was my first betrayal.

But now I must admit the truth, because I am very much afraid that Phillipe is on his way to you at this moment, intent upon upsetting your life in whatever way he can. Forgive me, but I told him. Because of my own needs, I broke my vow, destroyed my honor, and made him a bastard—all with a single sweep of my hand. And that was my second betrayal.

I warn you, Antoine, the boy hates you as he has never hated another in all his young life. I owe you at least this explanation, for I do not think you can comprehend how deeply we have both hurt him. He is strong-willed and unhappy, and his hatred is the only anchor he can cling to now that I, too, have deceived him. I warn you that he is your enemy; I ask you not to let him destroy you; I beg you to try to understand him, and I plead with you to keep him by you. Because, despite his feelings for you, I do not think he could bear it if you turned him away.

I am sorry for the pain I have caused you, and sorrier still for your wife, whose life I never meant to touch. But more than that, I am sorry for Phillipe, who is still a child and has not your ability to survive these constant trials.

I am also, unforgivably, sorry for myself. Now, through my own folly and weakness, I have lost my son—the only other person I truly loved. Perhaps, because of that, because my own desperate prophecy has come true and my life has become empty and cold; because, finally, I have loved you and you, me, a long, long time ago—perhaps these things will dispose you to forgive me someday. Just as I forgave you once, but could not tell you so.

Tell Phillipe I am sorry and that I love him. And you.

> Always,
> Nicole

Mores dropped the letter from nerveless fingers. His vision faded in and out with the pulsing of his blood, and he realized that he had not taken a breath for a full minute. For an instant, he was aware of nothing beyond the intricate workings of his own body; his mind steadfastly refused to function.

The unexpected racket as someone pounded on the door shook him from his stupor. "Who is it?" he growled, unwilling to be interrupted.

"William," came the answer. "I just got back from St. Paul and I heard," he paused, clearing his throat, "about the boy. Will you let me in?"

The Marquis picked up the scattered pages of the letter, folded them quickly, and thrust them into his pocket. He did not want anyone else to see it. It was absurd, but, in spite of what she had done to him, he wanted to protect her. Still.

Rising with unaccustomed stiffness, he unlatched the door, then turned back to the fire as William entered the room behind him.

"So Phillipe came here to tell you he is your son?" Van Driesche asked without preamble.

"He did," Mores responded, "but I still don't believe it." His voice was barely audible, a sign of his own uncertainty.

William stood absolutely still for a moment, watching the Marquis pace before the fire, his hands clasped tightly behind his back. Van Driesche knew how much of a shock this must have been to his employer, and his own eyes reflected a sudden weariness so intense that it gave his face a cast of despair. Sitting down on the edge of the desk with one leg swinging free, William took a deep breath and said, "I'm afraid it's true, my friend."

For a brief instant the only sound in the room was the crackling of the flames, and then Mores whirled to face the other man. "How the hell would you know?" he rasped.

"Nicole told me fifteen years ago when she was carrying your child."

The Marquis took a step forward, his black eyes fixed on William's face. "She told you?" Mores repeated incredulously. "She told *you?*"

William shifted his weight uneasily and nodded.

Clenching his hands into granite fists, the Marquis suppressed a shudder of fury. Now it was not only Nicole who had betrayed him, but his best friend as well. It seemed the whole world had conspired to keep this little secret from him. Everyone but he had known the truth, and they had made a fool of him. "My son," he murmured, "and no one saw fit to tell me. All these years I've had a *son!* Do you know what that would have meant to me?"

"I'm sorry," William began, "we thought—"

Mores snorted and waved a hand in dismissal. Then, without another glance, he turned away from the secretary as if he could no longer bear to look at him. . . .

Nicole lowered her eyes, unable to meet William's penetrating gaze. "Yes," *she murmured, tucking a blond curl behind her ear,* "the child I carry is Mores's." *She paused and* bit her lip while she gathered her thoughts. "But, William, he must not know it."

Van Driesche eyed her warily. Perhaps that was why she had encouraged the Marquis to travel outside France this year. Perhaps she was grateful after all that her lover was gone. But he simply could not understand her reasons. "Why not?" he asked.

Nicole waved her hand absently, causing her long blue sleeve to dance like a ghost in the still air of the garden. "He is so young," she said, "and impetuous. He lives in a dream world where romance is the only reality. He's not ready to deal with a child." Her heart was pounding erratically as she watched for William's reaction. It was so important that he see things her way. If the secretary were to tell Antoine what he had just discovered—she could not even bear to think about it.

Perching himself on the edge of a stone bench, William contemplated Nicole, aware of her inner turmoil and the driving force that seemed to propel her forward almost against her will. He did not speak; it was she who had so much to say.

"I don't want Antoine to feel obligated to me in any way, and you know he would. That kind of obligation would spoil his youth and make us both miserable. *And* the child. I'm right, William, you must see that. He just isn't ready for something like this."

With his hands clasped together between his knees, William considered her argument in silence. Finally, he asked, "What can I do?"

Breathing a sigh of profound relief, Nicole told him, "You can see that he stays out of the country for a year, until a few months after the child is born. You're going to join him in London, aren't you?"

"Yes. And it shouldn't be difficult to keep him busy traveling for that long. His parents have been encouraging him to do so while he is still young." He looked up at her, shading his eyes from the glare of the sun. "But what about when he gets back? Won't he guess when he sees the child?"

Nicole shook her head. "I don't think so. Antoine is the kind of man whose ego won't let him believe that anything that important could happen in his absence. Besides, I *am* married. Antoine will come back, find me with a new baby, and assume it belongs to Charles. After all, why should it not?"

Suddenly, a thought struck him. "How can *you* be sure the baby is Mores's and not your husband's?"

Nicole smiled secretly, placing her hand lightly on his shoulder. "I know," she said, "believe me."

"Well then, do you think it right to deceive the Marquis when he trusts you so much?"

For the second time she lowered her eyes and her face was touched with a shadow of doubt. "It's more than right," she declared, "it's necessary. For all of us. I want my family, William. I want Charles and his protection and the security he offers. And I want my baby. But most of all, I want to live a normal life composed of all these things. I desire this more than anything else. More than Antoine and his dreams and fire and romance. Do you understand?"

Glancing beyond her at the manicured gardens that spread like a tame, structured sea at her back, William cleared his throat and asked, "Does that mean that when we return you will refuse to see him?"

Nicole took a deep breath and, for an instant, her eyes were misted with tears. "If Antoine comes back to me after a year," she began, "and sees that I have my life and my family, but still wants me, I won't be able to send him away. I know that, William. I'm not quite strong enough to cut him out of my life entirely."

Van Driesche rose silently, attempting to disguise his displeasure, but he was not quite successful.

"You think I'm wrong," she accused.

"It's not my place to judge you," he answered stiffly. He saw by the flame of fear that lit her eyes that she did not believe him. "I want you to know, Nicole, that I will help you in any way you ask because, whatever your reasons, I think you're right—Mores isn't ready for this. He's not yet finished with being a child himself."

She came forward and clasped his hands, her gratitude shining in her wide gray eyes. *"Bless you, William," she said, touching his cheek with her warm lips, "I don't know what I should have done without you. . . ."*

"What shall I do?" Mores asked finally, breaking the silence that hung between them like a stone barrier. The Marquis had not yet managed to rid himself of a profound sense of betrayal, but he needed his friend's advice. He had always turned to Van Driesche for advice since he had been no more than seven and William all of twelve. And, despite the gnawing bewilderment that had paralyzed him for a moment, he knew somehow that Van Driesche would never advise him poorly.

"I think that you should keep Phillipe with you," the secretary said, choosing his words with great care. "Take him back to Dakota and try to establish a relationship with him—that is, if Medora is willing."

The Marquis closed his eyes. Medora. What could he tell her? That Nicole had been no more than a youthful fancy? But fancies did not result in boys like Phillipe. *Twice I have betrayed you—if you do not count my weakness in ever letting you touch me at all.*

"Well," William interrupted his thoughts, "what will you do?"

Mores met his friend's questioning gaze for the first time in several minutes. Running one hand absently through his hair, he muttered, "I don't know."

"So, you have unlocked the door at last. And high time, too." Von Hoffman puffed his way into the room, trailing a heavy cloud of cigar smoke. Kicking the door shut behind him, he stopped in the center of the floor and confronted his son-in-law. "Have you any idea what's been going on in the outside world while you've hidden yourself away to consider your sordid little dramas? Quite aside from the blow to your personal prestige that this bastard question has struck, are you aware that there is a plot afoot by the members of the Beef Trust to put us out of business? Or doesn't the business interest you anymore?"

Mores gaped at Von Hoffman, taking in the flushed redness of his cheeks and the taut lines of his face, but not the sense of his words. "Whatever are you talking about?"

"I am referring, my dear son-in-law, to the meeting of the Beef Trust that ended today, having successfully passed into law an act raising the shipping rate for dressed beef from 64 cents per 100 pounds to 77 cents. They were, fortunately, unsuccessful in their attempt to ban western beef all together."

The Marquis and William exchanged a long look. Such an increase in the rates meant the Northern Pacific Refrigerator Car Company would have difficulty competing with eastern meat packers. "But what is the point of—"

"The point," Von Hoffman explained impatiently, "is that this will hurt you more than them. They can afford it; they don't have to ship their cut beef across the country. These moves are aimed directly at you, Mores. The Beef Trust sees you as heavy competition, and they mean to eliminate you. It's as simple as that. Perhaps, in light of this new threat to our business, I can convince you to abandon the comfort of my study and venture once again into the world."

While the Marquis pondered this information, Von Hoffman puffed furiously on his cigar, enveloping himself in a pungent gray haze. "Well?" he snapped between puffs, "what are you going to do?"

William had asked the same question just a minute before and now, as then, he had no answer. "I don't know," he said slowly, "I have to think."

"Well, you'd better think quickly," his father-in-law warned, "before the whole world collapses around your ears."

Medora stood with her back to the fire, gazing out at the ice crystals that hung suspended from the window. Her dark wool gown hugged her body warmly, except where the skirt flowed out behind her, but she shivered just the same. She could hear the crackling, hissing sound of the fire that reached out with translucent yellow fingers to chase the cold from the room, but her hands were no warmer than the streaked glass that cut her off from the frozen snow beyond her window.

She had been badly shaken in the past half hour and her thoughts were a tangle of despair and anger that she could not even begin to sort into logical patterns. She knew it was her own fault; she should not have listened to a conversation clearly never intended for her ears. But she had heard William pounding on the study door, seen him admitted to the one room in this house that she had not been allowed to enter for the past three days. She had followed him to the door, deeply curious about her husband's frame of mind and disturbed by the stiff silence he had maintained in her presence for so long.

William had not shut the door behind him, and she had stood just out of sight, listening, unashamed, to their brief exchange. It had not been anything they said that had distressed her—the silences had been longer than the spoken words—but at one point, she had dared to look around the doorframe to see her husband's face. Just as he had cried, *"All these years I've had a* son! *Do you know what that would have meant to me?"* she had caught the expression that had turned his face into that of a stranger.

Not even Phillipe's arrival three days before had affected her as deeply as that look on Mores's face. She had been surprised then, certainly, and shocked, but she had not shared the Marquis's stunned horror over the news that the boy was his bastard. Medora had long known about Mores's affair with Nicole; she had made it her business to know, even before she married him. And surely it was not so surprising that the Frenchwoman should have borne him a son. Not surprising, but disturbing just the same. Yet not for a moment had Medora suspected the strength of the bond between her husband and Nicole—not until she had seen that look of pain and incredulity on the Marquis's face.

"My son," he had said, his voice heavy with grief. The memory made her grip the windowsill until her knuckles were white. Medora had not yet given him a son, but she had wanted to. She had wanted his first boy to be *her* triumph, but Nicole had robbed her of that victory. Nicole Beaumont, a shadow from the past, no more than a fond memory, had somehow managed to intrude herself upon the present in a most dramatic manner. And Medora knew that the other woman had a hold on Mores that could never be broken.

When her husband had said those two little words—"my son"—the pain in his voice had risen in her body like an ice-cold flame. She had realized with surprise that she was experiencing the first pang of true jealousy that had ever dared disrupt her well-ordered life. Never before had she felt so utterly helpless, so deeply hurt, so desperately fearful—except for the moment when she had been forced to watch her house burn to the ground. She might have wept, right there in the hallway, had she been another woman. But she was not. She was Medora Von Hoffman de Vallombrosa, and she did not allow herself the luxury of tears. Instead, she had turned away and gone to her room in silence, her self-control still uncracked.

Her eyes wandered across the tiny hills and valleys in the snow outside and she tried to think what to do. She could not speak to Mores just now; she would not dare. He just might recognize the source of the momentary torment that had subsided now into a dull but persistent ache. He might see her weakness after all, and that she could not allow. Not now or ever. Despite Phillipe Beaumont.

With sudden resolution, she turned away from the window and knelt before the fire in an attempt to warm her chilled hands at the hungry flames. Then she rose, straightened her already rigid collar, and, her lips set in a stiff line, left the room.

She found Phillipe where she had known he would be, leaning casually against the wall, staring out the drawing room window. He had been there, off and on, for the past three days, gazing off into some distant world that she could not fathom, his blue eyes shrouded with the secrecy of his own thoughts. He was waiting, she knew—waiting for something that he could not even begin to understand.

Phillipe did not move when Medora entered the room, although he was aware of her presence. He knew it must be she, because he recognized the soft rustle of her skirt across the rug. Gretta did not sound that way when she came into a room. In fact, no woman did. Except his mother. But that was a thought he refused to pursue.

"Phillipe," she said sharply, then paused, waiting for his response.

He turned to her slowly, as if there were no hurry. Crossing one booted leg over the other, he leaned more heavily against the wall. In apparent unconcern, he considered her hair— tightly braided and wound around her head like a false crown—and the dark, tailored cut of her dress. She was shorter than he and he liked that. It gave him an advantage.

When she saw that he was not going to speak, Medora said, "Why have you come here?" Then she repeated more softly, "Why?"

Phillipe raised one eyebrow, surprised by the directness of her attack. "I wanted to see my father, of course. And I was curious about the wild American West. France is dull these days, you know. So I came."

She knew he was lying, despite his light tone. He was a good actor, this boy, thoroughly adept at feigning an indifference he did not feel. But she was not fooled. "No," she said, "that's not why."

"Well, if you know my reasons already, I don't have to repeat them, do I?" He recognized the flash of anger, quickly suppressed, which lit her eyes. And he thought he saw something beyond that—some hidden pain that she did not intend for him to see. For a moment, he almost pitied her. This mess—which he now called his life—was certainly not of her making. It had all happened long ago, before she had even come onto the scene. Medora should not be his enemy; she was but another victim, like himself, of the Marquis's heedless existence.

Aware of the effort she was making to maintain her self-control, his features softened slightly. Perhaps he could make her an ally. But no, it was a foolish thought. This woman was still aligned with the Marquis, who was, in spite of everything, her husband. He could not let her see beyond his self-protective shell. It would be a fatal mistake. Tilting his head back, he smiled crookedly. "But, of course," he told her, "there will always be things which even you cannot guess at."

Medora sucked her breath in sharply. In that instant, when Phillipe smiled at her with superior self-assurance, she saw something that shook her to the very core. It was there, in the arrogant angle of his head, in the way in which he covered his weakness with a veil of obstinate cheerfulness, even in the slight cleft in his chin. This boy—despite his hatred of Mores, despite his anger and his all-consuming wish for revenge—was every inch his father's son.

"There!" Mores finished the letter with a flourish of his pen and laid it aside to dry. "That's the last of them, isn't it, William?"

Van Driesche glanced once more over the list in his hand, nodding in agreement. "Even if we've missed anyone, I can't imagine that one more letter would make any difference."

"And you don't think these will either, do you?"

The Marquis and his secretary had spent the last week engrossed in letter-writing and visiting the important members of the Beef Trust. There was little they could do at the moment, besides try to explain their position to the uninformed. Secretly, Mores intended to use a different method of persuasion when he got back to the Badlands. He meant to show his competitors that he could not be stopped by a few haphazard attempts to make his meat-packing business unprofitable. He would show them by refusing to give in. It was that simple.

"Excuse me, sir, but the mistress is on her way." Nell, the servant girl, stood in the doorway, shifting from one foot to the other. Even the servants seemed to have been affected by the somber mood that had crept through the house in the past two weeks.

"Thank you, Nell," Mores said, pushing back his chair and rising to his feet. He motioned the girl out of the room, then turned to William. "I would appreciate it if you would leave me alone now. I must see Medora in private."

Van Driesche unfolded himself from the wing-backed chair where he had been sitting. He knew Mores meant to bring up the question of Phillipe with his wife, and William would be glad enough to be absent during such an interview. With an encouraging half-smile, he inclined his head and left the room.

The Marquis drew a deep breath, his eyes focused on the doorway where Medora would enter. He had done what he could about the opposition of the Beef Trust, but had come no closer to solving the problem of Phillipe. He knew by now what he wanted to do, but his wife had to agree. And he was not certain she would do so. He had noticed a peculiar light in her eyes of late, and he could not understand what it meant. Still, he felt intense loyalty to and gratitude for Medora just now. Only she had not betrayed him. Only she was to be trusted absolutely.

Medora stood in the hallway gathering her courage around her like a warm cloak. The moment had come. Mores had asked her to meet him in the study, and she knew without a trace of doubt what she would find there. Closing her eyes in a single instant of weakness, she squared her shoulders and entered the room.

He was standing before the fire, his hands clasped behind his back, and the flames seemed to alter the outlines of his body, giving them softness where there should have been only sharp lines. His dark hair fell forward across his forehead, just touching the graceful lines of his black brows. And his eyes, which never for a moment left her face, were full of some grim plea. For what? she wondered. Mercy? Forgiveness?

"Medora." That single word fell between them like a drop

of clear water into a raging stream and she knew that, for the first time in many days, he was really speaking to her, not to some shadow just above her head.

She pushed the door closed and came to meet him, so that she could feel the warmth of the fire on her face.

"You know I want to talk about Phillipe," he began, watching the way her features blurred and softened in the firelight.

"I know."

"What am I to do for him, my love?"

She smiled slightly. He had asked the question as if there were many possible answers, many choices, all of them acceptable. But she knew what she had to say, regardless of her doubts and private torments. She knew, although he did not, that there was only one response she could give him now. Her green eyes widened as she swallowed once, then told him, "We must take him back to the Badlands with us, of course. He is your son and your responsibility. You can't simply turn him away."

Mores breathed a sigh of relief. It was what he had wanted her to say. He had not had to force her to agree; she had done so freely. For that he was deeply, ignorantly grateful. "Thank you," he whispered, reaching out to touch her shoulders.

Then, for the first time, she looked away. She simply could not meet his gaze. She did not want him to know what those few words had cost her.

Drawing her closer, the Marquis tilted her chin upward with one finger until he could see the soft parting of her lips and the subtle green glow of her eyes. Then, slowly, with his mind engrossed in plans for the future, he kissed her.

The touch of his lips did not bring to her its usual fire. Her skin did not tingle into sudden electric life. She knew that this was partly because of the cold shield that had formed itself around her heart in the past few days and partly because of Mores's unnatural distance from her. He was not really aware of her, at this moment, as a woman. He was grateful for her acquiescence, but that was all. His mind had been wrenched so far back in time that he could not struggle forward into the present and the harsh reality of her cold lips against his.

"I shall go and tell him," Mores was saying.

Before she could protest, he had left her, disappearing so quickly and silently that she wondered if he had ever been there at all.

For the second time in one week, she was tempted to weep—to give in to the kind of shuddering sobs that seemed to lessen the pain a little, allowing it to escape in the salt tears that bore the heavy burden of sorrow away with them. She wanted to—with all her heart she desired such a release—but she did not do it. She could not.

PART III

THE BADLANDS, SPRING OF 1884

TWELVE

"Rustlers!"

Johnny Goodall opened his eyes warily to find Dick Moore stumbling toward him in the darkness. Groaning as he lifted himself onto one elbow, Goodall tried to force the last vestiges of sleep from his mind. "How many?" he mumbled.

"Three, maybe four. They're headin' south, as far as I can tell."

"Get the horses, Dick. I'll be with you in a minute."

As Moore disappeared through the door, Johnny swung his feet to the floor and hurried outside. This was the third time in the past two weeks that he had been rudely awakened by news of rustlers, and he was beginning to find these nocturnal raids more than simply annoying.

Suddenly Moore loomed up before him, leading two horses that pawed and snorted restlessly while the two men mounted. "Lead the way," Johnny called. "You saw them last."

"Right."

Just as they wheeled their horses and headed out into the night, Goodall heard the approaching hooves of a third horse. Cursing under his breath, he glanced over his shoulder and recognized Maunders coming up behind him.

"Rustlers again?" Jake asked.

"Yeah." Goodall dug his heels into his horse's sides and leaned out so his chest hugged the animal's neck. The last thing he needed just now was Maunders's company, but he had little choice in the matter. Jake was the Marquis's employee, too, though for the life of him, Johnny could not think why.

"Which way are they moving?" Maunders persisted, drawing up beside the others.

"South."

As they rode through the darkness, the cold air seemed to pierce their clothing with painfully probing fingers, despite the sweat that rose along their necks and shoulders. Above them, the wind cried shrilly, urging them forward, while the sure-footed animals beneath found their way across the sloping fields, in spite of the mud that sucked hungrily at their heels.

All at once, Moore slowed his horse, putting out a hand to indicate that they should go more quietly. "I saw them about 100 yards from here, near the far gate."

Goodall peered through the gloom, soothing his animal into silence as he tried to locate the men who he knew must be out there, crouching, for the moment, in the safety of the darkness.

"It seems to me," Maunders began, in a voice that was just a little too loud, "that—"

"Quiet!" Johnny hissed peremptorily. But it was already too late. The thieves had heard them.

Suddenly the air was split with two sharp whistles, then the sound of hurried mounting as the rustlers swung themselves up onto their waiting horses.

"Damn!" the word just escaped Johnny's lips before he urged his horse forward with Dick close behind him. This meant the thieves had had to leave the cattle behind this time, but that wasn't much help if the men themselves got away.

The horses thundered forward across the uneven ground. Goodall and Moore leaned forward tensely, holding their breath back in their throats, their eyes fastened on the retreating backs of the three men up ahead. They could just see the outlines of the thieves in the dim starlight. Maunders stayed a little behind his companions, grasping his revolver with stiff, cold fingers. And as the land flattened out and the hills faded into the background, the distance between the two groups grew longer, then longer still.

"Damn!" Goodall repeated, but his curse was lost in the depths of the wind that shrieked by. These men, whoever they were, had good, fast horses, and they knew precisely where they were going. He knew that the Marquis's men would never catch the rustlers, at least not this time, but he prodded his horse forward just the same.

Finally, however, even Johnny had to admit defeat as the three thieves disappeared over a rise in the ground and were swallowed by the protective shadows of a murky dawn. The horses were panting heavily and their coats were matted with large patches of sweat. He could not push them any further.

Just then Maunders rode up beside him and the two men watched as the thieves reappeared over a distant hill, then sank back into a valley. "Damned Indians," Jake muttered. "They're gettin' braver every week. They might only get one animal at a time, but pretty soon they'll take the whole herd right out from under our noses."

Goodall shook his head and refrained from answering. He knew there were others who, like Maunders, blamed the recent increase in cattle rustling on the discontent of the Indians. Johnny himself thought it odd that thefts should have increased so greatly all over the Dakota and Montana territories in the past few months, but he knew the Indians were not to blame. Certainly the three men he had been following just now were not Indians; he knew that without a doubt.

He had caught several glimpses of the rustlers as the night sky lightened into dawn, and he had seen, in those few moments, that the men did not ride as the Indians did. Goodall knew the stature and grace of the Dakotas on horseback—the way the rider seemed to merge with the horse until the two were one single animal, moving toward a common goal. Not like the cowering, stooped shoulders of those three who had just escaped him. Johnny knew how an Indian crouched easily on the horse's unsaddled back, the dark streaming masses of his hair flying behind him like a jet black banner. Even the thieves who crept through the night and hid their faces from the sun had a certain indestructible pride of movement that they could not disguise. . . .

She rode with the wind at her back, bent forward gracefully, her head bent low against the horse's neck as if she were singing him fiery love songs to urge him forward. Although her brothers rode on either side, it was she who traveled bareback on the fine cream stallion, her hair—caught up in the gusts that rose behind her—weaving itself into the pale silken mane of the animal.

Johnny could not help but draw in his breath in admiration as he approached and, although he should have been wild with fury, the anger simply would not come. For he knew it was Kiwani, had known it from the moment he saw the Indians riding away. When he overtook them, blocking their path, the three reined in their horses and came to a halt. They sat up, tall and straight, waiting for him to speak, their eyes fixed on his face with hatred and suspicion.

"The horse is mine," he said in the Dakota language, indicating the girl's mount. "Perhaps it wandered from the stable and you thought it free." This was absurd, of course. He knew they had stolen it, but he did not want to antagonize them just now. He wanted, in fact, to win them over.

None of the Indians moved a muscle. They merely stared back at him disdainfully, implacably, unmoved by his announcement. He could see that they despised him—they did not try to hide it—and the knowledge made his insides twist into knots. He could not bear for Kiwani to hate him, not she whose image wove itself into his dreams at night. But her brown-skinned face was empty of emotion and her dark eyes shuttered against him, even though she knew—she had to know—how he felt.

Remembering the gift he had bought for her that morning, and which he had not yet removed from his saddlebag, Goodall turned to her. "Perhaps we can trade," he offered, "the horse for a piece of magic that I have."

Kiwani glanced at her brothers; she could not disguise the

flicker of interest that crossed her face. Neither of the men
responded. Clearly they did not intend to involve themselves.
It was then that Johnny realized that it had been her idea to
steal his horse; otherwise, surely her brothers would have objected to this offer.

Kiwani nodded, demanding, "Let me see."

He reached back to untie the bag and withdrew a large,
flat package wrapped in brown paper. Holding it out to her,
he warned, "Be careful. It will break."

She took it in both hands and unwrapped it slowly, turning
it over and over as she unwound the string. Then the paper
fell away and she gasped as the sun struck the smooth surface
of the object in a blinding flash.

"Like this," Johnny suggested, reaching out to tilt the mir-
ror at a better angle, so that her face was reflected there.

Kiwani stared for a long moment at the graceful lines of
her nose and the high curves of her cheekbones, enchanted
by her own image, which before she had seen reflected only
in still mountain lakes. "Ah," she whispered.

"It is for you," Johnny told her, "the only thing on this
earth as lovely as Kiwani."

And then, at last, she looked up at him with the gift he
had sought for so long in her gaze. *Now, for the first time,
he saw that the shutters had risen from her eyes—as if she
had forgotten, if only for a moment, that he was white and,
therefore, an enemy. . . .*

Maunders frowned, his scowling face contorted and unpleasant. "Goodall," he grunted, interrupting Johnny's wandering thoughts, "I don't know what you're thinkin' of, but
we'd better quit wastin' time and get back to the house to
tell the Marquis, don't you think?"

Peering at Jake from the corner of his eye, Johnny dragged
the reins over to turn the horse around. For once, the other
man was right; there were more important things than old
memories to occupy his mind. "The Marquis ain't back from
St. Paul yet," he said.

Maunders grimaced, shaking his head. "I don't know why that should surprise me. He's been away from Medora more often than he's been here in the past two months. But I s'pose he's busy workin' on his new project, eh, Johnny?"

Goodall nodded glumly. He knew that Jake was referring to Mores's latest obsession with building a stagecoach line between Medora and Deadwood. He had found himself a new business venture to keep busy, and that meant he was out of town more often than he had been. "I wouldn't be surprised to find out that he went straight from St. Paul to Washington before he comes back, either. He's still politicking for a government mail contract for the stagecoach line. He figures it's bound to fail if he doesn't get that contract."

With a sidelong glance at his companions, Maunders made a note of the information. He could see that Goodall was too tired to really know what he was saying anyway. "Hell," he said, grinning, "I think maybe the stagecoach line is just an excuse to keep him away from here. If you ask me, he's just plain afraid to face that bastard of his. Not that I blame him. That boy's prickly as hell. I think it's kinda funny, myself."

"Shut up, Maunders." Johnny nodded to Moore and urged his horse forward until Jake was left behind. That man made his blood boil almost every time they met, what with putting his nose where it didn't belong and gloating over other people's misfortunes.

"Wait, Johnny! I want to know what the Marquis is gonna do about this rustling. Or is he too busy to care? Somebody around here better start coming to some decisions and take care of this problem."

Goodall slowed his horse and shifted in the saddle so he could look the other man in the face. "I'm sure you're already doin' the best *you* can to take care of it, Jake," he observed, his voice heavy with sarcasm. The foreman had long been suspicious of Maunders, who had taken to spending most nights away from the bunkhouse where the other men slept. He even suspected, though he could not prove it, that Jake himself was intimately involved with the recent spate of cattle thefts. After all, he reasoned, who was it who had spoken up at just the wrong moment in a voice that had carried easily across the field, warning the thieves and giving them those few extra moments that had ensured their escape?

"Mama is crying again," Katherine Pendleton announced.

"What is it this time?" Greg could not hide the annoyance he felt at the moment. He had business matters to attend to, and Cory's abrupt changes in mood had begun to plague him a little too often of late.

"I don't know. Perhaps she's burned the pot roast for tonight's dinner. That's what it was the day before yesterday."

"Katherine, I don't want you to speak of your mother in that tone of voice," Greg snapped, pushing his chair back from his desk so he could see her more clearly.

Katherine shrugged and went to the window to draw back the curtain in order to let some light into the dim room. The day was warm, and last night's fire had been allowed to burn itself out, but the windows remained firmly closed and the study was uncomfortably close. Gazing out at the rolling grassland that ended abruptly at the foot of the distant cliffs, she continued as if her father had not spoken. "Or perhaps it's because of the number of cattle that have been stolen from us in the past month. Mama might be worried, you know."

"Katherine—"

"Or it could be that Madame la Marquise called for a visit and you spent the whole time watching her and then walked her out to her carriage."

"That's enough!" Greg rose precipitously from his chair, grasping his daughter's shoulders in a bruising grip. "In the future, you will keep your sordid little thoughts to yourself and your mind off matters that don't concern you."

The bright hot stream of light from the window illuminated his face, turning his eyes to deep silver and emphasizing the quivering tension in his nostrils and the taut lines of his mouth. Katherine smiled to herself, pleased that she had shaken his usual composure. "You asked me, Father. I was merely answering."

Greg released her shoulders impatiently. "I'm warning you, Katherine, I don't intend to listen to that sharp tongue of yours much longer."

Katherine recognized the implied threat in his words and backed away, shaking her head as if to free herself from the memory of the punishing touch of his fingers. "I should think you'd prefer my tongue to Mama's constant sniveling. Or perhaps it disturbs you that I'm not as blind as she is." She stood before him, leaning one hand casually on the edge of the desk, her face free of any telltale signs that might betray her thoughts. She was not afraid of him; she had decided long ago that her mother felt enough fear for both of them, and Katherine had determined that she would never be like Cory Pendleton.

With a stifled oath, Greg motioned toward the door. "Get out," he murmured, his voice dangerously low. "I have had enough of you for one morning."

For the second time, Katherine shrugged with unconcern and crossed the bare wood floor in the direction he had indicated. When she reached the doorway, however, she paused to call over her shoulder, "Mama is not quite as blind as you might think, and I'd have a care if I were you."

Greg stood perfectly still, wondering how well his daughter had really read his mind. No doubt she was just guessing, trying to distress him, as usual.

"Morning, son," Bryce said, entering the room unexpectedly. "I saw Maunders making his way up the hill just now. He should be here any minute."

Turning back to the desk in order to hide his thoughts, Greg began to sort through the papers that were spread across the top in disarray. "He probably wants to tell us about last night's cattle raid."

"That's where you're wrong, sir," Maunders declared, appearing suddenly in the doorway. He strolled, uninvited, to the only comfortable chair in the room and sank down into it with a pleased sigh.

Bryce and Greg exchanged a look before they turned to face the newcomer. Jake certainly had a sense of his own importance, Greg thought, noticing that Maunders's face wore its usual dark scowl despite his obvious good humor.

"What's the news then?" Bryce demanded. "I assume it's important, or you wouldn't have risked coming up here in broad daylight."

Maunders smiled crookedly, his eyes watchful beneath his heavy brows. "Well," he said, tapping his fingers on the arm of the chair, "it seems the Marquis is all wrapped up in this latest venture of his—a stagecoach line from Medora to Deadwood."

"We know that, Jake; it's hardly worth coming all this way to tell us something that's been obvious for a month or more."

Jake ignored him. "And he's spending a lot of money on the project, for the best horses and coaches and planners—"

"We know," Greg repeated, "you've already—"

"And," Maunders continued doggedly, "now he's on his way to Washington to negotiate for a government contract. He told Goodall the whole project would fail without that contract."

This time neither Greg nor Bryce spoke, but their eyes locked together for a long moment and then they smiled— slyly, knowingly.

"I thought you might be interested in that piece of news. I mean, seems like, after the Marquis sunk all that money into a stagecoach line, it'd be a real shame if it fell through, don't you think?"

Bryce nodded and reached into his pocket for the roll of bills he always kept there. "You were right, Jake. And we appreciate your concern." He pulled a couple of bills off the roll and handed them to Maunders, who quickly stuffed them into his own pocket.

"You know anybody in Washington who might be able to help you out?"

"You let me worry about that," Bryce told him shortly. "You should be concentrating your energy on those rustlers who've been bothering us lately. Seems to me that you should have turned something up by now. Hell, you've been out practically every night looking. Why haven't you caught them yet?"

Maunders shifted from one foot to the other, burying his hands deep in his pants pockets. "They're awful slippery," he muttered after a moment's hesitation. "Those Indians are damned clever at gettin' away without a trace. You know that."

Hiding a grin beneath a stern expression, Bryce agreed, "I'm afraid you're right, but I figured you to be smarter than any Indian, if you put your mind to it."

"Don't you worry, Mr. Pendleton, one of these days they'll make a slip, and when they do, I'll be on 'em like a swarm of stinging bees." As he spoke, Maunders sidled toward the doorway, pleased to be going now that his business was complete.

"I'll bet you will, Jake," Bryce told his retreating back. "I'll just bet you will."

When he had gone, Greg turned to his father in surprise. "You know damned well that Jake is involved in the rustling operation clear up to his eyeballs."

"I do."

"Then why are you pushing him like that?"

"Because, my dear boy, I've been thinking." He crossed the room to stand before the window, his hands clasped loosely behind his back. "We made use of the outlaws around here last summer, and quite effectively, if I may say so, even though Mores won in the end."

"And?"

"And it occurs to me that what worked once might well work again, if you see what I mean."

"You want to let the rustlers do our dirty work for us?"

Bryce turned to face his son, a malevolent smile on his lips. "Can you think of anyone better equipped for the job?"

Phillipe lay immobile, his belly pressed against the cold ground, his rifle cradled in the curve of his arm. Overhead, the early afternoon sun blazed across the cloudless sky, bleaching the blue expanse to pale yellow-white and burning itself like a brand into the sensitive skin at the back of the boy's neck. He remained still, lying in wait behind an outcropping of light brown stone. Beyond the rock, he could see the gently sloping expanse of prairie that was transformed, magically, from rolling grass to sculpted sandstone where the cliffs rose abruptly from the soft, green earth.

Below him, in the hollow of land where the prairie dogs had not yet marred the earth with their endless tunnels, grazed the seven prong-horned antelope that were the object of his scrutiny. He had followed them here, slowly, silently, keeping a safe distance, so as not to alarm them before it was time. When they stopped to graze, he had chosen his place carefully, and now he lay there, scarcely daring to breathe, as his eyes took in the picture of the animals feeding with unconcern, their rust and white heads bent gracefully over the short grasses and the new blossoms of the locoweed.

Satisfied, at last, that he was ready, he reached into his pocket and drew out the large scrap of deep purple cloth he had put there that morning. Then, holding his breath back in his throat, he lifted his hand and allowed the cloth to flutter easily in the breeze. With luck, the sharp eyesight of the antelope, along with their strong sense of curiosity, would serve him well.

It was several minutes before one animal raised its head, then paused for a moment when it caught sight of the purple cloth. Then the antelope began to move forward warily, drawn against its will by the piece of deep color that danced so lightly to the wind's tune.

Phillipe smiled and inched his rifle forward until it rested in an indentation in the rock, the barrel pointed with unerring accuracy toward the animal that was approaching. As it came nearer, he identified the short, curved horns that grew from its forehead and the small patch of black that touched its face just below the ear. As if hypnotized, the animal came on, oblivious to the threat lurking like a deadly snake beyond the far rocks.

When he judged that the animal was within range, the boy raised himself slowly to his knees and released the cloth. It fell to the ground and lay still, a violet stain against the green grass. With the rifle propped firmly against his shoulder, Phillipe sighted along the barrel, cocked the gun and swallowed deeply, his finger poised on the trigger.

It was then that the antelope stopped abruptly, nostrils quivering, and then, before Phillipe could respond, turned to flee. The boy swore vehemently and uncoiled from his position behind the rock. Moving without conscious thought, he saw the antelope gather its long legs together for a single, desperate leap toward freedom, and in the instant when the animal took to the air, Phillipe pulled the trigger.

The sun struck the rifle barrel with a touch of gold fire, just as the bullet exploded into the air, then found its target. The antelope's body jerked spasmodically before it folded in upon itself and fell to the ground with a heavy thud. From the corner of his eye, Phillipe could see the other animals fleeing as if possessed, their long, lean bodies no more than a series of rust-colored blurs against a pale blue sky.

Kneeling in the soft, muddy ground at the antelope's side, the boy winced at the deep red blood that flowed like a sluggish river from the wound his bullet had made. For a moment, as it always did, the blood became the creeping stain that had tainted Charles Beaumont's snow-white shirt, stiffening the ruffles into deep brown swells like the sun-touched domes of the Badlands at sunset. Phillipe closed his eyes, grasping his rifle as if he could absorb, through the smooth metal barrel, some of the fire that made it such a dangerous weapon.

The Marquis de Mores guided his horse along the bluff, but he was unaware, for once, of the impressive scenery all around him. He recognized the Chateau in the distance and it seemed to him that he had never seen it before. It was incredible that he should call such a place home; all at once it was no more than a plain white shell that harbored strangers within its bleak walls. He shook his head, reminding himself that it was better not to think just now. Better to keep oneself endlessly busy with the problems of the Northern Pacific Refrigerator Car Company than to lose oneself in disturbing thoughts about personal troubles.

Not that the business did not keep him adequately occupied. On the contrary, he had found himself constantly involved in making the meat-packing plant run smoothly despite the continued rumors of trouble from New York. Then, of course, there were the rustlers who plagued his ranch at night and the threat of diseased cattle that appeared by day. Finally, he had the new stagecoach line to organize. Enough, surely, to keep his thoughts away from the increasing distance between himself and his wife.

Nevertheless, each time he came home, the awareness of his troubled marriage fell upon him like a pall, and he found himself hoping, as he always did, that perhaps this time the coldness in Medora's eyes would have melted just a little. He did not understand her anymore; she had become a stranger since their return to the Badlands two months ago, and, like him, she had promptly buried herself in work. It was the boy, he mused, allowing his horse to pick its own way across the ridge. That was the only answer. It must be the boy. He had propelled himself into the center of their world and proceeded to tear that world up by the roots.

Mores pushed his white hat back on his head and ran his hand across his forehead. The problem, he thought, was that he did not understand his son either, and it was no longer pleasant coming home to his family. He had begun to stay away for longer and longer periods of time; there was always enough for him to do outside the Badlands.

He paused when he saw a flicker of colored movement in the valley below. It was a long moment before he realized that someone was stalling the herd of antelope grazing on the new prairie grass. Having located the hunter stretched out behind a rock, he urged his horse forward to get a better vantage point. He always enjoyed watching a good hunt; perhaps this one would distract him from his unpleasant thoughts.

He sat for a long time, perched easily in his saddle, admiring the graceful efficiency with which the hunter moved and the patience that kept the man from betraying himself too soon. It was only when the antelope leapt away and the man stood up to fire that Mores recognized Phillipe. He realized with a shock that the boy was a fine hunter and the Marquis wondered where he had learned the art so well. From Beaumont, no doubt. Nevertheless, here was something that father and son had in common; he knew from the way the boy moved that he loved the tension and excitement of the hunt well enough to do it properly, with an economy and agility of movement that made the experience into a kind of communion with one's deepest instincts.

Perhaps, after all, there was a way to reach the boy. With the first lightening of his mood in many days, he guided his horse down into the valley in search of his son.

Phillipe heard him coming but did not look up. He imagined his father to be in St. Paul, and the boy assumed it was one of the ranch hands who was approaching him. He did not mind such an intrusion; the magic was over now anyway and he was anxious to show off his prize to an admiring audience.

"That was well done, Phillipe," Mores called.

Phillipe stiffened, his fingers still gripping the barrel of his rifle. He knew that voice by now, even though he had heard it so rarely, and the deep, even tones reached out to destroy his pleasure in the hunt as surely as if this man had called him a bastard. He turned slowly to face the Marquis, his blue eyes dull and free from betraying emotion.

When the boy did not speak immediately, Mores swung himself down from the saddle and bent to examine the fallen antelope. He saw that the shot had been clean and the hide not too damaged by the bullet. Raising his head, he smiled up at his son and said, "I didn't know you were so accomplished a hunter. I thought for a moment there that you had surely lost him."

Phillipe stepped back, snorting in disgust. "I would not have lost him regardless. I'm too good a shot for that."

Recognizing the note of defiant challenge in his son's tone, Mores nevertheless maintained his pleasant expression. "Evidently," he agreed. "But now you are faced with the problem of how to get the carcass home. I assume your horse is some distance away?"

The boy nodded, his lips compressed into a thin line. "I can go get her though."

"But that's unnecessary. As you see, my own horse is here and more than willing to assist."

"You will soil your clothes with the blood," Phillipe muttered.

"I have others." The Marquis turned back to the animal, sliding his arms underneath the still-warm body.

"No!" Phillipe choked suddenly. "Don't touch it. I would rather leave it here to rot than have you touch it!"

Mores shook his head in surprise, but continued with his work. The boy was undoubtedly mad. Let the animal rot indeed, and such a fine specimen. It was only when he rose awkwardly from the ground, the heavy burden in his arms, that he saw the fury that disfigured Phillipe's face.

The boy stood with his rifle clutched in one hand and his feet wide apart on the ground. His face was flushed with the heat of his emotion and his eyes were flaming silver spheres. "Damn you!" he hissed. "You've ruined it!"

Before Mores could respond, Phillipe grasped the pommel on the horse's saddle and swung himself off the ground. In the next instant, he wheeled the animal around, digging his heels into the soft brown flanks, and left his father standing, the antelope still in his arms, to find his own way through the flying mud and grass that rose in a shower from beneath the horse's heels.

"Whatever made you do it?" Cassie asked, shaking her head in dismay.

"I don't know." Phillipe spoke, not to the cook, but to the bugs crawling through the grass at his feet. He had perched on the edge of the porch steps, watching Cassie as she prepared the beans for supper. She had brought her work outside, as she often did when the sun was warm, and, having found her whistling merrily to herself, Phillipe had stopped to tell her about his confrontation with the Marquis. He had not hesitated to do so because she was the one person at the Chateau whom he had come to trust. They had liked each other on sight, and Phillipe often found himself telling her more than he had planned to.

"Well," the cook shifted her bulky frame on the kitchen chair she had brought outside with her, "I think maybe you do know. If you consider real careful like, you might just come up with an idea." As always, she straddled the chair backward, her skirts pulled up above her knees, revealing the dilapidated hunting boots underneath.

Lacing his fingers together, Phillipe stared at the broken pattern they made on the grass. Perhaps Cassie was right and, if he really thought about it, he would find an explanation for his behavior. But just now he was at a loss to do so. He had done the one thing he had sworn never to do—revealed the depth of his feelings to his father.

"I don't know," Cassie continued thoughtfully. "I guess we all turn a little childish now and then." She broke off the end of a bean and tossed it over her shoulder to join the pile of discarded greens that had begun to grow there.

Phillipe looked up and grinned in spite of himself at the well-chewed stalk protruding from the corner of the cook's mouth. She had stuck a bean there several minutes ago, and now she chewed and munched and talked around it as if it were the end of a good cigar that she could not bear to throw away.

"My lands!" she cried, inadvertently spitting out the stalk. "If that don't beat all."

Following her shocked gaze, Phillipe saw his father coming up the hill carrying the antelope carcass. Cassie rolled her eyes, shaking her head again. "I guess we'll find out what he thinks about things now," she whispered, "but I got me a hunch that he ain't too pleased. Not with a black look like that twistin' his eyebrows into knots." She glanced sympathetically at the boy beside her. "But then, I guess I don't blame him, either."

The Marquis stopped a few feet away from the pair and dropped the animal on the ground at Phillipe's feet. The boy swallowed noisily, glancing up and down Mores's body. His clothes were stained with dried blood from shoulder to knee and his shirt hung limp from the sweat that had soaked through. The Marquis's eyes were midnight black, shadowed by his puckered brows, and a single blue vein pulsed regularly down the center of his forehead.

"You will begin at once to skin and clean this animal," Mores said without preamble, "and I don't expect you to enter the house until you're through. We do not hunt here merely for the pleasure of the kill; there are too many mouths that need feeding. And we never leave a dead animal to rot. Never. It's not only wasteful, but foolish besides. Do you understand me?"

Phillipe rose from the step and nodded dumbly. He could not have spoken at that moment even if he had wanted to. He had never heard the Marquis speak in such clipped, precise sentences and, despite his outward control, the boy knew that fury lay just beneath the surface. For once, he had no urge to break through Mores's calm exterior to get to the dangerous emotions below.

For a moment, the Marquis looked as if he might say something further, but then he seemed to think better of it. Turning to Cassie, he unhooked the hunting knife from his belt and tossed it down next to the carcass. "You'll see that he doesn't waste any of the meat, won't you, Cassie? And you know what to do with the hide."

"Yes sir, I'll see to it."

Mores glanced at his son once more, his anger only fired to greater depths by the look of mute surprise on Phillipe's face. Clearly, the boy did not have it in him to apologize. He probably did not even regret his actions. Damn him, anyway. The Marquis clenched his teeth to keep his restless tongue silent and strode to the kitchen door, pushing it open and slamming it shut at his back.

Cassie cleared her throat, submerging her hands in the bowl of beans. She carefully avoided watching as Phillipe knelt beside the animal and took up Mores's hunting knife.

"How do you suppose he got it here?" the boy asked after several minutes of strained silence.

"I imagine he carried it."

"All the way from the valley?" Phillipe could not hide the hint of admiration beneath his incredulity.

"Don't see how else he could of done it." There was another minute of silence, during which Cassie snapped the ends of the beans and tossed them over her shoulder, her leathery face creased in a thoughtful frown. "Well," she said at last, "I guess you finally succeeded."

Phillipe looked up curiously. "At what?" By now his hands were covered with blood and he held the knife awkwardly in his slippery fingers.

"Why, at makin' your father angry. Ain't that what you been workin' at since the minute you arrived here?"

Clamping his lips together, the boy looked away from her, plunging the knife deeper into the belly of the dead animal that lay stretched out, helpless, before him.

THIRTEEN

The next morning, Mores stood at the window, watching the dust dance through the stream of sunlight that illuminated his rather austere bedroom. He knew that William had left an hour ago to check on a problem at the plant, despite the early hour. Phillipe had gone with him, having discovered a sudden urge to see how the meat-packing business worked. The Marquis let the curtain fall across the window. He would not think about the boy now; it was a hopeless exercise anyway. Besides, now that he was alone in the house with Medora, he meant to make another attempt at breaking down the wall that had grown between them.

She was not in her room. The huge, ornate bed with its luxurious canopy—red velvet draped over French lace—was empty and the wardrobe door firmly closed. Nor was she in her tiny office. He made his way through the empty house, checking every room, until an unfamiliar noise brought him up short in the upstairs hall. It was a moment before he realized that what he had heard was soft laughter and that it was Medora's.

He found her in Athenais's room and he stood back from the doorway, just out of sight, amazed by what he saw there. Medora was kneeling on the floor in her nightgown, her hair hanging loose all around her, falling across her shoulders and down to the carpet in long, soft waves. She was bending forward slightly, speaking nonsense to her daughter, who lay giggling on the rug before her. With one finger, Medora touched Athenais's forehead gently, brushing the child's hair back from her face, and then she leaned down, smiling, as the girl grasped her finger in a tight little fist. Athenais was nearly a year old now, yet the Marquis had never seen Medora playing with her daughter before.

Mores stood absolutely still, watching in fascination. Never had he seen his wife look so soft and warm and loving, not even in the beginning, when they had made love together. Never had he seen an expression so full of delight, nor had he heard the trilling laughter that rippled up her throat, then escaped from between her parted lips in a rush of pleasure. Never, except for the night when she had delivered the child, had he seen her look so frail and vulnerable.

This was the Medora he had been seeking from the moment he first laid eyes on her. This was a woman whose heart was in her eyes and whose head was not, for once, full of practical matters. This was the woman he had looked for but had been unable to find in all the long days since he had come home. Hesitating only briefly, he stepped into the room and called her name softly, so as not to disturb the tenuous mood of the moment.

She looked up at him and he was afraid her smile would fade away, as it had done so often in the past two months. But when she saw the expression on his face, she seemed to rise from the floor without moving at all. Lifting the child, she turned and placed her in the crib and then came to stand before him, drawn against her will by the desire in his eyes.

He reached out to draw her toward him and his hands were warm through the thin fabric of her gown. Leaning forward, she brushed back her hair and tilted her head, exposing the long, white line of her throat. With infinite care, he touched her skin with his lips, then traced with his tongue the curve that began at her shoulder and ended just below her ear.

It had been a long time, but she had not forgotten. She knew how his hands would find their way across her body, sometimes massaging the tender skin, sometimes touching with the lightness of a feather, but always leaving a burning path behind as they moved lower and lower still. She remembered how his lips surrounded her erect nipples, the cleft between her breasts, the rise of her belly, and how his body seemed to melt into hers as his arms circled her.

Now, as always, her body responded until her senses were confused into a single, flaming desire to merge with him completely. "Perhaps we should go," she whispered, locking her hands behind his back.

But Mores shook his head. He was afraid that if they left this room, even for a moment, the spell would be broken and this soft and willing Medora would be transformed into the cold, prim woman who had shared his house for the past two months. And that he could not bear. "Please, Medora," he murmured into her hair. . . .

"Don't ever plead, my dear; that's not the way to achieve your goals." Von Hoffman sat in a wing-backed chair before the fire, watching his daughter closely, his hands pressed together fingertip to fingertip.

"But, Father, it's only polite to ask before you simply take something," Medora objected.

The sunlight poured through the slatted study window but it never quite reached her father's face. "You are eighteen now, Medora; it's time you learned about the real world. Out there, if you want something, you seize it before someone else beats you to it." He paused, tapping his fingers together thoughtfully. "I would not have been as successful as I have, my dear, if I had not learned early that if you don't ask, they don't have a chance to say 'No.' "

"But—"

"Don't be obtuse. You have to understand that your knowing precisely what you want and setting out to get it puts everyone else at a disadvantage. They're too uncertain and insecure to even try to get what they want. Don't ever be weak like the others. Be certain, determined, and absolutely unshakable in your demands. It's the only way to obtain the respect you deserve."

Medora's brows came together in a frown. "But what about love. You can't just force someone to care for you."

Von Hoffman allowed himself a superior smile. "You are *so* young, my dear. You have to learn, as I did, that if you are aggressive enough, you can make others believe anything you like. It's really quite simple—if you wait for someone to offer you happiness, you'll never have it at all. You have to make your own happiness and secure it any way you can. *Don't wait, don't ask, don't tremble in fear of being rejected and you won't be. . . ."*

At that moment, the child began to cry wildly, as if she had been abandoned, and Medora backed away from her husband. "I must see to her," she explained, attempting to ignore the look of unconcealed disappointment that touched the Marquis's face. Turning away, she lifted the baby from the crib, cradling Athenais in the curve of her arm.

When she looked back at him, Mores saw that the shutters had fallen across her eyes and she was once again a stranger. Without a word, he turned and left her.

Medora stood in silence, her eyes fixed on the doorway through which her husband had disappeared. And as the baby was lulled into stillness, she found herself wishing that he had simply taken what he wanted without asking and without hesitation.

Phillipe sat on his horse—a gift from his father that he had not yet acknowledged—viewing the outside of the packing plant with distaste. William had already left him to deal with some problems in the main office, and the boy felt oddly uncomfortable sitting here alone, although he had been alone, really, since the day he left France. It was Cassie's fault that he had come to the plant today. *"Maybe you're so ornery because you're bored,"* she had said. *"Why don't you get involved in your father's business? Or at least go see what they do down there. It just might do you good, you never know."* He hadn't dared tell her that he didn't intend to become involved in any business that his father ruled; Phillipe had a funny feeling she would not have believed him.

So now, here he was, having broken his resolve never to set foot in this town that he believed could only feel hostility toward him, though he had never considered his motives long enough to wonder why. Besides, he had been relieved to get away from the Chateau today; the stiff silence that prevailed among the various members of the household had begun to wear on his nerves, and he had been more than a little intimidated by yesterday's glimpse of the Marquis's anger. Still, Phillipe was not entirely pleased by the prospect of a tour of the plant. He considered the business of slaughtering beeves for the market to be far beneath him.

"Hello."

He looked up in surprise at the sound of a female voice and found himself staring directly into a pair of disconcertingly direct brown eyes. "I'm Katherine Pendleton," their owner declared. "Who are you?"

The name Pendleton caught his attention immediately; he had heard a great deal about this family in the past few months. He considered with interest her lovely oval face and the thick brown hair that she had tied back with a velvet ribbon. For a moment, she seemed out of place in this frontier town; her blue velvet riding outfit was much too expensive, and the grace with which she rested in the saddle was far too elegant for the mud and dust and poverty all around her. But then he realized that perhaps she had planned it that way. The drab setting made the jewel sparkle that much more brightly. "I'm the Marquis de Mores's bastard son," he told her.

She considered his answer for a moment, then smiled. She did not seem to be shocked by his bluntness, merely amused. "You seem proud of the fact."

Phillipe shook his head in vehement denial. "No," he said, "I just want everyone to know."

Narrowing her eyes as if to see him more clearly, she asked, "Why?"

"I'm hoping it will embarrass him."

"He doesn't seem to me like the kind of man who is easily embarrassed."

He eyed her sharply, curious about the slight smile that touched her lips and the knowing look in her eyes. Katherine returned his gaze with apparent unconcern.

"You resemble him a great deal, you know," she said, breaking the momentary silence. "You have his broad forehead and his chin."

"I don't," Phillipe snapped, now thoroughly disconcerted.

Katherine looked away, murmuring, "You wish you didn't; nevertheless, it's true." Then, abruptly, she turned back to him. "You don't like your father much, do you?"

For a moment, he thought he might answer, but then he drew himself up, gave her a tight little smile, and said imperiously, "That's not your concern."

She admired his regal bearing, but was amused at the ease with which she had made his defenses rise. He was, she realized, very insecure, and his antipathy for the Marquis was evident in every line of his face. Perhaps this boy could be an ally; he certainly seemed to feel no allegiance for his father. Besides, she liked his looks.

Phillipe recognized Katherine's amusement over her own thoughts, and he wondered if she were the kind of girl who always had a secret. He had known a few of those in France—his mother, for instance.

"Have you come to see the packing plant?" she asked unexpectedly.

"As a matter of fact, I have, but I think it would be more interesting if you came with me."

She smiled and shook her head. "I hardly think your father would approve."

"I don't particularly care whether he does or not," Phillipe insisted.

"Just the same—" she began, then paused to take a long look at the huge building before them. "It was a good idea," she said, "but of course it will fail."

"Why?" He found that he was truly interested in her answer.

"Because of the man who conceived it," she told him. "If my father had done it, it would have succeeded, but the Marquis is far too naive to run such a large business empire."

Phillipe was surprised at the note of bitterness in her voice; it seemed that she resented Mores as much as he did. But there had been something else beneath the bitterness—a certain obstinacy, perhaps even a challenge. For whom, he wondered? His father? Or himself?

As if in answer to his question, Katherine gathered the reins tightly in her hands, crying, "Race me to the far side of the river!" It was not a request, but rather, a command.

Clearly, this was no timid French girl peeking out from behind her fan, and he found that he liked her. Before he could respond, however, she was off in the direction she had indicated, her hair leaping wildly with the rhythm of her horse's pace. She glanced back once, grinning, and he called out, "Cheater!" as he kicked his own horse into motion.

Phillipe felt himself smiling for the first time in many days as he leaned forward in the saddle and let his horse narrow the distance between them. The cool morning air felt good on his face, and the wind beat about his ears like the flap of a bird's wing. He had not raced a horse for months, and the experience was heady, especially when his opponent was a girl like Katherine Pendleton.

She felt him closing the gap between them and Katherine dug her heels deeper into her horse's sides. She wanted to give him a good race, even if she gave in in the end. She lowered her head as she saw the cottonwoods looming before them. By now, their horses were neck and neck, and she could hear the rustling of the leaves quite clearly, even above the panting of the animals and the pounding of their hooves across the increasingly marshy ground.

Flashing him a wide, delighted smile, she felt the jolt as her horse plunged into the river. The water seemed to rise up to meet her, caressing her booted ankles and the hem of her skirt, and she laughed with pleasure, just as she pulled in slightly on the reins so that Phillipe reached the bank just a moment before her.

Phillipe allowed his horse to slow down of its own accord, then he dragged the reins fiercely over its neck until it turned and rejoined Katherine where she sat, damp and smiling, on the riverbank. "Good-bye," he muttered, urging his animal back into the water.

"Where are you going?" she called, surprised by his surly manner.

He did not pause, even for a moment. "You let me win!" he called back over his shoulder. "You didn't even try."

Katherine froze at the note of disgust in his tone. As he bent down to avoid the low-hanging branches overhead, a slow, burning fury began to build in her chest. How dare he speak to her with contempt? She had only meant to do him a favor by not damaging his delicate ego, yet he had simply turned away without a second glance and left her behind. The bastard!

Then, against her will, the fury transformed itself into surprised amusement. He *was* a bastard, after all. What could one expect? Perhaps Phillipe Beaumont was not just another boy with an ego of breakable glass. Perhaps he really appreciated women who were as strong as he. Katherine smiled slyly after Phillipe's quickly diminishing figure. She found that she rather liked the idea.

After the Marquis left Medora, he had barely gotten downstairs when the front door burst open and Theodore Roosevelt strode into the room. Before Mores could speak, the visitor burst out, "Rustlers hit the Elk Horn last night. They took some of my best horses." Aware, all at once, that the Marquis was somewhat distracted, Roosevelt paused to catch his breath. "The thing is," he continued more calmly, "I just talked to Goodall and he said they hit here, too. They got away with six horses."

Suddenly, Mores was paying close attention. "Damn them," he swore under his breath. "They might as well just move in, they visit here so often lately." Twirling the end of his moustache, he considered the other man's flushed, angry face. "It's time we did something about it, don't you think, Ted?"

"You're absolutely right. I've already found out from Goodall that they left here going north. Apparently it was too dark to follow the rustlers effectively and your men lost them in among the deep ravines north of town. Shall we go after them ourselves?"

Mores felt his pulses leap at the prospect of some action. He would be grateful for anything that might distract him from thoughts of Medora.

Roosevelt himself was anxious to be on the move. Behind his thick glasses, his eyes were glowing with excitement and he could barely hold himself still; he paced furiously back and forth, his hands clenched into tight fists. "I told the groom to get your horse ready. It should be waiting outside. I thought the less time wasted, the better."

"Then let's be off!" the Marquis called, echoing his guest's excitement, "and this time maybe we can catch those bastards with blood on their hands."

The men had been riding for two hours through the maze of rock and clay with only their hats to protect them from the harsh glare of the sun. They were surrounded on all sides by the chaotic pattern of chasms and precipices that seemed to be part of a brooding presence that followed them with grim intentions. Despite the brilliant morning light, the echoing thrum of their horses' hooves against the ground reverberated from the towering walls with ghostly intensity, and the shadows crept around them furtively, in answer to the low moan of the wind. It was as if the landscape had swallowed them alive, transporting them to the inside of a grotesque foreign world.

Roosevelt rode hunched in the saddle, trying to ignore the eerie sounds that nevertheless intruded upon his thoughts. Perhaps the rustlers were no longer here, he told himself. Perhaps they had already taken the horses and cattle and fled to Canada. But he knew that the outlaws had to have a place to hide out that was nearby, where they could hold the animals while they changed the brands and markings. And if any land on earth had been created to shelter outlaws, it was the barren Dakota Badlands.

Suddenly, Mores reined in his horse and motioned for his companion to stop. "Do you hear it?" he whispered.

Roosevelt inclined his head and concentrated for a long moment before he nodded. Somewhere, far distant and shrouded by the rock walls, he heard a hollow thumping sound that faded in and out at regular intervals.

Smiling grimly, the Marquis glanced at the barriers that circled them, cutting them off from their quarry. "The question is," he murmured, "where is it coming from? With the kind of echoes around here, it could be anywhere."

They sat together, listening for several minutes, and then the two men began to move forward, warily, taking care that their horses should make as little noise as possible. Mores nodded to himself when he realized that the sounds were getting louder every minute and then, abruptly, he found himself at the edge of a steep precipice. Far below, he could just discern a round pattern on the sandy floor of the ravine—the kind of pattern made by a barbed wire fence. He looked up at Roosevelt, who had clearly made the same discovery, and, as if at an unspoken order, both men dismounted.

Better to come upon the rustlers' camp on foot, without the betraying rattle of horse hooves on stone. Better to arrive unannounced, revolver in hand, before the thieves had a chance to run. Not that there were many places for them to go. The Marquis could see that the ravine had only two means of escape—the narrow openings at either end. Perhaps the rustlers had planned on never being discovered, buried as they were in the heart of a stone maze.

The men separated then, Roosevelt moving around to the east while Mores took the western approach. Slipping and sliding as he made his way down the face of the rocks, the Marquis followed the sound of the droning pounding below and prayed that it would continue long enough to cover his own noisy descent. Finally, he reached the bottom of the ravine and drew his revolver from its holster. The pounding stopped all at once, and Mores held his breath and hoped that Roosevelt was already at the other end, his gun in hand.

Then he peered around the rock that he was using as a shield and saw the brief flash of the other man's handkerchief. That was the signal he had been waiting for. Leaping out into the sunlight, he fired his pistol into the air, just as Roosevelt appeared from the far end. It was then, for the first time, that they saw clearly the nature of the camp spread out before them.

It *had* been a rustlers' hideout; in that assumption they had been correct. There was a makeshift shack near the base of the cliff and the building was so dilapidated that it looked as if it would collapse in the dust at any moment. The walls had been thrown together of odd boards and leftover wood like a giant patchwork quilt in gray and brown, and the door hung by a single hinge, tilting crazily as it swung slowly back and forth. In front of the shack stretched a long wire fence, half of which had been ripped from the wooden stakes and thrown to the dirt. From the confusion of hoofprints and debris on the ground, it was evident that this fence had once held cattle and horses within its boundaries, but now it was empty—except for the boy, eyes wild with fear, who sat with a hammer in his hand, staring at his attackers.

Mores cursed and approached the boy while Roosevelt went to examine the shack more closely. The boy was clearly no more than sixteen and he could hardly have looked less like a desperado if he had tried. His blond hair was in wild disarray, and many of the dirty strands stood straight out from his head, while a few fell forward into his hazel eyes. His shirt was thick with dirt, except where the holes revealed the skin underneath, and his pants were in no better condition.

Shaking his head, the Marquis knelt before the boy and demanded, "Where are they?"

"I don't know," the young man declared, eyeing the revolver in Mores's hand, "really, I don't. They left this morning, early."

So he was not even going to bother to pretend he didn't

know what the Marquis meant. Perhaps they had surprised him into telling the truth. "Then what are you doing here?"

The boy scratched his head, dislodging some dust that had long settled there. "My pa sent me to clean the place up. Take down the fence and—" He stopped abruptly, as if he had just realized what he was betraying to this stranger.

"It was rustlers all right," Roosevelt called blinking as he stepped from the inside of the shack. "They've got three running irons in there for altering the brands."

The Marquis looked back at the boy. "And to bury the tools?" he suggested helpfully, completing the child's unfinished sentence.

Clamping his lips shut, the boy glared defiantly at his captors, but never once did he look away from the barrel of the gun that was still pointed at his chest.

"Who are you?" Roosevelt asked.

"Peter Clay."

The two men exchanged glances. It was hardly likely that this boy was one of the rustlers. He was too willing to give out vital information. This group of thieves was far too well-organized to let someone like this into their ranks; they were experts and this boy was a bumbling amateur. Had the others been like Peter, the rustlers would have been caught long ago.

"Is your father a thief?" Mores inquired stiffly.

"Hell no," Peter asserted, "he's just a rancher hereabouts."

"Then why did he send you to destroy the camp and hide the rustlers' tracks for them?"

"They told him to," the boy explained matter-of-factly.

Roosevelt's eyebrows rose in disbelief. "Does he do everything that outlaws tell him to?"

"Why, sure." Peter shook his head as if the fact were obvious and Roosevelt a fool not to realize it. "If he didn't, they'd take all our cattle and probably burn down the house besides. Hell, you can't fight these rustlers, and if you do, you're bound to lose."

"And you don't know where they've gone?"

"Nope," he denied vehemently.

Mores and Roosevelt turned to face each other. "Shall we leave him?" the Marquis asked.

"I don't imagine he'll do us any good."

"No. Let's get out of here then."

They left the boy sitting where they had found him, scratching the dirt out of his hair and gaping after them in perplexed silence. When they had found their horses and started back out of the maze, Roosevelt muttered, "What do we do now? It doesn't seem like we have much of a chance with the small ranchers working for the rustlers."

Mores pulled thoughtfully on his moustache for a moment before he replied. "You know who Granville Stuart is, don't you?"

"Of course. He's the one who stamped out the Henry Plummer Gang in the sixties."

"Well, I've heard, though it's supposed to be a secret, that he's organizing a vigilante group and plans to round up the rustlers in Montana and the Badlands both," the Marquis informed him.

"And you're thinking—" Roosevelt prompted.

"I'm thinking we should go find the man and offer to join the hunt. Obviously the law can't handle the situation. But Granville Stuart can."

Roosevelt nodded enthusiastically. "Let's go tomorrow."

"Right," Mores muttered, "before another disaster befalls us and we're helpless to stop it."

"The railroads are raising their shipping rates."

Medora shook her head at William's piece of news. The rates were already exorbitant; they could hardly afford another increase. "But they promised not to. They said the rates would be stable for a while."

William shrugged. "They don't care. They know you can't fight them."

Pacing back and forth before the secretary's desk, Medora considered this newest development, her brows drawn together in a frown. "It's rather sudden, don't you think? And rather poorly timed."

"I know," William agreed, "but there's not much we can do."

Pulling her skirts in so they would not disturb the many piles of paper that littered the several desks in the room, Medora crossed the floor and paused by the window. The blind was closed in order to keep out the glare of the afternoon sun, but several lamps, set at strategic points around the cluttered room, managed to keep the shadows at bay. She rather liked the N.P.R.C.C. office that the Marquis had had built in town; it always had a look of important commercial activity, with people scurrying here and there, sheaves of papers in their hands. She wondered for how long that would be true.

Medora lifted the blind just a little and peered out at the dusty street. It too was full of activity; there were several horses tied outside the saloon across the way, some cowboys on foot, and a single carriage. She stiffened when she recognized the man who stood beside that carriage. Greg Pendleton. Again. Wherever she went of late, he seemed to be there, watching. When she went to the General Store, Pendleton inevitably had business there too; when she stopped in the office, he would buy a drink in the saloon and drink it on the wooden sidewalk, his eyes fixed on the building across the street. She had even met him at the seamstress's once—he had had an errand to do for Cory. Medora found his constant presence deeply disturbing, because she could not fathom its purpose. But one thing she knew—he did not intend simply to watch her indefinitely. He was planning some kind of action, and sooner or later he would abandon his passive role and move. Greg Pendleton was not the kind of man to stand still forever.

"Excuse me, William," she said shortly, "but I have something to take care of." In another moment, she had stepped out into the brilliant light and closed the door on the shadows behind her.

Pendleton saw her coming and a lazy smile touched his lips. From his vantage point under the sloping roof of the saloon, he recognized the determination in her movements and he knew, although he could not yet see her eyes, that they were glittering with anger born of hopeless frustration and more than a pinch of curiosity. He had known she would come to him like this; he had merely been biding his time, waiting. "Good afternoon, Madame," he said, inclining his head slightly.

"Mr. Pendleton, I want to speak to you."

"Evidently. But tell me first, since my curiosity is driving me quite mad, is your husband in St. Paul this week, or is it Washington?"

Medora's eyes narrowed suspiciously. "That's hardly your concern." She had not come here to discuss the Marquis's extended absences from home and she certainly did not intend to give him any information that might help him in his crusade to ruin her husband. She knew that his desire to see Mores and his family leave the Badlands controlled his every action, and she also knew that that was why he had been following her.

"But that's not true," Pendleton assured her. "I am concerned that the Marquis is neglecting his business interests."

Medora was still standing in the sunlight, but now she joined him on the sidewalk so that the shade hid her expression. "Nonsense. I am anything but a fool, Mr. Pendleton, and I want to know why you have been watching me."

His eyes raked over her, beginning at her kid boots and stopping only when they reached her face. He appraised her long and leisurely, the steel color of his eyes hooded by concealing lids. "I am merely sizing up the opposition."

Medora shivered, despite her intention to remain aloof. His gaze had seemed to shred the clothing from her body and she felt certain that, even if he could not actually see her naked skin, he was nevertheless imagining it in vivid detail. Struggling to suppress a brief flash of fear, she managed to say stiffly, "I imagine you've already had ample opportunity to do that."

"But there are things I still don't know," he drawled suggestively. His eyes ran up and down her body again, and his meaning was unmistakable. . . .

"There's so much I have to learn about you," Mores said, "I don't want you to hide anything from me."

Medora lay in their honeymoon bed, staring up with glowing eyes to where he stood, naked, beside her. Her eyes ran up and down his fine, lithe body and she found that she was not ashamed of her interest. He was, after all, her husband now, and a man well worth looking at. He was smiling tenderly, his moustache curling upward, his black eyes sparkling with a desire he could not hide.

"Come," she said, giving him her hand and, when he took it in his, she drew him slowly downward until he lay stretched out beside her. Only then did she throw back the sheet and let him gaze, for the first time, upon her unclothed body.

For a long, long time he did not touch her, but simply contemplated her smooth white shoulders, the graceful rise of her breasts, and the sloping curves of her hips and thighs. "I could look at you for hours on end," he murmured huskily, "and only then—"

She reached out to grasp his hand and guide it to the warm pulsing hollow in her throat. With a touch that resembled the tantalizingly indolent descent of a feather, he began to run his fingers over all the secret places of her body, leaving a path of warm, tingling sensations behind. With infinite care, he caressed her, gently and expertly, and all the while, as he set her skin alight with his touch, she watched him, drugged by his presence, his love, and his delight in her response.

And when at last he closed the space between them and she felt the trembling excitement of his body against hers, he whispered, "I believe you can teach me a great deal, my love, and, perhaps, I can also teach you." *His eyes were twin circles that had captured the firelight and held it there—a reflection of his desire and his devotion. . . .*

* * *

Take A Trip Into A Timeless World of Passion and Adventure with Kensington Choice Historical Romances! —Absolutely FREE!

Let your spirits fly away and enjoy the passion and adventure of another time. Kensington Choice Historical Romances are the finest novels of their kind, written by today's best selling romance authors. Each Kensington Choice Historical Romance transports you to distant lands in a bygone age. Experience the adventure and share the delight as proud men and spirited women discover the wonder and passion of true love.

4 BOOKS WORTH UP TO $24.96— Absolutely FREE!

Take **4 FREE** Books!

We created our convenient Home Subscription Service s
you'll be sure to have the hottest new romances delivere
each month right to your doorstep — usually before the
are available in book stores. Just to show you how
convenient Zebra Home Subscription Service is, we wou
like to send you 4 Kensington Choice Historical Romanc
as a FREE gift. You receive a gift worth up to $24.96 —
absolutely FREE. There's no extra charge for shipping
handling. There's no obligation to buy anything - ever!

Save Up To 32% On Home Delivery!

Accept your FREE gift and each month we'll deliver 4 bra
new titles as soon as they are published. They'll be your
to examine FREE for 10 days. Then if you decide to keep
the books, you'll pay the preferred subscriber's price of ju
$4.20 per title. That's $16.80 for all 4 books for a saving
of up to 32% off the cover price! Just add $1.50 to offse
the cost of shipping and handling. Remember, you are
under no obligation to buy any of these books at any tim
If you are not delighted with them, simply return
them and owe nothing. But if you enjoy Kensington Choi
Historical Romances as much as we think you will, pay t
special preferred subscriber rate of only $16.80 each mo
and save over $8.00 off the bookstore price!

We have 4 FREE BOOKS for you as your introduction to KENSINGTON CHOICE!

To get your FREE BOOKS,
worth up to $24.96, mail the card below
or call TOLL-FREE 1-888-345-BOOK
Visit our website at www.kensingtonbooks.com.

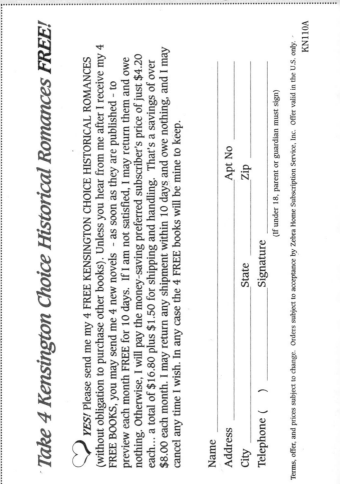

Take 4 Kensington Choice Historical Romances FREE!

YES! Please send me my 4 FREE KENSINGTON CHOICE HISTORICAL ROMANCES (without obligation to purchase other books). Unless you hear from me after I receive my 4 FREE BOOKS, you may send me 4 new novels - as soon as they are published - to preview each month FREE for 10 days. If I am not satisfied, I may return them and owe nothing. Otherwise, I will pay the money-saving preferred subscriber's price of just $4.20 each... a total of $16.80 plus $1.50 for shipping and handling. That's a savings of over $8.00 each month. I may return any shipment within 10 days and owe nothing, and I may cancel any time I wish. In any case the 4 FREE books will be mine to keep.

KN110A

Name _____

Address _____ Apt No _____

City _____ State _____ Zip _____

Telephone ( ) _____

Signature _____
(If under 18, parent or guardian must sign)

Terms, offer, and prices subject to change. Orders subject to acceptance by Zebra Home Subscription Service, Inc. Offer valid in the U.S. only.

4 FREE
Kensington
Choice
Historical
Romances
are waiting
for you to
claim them!

*(worth up
to $24.96)*

*See details
inside....*

PLACE
STAMP
HERE

Ilhɪlɪɪllɪɪɪllɪɪllɪllɪɪllɪɪllɪɪllɪɪllɪɪllɪɪl

KENSINGTON CHOICE
Zebra Home Subscription Service, Inc.
P.O. Box 5214
Clifton NJ 07015-5214

Greg Pendleton's gaze was insolent and self-satisfied, as if, merely by looking, he had learned what he wanted to know. Suddenly, a wave of fury began to build inside her chest. How dare he look at her that way? As if she were a common whore. As if he intended—her imagination balked at this and she felt a surge of some emotion that she could not identify. It rose with her anger until she thought she would choke on it. Somewhere, deep in the back of her mind, she knew she was overreacting. But he was smiling at her so mockingly, as if he could read her thoughts without effort. And that smile burned itself into her memory like the touch of a red-hot brand.

"My dear Medora," he murmured, "your face is really quite flushed. Perhaps you are ill?"

The words penetrated her raging thoughts with the accuracy of a well-thrown knife. Damn the man to hell, she prayed silently. He knew what she was feeling, probably better than she herself did. "If you will pardon me," she choked, "I have better things to do than stand here and allow you to insult me." With a violent sweep of her skirts, she stepped off the sidewalk and started away.

"Perhaps," he called after her, "but I doubt if you enjoy them as much."

She did not pause to answer, because his words had inspired a horrible thought that came from somewhere in the vicinity of her heaving chest. He is right, she told herself. She was nursing her anger, because it was, at least, a feeling—a real emotion—and she had suppressed her emotions for so long. With Mores she was afraid to feel, and so he had become a stranger, and a timid one at that. Medora knew instinctively that Greg Pendleton would never ask permission for what he wanted; he would just take it.

FOURTEEN

Katherine leaned forward to brush her lips across Phillipe's forehead.

"Stop it," he said impatiently, "I'm trying to concentrate."

Glancing at the chessboard in disgust, she muttered, "So am I."

Since the afternoon was warm and balmy, they had brought the board to a grassy knoll by the riverbank so they could finish their game with the murmur of the water at their backs. Now they were stretched out on the grass, leaning on their elbows with the sun dancing across their bodies as the leaves overhead fluttered in the breeze. They had met often in the past few weeks, despite the unpleasant conclusion to their first encounter. Refusing to be deterred, Katherine had waited a few days, then, finding Phillipe riding near the river, offered him a game of chess. It had not been long before they became friends.

Resting her chin on her hand, Katherine found herself thinking again how attractive Phillipe was with his piercing blue eyes and patrician nose, especially when, as now, his face was tensed in concentration. "Phillipe," she said impulsively, "have you ever been with a woman?"

This time he paused in his consideration of the chess pieces, although he did not look up. "It seems that you took me too seriously when I told you I didn't like it that you let me win. Now you'll do anything to distract me from the game so *you* can be the victor."

"Nonsense," she contradicted him, smiling, "you know you always win at chess. I'm only better when we race."

"If anyone is better at racing, it's your horse, not you."

Katherine eyed him for a moment, then decided he was only trying to distract her from the original question. "But have you ever done it?" she repeated doggedly.

At last he looked up to meet her curious gaze. "Have you?"

Tilting her head, she pursed her lips as if deep in thought, then an enigmatic smile spread across her face.

Phillipe recognized another of her secret looks and, as always, it intrigued him. He suspected that she had not really slept with anyone, even though her smile was clearly intended to convey that impression. Katherine was not nearly as worldly as she wanted him to believe, he knew. After all, she was not yet sixteen, less than a year older than he. Besides, she was a terrible snob, and there were not many suitable boys in the area. But her sophisticated air was part of her appeal.

This time, when she shifted her position so the board no longer came between them, he did not back away. Instead, he leaned forward, aware, all at once, that she meant to kiss him. Phillipe was not altogether inexperienced at this kind of thing. There had been a girl back in France, and the two of them had spent a good deal of time experimenting with kisses and soft, willing hands, but they had always been afraid to go much further. But now, with Katherine beside him, her breath like a summer wind against his cheek, he felt no fear.

As their lips met, lightly at first, Katherine was pleased by the tingling warmth that began to stir inside her. She threw her arms around his neck pressing her chest against his and permitting his lips to find their way down to the hollow of her throat. When he reached up to touch her breast through the thin fabric of her blouse, she gasped at the burning response that ran through her body. Raising her head eagerly, she sought his lips, clinging to them with her own as his tongue slipped into her mouth.

Phillipe lay back instinctively, pulling her over until she

was stretched out beside him. She seemed to draw the excitement up from his hips and her hands were burning brands along his back. "Katherine," he whispered, sliding his fingers through the gap in her blouse, feeling the silky flesh beneath.

Aware, all at once, of the extent of his excitement, Katherine blinked and backed away. "Not here," she said, "in broad daylight."

Clenching his hands at her sudden withdrawal, Phillipe struggled to hide his disappointment. "I should think that would make it more exciting for you."

"Perhaps," she responded, giving him another of her mysterious smiles, "but, nevertheless, we must wait."

He regarded her warily as the shadows from the leaves overhead quivered across her face. She was still playing a game of some kind; he knew it. " 'Til when?"

"Your father is having that big party tonight, isn't he?"

"Yes."

"And Von Hoffman will be there?"

"He will," Phillipe answered, "but I don't see—"

"I imagine he will keep the Marquis occupied. We could easily slip away together." She ran her tongue across her lips with sensuous promise.

He smiled slowly and nodded. "I see."

"So I'll meet you tonight then?"

"Yes, I think you will," he drawled in apparent unconcern.

"Good." Smoothing back her hair with steady hands, she straightened her blouse and rose from the ground. Then, just before she turned to walk away, she leaned forward to move her queen on the chessboard. Grinning, she blew Phillipe a kiss. "Checkmate," she said.

The Chateau was ablaze with lights that night, and there were guests from all over the territory. The house was finally finished—the last piece of Minton china and the last bottle of French wine had been delivered—and the Marquis had decided to have a huge celebration. He had brought out his finest wines, along with the expensive ruby red wineglasses, and thrown open his doors to as many of his neighbors as cared to attend. They circulated now from the porch, hung with dozens of colored lanterns, to the drawing room, dining room, and even the kitchen (though Cassie grumbled freely at this invasion of her private domain).

The guests were dressed in light summer suits and gowns because of the warmth of the June night air, and the women seemed to float in a sea of gauze and lace and silk. Nearly everyone held a glass in his hand, except for the dancers who circled to the soft strains of the violins, and the air was crowded with the babble of a hundred spirited voices.

Louis Von Hoffman watched the scene but did not become a part of it. He stood silently on the sidelines, glancing anxiously around until he located his son-in-law bent attentively over a woman's hand. Von Hoffman shook his head in disapproval. The Marquis was wasting time flirting while his business empire teetered on the brink of ruin. Von Hoffman had already expressed his anxiety to Mores, hinting that if things didn't improve, he might withdraw his financial support. The Marquis had merely smiled and told him not to worry. But Von Hoffman knew better than to imitate his son-in-law's cavalier attitude. He knew what the increase in transportation rates would mean, sooner or later, especially with the rustlers stealing the ranch blind as they were. Celebrations indeed!

"I have good news," the Marquis declared, appearing suddenly at Von Hoffman's side. "William tells me he just got word from Washington; the government has promised me that mail contract. The stagecoach line is bound to be successful now."

Aware of the enthusiasm that lit Mores's face, his father-in-law sighed. "What about the meat-packing business? That is, after all, why you came out here."

The Marquis glowered at this abrupt change in subject; they had been over this once already. "There's no need to worry about that. We're slaughtering fifty beeves a day."

"It should be eighty," the other man replied. "And now,

with the New York butchers threatening to boycott your beef—"

"I don't give a damn about the New York butchers. I'll bring them around. So long as Swift is buying, we have nothing to worry about."

Von Hoffman rubbed his chin, considering this bit of information. "Perhaps you're right," he muttered. "Swift might even be able to talk some sense into the butchers himself."

Mores grinned and murmured, "We shall both be multimillionaires before too long."

His father-in-law regarded him skeptically, but before Von Hoffman could voice his next objection, the Marquis turned away, losing himself in the milling crowd.

Medora had seated herself between Cory Pendleton and her daughter because she thought it would be the least likely place to find Greg. She was disturbed by the way his eyes had followed her all evening, especially when she realized that Katherine, pale and lovely in lilac silk, was aware of her father's interest. By now, Medora had recognized that Pendleton viewed her as more than simply an enemy, although his intention was still clearly to conquer her. And for the first time in her life, she found that she was intimidated by a man's penetrating stare. It was disconcerting indeed to discover that she was a woman like all others. She hated him for bringing it to her attention.

Cory herself was stiff and uncommunicative tonight; she sat in her chair as if she had been sculpted there. Her hands lay inert in her lap and her ankles were tightly crossed beneath her voluminous skirt; she might have been made of stone, except that her sallow skin gave her an ethereal look of another world. Only the slight rise and fall of her chest and the restless motion of her eyes betrayed the fact that there was life within her body.

Medora's gaze shifted from mother to daughter and back again, and she found that the lights and music faded into insignificance beside her own growing sense of apprehension. She was pleased to see Theodore Roosevelt approaching.

"Would you care to dance?" he asked, offering her his hand.

"I should be delighted." She rose, smiling, and followed him onto the tiny dance floor.

As they spun through the intricate steps together, Medora was reminded of the last time they had danced like this in New York, where the ice and snow had been piled against the windows. Here the doors were open to admit the warm night air and, through the windows, she could see several couples dancing on the porch.

Smiling absently at Roosevelt, who was perceptive enough to leave her to herself, Medora thought back to that other party when, just as now, she had been troubled by vague intuitions of disaster. She had been right then, of course, for Phillipe had appeared the very next day; but somehow, Mores had made her forget those things as they lay in bed with their naked bodies pressed together. It had been a long time now since she had lost herself in the sweetness of their lovemaking. But that had been her choice. He had wanted her many times, she knew that as certainly as she knew that she could not let him near. Quite simply, she was afraid to, now that Phillipe was here to remind her every day that another woman was tied to the Marquis more closely, and by a bond more unbreakable, than any Medora had woven.

At that moment, Mores's voice reached her through the music and she inclined her head to listen. "We are working on establishing a retail distribution center in New York," he was saying in a voice meant to carry across an open field. "And from there, the beef will be shipped to retail markets in the poor sections of the city. The way we've planned it, the meat will sell in the tenements for three cents per pound less than the usual price."

Medora closed her eyes for a moment, then looked up at her partner. "Will you forgive me, Theodore?" she asked. "I think I need little air."

"Of course." Roosevelt offered her his arm and escorted

her to the door. He hoped the slight breeze might bring some color back into her cheeks. She was looking dreadfully pale, and he felt a surprising surge of concern for her. He had come to like Medora in the past few months; she was possessed of such energy and forcefulness of character. He admired her tremendously, and he was aware that she had been unhappy of late. But he did not press her with questions about what was troubling her. He knew well enough that she was a private person who liked to keep her problems to herself. With a rueful shake of his head, he watched her cross the porch, then glide away into the night.

Medora made her way noiselessly down the hill toward the river. She hoped that the constant rippling of the water would drown out the sounds of the party behind her. She wanted, particularly, to escape the memory of her husband's voice. All at once, she had heard enough of his eternal optimism and his grand plans for the future. He was so blind, so utterly foolish where the business was concerned. Why couldn't he recognize the strength of the forces against him? Until he did so, she knew he could never fight them effectively. Mores believed, with a fervor that amounted to fanaticism, that he could solve his problems merely by refusing to see them as such. He continued to move ahead, oblivious to the pitfalls all around him, blustering his way through week after week. And she knew, as he did not, that his enemies were waiting with baited breath for him to stumble, just once, before they fell upon him like hungry wolves.

As the earth grew soft and damp through her light slippers, she came out of the morass of her thoughts long enough to hear the muffled tread of someone close behind her. She whirled, unafraid, and recognized Greg Pendleton. "Damn you!" she hissed, releasing all the pent-up frustration of a long and tedious evening. "Leave me alone!"

Pendleton did not seem surprised by the fury in her tone; instead, he appeared to welcome it. "I saw your face back there," he explained, "and I thought you might like someone to talk to."

"Like hell you did! You thought I was upset and that you might be able to take advantage of me."

"And can I?" he asked with interest.

"No!" She spat the word at him, remembering that only a moment before she had characterized him as a hungry wolf. He certainly took on that aspect now, with only the moonlight to illuminate his face.

"Do you know, for some reason I don't believe you. I think you knew perfectly well that I would follow you." His voice was like honey laced with venom.

Medora fought against the shudder that ran through her body. When she saw that he was going to touch her, she backed away. Groping desperately through her blank mind for something to say, she snapped, "I know only that you seem prone to follow ladies at parties when they venture out of the house." She was remembering that other night last year when she had gone looking for an intruder and Pendleton had watched her, intending, no doubt, to come after her. "Perhaps you think the only way to have me is to overpower me in the dark."

His jaws clenched with his sudden anger, but his voice was steady when he replied, "I don't want you quite that much, my dear. The last time I was merely observing a possible enemy to see how she might react, and I was curious about your little midnight expedition." He paused for a moment, as if measuring her response, and when she did not speak, he continued, "But I will admit that I suspect you are precisely the kind of foolish woman who refuses to recognize her own desires unless you are 'overpowered in the dark,' as you say."

With a sudden explosion of the rage he had encouraged in her from the beginning, Medora drew back her hand and slapped him soundly across the face. "You go to hell," she cried, her hand tingling from the force of the blow.

"Not unless I take you with me."

Before she could back away, his arms closed around her,

imprisoning her in his grasp. And then his head came down, forcing hers back until their mouths met in a brutal kiss. She gasped and tried to strike at him, but her arms were useless. When she kicked him fiercely with one slippered foot, he forced her legs out from under her and she fell to the ground. Pendleton knelt above her, grinning, then dragged her hands above her head and held them there.

His face came toward her as his body covered hers, and though she turned her head away, he kissed her cheek, her neck, her ear until, against her will, she found his lips pressed bruisingly against hers. She struggled, kicking at him wildly, overwhelmed by the rage his touch gave rise to, until she jerked her hands free. Her body trembled with the depth of her fury and she found his back, digging her fingernails in, hoping that soon the blood would come.

He grunted in pain, but his mouth did not release her lips. Her struggle seemed only to fuel his desire and his hands found their way beneath her bodice, reaching for her breasts.

"Damn you!" she choked as he sank his teeth into her earlobe with practiced efficiency.

Then, in a brief but piercing flash of moonlight, she saw the wild, hungry look of passion in his steel-gray eyes. Despite her rage at her own impotence, she recognized the vibrant light that glowed with his determination and his desire. She realized then that, despite his cruelty, his heartless nature, and the gleam of pure, shining evil in his soul, Greg Pendleton would always be a winner. He was a man who would never fail to get what he wanted because he did not care about the cost. And all her life she had been taught to seek out winners. The losers were the weak and the foolish, and that she must never be.

In that instant, the fanatic gleam in Greg's eyes reminded Medora, briefly, of her father, who had shaped her life from the moment of her birth. She recognized his strength with an insight that was painfully vivid. And it was that very strength, that power and indomitable self-confidence, that began to eat away at the wall of indifference that had held her apart from him. Fueled by her fear of failure, her own hunger and bitter resentment, she let her body smother the whispered warnings of her mind in a wave of unquenchable desire. He was evil—she knew it—but, for the moment, it did not matter.

All at once, she realized that she was clinging to him, that he no longer held her prisoner, and that she had no desire to flee from him. Burying her fingers in his hair, she reached hungrily for his mouth and covered it with her own lips. Somehow the fury had become desire, and the desire madness, and she waited impatiently while he loosened his clothing and raised her skirts deftly, always keeping her senses aflame with the tip of his tongue and the ends of his fingers. Then he was upon her, his skin against her skin, his face buried in her hair, his long, lean body pressed so closely next to hers that she thought she could not breathe any longer. As he moved rhythmically, she met his thrusts with her own, and her head began to pound with the heat of her response, until the madness exploded in a storm of long-suppressed desire.

There was no tenderness in their meeting like this, furtively, only passion like a surging waterfall. It swept them along in a flood of uncontrolled emotions—always a struggle, even to the end, when he collapsed beside her and the madness slowly faded into stunned disbelief.

Raising herself on one arm, she breathed raggedly, horrified now by what she had done. He reached out, blindly, to touch her shoulder, but she wrenched free of his grasp. "I hate you!" she snarled, backing away.

He sat up and glowered at her in silence while his breath seemed to freeze in the warm night air. Then he relaxed, smiling negligently. "If your hatred brings out that response in you, my dear, then I shall fuel it like a fire until it consumes you."

"Where have you been?" Cory demanded shrilly of her husband when he returned to the party.

Greg took her arm and guided her outside, glancing around as he did so to see if anyone might have overheard. From the expression on his wife's face, he guessed that she was about to make a scene and he wanted to get her away from the other guests before she exploded. He looked over his shoulder once, hoping that Medora had made it back to her room unobserved. She would have to change her gown before she rejoined the party; the one she had been wearing was ruined. Let her be wise enough to think of a good story, he said silently. But, of course, he knew she would be. That was why he had chosen her. Fortunately, he himself had avoided most of the mud and a vigorous brushing had freed his clothing of any visible traces of their encounter.

Cory forcibly removed her arm from his grasp, whirling to face him as they paused just beyond the reach of the lights. "You were with *her,* weren't you?" she rasped.

"With whom, Cory dear?"

"Medora!" She spat out the name as if it were poison.

"Of course not. I was alone. I decided to go for a walk, that's all. It was too stuffy inside and the night air seemed so inviting."

"Hah," his wife snorted in disbelief. "I know you, Greg. You were with her."

As always, Pendleton was amazed at how perceptive a woman as foolish as Cory could be. She had sensed his interest in Medora from the first moment the three of them had been together. It was odd how much she saw in this one respect when she was so utterly, utterly blind in all others. "I was alone," he repeated, aware that, in the face of his adamant denial, her fury would burn itself out.

"I don't believe you. I never *can* believe you. Not since Marisa. You're doing it again, Greg, don't you see? Betraying me again and again for those—"

"Quiet!" he hissed peremptorily. At the mention of Marisa's name, his eyes had hardened into glittering stone in the moonlight. It was a name he refused to say even to himself, yet Cory dared. She was a hopeless fool, but one day she would push him too far. "Don't speak of things you don't know about," he continued threateningly. "And I don't want to hear you use Marisa's name ever again. *Or* Medora's."

Cory lowered her eyes. She could tell that he was deadly

serious. "But your eyes are always on her. I've seen how you look at her." Already the righteous indignation in her voice had begun to fade to whining self-pity.

Struggling to control his anger, he forced himself to reach out and touch her cheek. "You are imagining things, my dear. You know I look only at you."

With a stifled sob, she crumpled against him, clinging as if he were the source of her lifeblood. "Do you love me, Greg?" she wailed.

"Of course I do. You're my wife." His arms closed around her automatically, for he knew if he did not hold her upright she would fall. But above her head, he gazed back at the house they had left behind, thinking of Medora and the painful bite of her nails in his back. While Cory wept herself out, he watched with interest as someone crept down the hill toward the river. From the size, he guessed it was Phillipe. The riverbank seemed to be a popular place tonight. Greg wondered who the boy was meeting there. It was hardly likely that he meant to take a moonlight stroll all by himself.

Then, suddenly, Pendleton clenched his teeth. Surely that girl treading so lightly across the sloping grass was Katherine, and yes, she was moving in the direction of the river. "Cory," he said sharply, "let me go!"

"Oh no!" she cried. "Don't leave me again. Please. I couldn't bear it!" Her fingers dug deeply into his forearms and she peered up at him through tear-soaked eyes.

Greg glanced once after his daughter, then sighed in resignation. Cory was in too dangerous a mood to be left alone tonight. She might do something foolish, and that could ruin his plans with Medora. Just now, there was nothing more important than those plans. Nothing. Let Katherine ruin herself, if that was what she desired, so long as she continued to get the information they so desperately needed from her boyish lover.

Phillipe waited with his back against a tree, listening to the gentle pulse of the river at his feet. He did not bother to watch for Katherine, for he knew she would come. It was not part of her game to leave him waiting here tonight, of that he was certain. He did not know exactly what she intended, but one thing he did know—she wanted him as much as he wanted her. Her body this afternoon had been warm and willing and ready for his, and he sensed that she was victim to a physical hunger that had come near to overpowering her. He knew because he had seen the same starved look in his mother's eyes once or twice when she had been unaware of his presence. Even then, he had known what it meant; instinctively, he had recognized Nicole's weakness. And now Katherine's. And his own.

"Phillipe," she called breathlessly, appearing like a wraith with her lilac gown flowing out behind her.

Although he could not see her clearly in the moonlit darkness, he knew her cheeks were flushed and glowing. Her eyes sparkled as she reached up to slide her arms around his neck.

"Did you think I wouldn't come?" she asked.

He thought he detected a note of hopefulness in her tone, as if she would have liked it if he believed that of her. "No." His answer was noncommittal, but he was intensely aware of the touch of her hands against his neck and the flowery fragrance of her hair. Perhaps this would be more difficult than he had imagined.

He circled her waist with his arms, pulling her closer as his mouth descended to meet hers. Tonight her body trembled with excitement, as if the music and lights had somehow snared her in their spell, and her lips were hot and anxious beneath his. God, but she was beautiful, he thought. Beautiful and hungry and wise beyond her years.

This time it was she who drew them down until they were stretched out on the damp earth of the riverbank, and *her* hands that fluttered over his body, seeking the secret places. His senses seemed to slide into a rush of tingling, burning sensations that threatened to take away his will. And when her fingers found their way downward and then stopped, massaging gently, drawing the blood from his head and into the nerves beneath her hand, he realized that this time she meant to go through with it. This time it was not a game for her, unless—unless—

Propping himself on one arm, he laid his hand against her cheek and whispered, "Katherine."

"Umm," she sighed, removing the hand and guiding it to her breast.

Phillipe swallowed convulsively and closed his eyes. "Tell me," he managed to choke out, "does your father pay you to do this, or is it only out of family loyalty?"

She blinked at him in confusion, her senses dulled by the overpowering impulses of the nerves in her body. "What?" And then his meaning hit her, struck her like a splash of burning oil across her face. For a full minute she was mute with horrified surprise and then the fury rose in her body and she lashed out at him, shrieking, "How dare you say such a thing? How dare you!" Now her mind had regained control, silencing the screaming hunger in her body, and she saw that he had done it on purpose, had taken her just so far and no farther so that he could humiliate her like this. He had never meant to make love to her at all.

"You bastard!" she snarled, striking his face a stinging blow with her open palm.

And then he was upon her, his face hovering like a disembodied spirit in the darkness. His hands moved from her shoulders to her throat and paused there, threatening to come together to choke the very life out of her. "Don't call me a bastard," he hissed, "ever! Do you understand me? Ever!"

Swallowing the scream that rose in her throat, she nodded. She could feel the pressure of his fingers on her throat and she knew he was deadly serious.

Phillipe saw the look that transformed her face from beautiful to ghostlike and it seemed to wake him from a dream. He withdrew his hands and rose, stepping away from her. What was he doing? Had he gone mad? She had called him a bastard, it was true, but that was not what had driven the rage into his head. No, it was the frustration, the hunger unappeased. Because he wanted her, even now he wanted her, but he could not give in to his desires. Not with this girl.

She was a Pendleton, after all, and therefore his enemy. It was then that he realized for the first time that somehow, in the furious battle of emotions that had just swept through him, he had chosen to align himself on his father's side. Unconsciously, he had made himself an ally of the man he hated most in the world.

Theodore Roosevelt sat on the edge of his bed, unable to sleep after the excitement of the party. Watching the shadows that played around the edges of the room, he realized that he had really come to love the Dakota Badlands. Here he was free to do as he pleased, and he had already proven to everyone's surprise and his own delight that he could succeed as a rancher, hunter, and horseman.

Of course, this elegant Chateau was still a dramatic contrast to his own simple cabin at the Maltese Cross Ranch, but he had come to appreciate that difference, too. In the past year, he had actually become friends with the Marquis and he knew without a doubt that of all the ranchers in the area, only Mores was as committed to stopping the rustlers as was Roosevelt himself. Too bad, he mused, that Granville Stuart had turned them down flat. Too bad that without him they had neither the organization nor the manpower to do this thing properly.

In the back of his mind, a nagging doubt continued to remind him of its presence, although he had long been trying to ignore it, and it had nothing to do with Granville Stuart and the rustlers. No, it had to do with the rumors that had circulated among the crowd after Medora's reappearance in a new gown. She had spilled wine on the other one, she claimed, but the women, gossiping among themselves, had come up with a different explanation. After all, they had said, Greg Pendleton had left the party and so had Medora, and then they had both returned within fifteen minutes of each other—by different doors, it was true, but just the same. . . .

Roosevelt would have laughed at such absurd stories, defending his hostess hotly, if he had not seen her disappear into the shadows near the river to be followed closely by the very man rumor said she had gone there to meet. He simply could not understand it. Not with Medora.

All at once, he heard a terrible racket from downstairs, and he wondered if it were morning already. But then he saw that it was still dark outside. Throwing a robe around his shoulders, he dragged open the door and ran down the hall, reaching the bottom step just as a breathless Dick Moore began to relay his piece of news to the assembled guests. Mores was there, with Medora beside him; Wilham hovered on the outskirts of the group while Von Hoffman and the Pendletons crowded forward.

" 'The Stranglers' struck in Montana tonight," Moore explained.

"Who the hell are they?"

"Granville Stuart and his men. They surprised a rustlers' camp and hung six men. From what I hear, that's only the beginning. Johnny says they've got a list of outlaws for each area in eastern Montana and western Dakota, and they plan to move through both territories until they've gotten every man on that list."

"What I want to know is, why didn't you think of something like this long ago, Mores?"

The Marquis recognized his father-in-law's voice, but he did not turn to meet his gaze. "I hardly think 3 A.M. is the time to discuss it," he replied casually, but inside, his response was more violent. He had been humiliated when Stuart refused to let Mores join his group. The man had laughed at him, calling himself and Roosevelt impetuous boys. Stuart had implied that they were not to be trusted and, although Roosevelt seemed to have accepted this decision, the Marquis had resented it deeply. And now Von Hoffman was insinuating that Mores had neglected his duties in yet another area. It was too much for one night. "Let's go to bed," he said wearily.

When everyone else had disappeared into their rooms, Bryce Pendleton motioned to his son to follow and slipped out onto the porch. A single colored lantern burned overhead, giving Bryce's face a strange reddish cast, transforming his features into a grotesque caricature of his natural expression. "Listen," he whispered tensely, "I want you to get me that list. I don't care how you do it, just see that it's done. And soon."

"Why? What are you planning?"

Bryce's eyebrows came together and his eyes narrowed to tiny blue slits. "I'm not quite sure just yet, but I have to have that list, I know that much. And after you get it, bring me Jake Maunders. We'll need his help."

"But—"

"Never you mind about why and wherefore, Greg, just do what you're told and concentrate your attention on your own part of the bargain—Madame la Marquise, for example. You've gotten a good start tonight; the rumors are already flying and if I don't miss my guess, that marriage will be in serious trouble soon, if it's not already. Just you keep your eyes open, boy. That woman will ruin you if you give her half a chance. You've got to keep your mind working all the time just to stay one step ahead of her." He paused when he noticed the disturbing light in his son's gray eyes. Then, drawing a deep breath, he asked abruptly, "Have you forgotten your mother?"

Surprised by the unexpected question, Greg shook his head and forced his mind back to the present and away from the memory of Medora's lips. "I have not forgotten," he said stiffly.

"I'm glad of that, at least," Bryce murmured. "Because to forget is dangerous, my son. Don't let it happen. Ever."

FIFTEEN

The Marquis lay in bed watching as the morning light crept through the glass door to dissipate last night's shadows. He had not slept well for several hours; his mind had been occupied with a hopeless series of conjectures and frustrations in which Von Hoffman's grim voice intertwined itself with the cries of the rustlers and Granville Stuart's laughter to keep Mores from getting any rest. And when he finally did close his eyes, it was to dream of a mob of New York butchers who waited with guns and clubs at the train station to turn away his carloads of beef. He awakened with a start. It was useless.

Then there were the ridiculous rumors about Medora and Greg Pendleton. Of course, he did not believe them for a moment. He knew his wife better than that, even if she had been somewhat distant of late. But still, the whispered gossip troubled him. He found that, as the night turned to morning, he longed for her as he had not done for many days. He wanted to see her, to ask if she had heard the rumors, to tell her he did not believe them. He wanted more than anything to feel her satin skin beneath his fingers and her warm breath against his face, and this time he would not allow her to retreat from him. He had to try to break down the barrier that had grown between them.

Rising while the biting chill of early morning was still heavy in the air, the Marquis slipped his robe loosely around his shoulders. Then, moving quietly, so as not to awaken her, he went to the door and turned the handle. He wanted to surprise her in bed, to catch her before the mists of sleep had cleared from her mind. Perhaps, if she awakened to find his hands on her body and his lips close to hers he could stop the shutters from falling across her eyes. Perhaps.

He pushed the door open soundlessly and saw at once that he would be disappointed. Her bed was empty, though the sheets were still rumpled and the pillows bunched in one corner. Then he turned to see her standing framed in the light of the outside door, staring at him in alarm with her robe in her hands. The sunlight caressed her arms, her flowing hair, and the long line of her neck as she slipped the robe on and pulled it closed, but not before he noticed the deep purple bruises that discolored her shoulders and the base of her throat.

For a long moment, Mores stood there immobile with the words of one of last night's guests running through his mind like a deadly refrain. *"She had to change her gown, my dear. She says she spilled wine on it, but we saw her going down to the river, and if you ask me, she simply ruined the dress on the riverbank."* Those bruises had not been there last evening, he knew; her gown had been low cut across the shoulders and her neck had been bare. Then how had they come to be there? An inner voice supplied the answer.

He saw that she had not moved. Her eyes were fixed on his face, but she did not even try to speak. Then, abruptly, he strode to the wardrobe, flinging open the doors with a violent wrench. He knelt on the floor and began to toss aside the clothes he found on the bottom until he came upon what he was seeking. The gown had been pushed to the back of the cabinet, where it lay in a pitiful little heap, far from the reach of the morning light.

By now the blood was pounding in his ears as he reached inside to drag the ruined garment from its hiding place. The bodice had been torn in two places and the lace hung limply from the sleeves. Mores bit his lip and choked back an exclamation when he saw that the back of the skirt had been stained with mud and soggy leaves that clung like leeches to the flimsy gauze. So it was true.

Whirling to face her, he held the gown up and asked, "Did he rape you?"

Medora stood where he had found her, with the feel of the sun warm on her back. She saw how his fingers clutched the dress until they were white, and how the tiny blue vein pulsed like a warning down the center of his forehead. She saw reflected in his expression her own horror at what she had done. She knew what Greg was, yet she had succumbed to him. And in doing so, she knew she had hurt not only her husband—who waited now for her answer to destroy him — but also herself.

"Did he rape you?" Mores repeated.

She could have told him yes. The man had overpowered her, knocking her to the ground against her will. He had taken advantage of her anger and forced her to receive his kisses and his passion. Yet, although she had betrayed the Marquis with her body, she could not bring herself to deceive him with a lie. "No," she said softly, "he didn't. . . ."

"Of course I did, Antoine. He is my husband," Nicole told him, leaning one arm on the mantel.

Her cream satin dressing gown had fallen open, exposing the silken body beneath. Mores winced and turned away when he saw the slightly red impression of Charles Beaumont's teeth in the rounded hollow at the base of her throat. The Marquis had known, of course, that she allowed her husband to make love to her, but somehow he had never seen the evidence before. The thought of another man leaving his mark upon Nicole sent a physical pain through Mores's body. He was a fool, he knew that, but he simply could not bear to share her. "I see," he replied in a voice like polished stone.

Aware, suddenly, of the depth of his distress, Nicole came to him, barefoot, and ran her hands across his chest. "It was nothing, dear one. Do not be so foolish. You know that I love you."

He drew in his breath at the touch of her cold fingers and the sight of her honey-blonde hair cascading over her shoulders and naked breasts. Her breath, when she leaned toward him, was incredibly sweet, and her eyes held promises of passion in their pale gray depths. Like a reed, her body swayed before him, elastic and supple and a slave to the dictates of her sensual nature.

Mores realized then that she did not simply "allow" Charles to take her; she begged him to. She was a woman who could not live without the exhilarating presence of a man consumed with desire for her. She loved the Marquis deeply, that he knew, but, all at once, that was not enough.

"Antoine?" she murmured seductively, her hands like fire upon his back, "What are you thinking, my heart?"

Silently, he answered, "That you are my soul, yet I shall never truly have you. Never." Then, with a strength of will he had not known he possessed, he backed away. *And, for the first time since he had known her, he refused the offer of her body, his face stiff with the effort to disguise his inner struggle. . . .*

There was no change in Mores's expression. None. He just stood frozen for an instant; then, drawing a single ragged breath, he ripped the dress down the middle and tossed it at Medora's feet. Without a word or look in her direction, he turned on his heel and left her there.

"Katherine, come here."

She hesitated in the hallway outside the study. Her father was the last person she wanted to face this morning. Somehow he always provoked her into indiscretions and her mood just now was already dangerous. The Pendletons had left the Chateau early that morning to return to their ranch, and for hours, Katherine's head had been swimming with fury, humiliation, and plans for revenge. No one made a fool of Katherine Pendleton and did not pay. Especially the bastard son of a foreign jackass.

"Katherine!"

Recognizing the note of command in Greg's voice, she sighed in resignation and entered the room. Her father was standing at the window looking out, his face lit by a rather smug smile. That smile antagonized her from the moment she saw it. How dare he be pleased with himself when she was so miserable?

"Did you learn anything from Phillipe last night?" he asked without turning away from the window.

Katherine tensed, clenching her hands together behind her back. She did not like the slightly ironic twist in his question, nor the way he spoke to her so offhandedly, as if she were a servant. What did he know about last night, anyway? "No," she replied, "he wasn't very talkative." Amazing that she could speak of Phillipe so calmly when she hated him so much.

"Then you aren't doing your job, my dear. Our purpose is not simply to frolic in the moonlight, you know. You must make use of your connections."

"Not anymore," Katherine breathed, "not with Phillipe."

Now, at last, he turned to look at her, his eyebrows raised in surprise. "You mean you didn't make him your slave in just one night?" His eyes ran up and down her body with interest and he added, "With that figure, you shouldn't have had much trouble."

Drawing her breath in painfully, she just kept herself from spitting in his face.

"You see, Katherine," he continued, leaving his post by the window, "we've reached a rather crucial stage in our plans just now, and we need every source of information we can get. So I think you'd better win Phillipe over thoroughly and, this time, for good."

"If you want his information so badly, *you* get it. I have better things to do."

"Don't push me this morning; I'm not in the mood to deal with your tantrums." Running a hand through his hair, he eyed his daughter closely. "Perhaps that's why you don't learn as much as you ought to from your little friend, if you're always subjecting him to your bitter tongue."

The pressure had begun to build in her head until her temples throbbed regularly. He did not care what he said to her, so long as he got what he wanted. "I suppose Medora was babbling the Marquis's secrets while you wallowed together on the riverbank last night?" she hissed.

With the swiftness of a lightning bolt, the smile disappeared from his face. "Don't," he said, his voice like cold steel.

Katherine ignored him. He had pushed her too far. "Tell me," she continued, "did the ice queen melt a little under your tutelage, or is she really frozen stone clear through?"

"Enough! You will not speak of that woman again so long as your mind is incapable of dragging itself out of the gutter."

Encased as she was in her personal cocoon of anger and frustration, she did not see the rage that climbed inexorably from his rigid chin to his glittering eyes, nor did she recognize the depth and intensity of the threat in his tone. "I thought that's where whores belonged," she snapped, "in the gutter. Or is it the mud?"

When she heard him slam the door and bolt it, some hint of warning finally penetrated her clouded senses. She looked up then, her pulse beating wildly against her throat, and saw him—really saw him—for the first time. The man who came toward her moved as if in slow motion, a towering mountain of rage, with his hands at his belt. She watched in astonishment as those hands released the buckle and drew the wide leather band from around his waist. In the instant when she realized what he intended, she swallowed a rush of dry, stale air and began to back away. But there was nowhere she could go.

"I have warned you, Katherine," he said with a deadly calm that belied the fury reflected in his twisted features. "Time and again I have warned you, but you just wouldn't listen." His hands played across the leather, pulling it taut; then gathering the ends together until the belt became a single, continuous loop.

Suddenly, his livid face filled her vision, blocking out the light, and for the first time in her life, Katherine Pendleton shrank from her father in fear.

* * *

Mores stumbled blindly across the sweeping expanse of grass that culminated in a steep bluff overlooking the river. He was numb from the inside out; only his thoughts seemed to have any life of their own. Medora had given her body to another man. For reasons which he did not believe he could ever understand, she had refused that same body to her husband, then turned and delivered it to Pendleton—the Marquis's greatest enemy. He simply could not comprehend it, and he suspected that he really did not want to.

He had left her without speaking because he had known with absolute certainty that, had he stayed a moment longer, he would have killed her—broken her neck with his bare hands. It was strange, but he had not even thought of beating her, although it might have relieved some of the gnawing pain and anger that consumed him now. He had not done it because he loved her, still, and he could not bear to put more bruises on that smooth white skin. He might have destroyed her, in that brief moment of madness that followed her calm announcement, but he could not have brought himself to mar her.

Without being aware of it, he had found his way down to the river. He realized it when the shadows of the leaves touched his face instead of the fiery intensity of the sun. He welcomed this unexpected coolness on his cheeks, though he could not hope it would stop the fever that ran through his body with sharply probing fingers.

It was a long time before he heard the song, and even longer before he realized what it was. The words rose as if from the heart of the river itself and the voice of the water was high and piercing and infinitely sweet.

A dawn appears; behold it.

He moved toward that voice without conscious thought, listening with his ears and his eyes and his body.

An elk am I; a short life I am living.

Beside him, the water swirled and rippled over the stones while the song fell like a shroud upon his turbulent thoughts. He knew what he would find when he reached the sunlight where the river widened. Or, at least, he hoped he knew.

I hear there are difficult things to be accomplished.
I seek them.

She was there, just as he had imagined, stretched out on the bank with her face above the river, singing. Her dark hair had fallen half into the water, where it floated languidly among the reeds. And she had folded her hands beneath her chin, extending her neck like the throat of a bird where the song pulsed deep and regular within.

"Ileya," he murmured, afraid to break the spell she had woven.

She turned her head gracefully to gaze at him and he realized that she was not surprised by his presence. Her face glowed as a smile spread slowly from her lips to her dark, shadowed eyes. Then she reached out, offering him her hand.

With a sigh that was barely audible, he went to sit beside her. "Where have you been?" he asked in a whisper.

"In the north," she replied simply.

"And why have you come back?"

Drawing her legs up to her chest, she shook her hair back from her face. "You helped me once when I was in need. And now I see in my dreams that you are troubled and, perhaps, in need. So I came."

This matter-of-fact explanation came very near to destroying all the defenses he had built up in the past few weeks to keep himself from losing control. While his son became every day more a stranger, while his enemies plotted to cripple him, while his wife turned to another, this girl—whom he had known for only two short weeks, and those a long, long time ago—had come to him without question because she sensed that he needed a friend.

"You are glad?" she inquired, contemplating the emotions that moved across his face.

"Yes," he assured her, "I am glad."

* * *

William looked up as the Marquis entered the drawing room. "I'm afraid I have bad news," the secretary announced without preamble.

Sinking down onto the sofa, Mores considered his friend in silence. He did not want to hear any more bad news just now; Medora's revelation was quite enough for one day. Besides, the Marquis had spent the morning walking with Ileya by the river, and somehow she had performed a miracle for him. She had led him for a full hour along the riverbank, barefoot in her buckskin dress, singing softly to herself. After their initial meeting, they had not spoken—the murmur of the water beside them had been all the conversation they needed—except once, when a flock of swallows had risen from among the leaves, darting fearlessly overhead like a group of drunken cowboys. Then Ileya had paused, touched her finger to her lips and told him, "There will be a thundershower today. It is always so when the swallows dance."

As they wandered together, with the shadows of the leaves on their faces, Mores had begun to realize that the girl had cast a spell upon him. Subtly, and without apparent effort, she had transformed the electric shock of his early morning discovery into a dull but persistent ache. It was as if she had drawn most of the poison away with the pressure of her fingertips and lost it somewhere on the muddy bank. And yet she had done no more than touch his hand. He had left her, reluctantly, in the hut downriver where she had stayed last summer, and come back to face the world where the Indian girl's magic could not quite reach.

"Mores?" William inquired. "Did you hear me?"

The Marquis sat up, focusing on Van Driesche with difficulty. "No, I'm afraid my mind was wandering. What did you say?"

"Yes, William," Von Hoffman said as he sidled in from the dining room, "by all means tell us what new disaster we have to face this morning."

The secretary glanced from his employer to Von Hoffman

and back again, then cleared his throat. "I've had a telegram from Chicago," he explained. "It seems the carload of beef that arrived there yesterday was rotten."

"What?" the Marquis cried, while Von Hoffman spluttered, "The entire load?"

"I'm afraid so."

"But how could that happen?"

"Apparently, the ice was never changed along the way."

Mores ran a hand across his forehead, stunned by the news. A full carload of beef—ruined. "I don't understand it," he muttered. "We had the icehouses working so smoothly."

"Then what in blazes happened?" Von Hoffman shrieked. "Have you any idea what that meat was worth?"

"I know."

"Well? What're you going to do about it?"

"I shall have to investigate, of course," the Marquis said quietly.

"Investigate! Can't you think of anything more than that? We are losing a fortune and all you want to do is play detective?"

Dragging in a shuddering breath, Mores answered, "One carload of beef is hardly a fortune, sir. And even if it were, what could I do about it? The meat is lost. Do you want me to weep over it?"

"I don't imagine you give enough of a damn for that kind of histrionics," Von Hoffman declared acidly. "And you needn't bother to investigate this little catastrophe either. I'm leaving for New York by this afternoon's train anyway, and I shall make inquiries along the way to try to determine what happened. I wouldn't want you to have to go out of your way for something so terribly unimportant. And now, if you will excuse me, I'll go finish my packing." Having delivered his little harangue, he turned dramatically and strode from the room, slamming the door behind him.

William shook his head, glancing at the Marquis, who sat with his hands between his knees, the fingers locked together as if in combat. "I'm sorry," the secretary told him, "but there's more."

This time Mores did not even look up. "What is it?"

"Two of the boilers are acting up at the plant, and we can't seem to find the problem. Also, production has fallen off considerably."

"Did you ever wonder if I were the victim of a satanic curse?" The Marquis gazed at his hands for a moment, then forced a smile to his lips. "Forgive me, William. I'm afraid I have a tendency toward morbid self-pity today." He paused, struggling with his inner demons, then looked up. "What we need here is action. Let's you and I go down to the plant at once and see what we can discover. I know I've been preoccupied with the stagecoach line lately, but I intend to remedy that immediately. And while we're there, perhaps we can begin to work on a plan for running the operation more efficiently."

William breathed a sigh of relief. This was more like the Marquis he remembered—the man who had begun this business a little over a year ago with such high hopes. Not the kind of man who gave up easily, even in the face of odds like these. This was the man who could save the N.P.R.C.C. if anybody could. He smiled with fresh enthusiasm. "I'll get the books." Then, as he started from the room, he turned back to add, "We might even take Phillipe with us. He's been around the plant several times lately, and he seems particularly interested in increasing efficiency."

The Marquis gaped at William, astonished by this bit of information. He hadn't had the slightest inkling that his son was interested in the business. But then, that was not so odd after all. In all the months since Phillipe had been here, the Marquis had never heard a civil word from the boy. Yet, apparently, he had talked to William. As the realization sank into his consciousness, Mores reflected that his fears were no longer fantasy. He had, in fact, become a stranger in his own home.

Despite the burgeoning clouds that lowered overhead—reflecting Phillipe's mood with uncanny accuracy—the boy left the house and made his way toward the clearing by the river where he used to meet Katherine. He had heard that the Marquis was looking for him and, in his present frame of mind, he did not wish to be found. Besides, he rather liked the way the dark billows raced across the sky, propelled by a violent but invisible wind that threatened to rend the clouds open, releasing their sodden insides onto the earth beneath. Phillipe's thoughts were as sullen and as volatile as the summer thunderstorm that growled menacingly in the distance, waiting for its moment.

As he watched the leaves that spun wildly past in some primitive dance, he wondered if his guilt had drawn him here. For he certainly was not proud of what he had done to Katherine last night beneath the protective cloak of darkness. He could not rid himself of the memory of her face at the moment when his cruel words had sunk into her bemused consciousness.

That was why he nearly turned away when he came to the clearing and saw that she was there before him. He knew she would not want to see him. Knew, in fact, that he was the last person she would want to find there. But he also knew that he must speak to her again, if only to tell her he was sorry, even if she scorned him or laughed in his face. Besides, there was something unnatural in the way she was sprawled facedown across the grass like a discarded rag doll, her hands stretched out before her.

A flash of lightning split the sky as he approached. He wondered how long it would be before the torrent came down upon them. Then a twig snapped beneath his foot and he saw Katherine's muscles tighten spasmodically, but she did not turn her head. "Katherine?" He spoke her name softly, as if his gentleness might appease her.

"Go away," she choked, her voice oddly muffled.

Even when he knelt beside her, she kept her head averted. Phillipe bit his lip; this was not like Katherine. She believed in facing her enemies head-on until one or the other admitted defeat. "Please," he began, realizing that something was very wrong, "tell me what's happened."

"Go to hell." Again, that deep, raspy voice that was so unlike her own.

"It's going to rain in a minute," he explained ineffectually. When she did not respond, he added, "Listen to me."

"I won't!" she cried, turning her head at last. "Not anymore."

"Katherine, please—" he repeated, but when he saw her face, the rest of the words died in his throat.

Her jaw was swollen to twice its size and a dark, ugly bruise stained her skin from her chin to her nose. Her lips were caked with dried blood that appeared to have come from a deep gash that had split her lip. But oddly, the thing that disturbed Phillipe the most was the puffiness that nearly swallowed her eyes and the red streaks across her cheeks, betraying the fact that she had been weeping for a long, long time. Katherine never cried; he was certain of it. "Dear God," he rasped, unconsciously laying a hand on her shoulder.

She cringed, shrinking away from him and he knew it was not anger that made her do it; she simply could not bear the weight of even so light a touch upon her back. It was only then that he realized what must have happened. "Did your father do this to you?" he asked, unable to hide the horror that was a stifling weight inside his chest.

Her eyes were hard and shiny cold when she replied, "Yes, he did. And now that your curiosity has been satisfied, would you please leave me alone?"

The effort of speaking had started the blood flowing again, and when the clouds rumbled ominously above them, Phillipe came to a sudden decision. Regardless of her dislike for him, she needed his help. He could not simply leave her here to be caught in the rain. "I'm taking you to Cassie," he informed her resolutely, "maybe she can help."

"I don't want your help or anyone else's," she hissed.

"You're getting it just the same. Can you walk?"

"Phillipe, if you so much as touch me, I'll—" she stopped abruptly when a shower of raindrops fell on them, followed by a malevolent streak of lightning that lit her face grotesquely.

"Be quiet," he said, taking her arm to help her up. "You're coming with me, and that's that."

She started to protest, but then the drops turned into a deluge and, with the deafening shudder of the thunder to encourage her, she rose awkwardly to her feet. She insisted on walking by herself, although she moved unsteadily, but as the savagery of the storm increased with every moment, drenching her and causing her to stumble, Phillipe reached over to lift her in his arms, determined to carry her all the way to the Chateau if necessary. He was oblivious to his own discomfort as he looked down into her sallow face. Phillipe saw that she did not intend to struggle anymore, simply because she could not, and he was relieved when she let her head fall against his shoulder.

"She'll be all right," Cassie announced, closing the kitchen door quietly behind her. The cook had taken one look at Katherine's face and taken her immediately to the cozy little room just off the kitchen. It was Cassie's bedroom, but she had not hesitated to give it up to the girl. Leaving Phillipe to pace anxiously in front of the kitchen fire, the cook had disappeared into that tiny room for a long time, coming out only occasionally to get a clean cloth or more warm water. Now she came to sit beside the boy, covering his hand with her work-worn brown one.

"You're sure?" Phillipe demanded. "She looked awfully bad."

"She is," the cook agreed grimly. "I had to sew up that lip with a couple of stitches, and, even so, she'll have a little scar there. But that was just the beginning. You didn't see the welts and bruises that cover that poor child's back and shoulders. I don't think I've seen a beating that ugly for many a year."

Rising precipitously, Phillipe swung away from her, his fists clenched at his sides. "Why did he do that to her?"

Cassie turned her chair around and straddled it, drawing her skirts up to her knees. "She wouldn't say at first, but then she let a few things slip. As far as I can tell, Katherine provoked him." She considered the boy in silence for a long moment, her brow furrowed with concern. "It seems to me, son, that maybe you should learn a lesson from this."

He whirled to face her. "I don't understand."

"No, I don't guess you do. But it's like this. Now you can see for yourself what happens when you push a person too far. A man can only take so much abuse, Phillipe, and then his temper takes over. Sometimes it wipes out his conscience entirely. Do you see what I mean?"

Phillipe considered this for an instant, then his eyes narrowed and hardened. His voice, when he spoke, was brittle. "You're warning me," he said.

"I'm sure as hell tryin' to."

He took a deep breath, looked beyond her, and asked, "Can I see Katherine now?"

With a sigh that shook her body from belly to chin, Cassie replied, "She doesn't want you anywhere near."

"I know that, but I don't care just now."

"Then why are you botherin' to ask?" She waved a hand toward the door in resignation.

Katherine was lying facedown on snow-white sheets, covered with only a thin blanket. Her head was turned toward the wall, and although he knew she had heard him come in, she did not look up. He sat gingerly on the single chair, laying his hand beside hers, but he was wise enough not to touch her. "Katherine," he whispered, "I want to talk to you."

Not even by the twitching of a single muscle did she recognize his presence. Instead, she lay there in frigid silence, her dark, damp hair falling like a stain across her shoulders.

Undeterred, Phillipe swallowed once, then said, "I want to apologize."

Still she did not move and some of his determination slid away. "And I want to know"—he paused, licked his lips, then continued—"if this happened because of me."

Now, at last, she rose up a little and turned to face him, the piercing light in her eyes an open accusation. "Yes," she told him triumphantly, "because of you!"

He winced, but did not look away. "I'm sorry." He reached for her hand but she withdrew it. "For everything. But Katherine, I—"

He stopped abruptly when the door was wrenched open. He looked up to see Medora hovering on the threshold, her face alight with surprise.

"What—" she began. But then she saw the girl's face and, as Katherine turned away, the blanket slipped, revealing the dark, ugly weals that marred her shoulders.

Phillipe rose, motioning for his stepmother to leave the room with him. She did so, moving mechanically, shocked by what she had just seen.

"Who did that to her?" she gasped when the door was safely closed and they stood in the empty hallway.

"Greg Pendleton." Phillipe spit out the name as if he would have liked to crush its owner with his boot heel. "But Medora, please don't tell my father Katherine's here. She wouldn't want him to know."

His stepmother nodded numbly, unaware of the boy's murmured thank you. When he had gone, she stood for a long time, contemplating the blank face of the door. Dear God, she thought, what had she done? She had made love to a man who could do that to a young girl's body, who could scar his daughter so badly, probably without compunction. With a shudder that ran from her neck to the bottom of her spine, she remembered the bruises that discolored her own throat. How could she have allowed such a man near when she had turned away her husband, who had never touched her with anything but tenderness?

But she knew why. She had slept with a man she hated because she had been afraid to make herself vulnerable to the man she loved. She was a hopeless fool who had nearly achieved, through her own weakness, the object the Pendletons had been seeking for so long—Mores's destruction. But perhaps, after all, it was not too late to make it up to him. She could not win him back yet—that would take time and infinite care—but she could at least help take some of the weight of his business problems off his shoulders.

Gripping the fabric of her skirt firmly, Medora nodded to herself. Her father had taught her long ago to be stronger than those around her, and she had learned that vivid, painful lesson while still a child as she watched the flames dancing wildly through her ravaged home. She remembered the scene, as she always did, with a shiver. But she had won in the end; she had stayed until Von Hoffman came to take her away, nodding proudly at his daughter's strength and completely oblivious to the horror she had had to conquer. She had managed that time, and she meant to win this time too—whatever it might take to achieve that end.

Peter Clay shuffled along the dirt path, glancing idly from side to side as he went. His father had sent him to look for a cow that had wandered away in the night, and every now and then, the boy remembered his errand, taking up the search once again, albeit half-heartedly. He was much more interested in gazing at the frail white clouds that straggled across the sky. He was hoping for another thunderstorm. The sound of the deep, throaty thunder and the brilliant flashes of lightning excited him, and he loved to huddle up with his nose pressed to the window, watching the havoc that nature wreaked outside.

Kicking a large stone out of his way, Peter buried his hands deeper in his pockets and listened hopefully for the sound of approaching rain. He was so absorbed with his own thoughts that it was some time before he noticed the cloud of dust coming at him from the far side of the field. Even when the haze transformed itself into three men on horses, he did not pay them much mind. They wouldn't be looking for him, after all. Nobody ever was.

Still, he was only mildly surprised when they reined in the animals, blocking the path in front of him. He stopped to gaze up at them, scratching his head with two fingers.

"Well, well, what have we here?" one man said, leaning precariously forward in his saddle.

Peter noticed then that all three men wore scarves over

their faces. That was strange, he mused, but then, maybe they didn't like breathing their own dust. *He* certainly didn't.

"Answer me, boy!" a deep voice demanded from over his head.

As far as Peter could tell, no one had really asked him a question, so he didn't see what the stranger was getting upset about.

"What're you doin' out here so early in the morning?" another voice boomed out.

Now that one sounded familiar somehow, but the boy couldn't quite remember where he had heard it. Peter considered the question carefully for a moment, then the answer came to him. "Chasin' after a cow," he said, his face lighting up as if an inspiration had struck him like a bolt from the blue.

The men exchanged glances, nodding knowingly. "Doesn't even bother to deny it," one said. "These rustlers ain't no scared rabbits," another replied, "they'll tell you all about it, just as bold as you please."

Peter grimaced and hurried to assure them, "I ain't no rustler. My pa's a rancher. We—"

"Shut yer trap, boy, we already heard yer confession and we don't need no more jabberin'."

Now, for the first time, Peter sensed the dangerous undercurrent in the air all around him. If these men really believed he was a rustler—"Wait," he insisted, "you got it all wrong. Like I told you—"

"Quiet!" the familiar voice demanded. "Let's get on with this." The man turned to the boy, his eyes just showing above the fabric of his scarf. "We can't just let thieves like this one get away with their stealin'," he said threateningly. "We've already seen what happens when we don't take action soon enough."

Another man shifted in his saddle, pointing halfway across the field. "There's a nice sturdy cottonwood over there."

Suddenly their meaning penetrated Peter's rather thick skull. These men were vigilantes, he realized in horror, the hairs on his neck standing straight in the air. He had heard about Granville Stuart and his men—how they came unexpectedly upon their victims and strung them up with nothing but a make-believe trial. And now, these men had mistaken him for a rustler. The boy stood like stone, frozen in the middle of the road. If only he could explain to them—

But when he saw one of the three unhook a long rope from his saddle and hold it up triumphantly, the boy awoke from his stupor and began to run. Don't wait to explain, his brain directed his feet, those other men had probably tried to explain, too. He had not gotten farther than three yards when a horse came up beside him. The rider reached down, grasping the boy easily around the waist. Then, without a thought or glance, the man kicked his horse in the direction of the cottonwood.

Peter opened his mouth as wide as it would go and began to babble, terror making his voice into a high-pitched whistle. "I ain't no rustler," he repeated again and again. "I'm just out lookin' for the cow. It's *our* cow!" He knew they were not listening, but he could not stop himself. His heart raced wildly while the blood pounded like thunder in his ears. "I ain't," he rasped pitifully, "I ain't."

He was only vaguely aware that the horse had come to a standstill and that his hands were being tied tightly behind his back. His eyes were focused in horrified fascination on the knot that one of the men was tying deftly in the rope. Those fingers, moving around and around, seemed to swell until they filled his vision. The boy stopped shrieking long enough to swallow convulsively as his Adam's apple bobbed up and down. They couldn't, his mind kept insisting; they just couldn't.

But, within moments, Peter had been thrust rudely onto a horse's back and he looked up in agony at the rope that seemed to leap over the branch above him, then sway slowly downward as they lowered it from behind.

"Ain't we gonna have a trial?" one man asked negligently. Peter held his breath, waiting for the answer.

"Hell no! The kid confessed. No need for a trial when you got a confession."

That voice, his bemused brain repeated dully, where have I heard that voice?

And then someone came up behind him and pushed his head downward, forcing the rope around his neck. Peter began to shake so hard that he almost fell from the saddle, but his companion obligingly pushed him upright again.

"I tell you, I ain't no rustler," he shrieked, aware that the men were backing away. For a moment, in his crazed fear, the sky became a patchwork of colored scarves hiding cruel mouths, and the air was full of harsh, wicked laughter. And then, mercifully, the world collapsed into blackness.

SIXTEEN

"What are you going to do?" Medora demanded, allowing her frustration to overcome her good sense.

Mores faced her across the empty breakfast table where he had spread out the latest financial reports concerning his several business enterprises. "About what?" he asked without looking up.

"Mores," she began more softly, "it's been over a week and you still won't talk to me."

He glanced up, raising an eyebrow questioningly. "That's absurd. We speak regularly."

"Yes, about guests and menus and cattle and stagecoaches, but never about—"

"Well?" he prompted, pretending he did not catch her meaning.

"About Greg Pendleton and—"

"I should think that that's a subject better left alone, don't you agree?"

She noticed how the waxed ends of his moustache curled gracefully upward, but even they could not disguise the bitter twist of his lips beneath. "You haven't let me explain."

For the briefest of instants, his eyes reflected a light that might have been a flash of hope, but then it faded. "Can you?" he asked tightly.

Opening her mouth to give him an answer, she realized that her mind had gone completely blank. She wondered if he was thinking back, as she was, to the moment when he had asked her another such question and then waited stiffly for her response. *"Did he rape you?"* And she knew as she watched her husband's face cloud over that she had no better answer this time. "I don't suppose I can," she murmured.

"Then I suggest we refrain from discussing it further."

"Shall we go on like this forever, then? Acting like strangers who hardly know each other?"

"I no longer dare to predict the future, my dear," he observed. "That is one thing living in the Badlands has taught me."

And then, as he rose and prepared to leave her, she cried, "You could divorce me."

He stopped with his hand on the door frame and turned to look at her long and hard, an unreadable expression in his eyes. His eyebrows came together while he sought for words with which to answer her, and then, fleetingly, a flash of pain set his eyes blazing and he whispered, "No, I couldn't. I'm afraid that's one thing I couldn't do."

With a groan that rent the air in two, Peter Clay opened his eyes and peered in confusion at the weeds and dirt beneath his clenched fingers. It was a long time before he could see any further than that, but finally, the huge expanse of the field and the blue sky beyond came into focus. I'm dead; are there weeds in Heaven? he thought inanely. But then the raw burning pain around his throat drew his attention and, as he reached up gingerly to feel the wound around his neck, he realized that, through some miracle, he was not dead at all. He knew that because his body ached from top to toe, and his pa had told him once that there was no pain in Heaven.

Slowly, as his consciousness came back to him, a deep, consuming fury began to wash over him in waves. He was alive, but just barely, and those men had meant to kill him. They hadn't waited, hadn't listened, hadn't let him explain; all they had cared about was having someone to string up like a helpless chicken. And they had chosen him.

He turned over so the endless sky was above him and he could see the same wisps of cloud he had watched that morning. Those bastards had done this to him without cause, and he meant to see that they paid for their mistake. It wasn't his fault that their plan had failed and he had lived. If they were foolish enough to leave their victims behind without making sure they were dead, then they deserved whatever they got. Only he could not think what that would be. Not yet, while his body still throbbed and he could not even turn his head for the pain that shot through his neck. But soon.

When at last he rose awkwardly from the dry earth, he glanced up, even though the agony ran like fire from his head to his spine. The rope was gone, taken along, no doubt, to be used the next time. Peter shuddered as a ring of icy fear closed around his heart. It had been so close. He shut his eyes as if in grateful prayer, but his thoughts were focused on the rage inside him.

He opened his eyes, having decided he should find his way home, where his mother would pity him and coddle him and put him to bed. But as he turned to go, he saw a piece of dirty parchment lying at the base of the tree. Curiously, he bent to pick it up, thinking that perhaps it was a letter one of the men had dropped. His eyes widened in bewilderment when he saw a list of names, but as he read it through, his pulse began to pound madly. Everyone had heard of Granville Stuart's list of targeted rustlers; it had become a legend in less than a week after the man began his grim campaign. Everyone also knew that he had not yet come to the Badlands around Medora, but that he was coming—and soon—to wipe the area clean with vicious efficiency, just as he had done in Montana.

But what Peter Clay held in his hand was that very list, with the names of all the men marked for death. He recognized a few of them, and as he stared in wonder at the parchment, a plan began to form in his mind. Most people thought the boy stupid, but he was wise enough to know the value of this discovery. Those men didn't know it, but when they left Peter Clay for dead, they had left behind the means with which he could thwart them. Here, at least, their search would be fruitless, because the boy intended to see that every man on that list was out of the area before "The Stranglers" had a chance to find them.

Three weeks later, the Marquis left the Chateau behind and turned his steps toward the river where Ileya waited. He left behind thoughts of the mysterious accidents that had begun to plague the packing plant—the two boilers that had broken down, the machinery that failed to operate, the meat that somehow never made it to the icehouse—and the knowledge that rustling had increased to epidemic proportions in the past two weeks. He left behind his fears of Von Hoffman's threat to withdraw his financial backing and the trouble with the route of the stagecoach line. Finally, he left behind his son who had become more secretive and hostile of late—and his wife who had become a woman he no longer recognized.

He left them to go and seek the Indian girl who, although she often wandered the country on her own, was always waiting for him when he came to her in need of comfort. He knew that her eyes would reflect the same inner knowledge of his secret thoughts and that, like magic, she would erase them from his mind. Ileya's hands on his head and the sound of her voice singing softly above him had become a drug that transported him to another world, and Ileya herself was the spirit of the water come to free him from himself. He was incredulous, even now, that she had come to him as she had—willingly and with pleasure.

But today, as he approached the hut, he saw that he would be disappointed. Ileya stood before the door, facing Johnny Goodall, who listened, scowling, while she spoke. The two seemed utterly absorbed in the girl's story, and Mores realized that they were speaking the Dakota language, and that Ileya was, for once, unaware of his presence. All her attention was focused on Goodall, who nodded glumly at regular intervals and sometimes stopped the girl to ask a question.

The Marquis recalled with sudden trepidation the afternoon not long ago when he had come unexpectedly upon these two facing each other with the rushing river in between them.

They had gaped at each other in surprise that had quickly changed to dismay, and then Ileya had turned to flee into the safety of the bushes at her back. Goodall had called after her, in her own language, but she had not appeared again. Yet, in that brief moment when they had stood staring across the water, Mores had seen a flash of recognition pass between them and the memory of that look came to him now as vividly as if he were seeing it again.

There was an abrupt and profound silence when Ileya looked up to see the Marquis watching. It was as if his presence had shut off some crucial valve that allowed the words to flow between them, and he felt oddly left out.

Johnny turned and fixed his eyes on Mores's face, awaiting his response. Goodall's own expression was one of mingled alarm, surprise, and just a touch of disapproval.

"You know Ileya?" the Marquis asked helplessly.

Burying his hands deep in his pockets, Johnny cleared his throat and answered with reluctance, "I've had occasional business at the Standing Rock Reservation over the years. I met her there." He paused, as if considering whether or not to continue and then added, "I was surprised to find her here."

Was that a hint of accusation in the man's tone? Mores wondered. Did Goodall think the girl was the Marquis's mistress? Surely that was the only explanation for the veiled look in Johnny's eyes. But Mores did not intend to set him straight. He did not need to explain himself to anybody.

"Well, if you'll pardon me, sir, I have work to do," Goodall muttered.

Mores nodded and turned to Ileya as Johnny left them alone. Perhaps the girl would break her vow of silence and tell him what had happened here. She rarely spoke to him at all, except in song, and usually he liked it that way. They seemed to have no need for words, but read each other's thoughts through some instinctive bond that stretched between them like a fragile glass thread. This time, however, when he looked into her face, he saw that it was closed against him—

an open book on which the cover had been slammed shut unexpectedly.

"Ileya?" he asked, filling the word with a multitude of questions. But she pressed her finger to his lips and shook her head mournfully, as if she regretted being bound by some force outside herself to keep him, for the moment, in the dark.

With nothing to illuminate her face but the mellow light that spilled through the window, Medora listened patiently to Johnny Goodall's story.

"So I think you were right," he said, "and the Pendletons are tied somehow to the rustling operation. A friend of mine has noticed lately that Pendleton cattle get stolen just as often as ours do, but their herds never seem to get smaller. I figure they let the thieves take the animals so it looks good to the rest of the ranchers, but the livestock is filtered back in later."

"Do you think we can prove it?" she asked, her voice barely audible.

"Yep, I think so. Of course, we can't really hurt them, but we can sure embarrass 'em and maybe put a stop to the rustling for good."

"Do you know how to do it?"

Considering her face in the muted half-light, he drew his breath in slowly, then let it out in a rush. "Not yet, but I'm working on it. Of course, it's dangerous threatening any rustlers. They can be pretty mean. Do you still plan to go ahead with Maunders?"

"Can he help you?"

Goodall nodded and Medora said, "Then we'll go ahead. And don't worry. I don't intend to let the Pendletons win this one, and I don't intend to be their fool either."

"Tomorrow night then?" he suggested, glancing nervously over his shoulder to make certain no one was nearby.

"Tomorrow," she repeated firmly.

* * *

Goodall crouched tensely with the fingers of the night cold on his neck and the sound of his own breathing loud in his ears. He kept his eyes fixed on the tumbledown shack below him, watching the flickering lantern light that showed through the cracks in the walls, and he was aware of every minute sound that came from inside. Occasionally, the man in the shack moved across the single room, and then the quavering lamplight was momentarily extinguished by his bulky shadow. As the chill in the air deepened, Goodall shifted his weight and flexed his stiff fingers to try to force his sluggish blood to move more quickly through his veins. Then, finally, he heard the distant thrum of horse hooves that told him the moment had come.

When a sharp, low-pitched whistle reached his ears, he glanced back over his shoulder, peering through the blackness until he recognized the two familiar shadows coming toward him. "Wait a couple a minutes," he whispered, "so I can make sure he's not armed." Then, as his companions nodded, he rose swiftly and silently, his hand poised above his revolver.

Making his way carefully through the weeds and debris, Goodall listened intently for any sound from within the cabin. It was important that they take the man by surprise; it had taken them three long weeks to get this far and he wanted nothing to go wrong. Ever since Peter Clay had warned the marked men and they had scattered, one after another, to avoid Granville Stuart's peculiar kind of justice, Johnny had been watching and waiting. He had not been surprised when the rustling in the area had increased of late, despite the fact that all the major thieves had disappeared. All but one. Goodall knew, as did almost everyone, that Stuart had not been responsible for the loss of that list, but, unlike the others, Johnny did not blame the Marquis for the Peter Clay incident. He had heard the men say that Mores had somehow learned the names, then terrorized Peter Clay into making them public, and all because Granville Stuart had laughed at him, rejecting his offer of assistance.

Johnny snorted in disgust. It was absurd, of course. The Marquis had no more been involved than had Goodall himself. It had to be the Pendletons. And tonight he meant to begin to prove it. With the information Ileya had given him, they should also be able to put a stop to the rustling operation all together. They would do it by confronting the one man who had not run in fear from Stuart's wrath. The man who knew better than anyone else the nature and size of the rustling business in the Badlands. The man whose name had graced the very top of Granville Stuart's list—Jake Maunders.

Kicking the door open with a crash that shattered the heavy stillness of the night, Goodall drew his gun and pointed it at Maunders, who sat behind a makeshift table staring at his intruder in surprise. Johnny wrinkled his nose in distaste at the cloying odor of sweat and stale liquor that hung in the room like a foul early-morning fog and glanced around, looking for weapons. The guttering light from the lantern revealed a rickety cot, the blankets thrown haphazardly into a bundle on top, a stockpile of empty whiskey bottles that had very nearly been swallowed in the dirt that lay in drifts on the floor. Then, in the far corner, he located the two rifles and the branding irons that he had known he would find here. Stepping over so that he stood between Maunders and his weapons, Goodall turned his attention at last to the man himself.

Jake sat carelessly on a backless chair in his shirtsleeves. His hair was disheveled, as if he had just run his fingers repeatedly through the thick strands, and there was a three days' growth of beard on his face. Clearly, before Goodall's entrance, his attention had been focused on the table before him, where a half-empty glass of whiskey sat at his elbow and a large pile of money lay beneath his hand. "What in the hell do you think you're doin'?" he growled, reaching surreptitiously for the gun at his hip.

"Give the gun to me, Jake," Johnny instructed him, "or I'd be more than happy to make a third eye straight through the center of your forehead." He toyed with the trigger for a moment to emphasize his point.

Reluctantly, Maunders removed the revolver from its holster and tossed it across the floor where it landed with a thump at Johnny's feet.

"What do you want, Goodall?" Jake snarled, his heavy brows closing down over his eyes like a black pall.

"I came to ask you for a favor." Goodall smiled at Maunders's grunt of disbelief and added, "And to ask what you know about Peter Clay's 'accident,' three weeks ago."

"I don't know what you're talking about."

"Then let me enlighten you, Mr. Maunders."

Both men looked up and Maunders's jaw dropped open when he saw the woman who stood framed in the doorway. With her dark cloak covering her from neck to shoes and the soft glow of her red hair making her face seem pale and translucent in the flickering light, Medora looked like a spirit conjured out of the darkness beyond. Her green eyes seemed to absorb the flames from the lamp and magnify them until they stripped the dingy little room of all its shadows.

"You see, we know that Granville Stuart had nothing to do with the attack on Peter Clay; he would never be quite so careless."

Maunders shrugged. "You never know. It seems to me that even the best—"

"Mr. Maunders," she interrupted, coming further into the room, "we are not all as naive as Peter, whatever you may think."

"I don't see what this has to do with me." He glanced at Goodall from the corner of his eye, then took a swig from his whiskey glass with apparent disinterest.

"I am merely telling you how much we know," Medora explained. "We are also aware that the reason your rustling has not declined since your accomplices left town is because the Pendletons are backing you and protecting you, and probably profiting from your activities as well. We came here tonight to convince you to help us prove it."

Maunders gaped at her for a moment, then threw back his head and laughed. "You're mad," he gasped between roars, "hopelessly mad."

Medora waited until he had laughed himself out and then

reached inside her cloak and brought out a single piece of paper. Fluttering it gently just out of his reach, she said, "I have here a description of his ordeal as written by Peter Clay. It seems that, the more he thought about his attackers, the more convinced he became that he recognized one from his voice. It took the boy awhile, but he finally matched up a name to that voice. Yours, Jake."

Leaning his elbows on the table, Maunders sniffed disdainfully. "Nobody would believe him. He's an idiot."

"Perhaps, but he's received a lot of sympathy since he was nearly killed, and people have suddenly started to listen to him. And besides, if you don't think Peter's word is enough to anger the locals into forming their own little posse to come looking for you, maybe you'd be impressed with Granville Stuart himself. Your name was at the top of his list, and he still means to find you. And you ought to know that there's not a man or woman in the Badlands who wouldn't bring out a red flag to show him the way to your front door. Even the Pendletons couldn't protect you if he actually came after you.

"Three times I've caught you making a mistake, Mr. Maunders, and I think this time you've gone a little too far. You have only two friends left in the world—Bryce and Greg Pendleton—and a group of enemies so numerous that the cheer at your death would be deafening. So, I think you'd better help me out this time, because if Peter Clay's father does not hang you, I intend to see that Granville Stuart does."

Maunders's eyes flicked back and forth between Goodall, who still held his gun trained on Jake's forehead, and Medora, who stood calmly in the center of the floor waiting for his answer. Her gaze was unwavering as it raked across his features and he knew that she had the power to make her threat a reality. She had the power and, what's more, he knew that this time she would use it. The feel of this money beneath his fingers was a fine and warming sensation, but it wouldn't do him much good if he found himself at the wrong end of a hangman's rope. Besides, there were always ways to get around difficult situations. He'd done it before and he'd do it again. But there'd be no harm in letting them think they had frightened him. He heaved a sigh and muttered, "What do you want me to do?"

"I know what you and Goodall are up to."

Medora glanced up at Phillipe where he sat in the wing-backed chair, his foot swinging negligently over one arm. The firelight played across his face with searching fingers and she was surprised to see that his expression was neither smug nor hostile. Instead, the boy seemed to be overly thoughtful, and his eyes were glazed as if his reflections had removed him from this room somehow and set him down outside among the stars. "And what, exactly is that?" she asked quietly, afraid to disturb Athenais, who was sleeping in her lap.

"You plan to catch the rustlers yourselves. I heard Johnny talking to you one night. *I* think you're mad."

Medora rocked back and forth, back and forth, and the chair creaked softly, mesmerizing her with its steady rhythm. She knew that it was cold outside, despite the fact that it was midsummer, but the fire in the black brick fireplace kept the drawing room warm and the child contented. Eyeing her step-son without turning her head, Medora smiled and murmured, "I wouldn't think that would concern you overly much."

"But it does." Phillipe sat upright and swung his legs to the floor so he could see her more clearly. "I want to help."

He was sincere, she could hear it in his voice, but she could not help but wonder at his motives. "Have you been bored lately, Phillipe? Don't you spend enough time working with the machinery at the plant and scolding the lazy butchers? I should think that would keep you busy a great deal of the time."

"It's not the boredom," he declared impatiently. "I just want to help. Besides, I'm sure it will be terribly exciting, and I don't want to miss all the action." He rose and paced across the room and when he turned again to face her, he sucked in his breath at the picture she made. Athenais was curled across Medora's lap, her tiny legs tucked securely underneath her and her hand clutching the long braid that fell over her mother's shoulder. And Medora's deep red skirt enfolded the child protectively like a sweeping scarlet blanket. . . .

The voluminous skirts of Nicole's pale blue satin dressing gown fell around her in graceful folds and brushed against Phillipe's cheek where he had rested it on the chair seat at his mother's knee. He had folded his legs beneath him and found a spot on the thick blue rug where he could lean close to her, inhaling the soft fragrance of roses that clung to her gown. With the ice blue satin cool against his face, he murmured, "I should like to stay here forever."

Nicole smiled, reaching out to run her fingers gently through his light brown hair. "Don't be silly," she admonished him. "You would be dreadfully bored."

The firelight danced upon the shiny surfaces of her gown like a playful spirit and then found its way to her hair, which fell loose upon her shoulders. "I could find enough to do," Phillipe informed her. "There is always the hunting and the parties."

"I don't think that will satisfy you for long. You will grow restless eventually."

"Never!"

When he looked up at her his eyes glowed with the kind of blind determination only the very young could feel and her breath caught in her throat because, all at once, he reminded her so much of Antoine. "Someday," she said, her eyes focused on some distant vision, "you will leave France behind to go seek excitement and romance wherever you can find it. It's in your blood, Phillipe, this dissatisfaction with things as they are. And you will find that this life is not enough for you, so you will start to build another, just as your father will. It's inevitable and you should be glad to have been touched with such a spirit."

Phillipe gazed at her, puzzled by her words and uneasy at the faraway tone in her voice. He did not understand. "I won't go," he repeated.

With a tremulous sigh, Nicole laid her hand upon his fore-head and whispered, "You are still a child, my son, and things will change a great deal before you grow older. . . ."

Phillipe looked very young just now, Medora thought, with his hands clasped before him and his eyes shadowed by his secret thoughts, "We are doing this for your father, you know," she told him.

He looked away, fixing his gaze on the golden-red flames that danced for him across the room. *You will find that this life is not enough for you and you will start to build another, just as your father will.* He blinked and turned his attention back to his stepmother. "I know. But I want to help."

"You mean your curiosity has overcome your anger?" When Medora saw how he stiffened, locking his fingers together in a painful grip, she relented just a little. "I'm sorry," she said, "but perhaps you can understand that I might mistrust your motives, knowing, as I do, how you feel about the Marquis."

There was a long silence, during which the fire crackled and spit, filling the void that had come between them. "I understand," he said at last, without meeting her eyes, "but I want to help."

Suddenly, Medora saw again the resemblance between this discontented boy and her husband. They were both victims of their circumstances, but neither was willing to give in, even a little. Her heart wrenched painfully inside her chest. She was intensely aware of the weight of her daughter's head against her breast and, as she swayed to and fro, a slow creeping need began to climb from her thighs to her throat. She wanted to feel her husband's hands upon her. Closing her eyes, she felt the firelight quiver across her lids, touching them with a false warmth. "All right," she said unexpectedly, "there is one thing you can do. But you may not like it."

"What is it?" Phillipe leaned forward eagerly.

"You still see Katherine, don't you?"

"Sometimes." His answer was slow and wary.

"I need you to keep her out of this, especially one week from tonight. I know that girl and, regardless of what Greg has done to her, she'll protect her family's interests if she can."

"Odd, isn't it?" he mused. He was thinking of the night when he too had chosen where his loyalty should lie—almost unconsciously and entirely against his will—and Katherine had been made to pay for that choice.

"Do you think you can do it?" Medora inquired, puzzled by the expression in his eyes.

"Yes," he said, his voice heavy with sarcasm, "for my father I can do anything."

SEVENTEEN

Medora looked up as the office door opened. She was alone today, enjoying the morning in town, away from the pressures that plagued her at the Chateau. She had gotten out the latest reports on the progress of the stagecoach line and was reading them through when the sound of the door creaking on its hinges startled her. She did not want to be disturbed just now. But when she saw who the visitor was, she drew in her breath sharply.

"Good morning, Medora," Greg Pendleton greeted her, sauntering forward with his usual self-assurance.

He stopped on the other side of the desk she occupied and, when she realized how he towered over her, she rose to push the chair away. "What do you want?" she inquired coolly.

His lips twitched slightly at her tone, but he kept himself from smiling. "I had to see you. It's been so long, and I wondered what you had been up to."

There was an undercurrent of gravity in his voice that belied his casual attitude, and Medora wondered what he had heard that had brought him here like this. She knew he had not come just to see her. "What I do is not really your concern," she informed him stiffly.

"I've told you before, you're wrong about that. I have made it my concern." He stepped around the desk that stood between them and took her hand, which lay cold and lifeless in his. "Come, Medora, don't you remember that something changed between us that night?"

Withdrawing her hand, she considered his eyes, trying to

probe beneath the steel-gray surface to the thoughts that lay hidden there. She wanted to back away—he was standing much too near for comfort—but she refused to retreat before this man. "That night changed nothing," she said, "except that it made me more your enemy than before."

"Why? Because you learned that you were vulnerable to me?" He took another step toward her and placed his hands on her shoulders, drawing her forward until he bent his head and kissed her.

When his mouth met hers, Medora meant to draw away, but somehow the fire in his lips began to burn through her defenses. For a moment she swayed forward, closing her eyes in anticipation, but then the image of Katherine's wealed back rose between them and hovered there, destroying the moment. Medora gasped and wrenched herself free of his grasp. "Get out!" she shrieked.

Greg smiled, reaching for her again, and when she put out her hands to push him away, he grasped them roughly and forced them around his waist. She struggled, her breath coming rapidly as the anger built in her chest until she thought she would explode with the weight of it, but he held her immobile, his fingers digging painfully into her wrists. As his lips descended toward hers once again, she realized that he enjoyed the struggle, that if she were to come to him meekly and willingly, he would turn away and leave her. But she simply could not bring herself to succumb.

"My dear," he whispered throatily, "your body doesn't seem to understand how much you hate me." Releasing one hand, he ran his fingers across the taut fabric of her bodice and she realized with a shock that her nipples were erect.

Medora shivered briefly, then gathered her wits about her and twisted her other hand until he let it go. She drew herself up stiffly; then, noticing a letter opener lying on the desktop, she picked it up and pointed it at his heart. "Leave me be," she hissed.

Suddenly all the amusement fled from his eyes and he glowered at her menacingly. "Don't play at those kinds of games, Medora; you'll lose every time."

Again, she realized that he was not just speaking of the letter opener she held between them. This time, when he took a step forward, there was no desire in his expression, just grim determination.

"I know that you're playing another game just now," he continued, "and that it has to do with the rustlers. I want you to tell me your plans, exactly, leaving out not the slightest detail. Do you understand?"

"You're mad. I don't even know what you're talking about."

"I'm warning you, Medora, I'll find out. Why don't we just make it easier? Tell me what you're up to and then I shall leave you in peace. Unless, of course," he murmured, eyeing the pulse that pounded in the hollow of her throat, "you want me to stay."

He grinned slyly and the twist of his lips sent a chill down the back of her neck. "Go to hell," she snapped.

"Tell me the truth," he demanded, grasping her arms with a cruel grip. "Tell me how you got your information and what you plan to do with it."

Maunders had obviously been talking, Medora thought, but it didn't really matter. They would still get what they wanted from him. She was relieved to discover that Pendleton didn't know who had betrayed him—even she didn't know; Johnny had kept stubbornly silent on the matter.

"You know I will find out who the traitor is eventually," he muttered in a voice that was dangerously low, "and then I shall—"

"Do what you did to Katherine?"

His eyes glittered as he bent his head until his face was only inches from hers. "Katherine provoked me. She needed a lesson. But a beating was not what I had in mind. No," he said, his tone deceptively soft, "the one who betrayed me will die, I promise you that."

Medora swallowed once, praying that Goodall could manage to keep the information to himself because she knew with absolute certainty that Greg meant what he said. And if their plan should be successful, the Pendletons would be even more determined to find the informant.

"Listen to me, my dear," he ordered, "I can see that you won't help me, but I want you to know that, whatever your absurd little plan is, I shall find a way to stop it. You have given me no choice."

The mournful notes of the piano crept through the closed doors, finding its way to the Marquis where he sat propped against the pillow on his bed. Medora was playing Liszt as she often did late at night, and the song beguiled him in spite of himself. Closing his eyes, he let the music wash over him, lulling him into drowsiness. In his mind, he could see her fingers flying over the keyboard with skill and grace and the unbending line of her back above the bench. She had secrets of late; he knew this, although they were not close. He had seen the way she withdrew inside herself at times, almost as if she had left the world where he existed. Once, or perhaps twice, he had had a desire to reach out and touch her hair or to run a finger across her lips, but he had allowed those desires to die out, unfulfilled.

Lost in his thoughts, he was not aware that the music had stopped, nor did he hear his wife enter the room next to his and set about undressing. It was only when the door opened, spilling the light unexpectedly across the floor, that he looked up.

Medora stood before him with her hair tumbled loose around her shoulders, the lamplight radiating from her body in soft waves. She wore nothing but a thin silk dressing gown of emerald green; through the fabric he could see the outline of her well-proportioned figure. It was almost as if the yellow light merged with the shimmering gown to give her skin an ethereal glow. Her lips were slightly parted, her eyes flashing turquoise with a desire that she did not even try to disguise.

"Mores," she breathed, "I have missed you."

The Marquis looked away, but the image of the sensuous curve of her breasts beneath the fabric would not leave him.

"I'm weary," he told her, just managing to keep his voice steady. "Please leave me."

Shaking her head sadly, Medora left the doorway to kneel beside him. "You would sleep better in my bed." She laid her hand on top of his and, when he did not withdraw it at once, leaned down to kiss his fingers—one at a time. "Please," she murmured.

He had never heard her plead with him before; she was too proud, too strong, too self-sufficient. But now she was kneeling at his feet, her sweet breath caressing his skin, her eyes wide and expectant. The scent of her hair was heavy in his nostrils, and she was waiting for his answer. She had made herself vulnerable to him and he knew instinctively that if he sent her away now, the blow to her proud spirit would be crippling. And he could not bring himself to do it. Whatever she had done, he could not bring himself to deny her. Not when she was so alluring and her hand on his was so warm.

He rose from the bed, drawing her up beside him until her body was pressed against his and his hands had found their way across her shoulders and down the sloping curve of her back. "I want you, Medora," he said and, as he lowered his lips to hers, he added gruffly, "damn you to hell."

For the first time in many weeks the Marquis awakened in his wife's bed. He lay still with his eyes closed, remembering the many paths her hands had traced over his body the night before, until he felt her stir beside him. Her hand still rested on his chest and he raised it lightly to his lips. "Good morning," he said.

"Mores?"

Turning his head he saw that her face was shadowed with a frown.

"I want to tell you—" she began.

"Hush," he told her, "you'll spoil it." His lips curved into a smile, but inside he struggled against depression. He did not want to hear what she had to say, not if she meant to try to explain her relationship with Pendleton—and some instinct told him that she did. Last night she had made him forget the past, and he did not want to be reminded now. He was content, at the moment, to live in the present. It was the only way he could continue to survive.

"But I thought you should know," she insisted, aware that he knew what she meant.

He shook his head, reaching out to brush the hair away from her face. "Let it go, Dory, please."

Medora's heart sank. The only way he could accept her again was to ignore what she had done. If only he would face it squarely, instead of running away from the truth. But that was how he faced all his problems, she thought sadly. It was the only way he knew how. And as long as she could not speak of Greg to him, her own guilt would continue to haunt her.

"Please," the Marquis repeated. And this time it was he who was pleading with her.

The mood at the breakfast table that morning was lighter than it had been for some time. Mores had clearly ceased his brooding and he smiled at his wife each time their eyes met. William was relieved that some of the pressure had lifted, and even Phillipe was in a pleasant frame of mind.

"How are the boilers working?" the Marquis asked him in an attempt to draw the boy into the conversation.

"I think I've fixed them both, with William's help, of course. We slaughtered seventy head yesterday, so the plant is operating more adequately now," Phillipe answered airily.

Mores and his secretary exchanged an amused glance at the boy's use of the word "adequate." Apparently, Phillipe was never satisfied with anything less than maximum production. But the two older men had long known that they had to go slowly. There was too much working against them to allow the progress to be smooth.

"I have an appointment," Medora announced. "I'd forgotten, but I mustn't be late. If you'll excuse me." She pushed back her chair, blew a kiss in her husband's direction, then hurried from the room.

With a bemused smile Mores watched her go. He could not believe that she had come back to him, had made herself his friend and lover again, all in the space of a single night. She was beautiful and she loved him and he had forgiven her. Now, he thought—unaware of the longing look that had touched William's face at Medora's departure—now everything would be all right. It had to be; Medora was his wife once again.

The three who remained at the table looked up together as the thrum of horse hooves on soft grass came to them through the window. Medora rode into view, her back stiffly correct, the skirt of her riding dress flying like a captured bird around her legs. William and Mores and Phillipe watched her as if hypnotized by the graceful rise and fall of the horse's hooves and by the woman who was, clearly, the animal's master. A gleam of admiration twinkled in the Marquis's eyes.

Then, abruptly, a shot rang out, splitting the morning air like a bolt of screaming lightning from the heart of a clear blue sky. The horse reared with a frenzied shriek and then hung there, poised in midair for an instant before his hooves came plunging back to earth. Medora clung wildly to the reins, but the animal had gone mad; when it leaped upright a second time, she lost her grip and was thrown violently from its back.

Mores was out of his chair in an instant, with William and Phillipe close behind him. He ran blindly, nearly wrenching the door from its hinges in his haste, until he knelt beside the motionless form of his wife. She lay sprawled awkwardly, her arms flung out before her, her face drained of its natural color. The Marquis slid his hands gently beneath her shoulders and turned her to face him. Leaning his head against her chest, he listened intently for the sound of her breathing or the beating of her heart. For a moment he closed his eyes, perhaps in prayer, then he shouted, "William! Get the doctor!"

Mores knew that the secretary stood at Medora's feet; his

long shadow fell across her body. "Is she dead?" William choked.

The Marquis looked up, startled at the rasping question. As he sat there with his wife unconscious in his arms, he saw for the first time the pallid grayness of the secretary's cheeks, the lines etched deeply into his forehead and the agony reflected in his eyes. And there was one thing more. Behind the stunned grief lay a burning fire that drew his heart up from his chest and displayed it like a bright gold banner across the dark brown field of his eyes. Only then, with the message echoing across his vision, did Mores see what he should have known long ago—that William loved Medora with a longing so intense that it might easily destroy him. "No," the Marquis told him, "she's alive, but she needs a doctor."

William shook himself when he saw the look that passed over his employer's face, and Van Driesche knew that, in that one brief moment, he had revealed the secret that he had struggled for so long to conceal. Without a word, he turned away and went to find the doctor.

With a last look after his retreating friend, Mores lifted Medora from the ground and carried her in through the empty house to her room, where he laid her among the still disheveled covers from the night before. He stood staring down at her in bewilderment, unsure of what he should do for her. Just as when she had lain before him wracked with labor pains, he could not help her, because he did not know if she were broken inside. He only knew that the sound of her irregular breathing was more precious to him just now than her soft voice telling him she loved him. As long as that sound repeated itself in the stillness of the tiny room, he knew that she was alive. And that was all he asked, at least for the moment.

Suddenly, Phillipe burst into the room, his hair in disarray and his eyes wild. "How is she?" he gasped, attempting to catch his breath.

Mores looked at his son as if he had forgotten his existence. "I don't know yet," he said, "except that she's alive."

The boy nodded, reaching out to cling to the bedpost as if he needed to restore his balance. "I went looking for the one who shot at her," he explained at last.

The Marquis scrutinized Phillipe's face with more interest. "What did you find?"

"Nothing really. Just a place where the bushes had been broken, as if someone had been crouching there. But by the time I got there, whoever it was had disappeared. I didn't know what direction he had taken, but I ran after him just the same."

"Thank you for trying," Mores said, attempting an approving smile.

Phillipe saw the concern and fear that had changed his father's handsome face into a pale, drawn imitation of itself. He saw that Mores held his wife's limp hand as if to let it go would be to give her up for lost. He saw the flickers of indecision that appeared in the Marquis's deep black eyes, and, for the first time in his young life, the boy pitied this man whose arrogance and stiff-necked pride had somehow evaporated in the moment when Medora fell from her dying horse.

"She's all right," Mores announced to William as he joined him on the porch. Darkness had already fallen, and the secretary leaned against the railing without acknowledging his friend's presence, but the Marquis knew he had heard.

"She has a concussion, a sprained wrist, and a lot of bruises, but no broken bones. She's lucky."

"Have you found the man who did it?" William asked, hoping that his voice would remain steady.

"No." Mores frowned, lit a cigar, then took a few puffs before he continued. "But whoever it was, he wasn't much of a shot."

"Maybe he was only trying to frighten her."

"Perhaps." The Marquis rested his shoulder against a post and tapped his cigar ashes over the edge of the porch. He was disturbed by Medora's stubborn silence on the question of who her assailant might have been. She said she had no idea, but Mores sensed that she was lying. He could tell by the shadows that veiled her eyes and the tense line of her jaw. Secrets, he thought, secrets and hidden plans and lies and betrayals. Why wouldn't she tell him the truth? Why?

"If you'll excuse me," William said, interrupting his thoughts, "I'll go back inside now."

The Marquis heard the tautness in his voice, but he could not see Van Driesche's face through the deep night shadows. "I'm sorry, William," he said impulsively, "I didn't know."

Van Driesche paused in the middle of a step. He knew without being told that Mores was referring to William's feelings for Medora. He had been such a *fool* to let them show. "It wouldn't have made any difference if you had known."

Puffing carefully on his cigar, the Marquis considered William's assertion in silence. Then, as the seconds passed by, he murmured, "No, I don't suppose it would have." After another moment he added, "But I'm sorry, just the same. I understand what you're feeling."

"How could you?" William cried, whirling to face him. "She *loves* you!"

Mores's face was invisible in the darkness; only the glowing tip of his cigar revealed his presence. Secrets, he was thinking. Lies and secrets and Greg Pendleton with his hands on Medora's body. He had thought he could forget it, but it wasn't so. "Yes," he murmured. "Aren't I lucky?"

Before the secretary had time to wonder at the ironic tone in the Marquis's voice, the man had spun on his heel and disappeared.

Two days later, Johnny Goodall found Medora sitting alone in her office contemplating a watercolor she had begun a week before. She did not look up, although he stood in the doorway for several moments, his hat in his hand. Finally, when he cleared his throat, she swung around to face him. "How are you feelin', ma'am?" he asked politely.

"Just fine, Johnny. The fall bruised me, but there was no other real damage."

Pushing his hair back out of his face, he shifted his weight from one foot to the other. "I've been tryin' to see you since it happened, but they kept me away."

She stood then, her brow creased with concern. "Is something wrong?"

"No, ma'am, not with me. But, of course we'll have to give up our plans for the rustlers now."

Staring at him in disbelief, she asked, "Why on earth should we do that?"

"Well," he muttered, rubbing his chin, "because they tried to kill you."

"And that gives us every reason to go ahead. It proves that we have them scared and that whoever shot at me—"

"I'm sure it was Maunders, probably in Pendleton's pay."

"All right then, it proves that Maunders is getting desperate, and that can only be good for us."

Goodall shook his head without bothering to hide his skepticism. "You don't seem to understand," he said patiently. "They tried to *kill* you!"

"Look at me, Johnny," she demanded, moving easily across the room. "I'm alive and unhurt. If they were trying to kill me, they failed, and that makes them the losers. If they were only trying to frighten me, I'm not going to give them the satisfaction of even such a small victory. I cannot be frightened out of doing what I think is right, and we're going ahead with our project."

He clenched his jaw, as if to stop himself from speaking his mind, but then he replied firmly, "No."

"Johnny, we've worked a long time. We can't just—"

"No," he repeated. "Things have changed. It's gotten too dangerous, and I won't let you risk it anymore."

She turned her back on him, then whirled abruptly, her eyes ablaze with emerald sparks. "You haven't any choice," she cried, clenching her hands into fists at her sides, "because if you won't help me I'll do it alone. I mean it, Johnny. I'm going through with it. . . ."

* * *

"I can't let you go, Kiwani. It isn't safe."

She turned sadly away from him and continued pulling the comb through her long, dark hair. "I'm sorry, my husband. I will not argue with you, for it is not right that a woman should raise her voice. But I must go and see for myself whether or not my brothers died at Little Bighorn. They may need me."

Johnny felt the breath catch in his throat as the morning sunlight fell through the window, touching her deep brown face with a soft glow. *"I* need you," he said.

Kiwani left her comb and came to stand before him, placing her hands on his shoulders and brushing his lips with hers. "I shall miss you, Johnny, but I shall be home as soon as I learn the truth."

"You know how dangerous the mood of the whites is since the massacre. They hate any Indian and would as gladly kill you as a bobcat that had threatened their livestock. Suppose that happens, little one? What then?"

She smiled mysteriously. "Then it shall be so, my husband. I cannot change what God has ordained."

"And what about our daughter?" he asked, attempting to keep the desperation from showing itself in his voice.

"She has grandmothers and aunts who will care for her. She will not want so long as she is among her people."

"You want her to be raised with the tribe?" he rasped, but his thoughts said, "You want her to be raised apart from me?"

"That is my wish, should I lose my life during my search. But even if that should be so," she soothed, "I shall die happy, knowing I did what I thought was right. Cannot you understand?"

"I won't let you go."

Kiwani stood before him without moving, her expression remote, and he knew that she had made her choice.

"You are my *wife!*" he breathed in one last, hopeless attempt to make her see reason.

"I am a Sioux," she replied, "and I must go." Then she

aised her hands and placed them against his cheeks. "You
vill not stop me, because you know that I love you above
ıll others, as you love me, and that that affection which we
ɔear each other would curl like a dried-out plant and die if
ɤou were to hold me here against my will. You know that,
ɔohnny, as surely as I do. And you will let me go."

Kiwani leaned forward until her lips met his in a long,
ɔassionate farewell kiss that drew the fiery fear up from his
ɔelly until it lodged in his throat. Then she drew back for a
noment, contemplating his features with infinite care, as if
o burn them forever into her memory. In another instant, she
ɪad turned away to disappear silently on moccasined feet, her
oft buckskin dress swaying against her bare legs.

*Long after she had gone, he stood there like stone, and he
ɔould not rid himself of the memory of her piercing, liquid
ɡaze. . . .*

The sparks in Medora's eyes had subsided into glowing
ɛmbers and, recognizing the doubts that made Goodall so un-
ɛasy, she said more quietly, "It's too important to let it go,
ɔohnny. And perhaps this attempt on my life will even prove
o our advantage."

He shook his head. "I don't see how."

"They'll think that we *have* decided not to move. They'll
ıssume that I am cowering in my room, afraid to peek out-
ɪide. Perhaps they won't be ready when we do strike."

Johnny crossed his arms, regarding her with dismay. He
ɪad seen the look in this woman's eyes before, and he knew
ɪhat he had lost. If she were foolish enough to carry out her
ɪhreat to do it without him—and he was very much afraid
ɪhe would be—then he would have her blood on his hands
f anything went wrong. "All right," he agreed grudgingly.
'But we do it my way—slow and careful."

"Yes," she said, her relief evident in her voice. Smiling,
ɪhe offered him her hand. "But I'm worried about Maunders.
ʌpparently he already spoke to the Pendletons or they

wouldn't have dared attack me. How are you going to make certain that he doesn't warn them next time?"

Goodall smiled grimly and assured her, "I'll see to it ma'am, don't you worry. I'll make sure old Jake don't utter a word."

EIGHTEEN

Ileya dove beneath the water, disappeared for a moment, then rose to the surface, parting the water with her slender hands. She sliced her way across the river with powerful strokes as if she felt the water were her enemy and she sought to conquer it. Sitting on the bank with his back against the trunk of a cottonwood, Mores watched her with a touch of concern. Many times before he had come here like this to watch the girl while she swam, but never had he seen her concentrate so intensely on every motion of her arms and legs. Usually the water soothed her, acting like a balm upon whatever troubled her spirit, but today her body moved with a certain restrained violence. That violence was like an open challenge to the river, which before she had always felt to be her friend.

When she finally left the water, he drew in his breath, as always, at the soft brownness of her naked body. She had never hidden it from him because she had sensed that he would not take advantage of her and, besides, she hated the confinement of unnecessary clothing. It was a measure of her confidence in him that he had never thought of possessing that lithe, slender body, though he admired it often. To the Marquis, Ileya had nothing to do with fleshly appetites; to him she was part of another world.

She came toward him, her long hair dark and dripping, and retrieved the towel from where she had left it on the bank. Mores watched in surprise as she rubbed the water from her skin; usually she simply lay back on the grass with her hair spread out behind her and let the sun warm her dry. But today was not like other days. Today something was troubling her and, whatever it was, it had taken her out of the magic world where she usually existed and dropped her, cruelly, into the heart of the world of men.

"Ileya?" He spoke her name softly, afraid to ask the question that circled in his mind because he knew she would only refuse to answer. It was she who made the rules and he who followed, and he knew that her privacy was her most treasured possession.

Slipping her buckskin dress over her head, she shook out her hair and came to sit beside him. For a long moment, she met his questioning gaze with dark, liquid eyes, parting her lips slightly as if she meant to answer him, but then she looked away. Ileya stared moodily at the river in silence until a chill ran down her spine and she wrapped her arms protectively across her chest to stop the trembling in her hands. Mores touched her shoulder then, and she met his eyes only briefly before she whispered, "I am cold. Please hold me."

It was something she had never asked of him before, and he hesitated while a thousand questions chased each other around in his head. He realized with a shock that for once, Ileya needed *him*. What had happened to change her? Whatever it was, he knew she would tell him when—and if—she chose to do so. Reaching out tentatively, he slid one arm around her shoulders. When she leaned close to him, allowing her head to fall against his chest, he shifted slightly until he held her firmly in the circle of his arms.

For a long time, she clung to him, shivering, absorbing the warmth from his body like a drug that moved through her blood dissipating the chill that seemed to have settled into her very bones. Mores rested his chin on the top of her head and struggled to keep the shudders that wracked her from penetrating his own limbs. But he found that it was to no avail; her pain, her fear had become his and he could no longer tell where his own body stopped and hers began. She was as much a part of him as the fish were part of the river and the clear smooth stones beneath. It was as if the blood had flowed from her body into his, and his into hers, because now it was he who shivered and she who was still. But then, slowly, as they huddled together in the shade of the tree, the coldness left them and their bodies became two again.

For a long, long time they sat there, unmoving, while the dampness from the ground beneath seeped into their clothes. Mores and Ileya were unaware of their discomfort because they were so lost in amazement at the thing that had just happened between them. Neither had ever felt such absolute communion before, and both knew they probably never would again. They had not intended it; it had simply come upon them regardless of their wills and swamped their senses with a feeling of union so profound that they could not even attempt to describe it. The spirit of the river, whom Ileya worshiped with her every breath, had wound through their lives for an instant, leaving behind this gift, this miracle that had melded their thoughts into a single pulsing heartbeat.

The Marquis did not want to move or even breathe because he knew then this moment would be lost forever and he could not bear to let it slip away so soon. But then Ileya stirred beside him and raised her head and Mores was bewildered by the mournful light that touched her eyes. "What is it?" he asked.

She paused for a moment as if she would not answer, but then she whispered, "There is an old Indian song and it is very brief. It says, *'I catch, but cannot hold you.'* "

He opened his mouth to protest, but she covered it with her palm. "No," she said, "do not spoil it with promises that you cannot keep. I am content to have had this moment. And now it is getting late and you must go back."

"Ileya—"

"Please," she said, pulling away from him. "It is time for you to go."

Perhaps if he had argued, he might have convinced her to let him stay, but he could not bring himself to mar this day with dissension. She had asked him to go and he would do so, but not willingly. Never willingly. "Tomorrow," he murmured.

She reached out to touch his cheek, her caress as light as the brush of a bird's wing, then turned away and was gone. But as he made his way through the trees toward home, he heard her voice rise up out of the water like a song.

> *Friend,*
> *Whenever you pursue any course,*
> *Friend,*
> *May I be there.*

He shivered when he heard it and wondered why it should sound so much like a message of farewell.

Katherine crouched low against her horse's body with the air rushing like frozen laughter across her face. She loved the feel of the swift animal beneath her and the manic cry of the wind above. Here she was lost in a world of sensations that had no connection with fear and jealousy and hatred. Here she was completely herself, consumed by the physical needs of her sensual nature. Here, in the deep, black night, she was safe from prying eyes and restraining hands. Here, she was Katherine—wild and beautiful and absolutely free.

By the time she saw Phillipe waiting with his horse beside him, Katherine was breathless from her long ride. She reined the animal in and practically tumbled from its back only to find herself laughing within the circle of Phillipe's arms. "I thought you wouldn't come," he said, surprised to find her body pressed against his and her arms fastened around his neck. Since that night long ago she had touched him only occasionally and even then her eyes had always been wary. Never again had they come close to the kind of intimacy they had shared in those few moments before he had shattered the spell that bound them.

"I wanted to prove to you that I can win a race at night, too. And even you couldn't win a chess game in the darkness.

Come," she said, "I must let my horse rest while I catch my breath. Let's sit under the tree."

She clasped his hand as they walked and he could feel the pulse racing through her fingers. Her skin was icy cold, but he sensed that underneath a kind of radiating warmth was building, waiting to be released. He was aware that she was chattering at him but he could not make out the words; his head spinning with her presence and the feel of her skin against his fingers. It was almost as if she had forgotten the past. As if she had abandoned herself to the present and the dictates of her body.

Before they had reached the shelter of the spreading branches of the tree, he had released her hand to slide his arm across her shoulders. She had not resisted, but leaned into him, slipping her own arm around his waist. As they ducked under the low-hanging branches, he turned to face her and he saw how her teeth gleamed when she smiled. He moved toward her, but she put up her hand to stop him.

"Tonight you really want me," she declared, her voice still husky from her exhilarating ride, "don't you?"

He bit his lip in frustration, afraid that this was just another episode of the game that was played out between them every time they met. Tonight, for the first time, he did not want to play. Tonight he wanted to forget the competition and declare a truce. It did not even enter his mind that he was here because Medora had asked him to be. "You know I do," he breathed. He knew she would not give in unless he made himself vulnerable to her. He did not mind confessing his desire; she could see it burning in his eyes anyway.

"You're certain this time?"

"Katherine—"

"I want to know if you're sure."

"Stop it," he insisted, "you're wasting time."

"But I want to know—" Her words were cut off abruptly by the pressure of his lips on hers. He had realized, finally, what she was waiting for. She did not want to give him her body; she wanted him to take it.

His arms closed around her as he drew her inexorably

downward, his heart beating heavily against her chest. He teased her mouth with his tongue and his hands found their own path across her heaving breasts and her belly and the soft roundness of her thighs. The blood pounded in his ears as the sensations ran along his body wherever she touched him with warm, searching hands. "I want to see you," he whispered. "All of you."

She dragged her fingers through his hair and smiled as she felt the tingling presence of his hands on her shoulders. "You first," Katherine told him. "While I watch."

For a moment he hovered above her, trying to see her face through the dusky light. Was this another trick? Was she trying to get even after all? But when she reached up to run her hand slowly along his leg, massaging gently as she went, he decided to take the chance. In seconds, he had discarded his clothes and then he stood motionless for a moment, feeling her eyes devour the sight of him.

Unconsciously, Katherine licked her lips as she took in the broad expanse of his shoulders and chest, narrow waist, and well-formed hips. She swallowed deeply as her gaze rested on the dark area between his legs, and then he lowered himself beside her and began to unfasten the buttons of her blouse. She lay still, enjoying the unfamiliar feel of being undressed, slowly and sensuously, by hands other than her own. He did not touch her skin again until he had removed every piece of clothing and she lay naked before him. He gazed for a long time at the young, slender curves of her body, from her dark flowing hair to the tips of her toes.

And then, beginning at the base of her throat, he traced a path with the tip of his tongue over her smooth white shoulders, down across the soft rise of her breasts and the sloping roundness of her belly. His hands seemed to dance over her skin, setting it burning, and when he uncurled his body and pressed it against hers, she welcomed him gladly. The touch of his skin seemed to invade every part of her and she was hypnotized by the circular motion of his tongue in her mouth. Her nerves were screaming, shrieking for something that she could not even understand, but she knew that she wanted it now more than she had ever wanted anything in her life.

She shuddered, briefly, at the pain that shot through her thighs like a heated brand when he entered her, but then the gentle, rhythmic motion of his body and the electric touch of his hands made her forget. With her hands locked around his neck and her hips rising to meet his, she forgot that she hated him, that he had betrayed her, that he was her enemy. She forgot that she had sworn never to give him what she knew he most desired. She forgot, in the explosion of blinding fire that left her breathless and lost, that she had vowed to destroy him.

"Peter? Are you ready?"

Peter Clay was leaning forward with his head resting on his horse's neck. He stared idly at the ground below and tried to detect a trace of hoofprints. If Maunders had come this way, surely Peter would know it. Never mind that he could not even see clearly the man who waited just beside him; if Maunders's horse had been by, it would have left prints that glowed in the dark. At least, he thought it would—a man as evil as Jake Maunders had to leave a trail, didn't he? A man like that couldn't slink through the night without a sign.

"Peter!" Goodall repeated in a hoarse whisper. When the boy sat up halfway to peer questioningly at him, Johnny wondered if it had been wise after all to bring him along. But then, that had been part of the deal—Peter's written account of the attack for a chance to catch Maunders and his cohorts. As if Peter could catch anyone single-handedly, Goodall thought. He might very well get himself killed before the night was over.

"I think I hear him coming. Are you ready?" Johnny asked tensely.

"I'm ready to pump his belly full of bullets," Peter replied enthusiastically.

"But not yet," Theodore Roosevelt admonished him. "Stay with me until Goodall gives you the signal. You understand?"

"Sure I do, but it don't mean I like it."

"He's nearly here," Goodall hissed, turning to Roosevelt, "are they back there?"

"They're all here. And don't worry, he'll never know they're behind you."

"Good." Johnny nodded once, then plunged his horse through the bushes so he blocked Maunders's path. Pulling out his revolver, he waited, his heart thudding fiercely.

"What the Hell—" Jake cried when he saw Goodall.

"It's tonight, Jake. We go tonight."

"But, I thought—" the other man began, then clamped his lips shut.

"You thought we'd tell you ahead of time so you could warn the others, right? You thought we'd be stupid enough to let you get away with spoiling our plans? Sorry to disappoint you, but it's tonight. And you're gonna do your part, just like you promised. Now lead me to the rustlers' camp."

Maunders eyed him warily, his thoughts whirling in an attempt to come up with some means of escaping this obligation, but, for the moment, Goodall's gun was pointed at his heart and he knew the man would not hesitate to shoot. Time to think, that's what he needed. With a snort, he edged past Johnny and continued down the path with Goodall and—had he only known it—seven other men close behind him.

After several false starts, when Maunders tried to lead him in the wrong direction, Goodall finally heard the shuffling and snorting sounds that meant a group of animals were nearby. Maunders had decided the man was practicing some kind of black magic; he seemed to know the instant Jake took a wrong turn. But, of course, it wasn't magic. Johnny had just taken the time to find out where every single camp was beforehand. There were at least six in the area, and the thieves used a different one every night. Johnny had needed Maunders only to lead him to the one that was being used tonight.

As they approached the deep bushes that surrounded the camp, Goodall reached into his pocket and withdrew a heavy scarf. Then he nodded briskly and a man appeared from somewhere behind him. Tossing the scarf at the newcomer, he whispered, "Gag him so he won't warn them. And keep him here until I tell you different."

The man nodded and dragged Maunders from the back of his horse, protesting loudly, but not quite loudly enough. Johnny had stopped far enough away from the camp that the bushes and the restless stamping of the cattle covered the sounds of the men's approach.

When Goodall heard Roosevelt come up behind him, he turned and nodded to indicate that all was well and the two crept slowly forward on their bellies until they could see into the heart of the camp. There were still several men working with the cattle and horses, so Johnny waited, listening for any sign of trouble from behind, where he had left Maunders—and Peter Clay. The lowing of the animals and the whistling of the birds overhead filled the night with sound and a sense of motion, so that Goodall never had time to be afraid. Yet he knew that if he were found, he would be killed. He and Roosevelt and all the others. Nevertheless, he was glad Mr. Roosevelt had chosen to come along. It gave the plan legitimacy somehow.

Suddenly, he felt the grip of cold fingers digging into his arm and he looked over at his companion. Goodall let his breath out silently. It was time then. They would wait a few minutes, just to be sure, and then they would finally have their chance.

When the sound of the men had dwindled into nothingness, Johnny rose and whistled shrilly. Quickly, the others appeared and made their way into the center of the camp. "You have the paint?" Roosevelt asked the first man to pass him.

"Yes sir."

"Remember, put it where it won't show until you look closely."

"Yes sir."

Goodall noted with satisfaction that there were only about fifteen animals held in by a barbed wire fence. That was good. It wouldn't take them long to mark all fifteen. Then they could get out of here and leave the field to Granville Stuart, who sat behind him now, poised like a king upon his horse's back, waiting. This was not the kind of subterfuge Stuart liked, Johnny knew, but the man had little choice. And perhaps he would like the whole setup even less when he saw who was controlling this band of rustlers. Stuart was a friend of Bryce Pendleton's. But not for long, Goodall told himself. Not for long.

And now the time had come for Johnny to deal with Maunders. The man who had bled the Marquis dry for a year and a half; who had betrayed all his friends and befriended all his enemies; who had stolen and cheated and even killed to keep his little rustling business going; and who had tried to take Medora's life. Goodall knew what to do with a man like that. And he had waited for a long time.

He started back toward his horse, but before he had taken five steps, a man came stumbling toward him from out of the bushes. "Maunders got away," he gasped. "I tried to go after him, but—"

"Which way?" Goodall demanded sharply. When the man pointed to the west, Johnny began to run, his hands clenched into granite fists at his sides. If Maunders somehow managed to get back to warn the Pendletons or the other rustlers, all this would have been for nothing. Far worse than nothing, because it had nearly cost Medora's life. Johnny had to catch him; he knew no one else would. As he fought his way through the thick underbrush, he did not even pause to wonder where Peter Clay was.

Goodall ran blindly, listening with every ounce of concentration he could muster for the sound of someone fleeing before him. He was only mildly relieved to note that the horses still stood calmly where he had left them. At least Jake was on foot.

At last he found a place where the branches had been snapped across in several spots, evidence of Maunders's passage. Goodall slowed a little, peering into the darkness before him, listening for a sound, any little sound that seemed out of place. His lungs were screaming from the unexpected exertion when, abruptly, an arm whipped out of the bushes at his side and fastened itself around his neck.

"You're a damned nuisance, Goodall, you know that?" Maunders hissed in his ear. "I'm real tired of finding you at my heels every time I turn around, and I figure, since you ain't the type to listen to reason, that there's only one way to make sure you don't do it no more."

With his free hand, he removed the gun from Johnny's holster. Then, with the force of a cold north wind, Maunders shoved the other man to the ground and pointed the gun at the center of Goodall's chest. "Sorry, old friend," Jake said, smiling, "but you should of known you couldn't win against Old Jake Maunders. It's—"

The rest of the words died in his throat as a gun exploded from the bushes to his right. The bullet hit him square in the center of the forehead and before his eyes glazed over, they registered an instant of horrified surprise. Then his ugly, scowling face was covered in a wash of blood that filled his open mouth and spilled down his chin as he collapsed, motionless, in the dirt at Johnny's feet.

For a long moment, Goodall lay where he had fallen, gaping at Maunders's lifeless body. Then he turned his head at last and found himself staring up into Peter Clay's grimly smiling face.

"I told you I was ready," he explained. "I said I'd get the bastard, and I did." His voice was matter-of-fact, and he gazed fondly at the pistol in his hand for a moment before he dropped it next to Jake's limp, outstretched hand. "Don't need this no more," he said. "I got what I came for."

Three days later, the Pendletons were disturbed at breakfast by the noisy pounding of a fist on the outside door. Bryce looked up, his eyebrows arched questioningly, but Greg looked as blank as his father. Annoyed at the frantic energy of their visitor's knocking, Bryce said, "You'd better open it, Greg, before they kick it down."

Rising reluctantly, Greg strode across the room to throw open the door. "What is it?" he demanded in exasperation.

But then he saw who stood facing him across the threshold and surprise made him speechless.

"Morning, Greg."

"Granville. What in the hell are you doing here?"

"Chasing rustlers."

This matter-of-fact response, along with the carefully blank expression on his old friend's face, left Greg somewhat shaken. "What—" he began.

But Stuart interrupted him. "I think you should get Bryce and the two of you should go for a little ride with me." When Greg opened his mouth to object, Stuart added, "I'm not in the mood to argue just now. So why don't you just make it easy on both of us and come along?"

As Pendleton left the doorway, Stuart shook his head regretfully. In spite of the evidence, he had not really believed that the Pendletons were to blame for the most recent rash of rustling in the area. Not until he had seen Greg's face. For the first time since he had begun his campaign to wipe out the rustlers, Stuart found that he disliked his self-appointed task. But then, it hadn't been his choice to flout the law. No, the Pendletons had made that choice for themselves. And there was nothing he could do.

As they rode to the south pasture Greg and Bryce pelted the man with questions, but he maintained a stubborn silence. Then Greg saw the line of horsemen stretched across the field like soldiers at attention, waiting for their orders. He glanced down the line, noticing that no one moved to wipe his brow, even though the sun was beating down with punishing intensity. It glinted off the rifles cradled carefully across the pommels and sucked up the early morning dew only to replace it in a thin film of sweat on each man's forehead.

Suddenly, Greg knew why he and his father had been brought here, why these men were frozen like bronze statues before him. He could read his own fate in their faces. At the end sat Johnny Goodall, who could not hide his pleasure, as well as his profound relief; clearly he had come merely to witness his final triumph. Beside him was Peter Clay, smiling, as if he were out for a pleasant morning ride. Next came four strangers, all with faces like stiff, bleached sandstone and eyes like ice—their very absence of expression betraying their unyielding characters. Then there was a man with head lowered and hands tied: his condition told its own story. Finally, at the far end, sat Theodore Roosevelt. His mouth was set in a stern line, but his eyes revealed the depth of his distress and disappointment. All these things Greg took in in an instant—a moment that seemed to capture time and hold it still—while the bees hummed softly in the warm, bright air.

Then the three newcomers came to a halt facing the others and Bryce blurted, "What the hell kind of game *is* this? What's going on here?" He turned in his saddle so he could see Stuart's tanned leathery face, his own expression reflecting his annoyance.

Stuart cleared his throat and surveyed the line of silent men. "It's rather a long story," he said.

Waving his hand casually, Greg replied, "Then let's hear it," although he thought he had already guessed its content.

"Well," Stuart rubbed his chin thoughtfully, as if he had not already rehearsed this speech three times in his head, "it all boils down to the fact that Mr. Goodall here and his associates set out to prove that your family was involved in the epidemic of rustling that's been plaguing Medora since the thieves left town last month. He had it figured that you arranged for Peter to find the list and warn the local rustlers so they'd scatter and leave the field open to you and Jake Maunders." He paused, squinting into the sun as if seeking inspiration. "You two must have laughed yourselves silly when you heard the people blaming Mores for that little episode."

When there was no immediate response, he continued. "Goodall thought that all he had to do was prove you were stealing your own cattle and having the thieves return them later. And we proved it today.

"A few nights ago, we got into an active camp with your friend Jake Maunders's assistance. By the way, he was killed in the struggle. I'm sure you'll mourn him, even if nobody else will. After we got in, we marked every one of those animals with white paint, just inside the right rear leg, where you have to look carefully to see it. And then we waited and followed those cattle from camp to camp until they were brought back here this morning just before dawn. Of course, some of the stolen livestock was taken up to Canada to be sold, but none of them bore the Pendleton brand. Just these six right here have that brand. And if you'd like to, you can check for yourselves to see that they also have our mark."

Greg and Bryce looked at each other for a long moment, their faces carefully blank. Then Greg nodded at the man whose hands were tied. "What about him?"

"He's our witness. He used to work for you through Maunders. I guess Jake figured no one could connect the operation with you if you didn't even know who was doing the job. But when this fellow here heard that Maunders was dead, he couldn't wait to give us all the details about how the operation worked. I'm afraid we've got you cold, Greg."

Greg's lips twitched briefly and his eyes glittered like heavy glass with the sun raking across it. For the second time, he examined the faces of the men who sat across from him. They seemed to be incapable of action just now; they were waiting. For what? he wondered. They couldn't really do anything to hurt the Pendletons. The family was too strong. No, it wasn't action they were waiting for. They had come to see the mighty Pendletons put in their places.

Not for a moment had Greg feared these men, but as he sat there with the sun pounding like a sledgehammer across his forehead and the knowledge that their eyes never left his face, he felt the first stirrings of anger. A deep, burning humiliation had lodged itself hungrily in his gut and begun to gnaw away at the little bit of wisdom and restraint that he still possessed. They couldn't do this to him. Then it struck him; what did he mean "they"? It was *she* who had planned this humiliation and waited for the moment and carried it out. As if she had known from the beginning what would hurt him the most. . . .

* * *

He had waited an hour and still she had not come. But he did not believe Marisa would leave him like this much longer. She would not dare. After all, it was *he* who was doing her a favor by agreeing to meet her here. She would come. Soon.

As he lay back, staring upward through the branches heavy with leaves, he saw her face above him—pale skin and merry black eyes in a halo of dark hair. He thought of her hands and how they had played across his back and shoulders, teasing him into desire, while she turned her head so that her lips were just out of reach. She had maddened him with magic fingertips, then pushed him away. But she had been wise enough to hold back his fury with her promise to meet him here beneath the oak just at dusk.

Two hours now and the anger in his chest had begun to throb. Perhaps, after all, she had never meant to come. But then he heard her voice in the shadows, rippling like the song of a brook across stones. She was here. She was coming. But he would make her pay for his long vigil, alone with only the whistling wind for company. He would force her to plead for forgiveness. He would—

She appeared like a wraith under the leaves and he saw with a jolt that she was not alone. Marisa faced the man with both his hands clasped in hers, leaning forward until their lips met in a long, hungry kiss. And only when their mouths had parted did she turn to look up at Greg's barely suppressed exclamation.

Through the gloom she saw him standing, his fists clenched at his sides, and her face transformed itself into that of a grinning cat about to pounce upon its prey. "Greg," she whispered, turning back to her companion, "I told him I would meet him here, but I forgot. You see, I felt your lips on mine and I forgot poor Greg completely. He has been waiting here alone for hours, but I didn't come." Smiling into her lover's eyes, she added, "Isn't it sad for him?"

Then the man leaned down to kiss her once again and, at the end, she raised her hand to Greg in an offhand gesture of farewell, disappearing into the darkness that had spawned her.

As Greg stood there, frozen with rage, the blood pounding wildly in his ears, he heard her laughing. Her laughter seemed to rise and meet the wind above her, echoing its mocking cry, until he was deaf with the sound of it. *And when, at last, the laughter had been sucked into the night, he swallowed twice and swore that no woman would make a fool of him again. . . .*

A pale white face ringed with thick red hair rose in his mind and the brilliant green eyes seemed to penetrate to the very center of his fury. It was Medora who had brought him here, and he would not forget.

"What are you going to do about it?" Bryce demanded suddenly. He was not really concerned; he knew what Stuart would say.

"Not much we *can* do. We can't prosecute; your influence would ensure that the case was thrown out of court before it ever got there. And we certainly can't string you up, which is, I suppose, what you counted on." Stuart paused and looked over at Roosevelt, a question gathered across his brow. "But I don't think the Pendletons are the kind of men we want in the Montana Cattlemen's Association. It'd probably be best if you let your membership lapse. Don't you agree, Ted?"

Roosevelt glanced at Greg and Bryce with just a trace of regret. "I agree. Seems like, if we let them stay, we'd be condoning this, and I just don't think we can afford to do that."

Stuart nodded grimly. "You see," he declared, "this whole little episode didn't cost you very much. Just the expense of traveling to meetings out of state, and maybe a friend or two. I don't know about you, but that price would be too high for me." He wheeled his horse and, one after another, the others followed. He stopped only once to call back over his shoulder, "I don't imagine I'll be seeing you again soon. Good-bye."

Then he rode away without a backward glance and left the

Pendletons sitting alone in the middle of the field—two time bombs ticking away the seconds until they exploded with the flames of ice-cold fury that consumed them.

Fragment of text in the margin of the Pendleton trap
woman in the passage behind him and she exclaimed, "there
like a man that has just escaped disaster"

NINETEEN

"Why in God's name didn't you tell me?" the Marquis demanded.

Medora faced her husband across the drawing room, astonished by the rage that darkened his face. "We thought it was best to keep it quiet."

"We thought!" he exploded. "It seems that everyone but me was aware of what you were doing. The Pendletons are *my* enemies too. Did you think I would try to stop you?"

"No. As a matter of fact, I knew you would want to be involved."

"And, of course, you couldn't risk that," he snapped bitterly. "I might have ruined it for you, is that it?"

"No," she repeated, crossing the room to where he stood. She put her hand on his arm and murmured, "Mores, you had a great deal on your mind with the business and the stagecoach line, and I didn't want to distract you just now. It was the business that needed your attention, not the Pendletons and their sordid little attempts to ruin us."

He shook her hand away, surveying her face for several seconds while he struggled to control his anger. "You didn't trust me," he said at last. "You had to do it behind my back. And maybe that's because you were only concerned with your own desire for revenge against Pendleton and not the welfare of this family. Maybe you wanted to do it alone because that way you didn't have to share the glory—or the satisfaction—with anyone else." He saw the mask of rigid anger drop like a curtain over her face, but he could not stop himself. She had done all she could to exclude him from her thoughts and problems and, this time, she had pushed him too far. "Or perhaps you have simply gotten out of the habit of sharing things with me. Especially where Greg is concerned."

Medora grasped the fabric of her skirt with stiff fingers while the color drained from her face, then came rushing back in a wave. She took a step backward, afraid that if she stayed too close to her husband she would strike him. She breathed deeply once, then twice. "You—" she began.

"She was only trying to help you!"

Both Mores and his wife looked up at Phillipe, who had come into the room unnoticed. He was poised like a cat ready to pounce and his eyes blazed with righteous indignation.

"Get out," the Marquis ordered stiffly. "This is not your concern."

"But it *is* my concern, because you're wrong. Medora didn't—"

"I don't think you're hearing well today," Mores said, a dangerous glint in his eyes. Taking two steps forward, he pointed toward the door. "I told you to go."

Phillipe stood his ground. He did not intend to back down now. "I have something to say and I'm going to say it. I just want to help you, as Medora does."

"I don't need your assistance, Phillipe," his father snapped. "I'm quite capable of handling my own problems, which, if you don't leave this room at once, you're going to discover— to your chagrin." The Marquis was barely breathing, so rigid was his anger, and his eyes had become deep pools of black stone.

Biting his lip, Phillipe glanced quickly at Medora, who nodded toward the door, and he could see that she was right. All at once, Cassie's warning flashed through his mind. *You see what happens when you push a person too far: his temper takes over and sometimes it wipes his conscience out entirely.* This was not the time, he realized. Not yet. Spinning on his heel, he walked away. But he could not resist turning back for one last word from the safety of the doorway. "Do you know what I think? I think you don't let anyone help you because you can't. That would be like admitting to yourself that you're not some kind of god after all, and you couldn't do that. Your world would fall apart." And then the boy ran.

The Marquis stood frozen for an instant, clenching and unclenching his hands like a piece of defective machinery, before he started forward.

"Mores!" Medora cried warningly as she dug her fingers into his arm. "Let him go!"

He peered at her blindly while his vision came and went in jolting waves.

"Please!"

And then, somehow, his sanity returned. Perhaps it was the painful pressure of her fingers on his arm or the pleading note in her voice. Perhaps it was the flicker of some deeply hidden instinct that warned him not to destroy his relationship with his only son permanently by any act of madness. Or perhaps it was because, somewhere in the far reaches of his mind, the Marquis knew that Phillipe was right. Mores let the rage drain slowly from his body, then he sat down in the wing-backed chair and buried his head in his hands.

Medora stood watching him uncertainly, knowing that just now she could not touch him and aware that, somehow, withholding the knowledge of the Pendleton raid had hurt him as deeply as her original betrayal with her body.

"Mores!" William came into the room unexpectedly, waving two yellow telegram forms in the air. "I have to talk to you."

The Marquis raised his head unwillingly and glowered at the secretary. "Not now. I can't think just now."

William shook his head. "You have to. I just received two extremely distressing messages, and I'm afraid you must act at once."

Perceiving that her husband did not intend to respond immediately, Medora asked, "What's happened?"

"For one thing, the government mail contract they promised us has just been given to the town of Pierre."

"What?" All at once Mores was on his feet. "How can they do that?"

"They did it, that's all. They know there's nothing you can do about it."

"But the stagecoach line—"

"—will die a natural death. As I said, there's nothing you can do."

The Marquis dragged in a ragged breath, then cried, "Yes there is. I'll find something. That line will survive if I have to hand feed it for the next year."

With a sigh, William continued doggedly. "Also, another carload of meat arrived in Chicago—rotten."

Mores closed his eyes, but his expression spoke volumes.

"It seems the men you hired to staff the icehouses along the route have not been showing up for work," William explained.

"But why?" Medora gasped.

"Because someone paid them not to. I think the only solution is for the Marquis to go out there, hire a new batch, and maybe pay them a little more this time. At any rate, I know the problem won't be solved without your presence, Mores. They need to know you still exist."

The Marquis nodded somewhat numbly. "I'll leave late this afternoon," he said, "but there's something I have to do first." As he passed Van Driesche, he laid a comforting hand on his old friend's shoulder. "Don't worry, William," he said. "We'll beat them yet. It just may take us a little longer than we thought, that's all."

The air was so still that Medora was startled when a magpie took to the sky with the flapping of wings and a piercing cry. She guided her horse at a leisurely pace toward the canyons north of town, enjoying the tranquility of midday and the broad sweep of blue sky overhead. At the moment, she did not care where she was going; she merely wanted to escape the stuffy house and its troubled occupants. She wanted to feel the hot sun beating down on her face and the sweat that had begun to bead beneath the collar of her blouse.

Tilting her head back, Medora closed her eyes and let the

sun find its way into every plane of her face. She delighted in the heat that pulsed through her skin and the sweat that stood across her forehead, even though she knew that this prolonged exposure would burn her fair skin. Because she also knew she would welcome the physical discomfort; at least she would know she was feeling something—anything besides depression and frustration and hopelessness. The tall brooding rock pillars that surrounded her gave her a sense of strength and security. They were ancient, sturdy, and unbreakable, and only the winds of a thousand years could wear them slowly away. Somehow it was a comforting thought.

Although she tried to fix her attention on the bands of mellow color that wove like endless ribbons along the cliffs and valleys, her thoughts kept returning to the Marquis. She loved her husband, Medora told herself, but he was such a fool. Even now he would not admit the kind of adversary he was up against. Even now he would not see that no trick was too cruel or destructive, so long as it achieved the Pendletons' purpose. Even now he did not recognize that he was fighting a losing battle against an enemy who had no moral regrets or crippling human feelings.

And Mores would pay for his blindness, in time. They all would. All except the Pendletons—especially Greg. He would never really pay for anything he had done. Greg would succeed, despite her efforts.

It was only when she paused again to listen to the stillness hovering over the Badlands that she heard the regular clip-clop of a horse behind her. For a moment, she did not turn to see who was following her; she did not want to know. She was here alone, surrounded only by mute towers of solid stone, and they offered little protection should her pursuer be the man she feared. But then, finally, she turned to see him coming inexorably forward, his eyes fixed on her face. It was Pendleton. Of course.

She did not want to see him—not here and now, perhaps not ever. Someone had tried to take her life, and only Greg would have profited from such an attempt. *Whatever your absurd little plan is, I shall find a way to stop it. You have given me no choice.* Now he knew about the plan and she had won.

Kicking her horse with grim determination, she guided it down to a long stretch of valley, urging the animal forward with her breath held back in her throat. She leaned down, clutching the pommel with damp fingers, and recognized the sound of resolute pursuit. The hooves thrummed over the sandstone rhythmically, but she was not lulled into false security by the regular hum.

Medora's body had begun to sweat steadily and she knew that the horse must be equally uncomfortable, but she did not let him slow his pace. Welcoming the rush of dry air against her ears, she fled with every ounce of will focused on escaping an encounter with this man. Yet she knew, even as she urged the animal to go more rapidly, that she could not escape. He would catch her and she would be helpless, just as she had been before.

Finally, when she saw the striped sandstone rising sharply before her, she had to allow the horse to slacken its pace and then to stop. Glancing around in despair, she saw that she had ridden herself into the wrong end of a stone prison. Pendleton was blocking the only exit. Before she could even gather her thoughts enough to panic, he was beside her, grasping her horse's bridle in his hand.

"You're the victor today, my dear," he breathed hoarsely, "so why are you running?"

She could not read his eyes, which were smoky gray—the color of the stone cliffs at night. "Because I want nothing to do with you."

Then, amazingly, he smiled, though a bit stiffly. "You may have won this round, Medora, but if you keep lying to yourself—and to me—you'll surely lose the others." He leaned toward her and she saw how his shirt clung to his wet skin in patches. "And there *will* be others."

When she did not answer, he considered her flushed face, beaded with sweat, and the rigid line of her mouth as she looked away. "You didn't think you had actually beaten me, did you?" he asked incredulously. Then he shook his head. "No," he said, *"you* could not have been so foolish."

Medora forced herself to breathe regularly. She must not let him see that she had been afraid, even for a moment. It was too great a risk. "I must have had you frightened for a while," she replied smoothly, "or you wouldn't have tried to kill me."

"What?" His eyes opened wide while the color crept out of his face, a drop at a time. "What kind of nonsense are you talking? *Kill* you?"

Disturbed by the pallor of his skin and the look of stark disbelief in his eyes, she wondered, for the first time, if perhaps he did not know. "Yes," she said simply. "There were witnesses, but no one saw the assailant, of course. Although we rather thought it might have been Maunders, working under your orders."

Greg scrutinized her face, searching for some sign that she was lying, and she realized that, for the first time since she had known him, he was visibly shaken.

"What happened?" he demanded.

Puzzled by his response, she nevertheless told him the details, all of them, leaving out not a single bruise or ache. When she had finished, he looked away for a long time—so long, in fact, that she thought he had forgotten her existence.

"It must have been Maunders working on his own initiative," he murmured at last, speaking to the lifeless stone. "I swear to you I never ordered him to kill you or even to frighten you. Never." There was another long moment of silence and then he turned to face her. Twitching his lips into a forced smile, he said, "The game would hardly be any fun without one of the key opponents, after all."

She saw that he was trying to ease the tension between them—apparently her revelation had truly shocked him—but she was not willing to let him do it. "My husband is your major opponent, not me."

Greg shook his head. "He *should* be, my dear, but we both know he isn't. *You're* the one who will try to best me, time and again, and that's because you're the only one with any chance of winning. Unfortunately, you'll lose, time and again, because you won't be able to help yourself."

Medora knew that he was right about everything—and she realized with dismay that she admired him for his perceptions and his perpetual razor-sharp wit. He was a man who knew what he wanted and, more important, he knew how to get it. When he leaned toward her, his hand closing firmly over her hands, she tried to pull free, but his grip was painfully tight. She knew he was her enemy, her husband's greatest adversary—a man without a heart. Medora turned away. Suddenly his touch was like ice—cold and empty. She knew now that to have courage and wit without human warmth was worse than having nothing at all. "I'm sorry, Greg," she said, "but I have no more to give."

Mores had been walking for over an hour, hoping the tension in his muscles would ease a little. When he had realized that he would have to leave the Badlands this afternoon, he had vowed to see Ileya again before he went.

But first he had walked because he did not want her to see him in his present distracted state of mind. He did not want to go to her thinking of Medora and Phillipe and his own anger and hurt. The business he did not think about at all; that would work itself out. And now, finally, the muscles along the back of his neck began to relax, and when the wind came up unexpectedly, he let it run over him like a rush of warm water, easing the taut stiffness of his body. Suddenly, the deathly stillness of the afternoon was broken, shattered like a thousand fragments of fragile glass, swept away by a single shrieking breath of wind.

The Marquis turned his steps toward the river, drawn inexorably by the sound of the water Ileya loved, but when he reached the edge of the clearing where her hut stood, he paused, listening to the wind overhead. He was glad these gusts had come to brush away the silence—the absence of sound and motion had become oppressive to him. But now it did not matter, because he would see Ileya. He would see

her and the hush would become a blessing and the stillness
a kind of magic.

He went forward and pushed the swinging door inward.
Then, all at once, it was as it had been before. Everything
was gone—her flowers, her dried leaves, even the subtle fragrance of her body. The hut was empty, as were the clearing
and the singing, rushing river. He knew then that she was
gone—again—and it was as if she had taken with her the
very soul of the water and the trees and the moaning
wind. . . .

*The room was sterile now—he felt it when he crossed the
threshold—sterile and cold and hopelessly ordinary.* It was
only then that he began to believe that Nicole had left him
and that she did not mean to come back. If she had planned
to return, she would not have taken the very heart from this
room as she had done—not just her possessions, but her
moods, her laughter, the scent of her hair. He knew instinctively that Nicole could not exist in a room such as this; she
was too warm, too sensuous, too vital to live in the midst of
so much barrenness. With a single sweep of her beringed
hand, she had made this room—this world—a wasteland.

He ran his hand across the blank face of the bureau where
her brushes and perfumes used to lie. Like everything else,
it was cold and empty. The bed had not been slept in. It stood
there like an accusation, too neatly made, without a wrinkle
to mar its placid surface. The walls, the curtains, even the
rug beneath his feet had lost their magic and the warm, soft
blues had faded to indeterminate gray. His breath dried in his
throat and lodged there, but he did not try to force it upward.
And then he saw that he had been wrong; she had not taken
everything after all. There, on the tiny bedside table, dark and
somehow forlorn against the cold marble top, lay the silver
music box.

He knew she had left it there for him, a sign, perhaps, that
she had not forgotten their past completely. She had taken
everything else and left him this one gift, but even it was

only a memory. *With fingers that were strangely steady, he lifted the ornate lid, closing his eyes as the song that had been trapped within came rushing out in a wave of tinkling notes—free and lovely and absolutely alien. . . .*

The voice of the wind was the voice of a stranger, and Mores turned away from the doorway, his feelings oddly numbed. Ileya was gone and she had known she would be going, he saw that now. Her song had, after all, been a message of farewell.

"She had to go, you know."

The Marquis whirled to find Johnny Goodall watching him with concern. How long had the man been there? he wondered. And how could he know what Mores was thinking? Perhaps it showed in his face.

It did not occur to him that Johnny himself had known the same compelling, enchanting communion with another Indian girl a long, long time ago, and that he knew, as perhaps no one else did, what it meant to lose that momentary magic. Coming to stand beside his employer, Goodall explained, "It was Ileya who discovered the Pendletons' secret and revealed it to me. She made it possible for us to catch them in their tricks, and she knew they were looking for her. She had to go."

Mores considered Johnny thoughtfully. "But how could she know what they were up to?"

"She wandered at night. Perhaps you didn't know that. Several times she saw the rustlers working, both at taking the cattle away and bringing them back. She realized what they were doing and came to me. I don't know how, but I think they know she was the one who betrayed them."

The Marquis took a deep breath, glancing back at the empty hut. "She won't be coming back, will she?"

Frowning, Johnny muttered, "Not if she values her life."

With a curt nod at his companion, Mores turned toward the river. Perhaps, after all, if he stood in the places where she had stood, he could recapture her, if only for a moment.

And as he ducked beneath the cool, waving branches, the water seemed to take up his thought, murmuring,

> *Friend,*
> *Whenever you pursue any course,*
> *Friend,*
> *May I be there.*

PART IV

THE BADLANDS, SPRING OF 1885

TWENTY

Phillipe smiled and waved when he saw Katherine coming toward him. He was hoping her presence would distract him from his worries.

"It's so warm today," she said, linking her arm with his, "that I've thought of something marvelous for us to do."

"I'll bet," he groaned. "What is it this time?"

Katherine glanced up at him, smiling mysteriously. "You'll see."

Looking down into her sparkling eyes, Phillipe realized all at once how much he had missed her. It had been a long, dull winter in New York with the Von Hoffmans, despite the constant problems with the butchers that had occupied the Marquis, and Phillipe had been glad to get back to the Badlands. He and Medora and William had been here two weeks now, waiting for Mores to join them. His father had had to stay back East to try to settle, once and for all, the problems the butchers were making for the N.P.R.C.C.

Phillipe had seen Katherine twice since his return, but it was only now, when the Marquis's problems had threatened to drag him into a morbid depression, that he recognized how much he enjoyed these interludes with the girl. Locking his fingers with hers, he stepped in front of her, demanding, "Did you miss me over the winter?"

Katherine grinned and shrugged noncommittally. "The time passed quickly enough. You aren't the only boy in the Dakotas capable of entertaining me."

Her reply was sharp, but he knew she was only keeping up the facade. She could hardly admit that she was fond of him; that would make her vulnerable. And as long as the game continued between them, he knew she would never willingly do that. "Don't tell me—let me guess," he said, raising his eyebrows in mock dismay. "You've fallen in love with Peter Clay!"

Katherine snorted in disgust and pushed him away. "You're horrid, and terribly arrogant besides."

Grasping both her hands in his, he replied, "And that, my dear Kathy, is precisely why you're so enchanted with me."

She considered him for a moment, as if she couldn't decide whether or not to be angry—then she laughed. It was too lovely an April day to spend it fighting. "So you keep telling me, anyway," she retorted. "If you say it often enough, I may come to believe you, in time."

Her smile was brief and her eyes veiled. Phillipe realized that she loved tormenting him too much to give it up just because the sun was warm, the flowers were blooming, and her hand fit so perfectly into his. He leaned forward to kiss her, but she turned away and started toward the river.

"Come on," she said, tossing an inviting smile over her shoulder, her dark eyes smoldering with promises.

Phillipe followed her willingly, curious about what she was planning and lulled into compliance by the whisper of the wind through the cottonwoods and the babbling of the river at his side. One thing about Katherine's surprises, he thought—they were never dull.

Ten minutes later, she ducked under some low-hanging branches and drew him into a tiny shadowed clearing that the trees hugged tightly, their new leaves forming a protective canopy overhead.

"Here it is," Katherine announced, waving a hand to indicate the deep pool that lay at the heart of the clearing.

Phillipe eyed her suspiciously. "What are we going to do with it?"

"Why, swim, of course. Don't you think it's a perfect day for it?"

"But we didn't bring suits."

Katherine swayed forward to run her hand across his chest. "Would you mind terribly doing without them? The water may still be cold, but I'm sure we can manage to keep warm somehow." She traced the outline of her lips with a languorous movement of her tongue.

"I believe you *did* miss me," he told her, grinning.

Katherine did not bother to respond. She was already unfastening the buttons on her dress. Without further delay, Phillipe followed her lead, and he was diving into the water before she had begun to remove her underclothing.

"Christ!" he shouted, shaking the water out of his eyes. "You could freeze a whole beef in here and it would never know what hit it."

Tossing her chemise on the ground, Katherine plunged in beside him, laughing when his arms closed around her. For a moment, they huddled together, shivering, and then she brushed his lips with hers, murmuring, "I'll race you across and back three times. That should get the blood flowing."

Before he could protest, she had pushed herself away from him and was swimming briskly through the chilled water. Unable to resist any challenge that she flung him, Phillipe stretched out his body and began to stroke vigorously. The water seemed to wrap him in cold fluid fingers, but he concentrated on increasing his speed rather than on the goosebumps that rose along his neck. He could feel Katherine nearby, her feet kicking up an explosion of icy water, but he did not look over to admire her naked body. That, he knew, would come later. Just now the race was all that mattered. With Katherine it was always so: the challenge, the competition, the victory—and only then would she allow herself to surrender.

But this time, neither was the winner. They both reached at the same time for the gnarled old root that marked the edge of the pool, and they clung there, laughing, facing each other with the heavy root between them.

Phillipe swallowed huge gulps of air in an effort to regain

his wind, then spluttered, "So we're evenly matched for the first time."

Katherine shook the dripping hair away from her face and covered one of Phillipe's hands with her own. "Not for the *first* time," she replied, her voice husky. "There have been others." She smiled sweetly, exposing her even white teeth, while her fingers began to trace a sensuous pattern on the back of his hand.

He did not need to answer. Moving as if of one accord, they made their way back across the pool to the grassy knoll on the far side. Rising out of the water, they collapsed onto the grass with their arms wrapped firmly about each other's waists. The water rolled from them in rivulets, making a puddle in the soft ground beneath them, but Phillipe and Katherine did not notice. Their attention was focused upon the slippery touch of skin against skin and the warmth that willing hands drew like magic from shivering limbs.

Phillipe felt the cold, wet limpness of her hair, which had fallen across his shoulder, and he brushed it aside, running his fingers through the long, dripping strands. He thought Katherine was lovely with the drops of water sprinkled across her cheeks and forehead, and her lips were moist and supple and inviting. Lowering his mouth to hers, he buried his hands in her hair just as her palms began to massage his lower back—rhythmically, sensuously. "Kathy," he whispered against her lips, "you had better be careful. I think I'm falling in love with you."

Laughing, her hands warm on his back, her breath sweet on his face, she answered, "What's taken you so long?"

Later, when the passion had raged itself into silence, they lay side by side on the grass with the cool, caressing patterns of the leaves on their skin. Propping herself on her elbow, Katherine contemplated the smooth, relaxed lines of Phillipe's face. His eyes were closed, the brown lashes resting on his cheeks, and his lips were curved into a delightfully satisfied smile. Somehow, she thought, he had become even more handsome over the long winter. Perhaps it was because he was older, but she did not think so. She suspected that she herself was seeing him differently. Was she falling in love with *him* too? She hoped not. Love—as she had learned from observing her mother's obsessive affection for Katherine's father—was a debilitating disease; it made one into a hopeless simpleton without pride or self-esteem. Clenching her teeth, Katherine promised that that would never happen to her. Never.

"I thought your father was coming home today," she said at last, attempting to redirect her thoughts. "Why didn't you stay there to greet him?"

Phillipe stirred slightly but did not open his eyes; even so, the shadow that touched his features was plainly visible. "I didn't want to be there when he heard the news," he mumbled, brushing the question away as if intent on ridding himself of an annoying insect.

Pursing her lips thoughtfully, she tried to stop herself from asking the question that rose in her throat, but she was unsuccessful. "Trouble?" she inquired, unable to disguise her curiosity.

Phillipe opened his eyes at the hopeful note in her voice. He could tell that she had tried to hide it but had failed. "You promised, Katherine," he reminded her, "that we'd be friends without our families hanging like swords above our heads. It's supposed to be just you and me, not the Pendletons and the Vallombrosas."

"You don't want to tell me," she accused. "It must be important."

Biting his lip to keep from snarling at her, Phillipe turned away in disgust. He should have known it wouldn't work. Katherine simply could not separate their friendship from her loyalty to her family. Their personal competition had somehow become hopelessly intertwined with the struggle between the families. He supposed he had always known it would be this way. With her there was always that touch of self-interest to come between them, and he knew without a doubt that it would be there forever. She couldn't destroy it no matter how much she tried. She could never deny her Pendleton blood.

Unfortunately, there was no one else he could turn to. It

was hopeless; everywhere he turned, life was a competition with desperate rules and no restrictions. Only Cassie was really his friend. And, sometimes—when she forgot who he was—Medora.

Katherine recognized Phillipe's disappointment and she realized that she did not want to lose him altogether. Not this afternoon, when they had come so close to forgetting the obstacles that came between them. Not now, when his blue eyes were so deep and glowing and the cleft in his chin so incredibly attractive. "I'm sorry," she said, brushing his arm tentatively. "I won't ask again."

When he turned back to her, attempting to hide the hopeful flame that flashed in his eyes, she decided to distract him from his own distressing thoughts. "We'd better go soon," she said. "If we lie here naked long enough we might get attacked by the mountain lion that's been harrying the ranchers lately. I hear he's been seen several times by the river."

Taking his cue from her light tone, he replied, "You seem to like the idea, but I'm sorry to inform you that he's mostly interested in horses and cattle, not soft young ladies."

"Still," she said, "it would be exciting to see him close up, just once, don't you think? He must be huge to do as much damage as he has. Do you think you'll go on the hunt when they look for him?" Her eyes misted over with the thought of the hunt and she licked her lips unconsciously.

Phillipe smiled at her enthusiasm and lack of fear. "I'll be there," he told her. "I wouldn't want to miss all the action."

She lay back down, flinging her hair over her shoulders so that it spread above her head in thick, damp waves. "You never do," she murmured. But her mind was not on Phillipe; instead, her thoughts were occupied with trying to guess what news could be so disastrous that Phillipe did not dare to be around when his father heard it.

"He can't *do* this to me!" the Marquis shouted, striking the mantel with a clenched fist.

Medora glanced furtively at William, asking silently for his assistance, before she said, "I'm afraid he can, and what's more, I'm fairly certain he will."

Mores shook his head in disbelief. It simply couldn't be true. He had spent so much time this winter negotiating with the butchers and Swift, patching up the aspects of the N.P.R.C.C. that had begun to sag with their own cumbersome weight, and attempting—successfully, in the end—to breathe life back into the dying body of his meat-packing empire. And now, just when he had begun to think that his efforts would bear fruit, he had come home to find that his father-in-law had betrayed him after all.

Apparently, Von Hoffman had known that Mores would be tied up in New York for at least a couple of weeks, and he had taken the opportunity to make a tour of inspection at all the various offices of the Marquis's business connections. Von Hoffman had waited, purposely, until his son-in-law was occupied elsewhere and then he had moved ruthlessly through the commercial empire looking for inefficiencies, waste, and flaws in the operations. Now, having completed his little tour, he had left for New York again, but not before informing his daughter that he intended to withdraw his money from over half the Marquis's interests. He was tired of pouring money down a bottomless hole, he had informed her, and he simply refused to do it any longer.

With an effort at controlling the despair that swept over him at Medora's news, the Marquis managed to choke out, "What is he thinking of?"

This time it was William who answered. "Von Hoffman said practically everyone knows that the business is in trouble. He's already read several reports of our failure in major newspapers."

Mores winced, burying his hands in his pockets. That much was true enough, he thought, feeling the folded newsprint beneath his fingers. He had seen the accounts himself, all the way back from New York, but he had thought his present agreement with the butchers would have stopped any further rumors. With a narrow look at Medora, he swallowed and began to pace restlessly. Unfortunately, the reporters had not been satisfied with speculations about business failures only; they had assumed that the Marquis was beset with personal failures as well. The sad part was, they were right.

But that was no excuse for Von Hoffman's secretive behavior and his callous manner of stabbing his business partner in the back. Why couldn't the man have told Mores what he was up to? Why do all this when his son-in-law's head was turned? It seemed the Marquis could never get away from this kind of betrayal. Everywhere he turned, there was someone waiting behind him. Everywhere he looked, there was another enemy to be thwarted. Everywhere—even in his own home he was not safe. "Well," he said stiffly, "I can only hope he changes his mind. In the meantime, we'll just have to make the best of our resources."

Medora suppressed a sigh of relief. "I'm glad you're finally willing to face the facts."

Glaring at her suspiciously, Mores muttered, "Don't assume that this means I'm giving up, my dear. And as for facing the facts, I can hardly help but do so when every newspaper in the territory is screaming them at me." At her perplexed expression he took several deep breaths, then withdrew his hand from his pocket. "By the way, I thought you might be interested in this little article from the Bismarck *Tribune*. That is, if you haven't seen it already."

Tossing the newspaper clipping at her, he stood watching as her eyes skimmed over the brief story. He knew it by heart, so he was not surprised at her sharp intake of breath or the way every drop of color left her fair skin.

CRUMBLING EMPIRE LEADS TO DISINTEGRATION OF MARRIAGE, the headline read. Then:

> *Tribune* reporters learned today that the Marquise de Mores, wife of the meat-packing king from the Dakota Badlands, plans to sue her husband for divorce within the next two months. It is expected that the Marquis will absent himself from the proceedings by participating in a year-long tiger hunt in India.
>
> Those who know the couple are little surprised that

Louis Von Hoffman's daughter should choose to disassociate herself from her husband's numerous failing business projects. Clearly these financial disappointments have taken their toll on the once romantic pair who set this territory on its ear but two years ago.

Medora looked up to meet her husband's piercing black gaze. "It's not true, of course," she told him.

"Of course not. But I can't help wondering where they got the idea. These reporters don't usually conjure their stories out of the air."

"Mores," she said, rising to face him, her eyes blazing emerald sparks, "are you suggesting that I—"

"I'm merely suggesting that whatever problems may exist between us, we keep them to ourselves, rather than allowing the jackals out there to feed off our indiscretions."

Clearing his throat nervously, William slipped out of the room, but the Marquis was hardly conscious of his departure. Mores's attention was focused on his wife, who gazed at him in astonishment, her green eyes wide with disbelief.

"You can't really think that I told them this, can you?" she whispered, indicating the tiny piece of newsprint.

At the bewildered tone of her voice and the stunned expression on her face, he suddenly came to his senses. What was he doing, anyway, taking out his disappointment and fury for Von Hoffman on Medora? None of this had been her doing, after all. "I'm sorry," he said. "I'm afraid my judgment has not been very clear of late. Of course I know you had nothing to do with this. It's just that your father's actions have been rather a shock for me. Perhaps you can understand that."

"I understand," she said stiffly.

Mores's brows came together in a frown and he reached out to touch her shoulder lightly. "I suppose that's all I can ask just now."

Despite herself, Medora felt a flash of pity for this man who had already borne so much. He might have turned on her long ago, but he had never done so—not even when he saw with his own eyes the evidence of her betrayal. It was not surprising that he had spoken cruelly to her a moment ago. What *was* surprising was that he had waited so long. She took the hand on her shoulder and kissed the palm. "You could have asked a great deal more, I think, but you didn't," she told him. "Let's forget this afternoon, shall we, and start over again?"

He smiled and nodded, but he knew that his acquiescence was a lie. They could not start over; they had already gone too far along their chosen path. In that one respect, at least, the Pendletons had won.

The Marquis found William waiting on the porch, staring blankly at the sloping ground before him. "I'm sorry you had to witness that little scene, really I am, but I seem to have lost a great deal of my ability to conceal my feelings of late."

Van Driesche nodded without looking up, and Mores realized that there was no point in pressing the issue further. He had made his apology; it was up to William to decide whether or not he would accept it. "Where's Goodall?" the Marquis asked, having decided to change the subject. "I'd like to speak to him."

William hesitated for a moment, then turned to face his employer. "I don't know where he is."

"What do you mean?"

Running his hand across his forehead, Van Driesche explained, "About four days ago he got a letter of some sort. I don't even know from where. It seemed to upset him a great deal. The next thing I knew, he was asking for a week off to take care of some personal business, and then he disappeared. I haven't seen him since."

"Didn't you ask what was bothering him?"

"I did, but he refused to answer. Just said he'd be back in a week." William squinted into the blazing sun of late afternoon, his eyes reflecting his concern. "I've never seen Johnny looking so distressed, Mores, and it disturbed me more than I like to admit. He's usually so stable and self-possessed."

"Not always," the Marquis muttered, remembering the look

of surprise that had crossed Goodall's face the first time he had seen Ileya. "I've always thought that Johnny was hiding something from us. Almost as if his personal life was too private for him to share." With a sigh, Mores pushed his hands into his pockets and turned to look at the river that rushed by far beneath him. He could hardly conceive of any more problems just now—he already had enough to last a lifetime—but he sensed that Johnny's absence meant trouble.

Cory Pendleton jabbed the knitting needle viciously into the center of her ball of yarn. Pushing the half-finished sweater off her lap with an impatient hand, she glowered at her husband from beneath pale blonde lashes. "Have you seen her yet?" she demanded. The suspense of wondering had finally become too much for her. She had bitten her lip a hundred times in the past few days to keep herself from asking him, but she found that she could not wait any longer.

"Who?" Greg asked, glancing up at her in surprise.

"You know who. *Her.* She's been back for two weeks. Have you seen her?" Her fingers played nervously among the folds of her skirt while she waited for his answer, her heart thrumming wildly against her chest.

"If you mean Madame la Marquise, no, I haven't seen her. But you could pay her a visit if you like."

Cory spluttered out an incoherent response and began to laugh hoarsely. "I wouldn't see her of my own free will if I had the only antidote to a deadly poison she was dying of. Pay her a visit indeed!"

Narrowing his eyes in distaste, Greg noticed how, with the bright hot afternoon sun illuminating her features like an unwelcome revelation, his wife's face had suddenly become distorted into that of a stranger. Her flushed cheeks seemed to stretch into long, hollow valleys and her pale blue eyes gleamed like the eyes of a madman. Drawing in his breath at the unexpected transformation, Greg closed his eyes for a moment; when he opened them, she was merely Cory again.

And probably comparing herself to Medora at this very

moment, he thought. What a fool his wife was. When Medora was in the room, Cory did not exist. It was is if Medora absorbed all the light and energy into herself, leaving none for any other woman. It was that very energy—her inner light—that had drawn him to her from the first. She could never be ordinary; it was against her nature. Medora, he thought, repeating the name silently again and again. It had been nearly six months since he had seen her face. Too long. Far too long.

"Greg, could I speak to you for a moment?"

Bryce's sharp voice cut into his thoughts, wrenching Greg back to the present and the reality of his jealous wife who watched him like a wildcat intent on protecting her mate from his own inevitable destruction. At the moment, her claws were hidden, but he knew they were there. She was only waiting until the time was right to pounce. Shaking his head to free himself of his morbid fancies, Greg rose to follow his father from the room.

As he reached the doorway, Cory called after him, "I won't go visit her, do you hear? I won't!"

"Of course not, my dear. You needn't go if you'd rather not." Closing the door behind him, he rolled his eyes when Bryce met his gaze with a silent question. "I do believe she's mad," Greg whispered.

Bryce shrugged. "I sometimes wonder how she managed to bear a child like Katherine." When they entered the study he kicked the door shut and turned to face his son. "But I didn't bring you here to discuss Cory's eccentricities."

Seating himself on the edge of the desk, Greg swung one leg negligently forward and backward. "What is it then?"

"The Marquis is back," Bryce informed his son, "and want to know what we're going to do about it." He did no sit down but paced restlessly before the cold black fireplace his forehead creased in concentration.

"Von Hoffman is withdrawing half his financial backing isn't he?"

"He is."

"Well, I should think that would be sufficient to break th

Frenchman's spirit. He can't last very long without money, you know."

Bryce shook his head. "If you can say that, you haven't yet learned to know Mores. He's the kind of man who thrives on problems—the more you make for him, the harder he pushes forward. I'm warning you, that man won't give in until we've broken his back in three places and stolen his crutches besides."

Peering at his father curiously, Greg asked, "Then what are you thinking we should do?"

"Well, my mind's been coming back again and again to poor Riley Luffsey and his premature death at Mores's hands."

"Come on," Greg snorted, "that was two years ago. What would be the point of bringing it up again?"

"The point, my unperceptive son, is that a lot of the townspeople are like me: they haven't forgotten Riley's murder. And just at the moment, they're scared half to death by the rumors of the collapse of Mores's empire. That means that they're dredging up old memories, old hatreds, old resentments. People who live in the Badlands can harbor a grudge for a long, long time, Greg. And you know as well as I do that they never forget. Never." Leaning against the cool stone of the fireplace, Bryce grinned and shoved his hands into his pockets. "The Marquis is just about to learn that particular lesson," he added smugly, "the *hard* way!"

"Excuse me, but could I talk to you for a minute?"

Medora and the Marquis glanced up in surprise when Goodall appeared unexpectedly in the doorway to the study.

"Come in," Mores offered, indicating a chair. "I thought you were still out of town."

"Just got back," Johnny replied as he entered the room.

Neither Medora nor her husband gave the slightest outward sign of their surprise, but both were shocked by the changes in Johnny since they had seen him last. The man seemed to have aged ten years. The furrows in his grayish skin were deeper and more numerous, and his eyes were shadowed with the signs of some inner torment. Even his sandy hair was turning white. For the first time since the Marquis had known him, Goodall looked uncertain, even confused. He took the chair Mores had offered and sat for a moment, running his hands around the edge of his hat brim. It was several seconds before he finally looked up, cleared his throat, and said, "I have a problem and I need your help, if you'll give it."

"We will if we can," the Marquis assured him. "You've certainly done enough for us."

"The thing is," Johnny began, rising with his hat still clutched in his hands. "I was married once, a long time ago, to a Sioux Indian girl named Kiwani." Better to plunge right in, he told himself. "And she went off after the battle of Little Bighorn to try and find her missing brothers." He paused, drawing a deep breath. "She never came back."

"I'm sorry, Johnny." This time it was Medora who offered him sympathy, but that was not what he wanted.

"It was a long time ago," he repeated. "Anyway, she left me with a young daughter, Mianne. Kiwani asked that the girl be raised by her Indian relatives if anything should happen to her, and Mianne has been living at the Standing Rock Reservation ever since." Now that he had started, he did not want to stop until he was through. "Until now. I got a letter last week informing me that the last of the girl's aunts had died and that Mianne seemed"—he swallowed once, licking his lips uneasily—"unhappy. So I went to get her and brought her back here. I didn't know what else to do." He turned then to see their expressions and was reassured by the concern in their eyes.

"Of course you brought her here," Mores said. "She should be with her father."

Goodall nodded dumbly. "When I first saw her I was stunned. She isn't the same girl I left there six years ago." He shook his head, obviously still dismayed by the transformation that had taken place in his daughter. "I brought her back with me, but I don't know what to do with her now. She's—a difficult child."

"How old is she?" Medora asked, sensing that it was safe to interrupt.

"Fourteen, I think." Johnny looked at Medora and his eyes were dark with pleading. "I was wondering if maybe you could take her in hand, ma'am, just for the time being, until she settles down a little and gets used to living off the reservation. I wouldn't even know where to start, myself."

The Marquis exchanged a long look with his wife and then both nodded at once. "I'd be happy to, Johnny. As Mores said, you've done us enough favors in the past."

Goodall shifted uneasily from one foot to the other. "That may be, ma'am, but I don't think you quite understand about Mianne. She's wild, undisciplined, and very unhappy. I imagine she'll be quite a handful."

This time the message that passed between Medora and her husband was unmistakable. They were thinking of Phillipe.

"We have had some experience with children of that kind," Mores told him. "I think we can probably manage another."

"But you don't—"

At that precise moment, as if in response to her father's unfinished explanation, Mianne Goodall erupted from the kitchen, shrieking madly. Cassie was close behind her, but she could not catch the girl, who had learned the intricacies of escape almost before she learned to talk. Mianne stormed through the dining room, intent on leaving the cook behind, until she saw the three people standing in shocked silence in the drawing room. Then she paused, her eyes flicking quickly over the little scene, and crouched before her father. It was then that she drew the gleaming butcher knife from among the folds of her skirt, raising it threateningly above her head.

Medora gaped at the girl, stunned, despite all of Johnny's warnings, at the picture she made crouching there like a lion ready to pounce. Her long, thick hair was braided tightly on one side, but the other braid had come loose. The freed hair hung in tangled disarray across Mianne's shoulder and the strands were full of leaves and twigs, as if the girl had rolled over and over on the ground. Her face was covered with a layer of dirt so thick that her features were nearly indistinguishable and her fingernails were edged in heavy black. One arm of her blouse had been torn off entirely and the other had broken through at the elbow, while her plain skirt had been ripped down one aide from her hip to her ankles. Even from where she stood, Medora could see that Mianne's feet were bare and, from their color, she guessed that they had been uncovered for some time.

It took a moment for the astonishment to wear off; then Mores began to move forward slowly, his eyes fixed on the blade of the knife that hovered now just inches from Johnny's chest. But before he had taken more than two steps, the girl had whirled on him, brandishing her knife with uncanny skill. When he saw the stubborn line of her jaw and the way her black eyes flashed a deadly warning, he paused, glancing helplessly at Goodall.

With her attention wavering between the Marquis and her father, Mianne was fully occupied and did not realize that Phillipe had crept into the room behind her until he leapt at her, locking his arms around her body and pinning her own arms to her sides. "Drop the knife," he hissed in her ear, but she snarled, trying to wrench herself free of his grasp.

"Christ!" Phillipe gasped, finding it difficult, despite his size and weight, to hold the girl. "Somebody take it away from her!"

Goodall lurched forward then and pried the knife from his daughter's clutching fingers. When he stepped back, the glistening blade in his hand, Mianne twisted her body violently and broke Phillipe's hold on her. Whirling, she reached for his face, her hands poised like claws. The rage in her flashing eyes alerted him in time and he ducked out of the way, somehow managing to grasp her wrists in an iron grip. Then, while she kicked and flailed, swearing at him fluently in Sioux, he backed her against the wall, holding her there with the weight of his body. He raised her arms above her head, pinning them to the wall, and rasped thickly, "You're not going anywhere so long as you continue to struggle. I don't plan to let you mar my face today—or anyone else's, for that matter."

Mianne spat at him and a muscle in his jaw began to twitch, but he did not release her. Phillipe glanced over his shoulder to find that everyone was staring, unable to decide what to do. Probably, he thought, they should get a thick piece of rope and tie this madwoman up, whoever the hell she was. He could not understand how she had gotten into the house. Finally, he felt the girl relax somewhat and he gazed down into her face, attempting to read her thoughts there. But she was far too adept at hiding her feelings; her features remained impassive and blank. When he saw that Cassie had come up on one side of him and Medora on the other, he drew a deep breath and stepped away, releasing his grip on the girl's wrists just as Cassie enveloped her in a generous pair of arms.

"We'll take her upstairs, Cassie, and see what we can do," Medora said, while the cook nodded grimly.

As the three of them left the room, Medora turned back once to give Johnny a reassuring smile. "Don't worry," she told him. "We'll manage."

Goodall glanced at the Marquis, shaking his head in disbelief. "I'm sorry, sir. I didn't think she would do something like this. Believe me, I didn't know." He looked down at the butcher knife in his hands and sighed raggedly. "I shouldn't have left her at the reservation so long."

"It's not your fault," Mores insisted.

Phillipe watched the girl disappear, held tightly between Medora and Cassie to avert further disaster, and he rubbed his scratched hands absently. "Jesus!" he exclaimed. "I've heard the Indians out here are savages, but I never really believed it until today. That girl would have scratched my eyes out if I'd given her half a chance."

"Yes," Goodall murmured in despair, "I believe she would have."

TWENTY-ONE

The wind danced through the leaves overhead, echoing the rustle of water on stones that rose from the river beneath, and the Marquis walked beside the water, enveloped in a cocoon of natural music. He often came to walk here lately, his rifle in his hand—he had heard that the mountain lion that had become a regular visitor at the ranches in the area sometimes stopped in the shade of the river and Mores did not want to be caught unprepared. The Marquis had discovered that when he followed the path Ileya used to walk, listening to the murmur of the river, it was almost as if she were beside him again, smoothing the wrinkles from his forehead and the worries from his mind. It seemed that her last wish for him had come true. He found that when he needed her, her spirit was always there.

Mores came to the river seeking the tranquility that always came upon him when he lost himself among the trees, but today he felt an unusual sense of urgency. He moved along the bank warily, listening for a sound that never came, waiting for something that he did not understand. Then, in the moment when he started to turn back, some hidden instinct drew him forward into the clearing and he saw her. For an instant, he was frozen with blank astonishment, but then his heart increased its tempo, pulsing out a startled message. Ileya was back.

She lay stretched out on a sloping rock with her braided hair hanging over the water. Her pale buckskin dress seemed to blend with the surface of the stone, so that only her head and arms were clearly visible, and her hands were rigid, held out before her as if in supplication. She did not move at all, not even to blink her eyes. For a horrible moment, he thought she was dead. But then he saw the object of her attention—the vision that held her immobile. Crouched across the water, not more than fifteen feet away from her, was the largest mountain lion Mores had ever seen. At least nine feet in length, it hovered on the opposite bank, flicking its rust brown tail now and then, watching Ileya with cruel yellow eyes. The two were locked in some silent combat; both beings were focused only on the other and both were motionless, as if waiting for a bolt from heaven to break the expectant hush that had fallen between them.

The Marquis knew that the mountain lion would not remain this way forever. It was only a matter of time before he stretched out his long brown legs to make the single flawless leap that would close the gap between himself and Ileya. With infinite care, Mores lowered his rifle and took aim, praying this fragile moment would last long enough for him to fire. Swallowing a huge gulp of air, he cocked the gun and prepared to shoot. But then, in the instant before he squeezed the trigger, Ileya's head snapped around. Catching sight of the Marquis with his weapon ready to fire, she shrieked out something in Sioux and gestured wildly to the cat. With a swiftness that made Mores draw in a painful breath, the animal disappeared. The Marquis's bullet landed harmlessly in the marshy earth on the far bank.

Lowering his rifle, Mores turned to stare at Ileya in disbelief. She stood upright now, facing him, and she was clearly furious. Her body trembled with the force of her anger, her cheeks were flushed and her eyes blazed. The Marquis had never seen Ileya angry before, and never had she looked at him in anything other than tenderness and concern. But he knew without a doubt that her fury was for him and not the mountain lion. It was almost as if she had warned the animal, siding with him against Mores and his deadly rifle. He simply could not understand.

He realized then that all the joy of her return had left him.

The quality of her silence had swept it away as surely as a wild Badlands wind ripped through the cottonwoods, taking the leaves as tribute when it left. For a long moment, her hostility tainted the air between them. Then, when the Marquis dropped the rifle into the grass, the tension seemed to drain from her body in a rush and she stepped down from her rock and came to join him.

"Forgive me, my friend," she said. "Sometimes I forget that we are of different worlds. No doubt you thought you were protecting me."

He looked down at her, his brow furrowed in confusion. "That's what I thought," he agreed. "The mountain lion would have attacked you."

Ileya shook her head. "I was not in danger. The cat and I were merely observing each other."

"That cat has killed at least a dozen cattle, several horses, and a couple of deer in the past two months. How can you be so certain he did not intend to harm you?"

Smiling enigmatically, she put her hand on his arm. "Because I know," she replied simply. "But let us forget him now. I am here. That is what matters."

As her fingers wove themselves among his and she leaned against him, closing her eyes, he knew she had spoken the truth. This moment, and the silence that fell upon them, was all that mattered. They sat for a long time, letting the song of the river wash over them like a soothing balm, while the wind rustled the leaves overhead. It was only when Ileya rested her head on his chest, wrapping her arms around his waist, that he remembered what Johnny had said when Mores asked if she would ever return. *Not if she values her life.*

Phillipe stood hidden in the shadow of the cottonwoods, watching Mianne dart toward the river. She ran as gracefully as an antelope, her feet barely touching the ground. And as she went, her tightly braided hair came undone until a fistful of coal-black strands were flying in the wind. The boy smiled to himself. No matter how often Medora braided the girl's hair, it always seemed to work itself free. Like Mianne herself, it simply could not bear to be confined.

Phillipe had found that this strange, hot-blooded Indian girl held for him a curious fascination. After three weeks in Medora's care, she was a great deal cleaner and quieter, but she was still an enigma to him and everyone else in the house. She chose to stay alone, maintaining a careful distance between herself and the world around her, and Phillipe was intrigued by her eyes, which were hollow, dark wells that revealed nothing of her thoughts. Many times he had seen her sprinting across the grass as she did now, and it seemed to him that there was always a quality of flight in her movements. She was fleeing, always fleeing, from a pursuer only she could see—an enemy as elusive as the wind itself.

In the moment when Mianne reached the shelter of the trees at the riverbank, she stumbled, then paused to examine her foot. Phillipe shook his head. He had warned her, as had Cassie, that she would get stickers in her feet if she insisted on going barefoot. But Mianne had ignored them. From where he stood, he could see her probing the foot carefully, her face twisted into her habitual scowl.

On an impulse, he left his hiding place, approaching her warily. He had not yet forgotten the blazing yellow light that had transformed her eyes into those of a wild animal the first time they met. "Mianne," he said softly, hoping he would not frighten her away.

Her head snapped back and her nostrils quivered for an instant, then she turned to duck beneath the trees in an effort to escape him.

"Please," Phillipe murmured, following her closely. "You obviously have something in your foot. Let me look at it." He fished around in his pocket until he found his penknife. Holding the knife up where she could see it, he said, "Maybe I can get it out for you."

Mianne retreated from him, teeth clenched. Reaching into her own pocket, she withdrew a dagger. As she backed away, the girl crouched defensively, holding the knife between them like a warning. "Don't touch me," she hissed.

Unconsciously, Phillipe's body imitated hers and he faced her, knees bent and shoulders hunched. "Don't be a fool. I just want to help." His pulse began to race as he watched how the shadows of the leaves played over the dagger blade. He knew instinctively that Mianne would not hesitate to make use of that blade. "I won't hurt you," he added.

She shook her head furiously. "Leave me alone!"

They circled for a long moment like bitter enemies waiting for the moment when one of them should stumble or look away. Crouched like wildcats, every muscle in their bodies taut and ready, they waited to spring. Then, abruptly, Phillipe stopped. Drawing himself up to his full height, he inquired coolly, "Why are you so afraid of me?"

Mianne froze, allowing her breath to escape in a cloud of surprised anger. "I'm not afraid of anyone," she cried, throwing out her chin defiantly.

With a stiff little smile, Phillipe said simply, "Liar."

"I'm not afraid," she repeated vehemently. "Even the ones who laughed at me said I was brave."

"I don't think you are," Phillipe continued calmly. "You can't even face me without a knife to hang onto. And you won't let me near enough to look at your injured foot. Normally, you won't even speak to me. It must be because you're afraid."

She shook her head stubbornly.

"If you're not, then prove it. Let me see your foot," he insisted, his eyes flashing a taunting challenge. . . .

"You say you do not fear the water," Mahpiya, the eldest brave said mockingly. "Then show us that it is so." Reaching out with a long, broken branch, he shoved a loose piece of ice farther from the shore, then grinned at Mianne and added, "You see, already the air is warm enough to melt the ice. Surely you cannot be afraid of such a little chill."

The other boys smiled, their eyes fixed on Mianne's impassive face. They would make her wince yet, Mahpiya thought. They would shatter that veil of outward calm and prove her to be the cowardly half-breed that she was. No one would really be foolish enough to swim in a lake still half covered with ice. Not even Mianne.

But the girl did not respond to their taunting. Instead, she kicked the moccasins from her feet and started toward the shore. She knew she was mad. She knew she would be ill later. But she could not turn away. Squaring her shoulders, she marched forward without faltering, her head high.

For an instant, the boys grew silent, their mouths agape. Surely she would not really do it? But when she paused as her feet touched the damp, sandy soil, they snickered again. She had just wanted to tease them a little, Mahpiya told himself. That was all.

Then, abruptly, Mianne raised her arms above her head and, bending sharply at the waist, projected her body toward the water. The boys stood shocked and immobile while her graceful form moved through the air, then split the still gray lake with a tremendous splash. She disappeared briefly, then her head broke the water again as she swam strongly to the edge of the ice, turned around, and made her way back to shore.

She rose from the lake with water rolling off her in icy waves, and the cold air pierced her lungs with sharply probing fingers, but she refused to shiver or tremble. She would not give them even so small a victory. Without a word, she picked up her moccasins, shook out her hair, and walked down the aisle they had inadvertently made for her. She did not look up at them even once, for she knew what she would see in their faces.

As for herself, she kept her features carefully blank, despite the cold that had turned her bones to ice, and her eyes were glittering, impenetrable obsidian. She did not need the stifled gasp of admiration to tell her she had won. She knew it. But she also knew that this was not the last time they would taunt her into performing some risky act. They could not help themselves; it was in their blood. Just as the indestructible pride of spirit was in hers. *They could try, time and again, but they could never break her—always, in the end, she would be the victor. . . .*

Mianne drew in a deep breath. She knew Phillipe had won. Simply by making it a challenge, he had forced her into submission. She could not say no, because that would make her seem a coward. And a coward was the one thing Mianne Goodall refused to be. Ever. She let the dagger slide from her fingers to the soft marshy ground at her feet; then she folded her legs beneath her and looked up at Phillipe. Her eyes held all the stubborn defiance of a sacrificial victim who refuses to go quietly to her fate, but who knows that, for the moment at least, there is no other choice.

The explosion of rifle fire shattered the stillness into fragments, echoing off the stone cliffs like an unexpected burst of thunder. A hundred yards across the clearing the white-tailed deer raised its head for an instant, frozen by the shock of the bullet's impact, then collapsed into the stream from which it had been drinking. The animal's rust-colored coat was twice sodden—by the seepage of clear crystal water on one side and the wash of dark ruby blood on the other.

Phillipe leaned back in the saddle, silently applauding his father's skill with a gun. The boy had learned a great deal about the Marquis in the past few days while they hunted together with Theodore Roosevelt and several of the men from both ranches. Again and again, the boy had seen Mores's talent for horsemanship, his expertise with a rifle. Against his will, Phillipe had come to admire his father's ability. Now, for the first time he began to wonder if perhaps, after all, this was the kind of man he would have chosen, had the choice been his. Turning away from the sight of the men lifting the deer from the water, the boy squinted up into Mores's face. "That's the third deer in the past two days. By the time we get finished, we should have enough meat to feed the whole town for the next year."

The Marquis smiled, shaking his head. "You'd be surprised how much those men can eat. I doubt if we'll have more than we need."

Mores had agreed to participate in this two-week hunt for several reasons. To begin with, Phillipe had asked to go along and the Marquis hoped to find an opportunity to somehow reach the boy. Then again, he himself had needed to get away for awhile from the problems at home. By now, the stagecoach line was little more than a memory, the packing plant was slaughtering only thirty beeves a day, and the plan for retail sales in New York had fallen through. Now that these things were known by the public, rumors of discontent had begun to filter through the town of Medora. Rumors about the rebirth of an old hatred in which the name of Riley Luffsey surfaced again and again like a sacred litany. Because of the unrest in town, William had advised Mores to leave for awhile. His presence only seemed to aggravate the dissatisfaction. He hoped William could handle the situation and soothe the troubled waters before the hunt was over.

"I've seen that mountain lion lurking nearby several times recently," Theodore Roosevelt announced as he rode up beside Mores. "Do you think we're getting closer?"

"At the moment, he seems to be moving west, ahead of us. Johnny thinks he's found the lair up in the hills there." Mores pointed with the end of his rifle. Like Roosevelt, he could not help a surge of electric excitement at the mention of the cat. So far, the crafty animal had eluded them, but the Marquis was determined to capture him before the hunt was over. For once, he had found himself a worthy adversary. "But we'll find him, don't worry."

Phillipe's eyes glistened with pleasure at the thought of the inevitable confrontation with the cat. It was for that moment alone that he had accompanied his father on this hunting trip. "It will be splendid," he breathed, grasping his rifle in a punishing grip.

The Marquis glanced at the boy in concern. He could see Phillipe's restless excitement; it hung between them like a pulsing, palpable force. And Mores, of all people, knew how dangerous that kind of driving desire for adventure could be. It was like a drug that swept through a man's blood, leaving him blind to wisdom or prudence or safety—to everything, in fact, but the compulsion to go forward, regardless of the consequences. "Phillipe," he said, "don't get any foolish ideas about this animal. He's dangerous and deadly and when we do find him, we have to move with care."

The boy was saved the necessity of responding when Goodall's voice reached them from behind a huge rock across the clearing. "I could use some help!" the man called.

Smiling, Roosevelt followed the sound until he disappeared.

Mores had just turned to continue his cautionary lecture to Phillipe when a blood-curdling scream sliced through the still afternoon air from the direction in which Roosevelt had just vanished.

Phillipe's eyes widened in horror. In the next instant, both he and Mores dug their heels viciously into their horses' sides. With the pitiless sun beating down on their necks, they headed unerringly for the stone barrier, just as a second scream erupted from behind the rock.

The horse whinnied in delight as Katherine's skilled hands guided the brush over the animal's sleek flank. The girl was aware of her father's lazy scrutiny, but she did not look up from her task.

"You do that well," Greg observed, leaning casually at the far edge of the stall. "I think perhaps you have a natural affinity for dumb animals."

His daughter recognized the sarcastic bite in his tone, but today she refused to be baited. "Perhaps," she agreed.

Greg chuckled softly to himself. He had been pleased with Katherine of late; she seemed to have learned at least a little discretion, and she had managed not to provoke him in a long time. Besides, there was no doubt that she was growing into an extremely attractive young woman and he knew she would be of great value to him sooner or later. Eyeing her well-defined curves critically, he asked, "Have you seen Phillipe lately?"

Pausing in her rhythmic brushing, Katherine glanced warily at her father. She knew the question was not an idle one, regardless of the offhand tone in which it had been asked. Greg was looking for something specific and she would have to take care. "We run into each other now and then," she replied.

"Do you?" His eyes narrowed at her studied reaction. He could see he had hit a sensitive nerve. "You haven't been foolish enough to fall in love with him, have you?" he inquired.

Katherine dropped the brush and turned to face him. "Of course not. Phillipe's just a boy."

"He's the *only* boy, as far as I can see."

Shrugging, she retrieved the brush from out of the hay at her feet. "Who else *is* there around here?"

"I suppose you have a point." Greg chewed thoughtfully on a piece of straw while he considered his next question. "Have you learned anything important from him?"

"No. He doesn't talk to me anymore," she told him, turning away so he would not see her secret smile.

"And I don't suppose he learns anything from you?" There was more than a hint of a threat in Greg's voice.

"Of course not. I've told you, I'm no fool."

"An interesting relationship," her father mused. "You give him nothing and you get nothing in return. What's the point of that?"

Katherine would not meet his eyes, but he saw the slow flush that spread across the back of her neck. Suddenly, he smiled. "I see," he murmured knowingly. "Perhaps the boy appeals to your baser instincts, eh? Satisfies other needs?"

She cringed at his condescending tone and the glittering look in his eyes. A slow burning anger began to climb up from her belly and, for a moment, she considered giving voice to the snide remark about Medora that rose to her lips. But, with a supreme effort of will, she managed to keep silent.

She had learned her lesson the last time. She did not intend to give him an excuse to beat her again.

"Have a care, Katherine," Greg warned. "Phillipe is a Vallombrosa through and through, even if he *is* only the bastard son. He's one of them, just the same, and he'll play their side right to the end. I would have you remember that, my dear, before you make a mistake that might eventually prove fatal."

The Marquis and Phillipe slid from their saddles, their rifles clutched in their hands. There, not more than ten yards from where they stood, lay Roosevelt, struggling desperately with a vicious, clawing red-brown cat that could only be the celebrated mountain lion. Goodall crouched a few feet away attempting to help, but the other man had fallen on his rifle when the cat pounced and Johnny could not reach it.

The hairs rose along Phillipe's neck at the inhuman grunts and wails escaping from the undulating confusion of man and beast before them. Instinctively, he followed the Marquis's example, raising his rifle to his shoulder and aiming for the hissing cat. He knew the danger in firing just now—he might hit Roosevelt instead of the animal. But if he did not take the risk, the man would surely be dead in a few minutes anyway. Gnawing unconsciously on his lower lip, the boy swallowed convulsively and cocked the rifle. Then, before he could talk himself out of it, he pulled the trigger less than a second after Mores.

The cat's body jerked spasmodically with a shriek so piercing that it echoed from the treetops. Then the animal rolled away from his victim, regaining his feet with difficulty. Trailing a jagged line of deep red blood, the cat turned away bounding into the maze of colored rock at his back.

In an instant, all three men were at Roosevelt's side, gasping, "How bad is it?"

The wounded man raised himself on one arm, swiping ineffectually at the rivulets of blood that ran across his chest from his shoulder. The cat had clawed through his shirt in several places and the long, ugly scratches were ominously frequent. "I'm all right," he choked. "Just need some disinfectant. Go get the cat."

By now Dick Moore had joined them and he nodded to Mores and the others. "Do like he says. I'll see to Mr. Roosevelt."

Phillipe's nostrils flared with fear and expectation. "I saw which way he went," the boy cried. "He can't get far with two bullets in him."

"Don't be too sure," Johnny said. "You don't realize how much strength those animals have until you see how far and how fast they run, even with the blood flowing out of their bodies in a torrent."

"Then we should follow him now, before he finds a place to hide."

Mores shook his head. "We have to do this carefully. We can't just charge in there after him. I don't think you know how dangerous a wounded mountain lion is."

"What're we going to do then, let him go?"

"Of course not," Johnny interrupted. "The thing is, we know which way he's going. I checked through the hills up there yesterday and I think I know about where the lair is. Since he's wounded, he's bound to head there. But we have to take it slowly, especially since I'm fairly certain there's another cat up there. Probably this one's mate. That makes the pursuit doubly dangerous."

Phillipe swore under his breath. "While the two of you are so busy being careful, that mountain lion is escaping. And the farther he goes, the harder it will be to find him. Let's go now, while we still have a chance."

With a stifled oath, the Marquis turned to grasp his son by the shoulders. "Listen to me, boy. We're going to do this my way—slow and easy—so we don't make any fatal mistakes. Before we start after the cat, Johnny's going to show us the best route to take and we're going to get some of the other men. While we do that, you will wait here quietly and not do anything foolish."

"We should go now," the boy repeated stubbornly, "and if you won't—"

"Phillipe! What you're thinking is madness. I forbid you absolutely *forbid* you to go after that cat by yourself. Do you understand?"

Phillipe nodded, shaking the Marquis's hand from his shoulders. Clenching his teeth in fury, he turned away and found himself a patch of dry grass where he sank down in disgust.

Already, the other men had begun to gather around, listening to Goodall as he described the best ascent through the mountains of stone that seemed to have been dropped in the center of the plain by the hand of some malevolent god bent on transforming the earth into a hazardous maze of dirt and rock. Mores leaned down next to Johnny, fingering the stock of his rifle absently. The next half hour was critical and, for once, he meant to exercise caution and keep every one of these men alive. But that cat was as good as dead; he swore that to himself. It was not until a short while later that the Marquis glanced back to the spot where his son had been sitting so unwillingly. With the pulse of the stream pounding like a deadly warning in his ears, he saw that the boy was gone.

TWENTY-TWO

Phillipe flattened himself against the cool stone, welcoming its reassuring presence. By now he was bathed in his own sweat and the bright sun overhead had become an enemy to be conquered, just like the wounded beast he had stalked across the twisting gullies and narrow precipice of layered rock. Running his arm across his forehead to wipe away some of the moisture, he eyed a few telltale drops of blood that stained the rock at his feet. The cat had been here, that much was clear, and not too long ago. The ruby drops had not yet seeped into the stone.

He had been right to come after the animal; he knew it. If he had waited with the others, the cat would have escaped them entirely, and that was something he could not allow. He had decided this, and no voice could sway him, no matter how rational or wise its words might be.

A shower of pebbles scattered across the rocks beside him and Phillipe peered up just in time to see the end of the cat's tail as it disappeared over the top of the hill. Grasping his rifle in damp fingers, he used the other hand to pull himself upward, sliding along the smooth surface of the rocks an inch at a time. He could see now that the trail of blood had become more pronounced; no doubt the wounds had begun to bleed more freely as the animal fled. So much the better, he told himself. Every drop the cat left behind meant that the animal was weaker and the mountain lion's weakness only increased Phillipe's strength. Breathing slowly, the muscles in his body screaming in protest, he dragged himself forward and waited

for the cat to tire or stumble or collapse. When it did, h
intended to be there.

For a long time, he followed the animal's ascent, leaving
his own trail of sweat behind on the rocks, and then he re
alized that he had not heard a sound for at least a full minute
Just ahead, he could discern a series of high, flat rocks, tilte
upright, that formed a natural stone wall on the hillside. H
approached the barrier on his hands and knees, his eyes flick
ing watchfully from side to side as he went. Just before h
reached the wall, he saw the broad stripe of fresh blood tha
ran between the rocks and he knew instinctively that the mc
ment had come.

Squeezing himself between the two nearest stones, h
caught sight of the cat sitting frozen in the center of a sma
flat area with only a single sagebrush bush to break the mc
notony of smooth gray stone. The back half of the animal
body was heavy with its own blood, which had formed a littl
pool at the base of its tail. For the moment at least, the cat
attention was focused on a shelf of rock above its head an
Phillipe guessed from the narrowing formation there that th
animal's lair must be located behind the rocks. Perhaps h
was gathering his strength to make the leap upward tha
would take him to freedom.

Phillipe raised his rifle with infinite care, hardly daring
breathe as he aimed the weapon and cocked it. Then, ju
when the cat rose from the ground in a graceful arc, leapir
for the shelf that meant escape, Phillipe pulled the trigg
with a shaking finger. At the rending eruption of sound, tl
animal stopped for an instant in midair, stretched out to h
full length, his head raised defiantly and his tail curled lil
a final caress around his back haunches. And then, with
shudder of disbelief, he came crashing back to the unfriend
rock beneath.

This time Phillipe knew his bullet had hit home. This tin
the cat would not rise and flee, leaving the boy in helple
silence. Mores had been wrong after all. It had not been
difficult, and never once had he been in real danger. Danglir
his rifle at his side, the boy crept forward, unwilling, ev

now, to disturb the animal's rest. He knelt at the cat's side and reached out to touch the fur, stiff now with blood, that seemed so out of place on this cold stone slab.

It was not until he heard the terrible hissing shriek overhead that he looked up in astonishment, just in time to catch a single, petrifying glimpse of the steel-gray cat poised above him on the ledge. Then, before he could gather the strength to breathe, let alone force his frozen muscles into movement, the animal leapt into the air, teeth bared and claws extended, hurling its body at Phillipe with unerring accuracy. In that instant, he thought of Roosevelt, torn and bleeding, his clothing hanging in scarlet shreds. But Phillipe knew that for him there was no one to stop the animal before it buried its deadly claws in his soft flesh. This time he was going to die. While the frantic beating of his own heart deafened him, he stared at those sharp claws until they filled his sight.

The boy did not hear the explosion that ripped through the air with unexpected force. He only knew that the flying ball of teeth and fury suddenly veered off course, collapsing with a dull thud on the inert body of its mate. Struggling to force the breath up out of his throat where it had lodged itself, Phillipe sank backward and closed his eyes as the waves of delayed terror washed over him, knocking him senseless. Those claws had come so close to tearing the life out of his body with several sweeps of a well-placed paw. In that moment, when the full horror finally gripped him, he did not even pause to wonder who his savior had been.

All at once, a shadow fell across him, blocking the hated sun from his sight. Phillipe opened his eyes to gape into his father's face. Mores towered over him, his rifle hanging loose in his hand and rasped, "Are you hurt?"

Phillipe shook his head. Although he could not force himself to speak, he was aware of the ice-cold fury that emanated from the Marquis's coal-black eyes until it touched every line and plane of his face.

"I told you it wasn't safe," his father hissed.

As the pounding of his heart subsided, the boy sucked a rush of warm air gratefully into his lungs. He knew he should respond to Mores, but just now he could not face his father's anger. Nodding dumbly, he rose and started toward the two dead animals.

"Where are you going?" the Marquis demanded.

"I want to see them," Phillipe explained, his voice no more than a hoarse whisper. He did not see the dangerous twitching of a tiny muscle in Mores's jaw.

"You're going nowhere except back to the wagon," the Marquis told him. Then he added, "At once."

Phillipe looked up at him defiantly. After all, he had just escaped death; he was immortal, was he not? Two dead mountain lions and not a scratch to show for it. "I want to see them," he repeated.

Mores took a step backward, blocking his son's way. "I'm warning you, Phillipe," the Marquis breathed. "I will not be ignored again. Go back to the wagon and wait for me."

They faced each other in silence, bright blue eyes staring into deep black ones, hands clenched and bodies taut. They stood as if carved from the stone beneath their feet—immobile, tense, furious—waiting for one or the other to make a move. . . .

"I did it!" Antoine cried triumphantly. "I brought her down safely." He stood, dripping wet, filthy and bruised, his clothing torn in several places, holding the bedraggled hunting dog in his arms. He was aware of his father's barely suppressed fury but, for the moment, he was too pleased with his achievement to allow the Duke to spoil it.

"I forbade you to go after that animal," the Duke declared icily. "Does that mean nothing to you? It was far too dangerous for someone of your inexperience." He spoke slowly, with infinite care, as if he were determined to keep his anger in check.

"It was not so difficult," Antoine lied. But he shivered convulsively when he remembered the steep, slippery, moss-covered rocks he had had to climb, with the pounding spray of the waterfall no more than three feet away. The hound had somehow fallen from above, catching herself on a damp stone ledge where she had lain, trembling and shivering, until the boy came. He knew his father was right; it had been madness even to try. But then, he had succeeded, and that made the victory all the sweeter. "Besides," he said, "I couldn't just let her die."

"And you thought your life was worth no more than that of a single hunting dog?" the Duke demanded. From the clipped tone of his voice, it was evident that his patience was wearing thin.

Antoine shifted the dog slightly. The weight had begun to numb his arms and the chill from his damp clothing was creeping through to his skin. "But we're *both* safe now."

"Only by the grace of God, and certainly not from the use of your own questionable intelligence." Turning to William, who had been hovering nearby, the Duke said, "Take the dog to the kennel and have her seen to."

"No!" the boy cried. "She's hurt. I want to stay with her. I'll take her."

His father's lips began to twitch ominously. "Will you defy me twice in one day? I warn you, such a course would not be wise. Do as I say, William. Take the animal away."

Reluctantly, Van Driesche lifted the shivering dog from Antoine's arms and started away.

The boy stood perfectly still, unblinking under his father's harsh scrutiny. But his eyes followed William and every instinct but one told him to go after his friend. But that one—the instinct for self-preservation—was somehow the strongest. So he did not move or speak, but faced the Duke squarely, jaw stiff and fists clenched. He was waiting, foolishly, to hear one word of praise for his courage or ability, but there was none. The Duke's implacable gaze was cold with fury, without the grace of a single glimmer of silent approval. *And all at once, the victory had been transformed into something small and insignificant beside the looming specter of his father's wrath. . . .*

For what seemed like an eternity, neither the Marquis nor his son moved so much as a muscle, while overhead the sun touched their hair with a whisper of fire. And then, at last, Phillipe realized from Mores's frozen features that this time, his father was right. The Marquis would win in the end. Eyeing Goodall, who hovered at the edge of the clearing, watching, Phillipe drew in his breath with a slow, painful whistle. They were waiting for him to crack, but he refused to give them what they wanted. The boy swallowed twice, picked up his rifle, and turned away, heading for the path that would lead him downward, away from the proof of his victory to the cold empty wagon at the foot of the hill.

"Are you mad?" the Marquis demanded, pacing furiously across the cluttered floor of the hunting wagon in which they slept. He had built it to be a home for himself and his wife on the long hunting trips they loved to take, but just now there was only himself and his stiffly hostile son. When Phillipe refused to break his stubborn silence, Mores added, "How could you risk so much for so little?"

Phillipe's eyes blazed turquoise fire and he shouted, "The death of that cat was not 'little.' It was worth any risk. You said yourself that he had become a constant threat to your livestock. How can you say it was nothing? Don't you care that I did it by myself and without getting hurt? Or did you want that victory for yourself?"

Mores fought to control the spark of anger that threatened to erupt into a bonfire in his chest. Choosing his words carefully, he replied, "I'm glad the cat is dead. I'm even glad it was you who killed him, but I repeat that it wasn't worth the risk."

"To what?" the boy snorted.

"To your *life*, you fool. Didn't you learn anything from the attack on Roosevelt? The man is very ill with the fever caused by his wounds. He's alive, but he could easily have been killed. And so could you."

"I wouldn't think that would disturb you, too much. I might even have rid you of one of your most pressing problems."

With a sharp intake of breath, the Marquis asked, "What do you mean?"

"You know very well what I mean. If I'd been killed, you would be free. I thought you'd be grateful I took the risk."

"That isn't true."

"Isn't it? Why not?"

The Marquis's thoughts were in turmoil. He could have answered that it was because every time he looked at Phillipe he saw himself. Because he recognized the boy's frustrations and his anger, his weaknesses and his strengths—they had long been Mores's own. He could have said it was because in all the years of his life he had never known another who felt and acted just as he himself had done. For he knew with absolute certainty that, had he been Phillipe, the Marquis would have gone after the cat by himself, just as the boy had done. He could have told Phillipe all these things, but he said, merely, "Because you are my son."

Phillipe shook his head. "Not by choice. I'm your son only because my mother was foolish enough to tell me her sordid little secret and I was foolish enough to come looking for you. You never wanted me; I just threw myself in your path and forced you to stop and take notice." He smiled bitterly. "I'm your son because you didn't dare refuse me. But I'm sure that if you could think of a way, you'd be rid of me tomorrow."

The Marquis listened with growing bewilderment to his son's harangue. For the first time, he saw some of the pain that ran always beneath the surface, making Phillipe into the hostile, insecure boy who could not resist a chance to challenge his father, to push him until, hopefully, he shattered with the impact. "If you really believe that," he said finally, "then you're more of a fool than I thought. I want to tell you now, Phillipe, that regardless of what you have done and said to me, regardless of your moodiness and your sharp tongue, regardless of the fact that you never really gave me a choice, I'm glad you came to me. Not for the world would I change that, and not for the world would I let you go again."

* * *

Medora let the door slam closed behind her as she hurried outside to meet Phillipe. Watching with concern as the boy dismounted, leaving his horse in Dick Moore's care, Medora waited anxiously for the news. "What's happened?" she asked when she could contain her curiosity no longer. "Why are you back so early?"

Phillipe scratched his head thoughtfully, considered several wildly imaginative explanations, then decided to tell her the truth. "Mr. Roosevelt was attacked by the mountain lion and my father sent Dick Moore and me to escort him home. We already stopped at the Maltese Cross and made sure he had a doctor." He paused for a moment, then continued, "But I have a suspicion the Marquis would have sent me back even if Roosevelt hadn't been ill."

As they entered the house, Medora attempted to interpret the expression on the boy's face. "Why?" she asked, sensing that Phillipe had quite a story to tell. "What else happened?"

To tell the truth, the boy was not quite certain himself what had happened back on that mountainside, or later, in the wagon. But one thing he did know—something *had* occurred and it had been important. Somehow, the Marquis had managed to change Phillipe's entire perspective, though the boy could not yet decide how his father had done it. He only knew that he had not really been sorry when Mores told him to accompany the injured man home. Phillipe had wanted to go, to give himself time to absorb his new impressions of the man who was his father.

By now he was strangely anxious to talk about the exciting and puzzling series of events that had taken place in the past several days. And so it was that he sat across from Medora in her tiny office and told her the whole story, leaving out nothing.

Medora leaned back in her bentwood rocker, amazed at Phillipe's openness with her. She sensed that he no longer looked upon her as an enemy and she was glad. She was certain this family would need to stick together in the days ahead and it seemed that, finally, the boy was willing to make that choice. Resting her chin on her hand, she smiled tentatively at him and said, "I asked you once before why you had come here, but you wouldn't answer honestly. Will you tell me now?"

He gazed unblinkingly into her green eyes, remembering that other time when she had first spoken to him at the Von Hoffman's house in New York. Then, as now, she had been wearing a plain, simple gown and her hair had been woven into the same thick braids around her head. Her gaze had been just as piercing, her expression as intelligent, but that woman had been a stranger and somehow, this one had become a friend. Had she changed so much that winter day, or was it he who had changed? "I came because I wanted to make my father's life as miserable as he had made mine," Phillipe told her bluntly. "I wanted to ruin him."

"And now?"

He looked beyond her to the late afternoon light that came fitfully through the window. "Now I see that others are doing it for me."

"And you've found that it doesn't satisfy you, does it?" she suggested.

"No. I changed my mind somewhere along the way."

"Why?" In the subdued light, her voice seemed to rustle past him like the whisper of water on stones.

"Because he won't break. No matter what they do to him, my father just keeps moving ahead as if he hadn't a single enemy in the world. He won't even bend," he explained haltingly.

"You admire him for that, don't you?"

The boy gaped at her in surprise when he realized she was right. It was not until that moment that he saw how deeply he had come to admire his father, who persevered, in spite of all the odds against him.

Medora saw the look of astonishment that crossed his face and she recognized it for what it was. In that instant, her heart went out to him because, like the others—herself and William and her father—the boy had been drawn into Mores's net of chimerical dreams. And, like the others, he would drown when the net burst, spilling them all into a cold and bottomless sea. "Phillipe," she said softly, "he'll break eventually. He has to. No man can stand up to this kind of assault forever. Not even the Marquis de Mores."

TWENTY-THREE

Medora glanced up from her paperwork in surprise when she heard a commotion in the front room. The house had been so quiet for so long that the sudden babble of voices sent a chill down her spine. Rising precipitously, she hurried toward the drawing room. She paused on the threshold, staring in bewilderment from William, who had been in Mandan on business for the past few days, to Mores, who was supposed to be hunting over fifteen miles away. "What—" she began.

"I had a feeling I'd better come back tonight," William explained. "I haven't been too successful at quelling the discontent here *or* in Mandan and I figured it would be best to stick close to home for the next few days." He glanced uneasily at the Marquis. "But why are you back so soon?"

Mores crossed the room in three quick strides and bent to kiss his wife's hand. "I got a message from Von Hoffman," he said. "He wants me here first thing tomorrow morning for some urgent business, so naturally I came back."

Medora and William looked at each other across the Marquis's head. Neither liked the sound of this sudden message from Von Hoffman, but, unlike Mores, they were both aware of the dimensions to which local discontent had grown in the past several days. Despite William's efforts, the people had become daily more restless, and threats against the Marquis had become as common as wishing one's neighbor good morning. And now, suddenly, at the height of this unrest, Mores had received a message telling him to come home. Something was wrong here.

"What kind of business?" Medora asked warily.

"Some papers he has to have signed tomorrow. They should arrive by special courier in the morning. But that doesn't matter now. I'm home; that's what's important." He waved his hand in a gesture of dismissal and said, "I'm famished. What's for dinner?"

"Mores, I don't think you understand—"

"Please," the Marquis sighed. "I don't want to hear your nervous superstitions or your dire predictions for the future. For the moment, I just want to enjoy the luxury of being in my own home again. The wagons are full of meat and skins, the mountain lion is dead, Roosevelt is recovering from his wounds, and the stars will shine beautifully tonight. It's time to celebrate, not to grieve."

Medora took the arm her husband offered, but not for a moment did she share his optimism. She was glad he was home and safe, but she could not rid herself of the feeling of bleak despair that had begun to gnaw at her insides. Despite Mores's unconcern, all was not well; she was certain of it.

Mianne sat in the nursery, tugging impatiently on the frilly silk gown that felt so soft and foreign against her skin. She simply could not understand the necessity for so many layers of confining clothing, and she itched to be free of the lace, silk, and satin, with only the wind and her buckskin dress to cover her. But tonight she would have to endure this temporary agony. She had sworn to do everything in her power to make herself attractive.

Phillipe had been home for several days now, but he had not spoken to her more than once, and then offhandedly, as if he had not really seen her. His disinterest made her furious. No one had ever dared ignore Mianne before. They had hated her and feared her, a few had even liked her, but no one had ever before refused to notice her at all. Tonight would be different, though; she had seen to that. Tonight she would force him to take notice. And once she had his attention—

well, then they would see who was the victim and who the conqueror.

Mianne looked up and smiled when Athenais came waddling toward her.

"Pwet-ty," the child said carefully, running a pudgy hand across the soft fabric of Mianne's silk skirt.

Taking the two-year-old onto her lap, Mianne hugged her affectionately. This child was the only person at the Chateau whom the Indian girl allowed herself to care for. Athenais— who, more often than not, was ignored by the adults and left to the care of her nurse—accepted her new friend gladly and without prejudice. Warm, loving, and generous, the child came alive each time Mianne stopped in the nursery to visit. And the older girl knew that here, in this one room, she was loved for herself. Here alone she was always welcome.

"Ummmm," Athenais murmured, wrinkling her nose with pleasure at the fragrance of Mianne's perfume. "Good," she observed judiciously.

The older girl was delighted with the child's approval of her changed appearance. "It's almost time for your supper, little one," she said. "I must leave you to your nurse."

Athenais's eyes lit up when her attention was caught by a single word. "Sup-per?" she cried.

Grinning, Mianne hugged her one last time, then set her on her still wobbly feet. "Yes, supper. But I shall come to tell you good night later."

As she turned and started from the room, the child grasped her skirt in a tight little fist. "Mianne pwet-ty," she repeated. "Come later."

"I will come, little one. *I* will not forget you."

Phillipe was sprawled on the bearskin rug before the fireplace, staring into the heart of the leaping flames, when Mianne stepped into the room. Against his will, his eyes were drawn toward her, and he was stunned by the picture she made. He had to look twice to assure himself that this was the same girl he had met by the river, and even then he could not fully believe what he saw. This girl, with her hair falling in soft curls across her shoulders, could not be the witch whose tangled braids had streamed out behind her in disarray. This face, with its perfectly proportioned nose, high cheekbones, and soft, yielding lips could not be the dirt-covered face with the wild yellow eyes. This swaying body, clothed in a lovely blue silk gown that clung to every curve, could not be the struggling, filthy form he had held pressed against the wall, afraid to let go.

But it was not only Mianne's physical appearance that had changed. It was not only the gown and the curls that had transformed her face from that of a child to one of a real beauty. There was also something in her smile, some tender light in her dark eyes that had not been there before. With the firelight playing across her face, Mianne stood before him, her lips slightly parted, and began to weave a spell upon his bewildered senses. Reaching out with a hand that was not quite steady, Phillipe grasped her hand and drew her down beside him where she sat quietly, smiling into herself and slowly drawing him within the midst of her web.

"Tell me about your life with the Indians," he said, groping for some topic that would keep her beside him.

Mianne shook her head. "That is in the past," she informed him. "I live only in the present."

"Your father, then. Tell me about him."

This time the mask fell back across her eyes, if only for a moment, and she hissed, "I hate my father. I will not speak of him."

Phillipe considered the shadow that touched her features and he realized that the new Mianne had not destroyed the old entirely. The raging animal was still there, just beneath the surface, waiting to come out. "Why should you hate him?" he asked curiously.

"Because he abandoned me," she answered without hesitation.

"But at least he married your mother," Phillipe pointed out, reminded of his own father.

Mianne leaned back, her eyes narrowed in thought. "Which

is worse," she inquired slyly, "to be a bastard or a half-breed?"

Biting his lip, the boy thought this challenge over for a moment before he answered. "If being a half-breed means looking like you, then I would say being a bastard is far worse. Don't you agree?"

"Yes," she said, grinning. "I should never want to resemble you."

All at once, Phillipe took her hand in his and held it for a moment, tracing a pattern on her palm with his finger. "Someday," he whispered, "I will make you my slave."

She snatched her hand away and her nostrils flared with sudden anger. "No one will ever do that," she hissed. But when she saw how his eyes sparkled, she knew that he was teasing her. "But perhaps," she mused, leaning down so that her hair brushed the back of his hand, "perhaps it will be the other way around. In the end it might just be you who will be *my* slave."

Before he could answer, they heard a noisy stomping of feet on the front porch. Someone pounded roughly on the front door, and when Medora dragged it open, a group of men spilled into the drawing room. Their hostility was evident in the way they held their hands clenched into fists at their sides and in the scowling expressions that covered their faces. A few even held revolvers. Phillipe was on his feet in a moment, moving to Medora's side. "What do you want?" the boy asked stiffly.

"We want the Markee, boy," one man snarled, "and we don't mean to let you keep us busy while he escapes, either."

"That won't be necessary in any event," Mores announced. "I'm here."

For just an instant, the men were disconcerted by the Marquis's elegant unconcern. He stood leaning against the door frame, one leg crossed negligently over the other, smoking a cigar. His curly dark hair was combed flawlessly into place and the ends of his moustache curled upward in perfect symmetry. But then the spokesman recovered himself. Glancing sideways at Medora and Phillipe, he cleared his throat and said distinctly, "Markee de Moree, I'm here with my men to arrest you for the murder of Riley Luffsey."

Much later—after his father had left with the men to be taken to jail in Mandan, after the voices of protest had faded into stillness, after plans had been made, discarded, and made all over again—Phillipe climbed the stairs to his room. With only the melancholy shadows for companions, he clung to the banister, raising one foot heavily in front of the other. His mind was a whirlwind of disconnected thoughts and plans and his body no more than a weary shell that harbored the burnt-out hole where his emotions used to be. This night had been too much for him, with its bewilderment, fear, anger, hope, and helplessness. And Phillipe honestly believed that one more surge of emotion would break him completely.

The Marquis was gone. They had come and taken him away with an ease that astounded the boy, and there had been nothing Phillipe could do to stop it. Nothing. He had been shocked at the rage that had possessed him in the face of his own inability to help his father; more than anything, he had wanted to destroy those men, one at a time, until they left the Chateau in peace. But of course, it had only been a fantasy. In the end he had had to let Mores go without a word of protest. And the knowledge of his own impotence had shaken him to the very core. The Marquis might refuse to break, but Phillipe was not quite so strong.

Pushing his bedroom door open, the boy stopped for an instant, surprised to see that his lamp was already burning. Perhaps Cassie had come up to light it for him. He was glad she had done so; tonight he did not want to struggle with the darkness. He gazed with the eyes of a stranger upon the dark oak bureau, the wing-backed chair, the oriental rug. It was almost as if, after the events of the past few days, he needed to reacquaint himself with his belongings, to remind himself of the boundaries of his world. Because, although he had been in this room a hundred times before, he felt as if this were the first time.

And then his eyes fell upon the bed, hung with light netting, and he saw it. Through the wavering shadows that hung along the walls and clung to the high bedposts, he saw the object that lay in the center of his quilt, placed there by a careful hand. Gnawing fitfully on his lower lip, he moved closer and drew the netting aside. For a moment, his mind refused to register the truth his eyes took in, and then he reached out to touch it.

Beneath his hand lay the head of a reddish brown mountain lion, stuffed and mounted on a piece of dark wood. Its evil yellow eyes had been replaced by amber glass that glowed magically in the dim light, and its sharp, deadly teeth were barely visible beneath the white fur that covered its lower face. Phillipe knew that it was the cat he had killed, and he thought it the most beautiful thing he had ever seen. Beside it lay a scribbled note, and although he picked it up and held it to the light, it was a long moment before he read it.

Phillipe,

I had this prepared for you in a hurry because I thought you might want to keep it as a trophy of your greatest hunting victory. There may never be another as fine. Well done.

—Mores

Dropping the piece of paper, the boy watched it flutter to rest beside the cat's head. His eyes burned and he discovered an uncomfortable lump in the center of his throat. Closing his eyes, he laid his head on the cool fabric of the quilt. It simply was not fair, he thought. For he was very much afraid that he had lost his father this time to the angry mob that waited hungrily somewhere in the darkness. Lost him in the very moment when he had only just found him.

Medora stood at the river's edge staring blankly into the ceiling of leaves overhead while her horse drank eagerly from the water. The train to Mandan would not arrive in Medora for another hour and a half, but she had been too impatient to wait at the Chateau. William had already left early that morning to see what he could do for the Marquis, but Medora had stayed behind to receive the expected papers from her father. She had been appalled when she opened the package, delivered by special messenger when the sky was still pink with the rising sun. The papers had been no more than a few financial agreements between the partners, and she could not understand the sense of urgency that had made Von Hoffman send his message to Mores. Had it not been for that disastrous message, the Marquis would have been wandering in the hills far away, safe from the assault of his enemies. Medora kicked a stone into the water. She was furious with her father; he had behaved like a fool.

"Good morning, my dear," a familiar voice called unexpectedly.

Medora looked up to find Greg Pendleton's steel-gray gaze appraising her idly. She bit her lip and looked away. She did not want to speak to him.

"Where are you going in your fine traveling suit?" he asked, apparently unaware of her rigid silence.

"To be with my husband," she replied shortly.

Pendleton rubbed his chin thoughtfully while a frown gathered in his eyes. "That would be most unwise of you. The mood in Mandan is dangerous, even to you. Surely you don't want to risk your own life for *him?* Especially when it would do you no good anyway."

Swallowing to keep from snarling in Greg's face, Medora turned to look at him. "That's my choice," she said, "not yours."

"Don't be a fool. He's gone, Medora, maybe for good this time. Let him go before he drags you down with him."

Her eyes narrowed and she eyed him speculatively. "You know something," she accused. "But then, you probably planned this from the start, didn't you?"

"Medora," he murmured, reaching out to grasp her shoulders, "forget about the Marquis and his silly little plans. Think about me instead. You know as well as I do that you and I belong together. That man is no more than a fool who doesn't even realize what he's got in you." His eyes burned with fiery intensity and his grip on her shoulders was bruising. "I've waited a long time, my dear. Don't make me wait any longer." And then, before she could protest, he bent his head to kiss her.

This time she did not wait for the fire inside to begin to burn. This time she pushed him away without hesitation, horrified by his calm self-assurance and his incredible arrogance. Brushing at her shoulder as if to rid herself of the memory of his touch, Medora said, "The Marquis is my husband."

Greg's nostrils flared and his lips twitched ominously, but he did not reach for her again. "And because of that he has earned your undying loyalty?" He could not hide the contempt in his tone.

"In a manner of speaking," she replied, "yes."

"It's a little late for that, my dear, don't you think? Your body seems quite willing to be disloyal every time we meet."

She had somehow known he would say it, but that knowledge didn't make the fury any less real. "That doesn't mean that I should leave him to be killed by his enemies when I might be able to help."

Greg shook his head in disbelief. "You'd do anything to help him, wouldn't you?"

"Yes. Anything."

His brows came together in a frown while his lips twitched into a kind of sneer. "I wonder if his Indian mistress feels the same?" he mused idly.

Medora recoiled as if he had slapped her. "What do you mean?"

"Come now, don't tell me you didn't know? I was certain that with your unfailing insight you would have discovered the girl long ago."

She stared at him in tight-lipped silence, her eyes wide with incredulity, and he smiled. "She's been his mistress since the first summer you came here," he explained. "He keeps her in a hut by the river where he goes to visit her regularly.

For three years he's been deceiving you, Medora. Three years."

"I don't believe you!"

"Shall we go look? The hut isn't far away."

"No," she hissed.

"You needn't be so distressed, my dear. I also happen to know that she's the one who betrayed us last year. She has an unfortunate habit of wandering in the night, and somehow she discovered our secret. We've let her be, for the moment, but I promise you, we plan to take care of her soon. So you see, your problem will be solved without your lifting a finger. Isn't it comforting to know that I always take care of your needs?"

"Get away from me!" she cried. "Take your damned sneering and gloating and get the hell away!"

Locking his fingers in his belt, he observed her distress with delight. It could only bring her closer to him in the end. "Don't let your husband's foolishness upset you," Greg advised her. "He isn't worth all this anguish."

And then Medora surprised herself and shouted, "He *is,* damn you! He *is!"*

Greg stepped away from her, taken aback by the vehement tone of her voice. He saw that she believed what she had just said, as surely as he believed in his own invincibility.

"Go away," she repeated. "Leave me alone."

Astonished at the turn of events, he turned away, scowling, and left her standing alone in the mud of the riverbank with the water rolling by endlessly at her feet.

Medora did not watch him go. Her attention was focused on the dull, pulsing pain that seemed to come and go with the erratic beating of her heart. She would not have believed that the knowledge of Mores's deception could affect her so profoundly, for he was not the only one who had turned to someone else for comfort. Yet Pendleton's revelation had left her chilled and shaking, as if her husband had dragged the very earth from beneath her feet. Why? she wondered. Why should this one betrayal hurt so deeply?

Perhaps it was because, as she spoke to Phillipe about his

father, she had come to realize that she herself was oddly impressed by Mores's unwillingness to give in. Perhaps it was because in the moment last night when her husband had stood before those angry men with such unconcern, she had seen a glimpse of a spirit of defiance so deeply imbedded that it could never be assailed. The Marquis's refusal to bow to their fury, his refusal to bend to their will, his refusal to allow them even a moment's victory, exemplified a depth of courage that she could not even begin to comprehend. This was not a man to be scoffed at, but rather one to be proud of.

"Medora!"

She looked up at the sound of her stepson's voice. She could see him approaching through the trees with several men behind him.

Reining his horse in, Phillipe leaned down and murmured breathlessly, "We want to go with you to Mandan."

Medora considered the boy in silence. Johnny Goodall was beside him, and Frank Miller and Dick Moore, as well as several others whose names she did not even know. They were waiting expectantly for her consent. "It will be dangerous there. No one with the Marquis's interests at heart will be safe."

"Mores is the one in danger," Phillipe exclaimed, "and if he didn't hesitate, why should we?"

She could see the stubborn light that seemed to reflect from Phillipe's eyes into the eyes of the others and she heard with relief the murmurs of agreement that rose from their lips. Giving them a small, winning smile, she thought, surely a man who had inspired such loyalty in his employees was a man who deserved her respect, whatever his faults. Perhaps, after all, it had been she who had been wrong, not he. "All right," she said, "let's go and do our best for him."

The torches that guttered outside the window cast grotesque shadows on the rough log walls of the jailhouse. Mores watched the dark eerie forms as they crawled along the ceiling and slid into the crevices between the rows of logs. The sinister images of those shadows playing across the far wall reflected his own state of mind with grim accuracy. He knew the men were gathering outside; their blazing torches were mute testament to their unwelcome presence. And he also knew that they had not brought him here to stand trial. They had played out their little drama to the last detail, locking him in the tiny jailhouse, calling for the grand jury to meet, even allowing his lawyer to visit him, but he knew it was all a farce. Those men outside had never intended for the Marquis to reach the courtroom alive. It had been prudence that had kept him from struggling the other night; he had sensed that they would shoot him on the spot if he gave them the slightest excuse.

So here he was again, two years later, reliving the nightmare in the same stuffy little room with the same group of madmen waiting for him just outside. Now, as then, he was infuriated by his own helplessness. He had only the single knife strapped to his leg—they had not searched him thoroughly enough to find it—and he knew that it would not be much good against so many. But he vowed that he would get to one or two before they got to him.

"Justice!" a hoarse voice cried. "We want justice this time!"

There was a chorus of assent and Mores shook his head in disgust. Those men had no interest in justice. It was not a sense of fair play that motivated them but rather greed, a desire for revenge, and simple fear. But it did not matter to them that their perceptions were distorted and their motives base. One way or another, they meant to have the Marquis's life before the night was over. He supposed that they had heard about the article in the Bismarck *Tribune* concerning the estrangement between Mores and his wife, and they were depending on that disaffection to keep Medora away this time. Surely a woman on the verge of divorcing her husband would not come to save his life?

The occasional ranting of single voices had begun to blur into a unified chorus of discontent and Mores rose restlessly from his uncomfortable bench. He buried his hands in his pockets, pacing back and forth across the dirt floor while cries of "Lynch him!" and "Justice!" swelled from the crowd. The sad part, he thought, was that he was not ready. There was so much he had left undone. He had not even said good-bye to Ileya. At the thought of the Indian girl, he paused and closed his eyes, concentrating on his memory of her face. Perhaps if he tried hard enough, he could bridge the gap be-tween them and absorb a little of her placid acceptance of life and all its trials. But for the first time, he felt no thread stretching from his mind to hers. For the first time, Ileya could not reach him. He was really alone. Despite the balmy warmth of the summer night, he suddenly felt cold through and through.

And then, above the chanting, threatening noise of the mob, he heard a series of taps against the far wall, as if someone were scrambling up the outside of the building to the roof. The noises continued, unnoticed by the crowd, and Mores found himself wondering if perhaps they meant to set their torches on the roof and burn the jail to the ground. He hurried to the window and gazed outside, but all he could see were the leering, malevolent faces that formed a sea of hatred from his window to the center of the street. Overhead he could hear the men sliding across the roof, but the crowd did not seem to notice.

Then, all at once, the nightmare was repeating itself all over again. The same expectant hush gripped the men outside, the same shocked inhalation of breath, the same swiveling of curious heads. And then she was there, standing like an avenging goddess with the flickering torchlight on her face. Medora shoved her way through the bewildered mob, forcing them to make a path for her, and like a flock of startled swallows, they fell back before her, unable to believe that she had really come.

Medora had loosened her hair, letting it fall all around her shoulders to her waist; the flames of the torches set it ablaze with dancing red lights and, for a moment, the men were surprised into awed silence. Her wild green eyes seemed to mesmerize them, holding them immobile, but then a man at the edge of the crowd broke free.

"Go away!" he cried. "We've got our business tonight and we don't want to hurt you!"

"I'm staying," she replied calmly, "and no one is going to be hurt unless you are so foolish as to attempt to forcibly remove me." Her voice was soft, but it carried to the furthest man as clear as a tolling church bell.

"Like hell!" one ruffian responded. "What'll you do, scratch our eyes out?" At the roar of laughter that greeted this witticism, he took several steps in Medora's direction.

"Stop!" Phillipe's voice called warningly from somewhere up above. "We have four rifles trained on you, and we'll shoot if you move in any direction other than backward."

Shading his eyes with his hand, the man gazed up at the roof in astonishment and he saw that the boy was telling the truth. The torchlight revealed four gleaming rifle barrels pointed threateningly downward.

"Ah, go on, Grady!" some members of the crowd called. "They won't really fire."

The man took another hesitant step forward and instantly the ground at his feet was peppered with bullets.

"Don't listen to your friends. They're not the ones facing our guns," Phillipe advised.

Without another word, the man slunk away into the darkness at the edge of the crowd.

"We have also called in the sheriff from Bismarck," Medora said, forcing her voice to carry over the shuffling sounds of discontent that had begun to ripple through the mob. "You might be interested to know that he and his men are standing just outside the crowd and their guns are also cocked and ready."

A few men turned back to look and met the blank stare of at least seven more shotguns. "She's right," they exclaimed. "Damn her!"

For several minutes longer the crowd seemed to hover before the jail in indecision, their gazes fixed on Medora's flaming eyes. Then, one by one, they admitted defeat and turned away, grumbling and cursing under their breath.

Phillipe, Goodall, Miller, and Moore, who were crouched on the roof, heaved a joint sigh of relief, but they did not abandon their positions. In case the mob changed its mind later, after a few glassfuls of whiskey had poured a dose of bravery into their guts, the Marquis's men meant to stay where they were until the rising sun set them free. Because only then would they know it was safe to go.

Just as before, the Marquis did not speak to his wife, who had seated herself just in front of the door. But he knew she was there—she and Phillipe. They had come for him after all. In spite of everything. And he knew they would be waiting when he awakened in the morning.

They were. And they were there when the grand jury indicted him for murder three days later. They were beside him at the hearing when he demanded a change of venue and when his request was granted. They were with him in Bismarck when the trial began and every day thereafter for three full weeks. Through all the struggles inside the courtroom and out, through all the publicity that plagued them like an incurable disease, through the hostility of the crowds and the hatred of the Marquis's enemies, they were there. And Mores's wife and son were waiting outside on the day when, finally, the jury found him not guilty and he knew that, this time, the verdict would stand.

The Marquis strode from the courtroom with his usual self-assurance, smiling broadly. And when he saw Medora and Phillipe waiting expectantly, he cried, "You see! I told you we could win!"

He reached out to shake his son's hand, but before he realized what was happening, the boy had flung his arms around Mores's neck. For a moment the Marquis was too surprised to respond, but then, with a surge of love and gratitude for the boy who had made his life so miserable, he closed his arms around Phillipe's shoulders and held him tightly. "Dear God," he whispered above his son's head, "it's good to be home."

TWENTY-FOUR

"You *fool!*" Bryce Pendleton bellowed. "You handed them the victory on a silver platter. And all because of that woman." He paced impatiently before the fireplace, his face distorted into an ugly scowl. "This is the second time you've allowed her to thwart us, Greg."

Greg stared bleakly out the window without bothering to turn and face his father's wrath. "I didn't think she would go to him," he explained, shrugging. But although Bryce could not see it, his son's expression was clouded with despair.

"How could you have misjudged her so badly? And why the hell didn't you keep her here forcibly, if that's what was necessary? You could have tied her up and thrown her in a shed for all I care. But to stand there and watch her ride away? You must be mad."

"Perhaps I am," Greg muttered, "but it wouldn't have done any good to keep her here unless I also hog-tied every man on the Marquis's ranch. Hardly a practical alternative, don't you agree?"

Bryce snorted. "I'm not likely to agree with anything you say today." Glowering, he added as an afterthought, "I can't believe you let a woman befuddle you so thoroughly."

"You've said it once and that's plenty. Drop it now."

Bryce considered his son's broad shoulders in silence for a long moment before he cleared his throat and whispered, "You've forgotten, haven't you?"

For an instant, Greg could not decide what his father meant, then, suddenly, Bryce's words from long ago came back to him. *Have you forgotten your mother? Because to forget is dangerous, my son. Don't let it happen. Ever.* With a painful jolt, Greg realized that he could not visualize his mother's face and that he had not tried to do so for a long, long time. "Of course I haven't forgotten," he murmured, but he knew it was a lie. Only the glare of the morning sun saw the anguish that ravaged his face. When Bryce did not respond, his son said, "What do we do now?"

Blindly, Bryce accepted Greg's answer and his abrupt change of subject. It was not that the old man was foolish, it was just that he did not want to know the truth. He could not face it. "I have instructions," he said. "It's come to the point when we have to resort to drastic measures. Anything we can do to stop that man. Do you understand?"

Greg released his breath in a deep sigh. "I believe I do."

"Good. The way I figure it, we harass and harry and block the Marquis at every turn and he's bound to collapse sooner or later. He's already swaying on the edge; all we have to do is push him over."

Mianne lay on her belly with a dried deerskin stretched out before her. All around her were scattered the paints and dyes she had dug from the earth and the brushes she had made with her own hands. Today she had discarded her elegant clothes and put on her simple buckskin dress again. As always, her feet were bare and her hair hung down her back in thick braids. With the sun on her head, she made a lovely picture, and Phillipe smiled to himself as he sat down beside her.

"What're you making?" he inquired, running his hand across the hide that had already been tanned into softness.

"A pillow," she muttered shortly. "I shall fill it with cottonwood floss and put it on my bed."

Phillipe stretched out next to her, bending his head to examine the colorful birds and geometric designs she had already painted on the pliable surface. "It's lovely," he told her, "but you haven't put in any flowers."

Mianne shifted her body away from his and reached for another brush. "Flowers are only for the whites," she said. She wished he would go away; she did not like to have him beside her. She had thought, for just a little while one night, that he might be her friend, but then he had abandoned her. For over a month he had stayed away, and when he came back it had been as if she did not exist. And so she had retreated back into her secret world and, rejecting white restrictions, she had become an Indian once again. But now, suddenly, Phillipe had rediscovered her.

"You're half white," he reminded her, "so you're allowed to have flowers."

"I am a Sioux," she insisted, "an Indian."

"But I thought you hated your tribe."

Peering at him from beneath her heavy lashes, she said, "I hate everyone. Didn't you know?"

"I don't believe you."

"Believe what you like. I don't care." She bit her lip painfully and turned back to her painting.

All at once, Phillipe was strongly aware of the soft brownness of her delicate face with the sunlight reflecting from her deep black eyes. She was lonely, he realized, and so beautiful that her very presence made his breath catch in his throat. "Mianne," he whispered, "look at me."

Against her will, her body responded to the gentleness in his voice and she turned her head to meet his curious gaze. "You are lovely," he murmured. "Did you know?" Then, unexpectedly, he leaned forward to brush her lips with his.

Mianne was startled into immobility, and Phillipe interpreted her gasp of surprise as one of pleasure. He pressed closer, reaching out to draw her to him, and the breeze whispered between their parted lips like a momentary caress. Then, abruptly, Mianne pulled away and rose to her feet, fleeing with every last ounce of her strength from the touch of the sunlight, the feel of Phillipe's warm mouth on hers, and the pulsing heat of her own desire, locked like a captive bird in her chest.

"Mianne!" he cried, springing to his feet, "wait!" But before he had taken more than three steps, he was brought up short by a taunting voice behind him.

"I don't think she wants you, Phillipe. Perhaps you should let her go."

He whirled to find Katherine standing a few feet away. She was wearing the same blue velvet riding habit she had worn the first time he met her, and her hands were planted firmly on her softly curved hips. Her mouth was no more than a thin, rigid line and her eyes snapped with sparks of fury.

For a moment, Phillipe gaped at her in surprise, awed by the anger radiating from every stiff line of her body. Then he realized that she must have seen that fleeting kiss. With a flash of delight, he recognized that Katherine was jealous. And he had always thought her above such things. But perhaps she was human after all. He knew well enough that she *could* be when she chose to. "Katherine," he said, moving toward her with his hand outstretched.

"You have something to say to me?" she inquired icily. "Perhaps you want to apologize for having forgotten that you promised to meet me in the clearing half an hour ago?"

Phillipe grimaced. He *had* forgotten. "I'm sorry," he said contritely, "but I—"

"You got distracted by your little friend," she finished for him, "and I slipped your mind completely." Her face was deeply flushed with her anger, and she wrenched her hand away when he attempted to grasp it. Suddenly her father's warning echoed in her mind. *Phillipe is a Vallombrosa through and through, even if he is only the bastard son.*

"Of course not," he soothed. "It's just that I thought I was to meet you at three instead of two."

"Liar!" Her eyes gleamed golden brown for an instant, then she lowered her lids demurely. *He's one of them, Katherine.* "Or perhaps you got your appointments mixed. Perhaps you didn't plan to meet *Mianne* until three."

"Don't be silly. I only found her here by accident and stopped to talk for a moment. She's lonely, that's all, and I pitied her."

"I *saw* how you pitied her!"

"Listen to me," he demanded, making one last attempt to possess himself of her hands and succeeding at last, "you know how I feel about you. Mianne is just a child. You're the one I want."

And he'll play their side to the end. Chewing thoughtfully on her lower lip, she scrutinized his face for a full minute. "All right," she said finally, "then prove it."

Phillipe smiled, sweeping her a dramatic bow. "I'm at your service." He was pleased with himself; it had been easier than he thought to mollify her. "But I think we'd better find ourselves a more private spot."

When he started toward a nearby group of box-elders, she followed willingly, but he did not see the sly little smile that flickered across her lips. *I would have you remember that, my dear, before you make a mistake that might eventually prove fatal.*

The moment they were safely within the shade, hidden by the low-hanging leaves, Phillipe turned to Katherine, sliding his arms around her. "You'll see," he murmured throatily, "that I'm only thinking of you."

She leaned into him and closed her eyes while he dropped kisses on her face and neck. Locking her arms around his waist, she seemed to abandon herself to the dictates of her hungry body. She sought his mouth with her own moistly parted lips, shivering when his tongue slipped inside. Then his hands began to roam down across her body, touching all the familiar curves and hollows with searching fingers. She could hear his quickened breath in her ear, feel the lurching beat of his heart, but it was not until she felt his excitement pressing against her belly that she backed away. "Tell me," she said, grasping his hands and holding them immobile, "does your father pay you to do this, or is it only out of family loyalty?"

He gasped, blinking at her in astonishment, while her words cut into him like the well-honed blade of a knife. He knew, in that instant, that she was finally achieving the revenge she had desired for so long. By flinging his cruel words back in his face, she had evened the score between them. "Katherine," he said pleadingly, "please—"

But, with a toss of her head, she released his hands, turned on her heel, and fled. For the second time in one day, Phillipe was left staring bleakly after his companion, his mind bewildered and his hands cold and empty.

"One boiler exploded, two separate attempts in the past week to burn down the packing plant, three more carloads of rotten beef, and the railroad's promise to double their rates. Don't you think it's time to recognize the signs and give up on this ill-fated business?" Medora asked.

The Marquis was sprawled in the wing-backed chair, gazing warily at his wife through the deepening shadows of dusk. "How can you ask me to give up when we've just won such an important battle? *They're* the ones who are on the defensive now. We should take advantage of it."

Rising precipitously, Medora came to stand beside him. "That battle was for your *life,* Mores. It's true that we kept you alive, at least for the moment, but that doesn't change the fact that the plant is only slaughtering twenty head a day. We're losing a great deal of money and there's nothing to replace it with. Why can't we get out now, before—"

"Because, as I've told you many times, I'm not the kind of man who gives up."

Medora sighed heavily and turned away. "Then you're a fool who doesn't know when to admit defeat. I've been thinking about this day and night, and I really believe we should go soon. It's not worth the risk of losing everything."

"To me," Mores said, *"victory* is everything. You should know that. I can't simply crawl away in silence and let the Pendletons believe they're the winners. I can't." He rose, grasping her shoulders firmly. "But you don't care about that, do you? You don't care that I could never look myself in the face again if I were to give in. All you care about is the money. Or perhaps deep inside you *want* the Pendletons to win. Perhaps you're more concerned about your lover's happiness than mine."

Pushing him away with a violent shove, she snapped, "Mores, you are so damned blind! You're determined to destroy us all."

"*I* am?" he snarled. "Well, at least I recognize the difference between a friend and an enemy. Perhaps you should learn to do the same." Turning his back on his wife, he started for the door.

"Where are you going?" she called after him.

"Out."

Medora's heart began to pound erratically. "Out where?"

"That's not your concern."

"You're going to see your Indian bitch, aren't you?"

Before she had even finished speaking he had whirled, crossing the room until he towered above her. His eyes shooting silver sparks of rage, he hissed, "Don't ever speak of her that way again."

She was appalled by the intensity of his response, numbed by the knowledge that, after all, Greg had told her the truth. Medora knew she should be silent, but her lips simply would not be still. "Why not?" she rasped. "Is the girl so sacred?"

The Marquis drew a deep shuddering breath and murmured, "Yes. To me she is sacred."

Closing her eyes to block out the sight of his face, Medora swallowed once. "It's true that she's your mistress then."

"No," he replied softly, "Ileya has never been my lover." But when his wife opened her eyes to stare at him in astonishment, he added, "She is much more than that—my only friend." Then he shook his head, buried his hands in his pockets, and left her.

Medora watched him go without protest. She could not have spoken in that moment even if she had wanted to. Her body and her mind and her emotions had been invaded by an icy numbness that crept through her blood as a snake creeps through the black night. But she knew that eventually—soon—the numbness would slide away, leaving her to be devoured by the pain that lay now, curled in stunned immobility around her heart.

Mores moved without being conscious that he did so. He knew only that he must find Ileya, for only she could free him from the grim shadows that had settled in his mind. He had realized as he stood gazing down at his wife through the melancholy desolation of approaching night that even she had become an enemy. He had known for a long time that she had betrayed him, but somehow he had never really believed she would abandon him entirely. He had seen from the cold light in her deep green eyes that she no longer believed in him. And that was the worst betrayal of all.

> *May this be the day*
> *which I considered mine.*

Ileya's song penetrated his consciousness, her voice as sweet as the voice of a nightingale. She was there, he told himself. Of all the others, only Ileya had not left him.

> *From the North the wind is blowing.*

Her simple words swept through his mind, wiping it clean of painful memories, leaving behind a soft refrain.

She was waiting on her knees at the river's edge, swaying with the rhythm of the wind overhead, singing with the pulse of the water below. The Marquis stood watching her in the last few instants before darkness enveloped her and the smile that curved his lips was infinitely tender.

Then, at last, she rose from her knees, coming to him silently, her feet no more than a whisper against the spongy ground. Without a word, she took his hand to lead him toward her hut, which stood waiting, the door swinging open. When they were inside, she left him for a moment to light a lantern, then she set it on the empty barrel that served her for a table.

Mores gasped as the light danced up her body, outlining

the lithe movement of her muscles and the undulating cape
of her hair. She was smiling, her eyes glowing with welcome
and, for the first time, he realized how lovely she was. Tonight
her beauty was a strangely vibrant thing—a soft, shining presence that had never been there before. He reached out to
enfold her in his arms and when she pressed against him,
locking her hands in the curve of his back, he remembered
the single moment long ago when they had somehow merged
into one being.

All at once he wanted that again—wanted to consume her,
to absorb her peace of mind, her quietness, her reserve. He
wanted to create another kind of communion with this amazing girl who found such pleasure in simple things like her
songs and the wind and the spirit of the water. She clung to
him, her body warm and trembling, and he knew then that
he had changed. Suddenly he was painfully aware of the
silken feel of her hair beneath his hands and the rush of her
breath against his cheek. Stepping back, he tilted her chin
upward so he could look into her eyes. "Ileya," he murmured,
"I want—"

She stopped him with a single movement of her hand.
"Everything I have is yours, my friend; you know that."

Her eyes were radiant circles of flame and her lips were
parted and moistly inviting. The Marquis realized then that
she could deny him nothing. Brushing the hair away from
her face, he bent to kiss her.

The meeting of their willing mouths was like a rush of
clear crystal water over smooth polished stones, the touch of
their hands the caress of a soft breeze. They clung together,
trembling, as if to let go would be to lose all that was warm
and pure and joyful. In moments, their clothing lay discarded
on the floor and they crossed the room together, arms
wrapped around each other, lowering themselves to the straw
mattress covered with only a single Indian blanket. Then, for
what seemed like an eternity, the Marquis knelt above her,
running his hands lightly across her smooth tanned skin, gently caressing her shoulders, her breasts, her belly and thighs.
With a tenderness that he not known himself to be capable

of, he learned the secrets of her body, allowing his fingertips to serve as his eyes.

"God, but you're lovely," he whispered huskily. "I never knew before how beautiful you are."

Then she reached out to draw him down beside her and their bodies fit together, hip to hip and chest to chest, as if they had been made for no other purpose on earth but to cling one to the other. Her hands found their own paths across his naked back, and everywhere her fingers touched, his skin glowed with a warmth that swept across him in waves, engulfing him until he was aware of nothing beyond the feel of her skin and the fragrance of her hair.

And when, at last, he entered her, she drew him so tightly against her that he could no longer tell where his own senses ended and hers began. The rocking, pulsing motion of his body seemed to merge itself with hers and, for the second time, he felt that his blood had become hers and the beating of her heart his. For a long, magic moment, they hovered there, enwrapped in a surging, flaming passion that made them one. Then the night exploded into a rushing waterfall that swept them away into the piercing, shimmering center of the light.

The Marquis awakened two hours later to find that the bed beside him was empty. He sat up abruptly, afraid that Ileya had left him, but she was there, sitting on the floor with her back to him. Tossing the blanket aside, he rose quietly and knelt behind her. With fingers that trembled just a little, he touched her lightly on the shoulder. "Ileya?"

She turned to gaze at him through the shifting curtain of her hair and he saw that her cheeks were streaked with tears. Not until that moment had it occurred to him that she might regret what they had done, but now the realization hit him with crippling force. Rising stiffly, he began to pace the soft dirt floor. How could he have been so blind? he wondered. How could he have forgotten how precious and rare their relationship had been before he made it common by giving in to his physical needs? And how could he ever face her again?

Ileya stood and went to lift the lantern from the barrel, motioning for the Marquis to take its place. "Sit for a moment," she said. "You do not understand."

Because he could deny her nothing, he did as she instructed him, but his heart was heavy with gnawing guilt. "I'm sorry," he whispered. "Can you forgive me?"

Shaking her head sadly, Ileya knelt at his feet and laid her hands on his knees. "Don't spoil it," she said. "Our meeting as we did is too precious to me. And there is nothing to forgive." When he did not respond, she added, "It was my choice, too."

He looked down at her then, giving her a little smile, but he could not find the words to answer her.

"Do you believe me?" she asked.

"No."

"Listen to me, Antoine. A woman of the Sioux must never weep for anything less than her nation going down in defeat, and although this is not so today, I would hardly break such a vow for a single hour in my lover's arms."

When Mores stared at her, uncomprehending, she reached out to lay her hand on his. "It is not for myself that I grieve, dear one, but for you. Your troubles are far deeper than mine and I do not know that you can bear—" She stopped herself with a quick indrawn breath, paused for a moment, then continued. "There are many things which you do not understand, but I would have you know that tonight, for myself, I am deeply happy. Happier, perhaps than I have ever been before in my lifetime. You have taken nothing from me that I did not wish to give. And I would have you remember that when the night has faded into morning and the sun stains the clouds deep red."

Cupping her hands between his, he asked, "Are you telling me the truth?"

"Always, my love. I would never insult you with a lie."

The Marquis leaned down to kiss her, but she drew away. "You must go now. Your wife awaits you."

Dropping his head so she would not see the bleak reality

he knew was reflected in his eyes, he said, "No. It's been a long time since Medora waited for me."

"Can you not work at dissolving these bad feelings between you? She is your wife."

Mores contemplated the girl's face curiously. This was not like her. Never before had she spoken of Medora. "No," he said, "I'm afraid I can't. The rift has grown too wide."

"But won't you try?" she pleaded. "For me?"

"Not even for you. And why should you want such a thing anyway? I don't understand."

Ileya twisted a finger in a thick strand of hair, gazing beyond him to the window at his back. "I see that it distresses you deeply, and I cannot bear for you to be unhappy. And then, sometimes, I am afraid that you will cut yourself off from her completely and be left alone."

"My dear," he murmured, running a finger along her cheek, "I am not alone so long as I have you."

She bent her head as if she could not bear to look at him. "Please," she mumbled without looking up, "I want you to go now."

"No, Ileya, let me stay."

She shook her head. "It is time for you to leave me," she repeated firmly. "Please."

When he saw that she was adamant, he agreed reluctantly to do as she wished. But when they stood before the hut and he knew that in a few moments she would disappear from his sight, he felt a wrenching sadness that shook him to the very core. He sensed a kind of living, devouring grief that held her body in its grasp and he simply could not understand. He could not bear the mournful look in her eyes, so he took her hand in his, thinking to comfort her.

The spark that passed between them in that instant was like a jolt of electric fire, and Ileya clung to his hand with all the strength she possessed. "I love you, Antoine," she whispered, "more, I think, than even you can understand." And when he turned and started away, the grief rose like a heavy stone upon her chest until she thought it must surely force the life from her body.

May this be the day,

she sang softly, the notes like pure, glittering diamonds in the air *"which I considered mine."*

The wind took up the words, painting them like a final shimmering lament across the deep velvet heart of the midnight sky.

Breakfast at the Chateau was an uncomfortable meal the next morning. Mianne ate quickly, without once looking up at her companions, and Phillipe realized she must have been more shaken by yesterday's encounter than he had thought. He himself transferred his attention back and forth between the Marquis and Medora, who spent the meal studiously avoiding meeting each other's eyes. William was so engrossed in thoughts about business problems that he did not seem to notice the wall of cold disinterest that had sprung up between Mores and his wife the night before, but Phillipe was painfully aware of its existence. What galled him was that he did not know what had happened to put it there, nor could he help to remove it. Once again, he was utterly helpless. As the meal dragged on in unnatural silence, he felt more and more like a stranger to the people all around him.

It was near the end of the meal, and not more than five words had been spoken at the table, when Johnny Goodall burst into the room, his hat clutched in stiff white fingers. "Could I speak to you for a minute, sir?" he gasped between gulps of air that never seemed to satisfy his greedy lungs.

Sensing the urgency in Goodall's tone, the Marquis nodded and rose from the table. He followed Johnny into the drawing room, where the man closed the door carefully behind him, turned, and muttered hoarsely, "They've got her, sir. The Pendletons have got Ileya!"

TWENTY-FIVE

It took a moment for the significance of Johnny's announcement to sink in, but when it did, Mores started for the door. "Where?" he asked.

"The last time I saw them, they were headed south down the river. Your horse is outside saddled and ready and I'll be right behind you."

The Marquis breathed out a gruff "Thanks, Johnny," and stepped outside. Leaping onto his horse's back, he urged the animal forward, his eyes narrowed as if, simply by concentrating hard enough, he could see through the heavy foliage around the river and locate the girl he sought. With Johnny at his side, the Marquis rode like a madman, unaware of everything but his desire to see Ileya safe once again.

It was less than fifteen minutes later when his wish was granted. As he came up over a low hill, he saw that there was a break in the trees on his side of the river. The cottonwoods seemed to have crept back in order to allow the morning sunlight to reach the water, and there, running along the bank with her hair whipping wildly behind her, was Ileya. She glanced furtively over her shoulder as she fled, and Mores sensed her urgency from the stiff, unnatural lines of her body. Pressing his horse forward, he started downward. He had to get to her before they did. She had escaped them for the moment, but he knew they would not give up so easily. Once they had decided to repay her for her treachery, they would not rest until it was done.

While Johnny slipped around the far fringes of the trees

in an effort to waylay the Pendletons, Mores continued to close the gap between himself and Ileya. By now he could see the tense expression on her face and the concentration with which she moved across the soft, marshy ground. For an instant, he actually thought he would get to her in time, but then a rifle exploded with a devastating shudder from somewhere in the trees across the river and Ileya crumpled forward onto the muddy bank.

Sliding numbly from his restive horse, the Marquis stumbled to the girl's side. He could see that already the blood was pouring from the wound in the center of her back, but he refused to believe his own eyes. Kneeling beside her, he lifted Ileya gently in his arms until her head rested against his elbow and he could see her pale, colorless face.

When she felt the pressure of his hands on her body, her eyelids fluttered open. For a moment, she stared at him blankly, as if she did not know him, but then a brief flame of recognition kindled in her dark eyes. And while the blood flowed out of her, taking with it her strength and her spirit, she reached up to brush a quivering finger lovingly across his cheek. "I was wrong, you see," she whispered. "I thought I would never see you again." Then her arm fell away from him and she gave him a smile of such incredible sweetness that it wrenched the agony up from his belly and into his throat. *I love you, Antoine,* she had said, *more, I think, than even you can understand.*

Ileya swallowed several times with difficulty, her eyebrows coming together in a grimace of pain; she just managed to mouth the single word, "Medora," before her eyelids descended heavily, blocking her pure, liquid gaze from his sight.

Mores shuddered convulsively, wrapping both arms around her in a grip that would have crushed the stones that lay at his feet, and yet he did not hurt her. He could not hurt her, for she had moved beyond the limits of human pain. In the instant when her body grew limp and flaccid in his arms, he closed his eyes, sucking in huge gulps of air to try to stop the flood of horror that had risen like a storm inside him. But all he saw printed on the back of his eyelids were a

hundred pictures of Ileya: She was diving into the still center
of a deep pool, ruffling the water with her presence; kneeling
beside the river, lost in the magic of her songs; floating in
the heart of the river, her hands like a caress upon the water,
the water like a caress upon her thick, black hair. It was
almost as if he remembered her always reaching for the river,
drenching herself in the healing water, desiring nothing more
than to become one with it. As she had, for a moment, with
him.

Opening his eyes at last, he gazed at her face and saw that
it was that of a stranger. He did not know who to curse more
violently, the man who had killed her with a gun or himself,
who had destroyed her with his passion. She had left him
once because her life was in danger. She had known even
then that she dared not return. Yet she had done so. She had
come back because she sensed that he needed her. Because
of his weakness, Ileya had died. And he knew with an insight
that was clear and piercing that in her he had lost a friend
such as he would never have again in his lifetime. *It is not
for myself that I grieve,* she had said, *but for you.*

Perhaps then she had known. Perhaps some primitive intuition had struck her in the night and that was why he had
awakened to find her weeping. If only she could have trusted
him enough to tell him. But of course that was absurd. She
had chosen her own path long ago and he knew that there
was no force on earth that could have stopped her. And now
it was too late. Too late to tell her all that she had meant to
him, too late to kiss away her tears and whisper that he loved
her as he had never loved another—or ever would. There was
nothing he could do for her now except hold her until her
body had given up its warmth and her spirit had left her
behind.

Pulling her close to his chest, he sat there on the damp
riverbank holding her, as he used to do, in silence. Without
the comfort of words, he kept his vigil, swaying unconsciously with the lethargic motion of the warm morning
breeze. Then, just as before, he felt the warmth flow from
her body into his as the death chill crept through her bones,

and he began to shiver, violently, as blood merged with blood and heat with coldness—one final miracle before he lost her entirely.

When his bones had turned to brittle ice inside his body, he looked up at last, aware, for the first time, of his surroundings. His breath caught in his throat when he saw the puddle of river water that lay just beyond Ileya's arm. Her blood had flowed from beneath her until it touched the water, dying it red, and Mores could see the image of the sky and clouds reflected there, discolored and distorted into scarlet billows. *You have taken nothing from me that I did not wish to give. And I would have you remember that, when the night has faded into morning and the sun stains the clouds deep red.* Dear God, the things she had known, yet kept to herself, carrying the weight of that knowledge all alone.

He saw then that the only part of Ileya still in motion were the long, midnight strands of her hair that had fallen into the water. The tendrils rose and fell, twisted and turned in a strange, undulating dance of death. Her hair was like a cape of night, a shadow on the water that moved softly and so smoothly that it seemed to have become part of the rhythm of the river. And he knew then that, in the end, her wish had come true and she had become one with the water she had worshiped for so long.

Medora sat staring despondently at the jumble of papers on the huge desk in the Marquis's study. She could no longer even begin to sort into some kind of rational order the bills, complaints, reports of profits and losses, and queries from investors. It was a hopeless task, and the longer she attempted to accomplish it, the more oppressive became the haze of despair that had been hovering just above her shoulder for the past several weeks. Finally, she closed her eyes and gave up, resting her head on the desktop because she was too weary to move it any further.

Even when she heard the screaming of hinges as a door was opened somewhere in the house, she did not look up.

was not until she sensed a compelling presence behind her that she raised her head and turned. Then she gasped in horror, clutching the chair to keep herself from falling. "Dear God!" she cried, and closed her eyes in an attempt to destroy the vision that had materialized before her like a nightmare.

Mores stood in the doorway, his clothing stained with blood, his face haggard, his eyes nothing more than lifeless spheres free from all color or light or movement. In his arms he held the blood-soaked body of a girl. Her feet were bare, coated in half-dried mud, and they dangled limp and lifeless, still swaying slightly from the motion of the Marquis's body. Her long, black hair fell across his arm, nearly to his knees; heavy and wet, it dripped regularly on the Persian carpet, leaving a small, dark puddle behind.

"What—" Medora managed to choke out.

"I thought you would want to see her," her husband answered. "To see your Indian rival when she could no longer hurt you."

Turning her head away, she choked back the bitter taste that rose in her throat. "What happened?"

"The Pendletons killed her." The Marquis spoke levelly, just barely able to keep under control the grief and rage that still swept over him in waves. "But I thought you knew that."

With the image of Ileya's unnaturally white face floating before her, Greg Pendleton's words came unbidden to her mind: *We've let her be for the moment, but I promise you, we plan to take care of her soon.* Clasping her hands together, she whispered, "Why bring her to me?"

"Because I wanted to see your face." His voice cracked briefly, but he forced himself to go on. "Did you tell them where to find her?"

He keeps her in a hut by the river where he goes to visit her regularly. "No. They already knew," she murmured.

Mores clenched his teeth for a moment at her response. She did not even bother to deny it. "Did you want them to do it? Are you glad?"

"Of course not!" *So you see, your problem will be solved without your lifting a finger.*

"Did you know what they were planning?" he continued relentlessly.

The one who betrayed me will die, I promise you that. Medora took a deep, shuddering breath. "How can you ask me such a thing?"

"Did you know?"

Rising from the chair as if in a trance, Medora looked away from him and did not answer.

Mores took a step forward. *"Look* at this girl!" he demanded. "Look at her and tell me the truth!"

As if drawn by some force outside herself, she did as he had bidden her. For an instant that seemed to stretch into eternity, Medora looked into Ileya's sightless eyes. *For three years he has deceived you, Medora. Three years.* "You are cruel," she gasped.

"Her *murderers* are cruel."

All at once she raised her eyes to meet his cold, grim gaze. "Are you suggesting that *I—* " *Isn't it comforting to know that I always take care of your needs?*

"DID YOU KNOW?"

Suddenly, all the moisture left her mouth and she thought for a moment that she would not be able to answer, but then she rasped. "NO! I didn't know, damn you! I didn't!"

He stood immobile, staring at her intently as if he were judging the truth of her denial. Then, abruptly, he turned and started for the door.

"Where are you going?" Medora cried hoarsely.

Pausing, he flung back over his shoulder, "To take Ileya's body back to the reservation, where she can be buried with the others of her tribe."

"But that's too dangerous. It's far away and they hate you out there. You might be killed."

Fighting back the incapacitating wave of bitter anguish that left his insides burnt and barren, he said, "Ileya was killed because of her loyalty to me. The very least I can do is risk my life for her."

As he vanished with his burden in his arms, Medora heard

as if he had spoken them the words he had chosen not to add: "And such a loss would not be very great, after all."

Greg Pendleton stood shrouded in the gloom, untouched by the glow from the single inadequate window. The murky atmosphere in the study had never distressed him before, but now that Medora stood across the room, he wished for a torrent of sunlight to burn away the shadows that hid her face from his sight. He had known she would come to him to-day—known it with an intuition that was rare in a man of his kind. And it had been so long since he had held her naked, quivering body in his arms. But she was here now and her presence seemed to fill the room. "You wanted to see me?" he inquired coolly, determined that she would not know how very aware of her he was.

"No," she told him bluntly, "but I knew I had to. I want to know why you killed that girl."

He was so taken aback by her question that it took him several seconds to gather his thoughts. "Don't try to interfere, Medora. There are things you can never understand," he said finally.

"I understand that you think nothing of taking a life for no other purpose than to satisfy your pitiful wish for re-venge."

Greg's nostrils flared and a muscle in his jaw began to twitch. "For Christ's sake, she was only an Indian."

"She was a human being, Greg, and her life was worth more than your sense of humiliation. If you wanted to pay someone back for that, it should have been me."

"No," he muttered, turning toward the window, "not you. Never you."

"Why not?" Medora demanded in a tight little voice. "It was *I* who ruined your rustling operation, not that poor girl."

Whirling to face her, Greg hissed, "That 'poor girl' was your husband's mistress! Why should you care that she's dead?"

Medora stared down at her hands for a moment, unable to

give him an answer. Why indeed? she asked herself. But she
knew why. It was because she had made a terrible mistake a
long, long time ago, and she was not certain how to make it
right. In truth, she had not come here for Ileya's sake, but
for her husband's. It was the only recompense she could make
for her obstinate blindness. Medora looked up at Greg and
said, "My husband loved her, you see, and somehow that
means more to me than your greedy, grasping family could
ever understand. Because you don't care about human feelings; you've never had any yourself. I honestly don't believe
that you've ever loved anybody."

He felt her derision for him like a pulsing physical force.
Her words pierced his defenses with devastating efficiency
and he whispered, "You're wrong. Terribly wrong. Because I
love *you* and always have."

For a long, tense moment, she was shocked into silence.
She had known from the beginning that he did not care for
her. It had always been a game with him—a contest between
two evenly-matched opponents to see who could manage to
collect the most points. And never once had it occurred to
her that he saw her in any other light.

Greg saw the disbelief that glittered in her eyes and his
insides twisted into raw, painful knots. "You possess every
quality I've ever wanted in a woman," he said, "courage, determination, intelligence, and an inner strength that puts all
others to shame. To me you are everything. And I love you."

Medora stood frozen, appalled by the smoldering light in
his steel-gray eyes. For, all at once, she knew without a doubt
that he was telling her the truth; she could read his feelings
in every movement of his features. Of all the words she had
ever expected to hear from him, those three had been the
very last. *I love you.* But then, he had been as wrong as she
had. *You possess every quality I've ever wanted in a woman—
courage, determination, intelligence, and an inner strength
that puts all others to shame.* She knew, even if Greg did
not, that her courage was a sham that disguised the one constant, debilitating fear that had haunted her for the past three
years—the fear that she would lose her husband. Determina

tion? Well, yes, she had been very determined; she had pushed the Marquis away, slowly and stubbornly, so that he would never be able to hurt her again. But intelligence? That was another mistake, because, in reality, she had been a blind fool and, what was worse, a coward. She had let the one man she had ever truly loved slip away, precisely because she could not bear for him to go.

As for her inner strength, it had only helped her to lay waste her own emotions, and his. It would never have happened, she knew, if he had not been what he was: a man who let his feelings rule him, a man whose emotions were of a depth and an intensity that few others ever attained, a man whose sensitive nature was a rare and precious thing in a desolate world like the Dakota Badlands.

This was the man she had destroyed, as surely as he had destroyed her when he said, *Ileya has never been my lover. She is much more than that—my only friend.* She had done it for a few stolen moments with Greg, who excited her, disturbed her, infuriated her, but who had never touched her secret inner being. He had been too cold, too self-sufficient, too unyielding to love. In other words, she told herself ruefully, he had been safe. His admission of his feelings for her, so long delayed and so adeptly concealed, did not move her. She felt only pity and a slight aversion. She did not know how she had come to be here, but she knew now that she had to go. Grasping the folds of her skirt in cold, stiff fingers, she gave him one long, pitying look and murmured, "I'm sorry, but that's just not good enough." Then she turned and walked away.

Greg swallowed once, gripping the edge of the desk with a force that should have shattered the wood. She was going. Because of Ileya's death, Medora was leaving him. For an instant, he considered telling her the truth; he knew it was the only thing that could make her turn around again. But even as the thought occurred to him, he knew that he could not do it. There were other loyalties he had to honor, and Medora would have to continue to hate him for the Indian girl's sake. But it was a lie. He had to let her go, even though he had the power to bring her back.

As he watched her disappear into the hallway, he closed his eyes to shut out the light. She might return, but never again for him. He was losing the one thing he had ever truly wanted in all his long and barren life. And when the door slammed shut behind her, a ring of cold stone locked itself around his heart. This time there would be no key to open it again.

As Medora checked the saddle for the last time, Phillipe came toward her from out of the gloom. "You wanted to see me?" he asked, eyeing her riding apparel curiously.

"Yes, Phillipe. I'm leaving for a few days and I just wanted to let you know. I'd like you to look in on Athenais now and then while I'm away. The nurse is efficient, but not very entertaining. Will you do that for me?"

"Of course." The boy reached out to rub the horse's neck absently, but his mind was clearly on Medora. "But where are you going?"

"To look for your father."

For a long time, he watched her out of the corner of his eye, his brows drawn together in a troubled frown. Then he said, "There's something very wrong between the two of you, isn't there?"

Medora put one foot in the stirrup, swinging herself onto the horse's back. She had been surprised by his question and needed a moment to think. Somehow she had forgotten there were other people in the house who could not help but be aware of the rift that had been growing for so long. "Yes," she told him reluctantly, "there is."

Phillipe nodded thoughtfully and his frown deepened. "And he left here in a rage?"

"Yes."

With a heavy sigh that sent the animal's mane dancing, he leaned his cheek against the horse's sleek red neck. "Is he coming back?"

Medora's heart went out to the boy she had resented so deeply for so long; the anguished question she had glimpsed in his eyes reflected her own personal torment. "I hope so. I'm going to try to find him now."

"And then you'll make it right again . . . ?"

"It isn't that easy to save a marriage that has begun to die, Medora," Gretta Von Hoffman said, twining her fingers together in her lap. "Believe me, I know. I lost your father a long, long time ago, my dear, to his schemes and his wealth and his ambition."

Medora leaned forward to lay her hand on her mother's, her own eyes brimming with sympathy. "You don't have to talk about it, you know."

Shaking her head sadly, Gretta murmured, "But I do. Because, you see, I couldn't bear to watch you make the same mistake. I want you to realize how rare a man Mores is—a romantic, a dreamer, a man with a real beating heart instead of an adding machine. Don't let him get away, my dear. His feelings for you are a treasure beyond price."

"I know that, Mother," Medora assured her.

"No," Gretta mused, "I don't think you do. I don't think you realize how barren life can be without tenderness, but I do. My life has been empty and cold for years, except for the joy you gave me. There was a time when I might have won Louis back to me, but I was too afraid of losing to even try. I'll never forgive myself for that."

"Mother, I don't—"

"Let me finish. I've waited a long time to tell you these things and I want to do it now before I lose my courage. I know your father told you that all you have to do is reach out and grasp what you want without hesitation and you'll find your own happiness, but he was wrong. Terribly wrong. You have to fight every minute of your life to achieve your desires, and sometimes that means giving in and letting your pride and obstinacy crack just a little. But believe me, it's worth the sacrifice. The love between you and your husband is more precious than anything else in this bleak world. More important than pride or courage or ambition. It is everything."

Medora rose, smiling, and leaned down to kiss her mother's cheek. "I'll remember," she said. *And as she brushed back a silvery curl that had strayed from its intended place, she realized, all at once, how sad and tired Gretta looked, and how infinitely fragile. . . .*

Medora thought Phillipe had never sounded so young and vulnerable before. Like her, he seemed to have discovered too late how much he needed the man he had once considered his greatest enemy. "I'm going to do my best, Phillipe. But I just don't know if that will be good enough."

TWENTY-SIX

The brooding spires and grotesque domes of stone seemed to shift position in the shimmering heat of late afternoon. Mores felt as if the twisting gullies that opened before him now and then were intent upon swallowing himself and his horse with a single hungry snapping of stiff clay jaws. All around him the landscape was a sinister, menacing force that intruded itself upon his thoughts like the ominous rumblings of a fierce summer storm.

Ileya was gone. He had left her cold, stiff body with the Indians, but had not stayed to see her buried. That was one sight he had refused to witness. He had said a last, silent farewell to her corpse—which the Sioux had dressed in a fine elkskin gown covered with beads and shells—then turned away from her. She was behind him now and, as his horse plodded slowly across the dry, parched ground, he knew that it was time to think about the future. Ileya's death had brought a sharp and violent close to a portion of his life. It would be different now. It had to be.

Out here, in the heart of the Badlands, time hung heavy and interminable on his hands, and, with the sun pouring its burning heat upon his head, he thought of going home. Home, his mind repeated dully; what was that? The Chateau, full of strangers—or the plant, full of flaws? For the first time in months, the Marquis took the time to really think about the business empire he had built around him and he wondered, with a sinking feeling of despair, what he had really achieved. Not money—he had lost that hand over fist. And certainly not prestige—he doubted if there were a man more despised than he in all of the territory. He had made a few friends, it was true, but most of them he had lost again. Just as he had lost Ileya.

Then, of course, there was Phillipe. And Medora. Ileya had seen it all. She had even warned him, but he had paid her no mind. *I see that it distresses you deeply, and I cannot bear for you to be unhappy. And then sometimes I am afraid that you will cut yourself off from her completely and be left alone.* As always, she had been right. He had gambled his family for an empire, risked everything for his dream. And in the end, Medora had been right too; he had quite nearly *lost* everything. Everything but his damned, arrogant pride.

It was not until that moment that he remembered Ileya's last word. *Medora.* Had she been trying to give him one final message? Perhaps she had only meant to remind him of her request the night before she died. *Can you not work at dissolving these bad feelings between you? She is your wife.* Twice she had tried to convince him and twice he had not listened. But he knew now that in her concern for him, Ileya had sought the only answer she could find for his loneliness—Medora. Her final wish for him had been that he somehow find his way back to his wife.

Yet Medora and he had grown so far apart that he did not know how to begin to bridge the gap. And now that his rage and guilt had subsided a little, he had to admit that he had been as much to blame as she had. They had both paid and paid, over and over, for the dream that he had refused to abandon until it had turned into a nightmare. They had struggled and strained and fought against each other and everyone else in order to meet the cost. And, all at once, he realized that the price had been too high.

It was early morning and the distant hills were still shrouded in cool morning mist when the Marquis saw a figure riding toward him. The rider materialized on a remote ridge like a vaporous gray specter framed by two carved sandstone pillars, and paused there as if waiting for some dark inspiration to spur him onward. Then, abruptly, horse and rider began to descend, gathering speed as they went, until they were racing across the empty plain with a speed that took Mores's breath away. The figure rode relentlessly forward, closing the gap between the only two riders in a long and desolate stretch of desert, and it was a long time before the Marquis recognized the copper glint of the sun on streaming red hair. Dear God! It was Medora. His hands gripped the reins furiously and his heart hammered painfully in his chest. Something must be very wrong at the Chateau if she had come to meet him like this. Perhaps Phillipe or Athenais—

Digging his heels into his horse's sides, he urged the animal forward with wild and desperate strength. He had thought he was past fear and sorrow, but he had been wrong. The sight of his wife riding toward him through the haze had sent an incapacitating surge of dread through his veins. "Medora," he called, when the two horses finally came together in the barren heart of the plain. "What's happened?"

She drew back violently on the reins, her breath coming in wrenching gasps, and gazed at her husband in silence. Now that she was here, now that he sat no more than three feet away, waiting for her response, she did not know what to say to him. For the moment, she was only aware of the blood that pounded deafeningly in her ears and the ice-cold flame that burned in her chest. She realized with a clarity of insight that was almost painful that, for the third time in her life, she was afraid. But she knew she had to conquer that fear, just as she had tried to conquer the fear of the leaping flames that had destroyed her home a long, long time ago. She knew that if she failed, the fear would devour her as surely as that fire had devoured her past. Biting her lip to keep it still, she looked up uncertainly at the man who held her future like a fragile butterfly in the palm of his hand.

"Medora," he repeated, "tell me."

Through the deadly intensity of her own agitation, she saw the panic that made his black eyes into bottomless wells, and some of her sanity began to return. "You were on your way home, weren't you?" she said.

Mores frowned impatiently. "Of course I was. But I want to know what's troubling you. Why have you come?"

The wave of relief that swept through her nearly knocked her from the saddle. He had meant to come home after all. Before she could stop to think, she breathed, "I thought you weren't coming back."

"Did that matter so much?"

It was then, finally, that her resolve broke completely and she began to weep.

Medora nodded dumbly and the Marquis reached out to grasp her hands where they rested on the pommel. Never before had he seen her weep as she did now, the tears covering her flushed cheeks in a crystal stream; he had always thought her to be incapable of tears. His heart constricted with a twisting bite of doubt when he saw how she dropped her head and hunched her shoulders, attempting to hide her weakness. Perhaps, after all, he had been wrong. The woman who sat before him now was undeniably human and unutterably vulnerable. "Medora," he murmured, "I think we should sit in the shade for a moment."

She did not protest when he took the bridle and led her horse into the shadow of a nearby cliff, nor did she push him away when he reached out to help her from the saddle. Medora was not really aware of what was happening until the Marquis's arms closed around her, firmly, protectively, and she buried her head against the beating warmth of his chest. Her own arms slid across his back and she clung to him wildly, with a strength that nearly forced the breath from his body. But Mores did not gasp or push her away; he merely stroked her hair gently with one hand while the other moved caressingly along her shoulders and back.

When at last she began to relax against him, he rested his chin on the crown of her head, closing his eyes to shut out the light. He found that he could not bear this kind of debilitating sorrow, not from Medora, who never allowed herself the luxury of tears. Raising her head, she looked up at him through the liquid veil that covered her eyes. His breath caught in his throat at the pure emerald glow of her sea-green gaze.

"I wanted to tell you how sorry I am," she murmured. "I didn't mean to—"

"No," he said, touching her lips with the tip of his finger, "no more apologies for now." He slid one arm around her shoulders and sat on the ground, drawing her down beside him.

"But I should not have said what I did about giving up on the business. I know how important it is to you."

Mores shook his head. "No," he declared, "I don't think you do." He was intensely aware of her warmth beside him and the curious light in her eyes. Staring off at some point above her shoulder, the Marquis drew a deep breath. "It's more to me than just pride, more even than my desire to do well financially." He removed his arm from her shoulder and ran a hand across his forehead. "You see, my life has never meant much to me."

At the look in his eyes, Medora's insides twisted painfully. If a man as passionate and determined as her husband felt life was meaningless, what did that leave for her, who could not even begin to understand the depth and violence of his emotions?

"So," the Marquis continued, "I've tried to keep moving, always moving furiously from place to place just to keep myself from having the time to think. There have been moments, of course, when this was not so—sometimes when I was with Nicole, once with Ileya. And when I met you, I actually believed for an instant that this time it would be forever. So I married you and came here." He paused to gaze at the mist that clung like a silken web to the far distant leaves of the cottonwoods, covering the bleak stone cliffs in soft, vaporous netting. "When I stood in the town of Medora—a town that I had built—and watched the door of the packing plant open for the first time, I thought that I had finally found a way to make my restless dreams come true. I believed I would really make something of myself at last. And I did—a damned fool."

Medora smiled grimly and shook her head. "You were no more of a fool than I was."

"Here we are," Mores said humorlessly, "a couple of fools. We make a perfect pair, don't we?"

Suddenly, Medora rose to her knees, placing her hand on her husband's shoulder. "Yes, we do," she asserted, her voice taut with inner urgency, "or at least we did. And perhaps we could again. You see, I have learned in the past few days that I need you, Antoine. And I came here to tell you that in spite of everything that has come between us in the past three years, I love you, and I don't want to lose you." She could not read the expression in his eyes, but she knew that she had to go on now, for she would never have the courage again. "But most of all, I wanted to ask you to forgive me."

He stared at her searchingly, as if he could judge her sincerity from the look in her eyes, then he whispered, "I think we *both* have a great deal to forgive, my dear."

While the uncertainty burned in the back of her throat, she touched his other shoulder lightly. "Please," she breathed, "please."

Only once before had he heard that word from her; Medora simply did not plead. Nor did she weep. He ran one finger across her lips in disbelief, as if to reassure himself that she had spoken, and he felt a whisper of her breath against his skin. Closing his eyes, he reached out to pull her toward him. She came willingly, eagerly, into his arms.

The touch of her husband's lips on hers was like slow burning coals. It brought back to her as if from an impossibly great distance the memory of the soft, tender feel of his hands upon her body. Pressing closer, she clasped her arms around his neck and let the throbbing warmth move through her icy veins. It had been so long since they had come together like this, and she was astonished at the answers her body gave him, at the tingling sensations that swept across her skin. It had been so long since they had lain side by side with nothing but their own heated breath to come between them. And Medora knew that it had taken no less than a miracle to bring it about.

"Antoine," she said, when at last he raised his head, "I want you to know that if you wish to keep the plant going, I'll do everything I can to help you."

Mores smiled, brushing the hair away from her face. "No. I've been thinking that perhaps we should close it down for a while and go back to France where we could start something new."

Leaning back so she could see his face more clearly, she asked, "Is that really what you want?"

"It is," he told her, "but only if you want it, too. You see, my dear, I think I've discovered that an empire isn't worth much without a family to carry it on when one is dead. I don't want to lose you and Athenais and Phillipe simply because I can't let go of a dream that was doomed from the start."

"You're really willing to give all this up?" she asked, gazing at the hills of stone that loomed on every side.

Clasping her hand in his, he said softly, "I have paid long enough for this one mistake and so have you. But no more, Medora, I promise you that." Then he took her in his arms and they fell back into the haven of the shadows, oblivious of the world around them, while the morning mist grew thin and disappeared, leaving the land to be devoured by the bright pulsing rays of the pitiless sun.

They stood on the porch, sheltered from the afternoon heat by the slanting roof overhead. One after another, they bid Mores and his wife good-bye: Frank Miller, Dick Moore, Mianne, Cassie, and Johnny Goodall. They would all be staying behind to keep the ranch going—Johnny and Mianne would live in the Chateau and see that it did not fall into disrepair while Cassie cooked for them as she always had. The others would work the ranch and keep the horses and cattle alive. But the packing plant had closed its doors for good, or so they thought. That had been the moment when the Marquis's rule of the Badlands had truly ended.

With William and Medora close behind him, Mores turned

at last to Teddy Roosevelt and shook his hand. "You seem to be fully recovered from your encounter with the mountain lion," he said.

"My wounds are nearly healed, but I'm sure I will not soon forget the attack," Roosevelt said. "I'm sorry to see you go," he continued, turning to include William and Medora in his regretful glance. "I'm afraid the Badlands will be a dull place without you."

"But I imagine you won't have to bear it for long," said the Marquis. "You'll probably be leaving this behind soon yourself."

Shaking his head sadly, Roosevelt murmured, "You're right, my friend. I love this place, but it's not much more than a fantasy world for me. Eventually, like you, I shall have to find my way back to reality." He gazed over Mores's shoulder, watching how the wind set the cottonwoods dancing. "But I shall always be glad I came. One needs to live a dream now and then; it makes reality a little more bearable." Finally, he turned to Van Driesche. "Tell me, William, do *you* mind leaving? You don't seem at all sad today."

"No," the secretary shook his head, "I'm relieved. I've missed France every day since we left her. Somehow the wind out here just doesn't let you rest, and I've never really been comfortable in the Badlands."

Mores slipped his arm around Medora's waist, taking a last long look at the deep blue sky, touched here and there with pale wisps of cloud; the stark, brooding cliffs that towered above the river; the sloping hills covered with buffalo grass and sagebrush, and the house he had built, which rose like an unnatural mutation from the land on which it sat. "I was," he mused thoughtfully. "For a while I really believed this was home."

Medora smiled up at him. "I know," she said, "so did I."

"Well, it's almost time for the train. We'd best be on our way," the Marquis announced. "Where's Phillipe?"

"Give him a minute," Medora advised, pointing to the end of the porch where the boy was locked in a bear hug insid

Cassie's strong arms. Mores nodded and the three started for their horses.

"I never thought I'd see the day that I'd admit that I was gonna miss a rascal like you," the cook groaned, slapping Phillipe's back with a work-worn hand, "but I will. Damn me if I don't!"

The boy clung to her a moment longer, but then she pushed him away. "I got no time for all this sniveling nonsense," she muttered, staring down at her work-soiled apron to hide the suspicious dampness in her eyes. When she saw Mianne slip behind her and disappear around the end of the house, Cassie squeezed Phillipe's shoulder. "Go after her, son. The poor girl's been waitin' all mornin' to see if you'd speak to her."

The boy stepped back and smiled incredulously. He knew that Cassie had said her good-byes and now she was done. She wanted him to go before she gave in to the sorrow that showed itself in the weathered skin of her face. With a last fond appraisal of her, from the top of her head to the soles of her worn-out boots, he did as she had bid him. He knew he would miss her, perhaps more than she would miss him. After all, she had been his first friend. But all thoughts of Cassie fled when he saw Mianne standing uncertainly beneath a nearby tree, watching him.

The girl had unbraided her hair for once, letting it fall loose around her shoulders. As Phillipe approached her, he realized again how fine and delicate her features were and how smoothly brown her skin. He thought that she must surely be the most beautiful girl he had ever seen, and he knew that it was her mixed blood that made her so. Her eyes were wide just now with some private grief that had turned them into liquid amber. Their penetrating gaze caused his heart to pause in its normal rhythm, if only for a moment.

"I've come to say good-bye," he told her, stepping into the cool, tranquil shade where he stood by her side. When Mianne turned her head away without speaking, Phillipe found himself wondering again what mysterious thoughts were swirling around inside her head. But he knew that she hid them too well; he would probably never see the secret side of her. And now, when he was leaving her behind, he realized that he wanted to. More than anything, he wanted to understand this pagan spirit who wove her Indian spells so well. Noticing that she still wore no shoes, he took her hand and said, "I've told you before that you'll get stickers if you insist on going barefoot."

"Then that is my choice," she replied, her voice hollow.

"But I won't be here to take them out anymore."

Mianne turned then and he was surprised by the mournful light in her eyes. For a long moment she did not answer; then she snapped, "Then at least I will no longer have to live in fear that you will enslave me."

Then, for the first time since he had spoken them, he remembered his words and the emotions that had brought them to his lips. *Someday, I will make you my slave.* With his eyes caught up in her piercing gaze, he whispered, "Don't be so certain Mianne. I will not let you go so easily. There will be other days."

She shook her head violently and tried to move away, but he grasped her shoulders, drawing her close. "Would it be so horrible?" he asked. But he knew that he did not want to hear her answer. Before she could open her mouth to protest, Phillipe covered her lips with his. And just for a single instant before she pushed him away, a bright, pulsing flame rose up between them, intense in its heat and frightening in its purity. But then Mianne shuddered, wrenching herself free of his grasp, and as his heart subsided into stillness, she turned to flee, her hair fluttering behind her like the half-formed wings of a raven.

The wagons full of heavy trunks had vanished into their own choking cloud of dust when Phillipe joined Mores, Medora, and William at the top of the bluff. Medora held Athenais in her lap, and for several minutes they all sat there side by side, looking out over the landscape below. The desolation was broken only by the majestic smokestack of the meat-packing plant, a few scattered buildings, and the sweeping presence of the river, covered by a canopy of green-yellow leaves. Only Phillipe turned away from this scene when he heard a horse approaching. But it was not until he saw Greg Pendleton coming toward them, alone, that he realized how desperately he had been hoping Katherine would come.

The disappointment hit him like a well-placed blow, leaving him shaken, and his eyes scanned the horizon one last time for a sign of her. But he had known she would not come. Known it with a certainty that refused to bend or break. Katherine had already said good-bye to him two weeks ago when she left him standing alone in the shade of the box-elders. For her, that had been the end of the game and she had been the final winner. But Phillipe suspected that the real struggle had only just begun, although he could not say why. And whether or not he ever saw her again, he would not forget that it had been her silken body he had known before all others. She had abandoned him for the moment, but he would not forget.

Greg ignored the boy, guiding his horse to the edge of the bluff where he stopped beside William. Both the Marquis and Medora turned to face him and he could not miss the flicker of anger that crossed their faces in that instant. But there was something else he saw there as well, some flash of wordless understanding that passed between the couple. They were not even touching, yet he sensed that they were intensely aware of each other. He clenched his teeth and forced himself to recognize that it had come back, just as he had feared that it would—that mysterious thread that bound them together in a web of affection that made all others strangers.

Somehow they had managed to go backward in time and it was there again—that feeling he had recognized between them three long years ago, and that he had done his best to destroy. That feeling he so despised as weak and foolish and unproductive. That feeling that, deep inside, he envied with every fiber of his being, and that he knew he would never have.

"What do you want, Pendleton?" the Marquis demanded, shattering the uneasy silence.

Greg drew a deep breath and forced himself to speak evenly. "I heard you're leaving Medora," he said, waving a hand to indicate the town that lay still and silent far below them. "I came to bid you good-bye."

"I'm leaving the *Badlands*," Mores replied, his voice strangely free of hostility, "but *Medora* is coming with me." Gazing at her with love and gratitude in his eyes, the Marquis added, "But I don't want you to start feeling too secure, Pendleton. Because we're coming back someday." He was pleased to see that both his wife and Phillipe nodded in agreement, and Medora reached out to take his hand.

Turning back to Greg, Mores continued, "You see, I'm simply not the kind of man who gives up, regardless of the odds. Remember that." Then, with the waxed ends of his moustache quivering slightly in the breeze, he urged his horse forward, while Phillipe and Medora followed. Just before they reached the path that would take them to the base of the bluff, the Marquis turned once more and cried, "We'll be back. I promise you that!"

The horses continued on their way and Greg sat for a long time, unmoving. They're going, he thought. We have finally broken them and they're going away, leaving the Pendletons as undisputed rulers of the Badlands. His family would continue—unbeaten and supreme. They had finally won. But as he watched Medora's diminutive figure shrink until it merged with the red-streaked cliffs at her side, the victory turned to dry bitter dust that was swept up by the wind until it disappeared into the oblivion of the endless Dakota sky.

BOOK YOUR PLACE ON OUR WEBSITE AND MAKE THE READING CONNECTION!

We've created a customized website just for our very special readers, where you can get the inside scoop on everything that's going on with Zebra, Pinnacle and Kensington books.

When you come online, you'll have the exciting opportunity to:

- View covers of upcoming books

- Read sample chapters

- Learn about our future publishing schedule (listed by publication month *and author*)

- Find out when your favorite authors will be visiting a city near you

- Search for and order backlist books from our online catalog

- Check out author bios and background information

- Send e-mail to your favorite authors

- Meet the Kensington staff online

- Join us in weekly chats with authors, readers and other guests

- Get writing guidelines

- AND MUCH MORE!

Visit our website at
http://www.zebrabooks.com

Put a Little Romance in Your Life With
Janelle Taylor

__Anything for Love	0-8217-4992-7	$5.99US/$6.99CAN
__Lakota Dawn	0-8217-6421-7	$6.99US/$8.99CAN
__Forever Ecstasy	0-8217-5241-3	$5.99US/$6.99CAN
__Fortune's Flames	0-8217-5450-5	$5.99US/$6.99CAN
__Destiny's Temptress	0-8217-5448-3	$5.99US/$6.99CAN
__Love Me With Fury	0-8217-5452-1	$5.99US/$6.99CAN
__First Love, Wild Love	0-8217-5277-4	$5.99US/$6.99CAN
__Kiss of the Night Wind	0-8217-5279-0	$5.99US/$6.99CAN
__Love With a Stranger	0-8217-5416-5	$6.99US/$8.50CAN
__Forbidden Ecstasy	0-8217-5278-2	$5.99US/$6.99CAN
__Defiant Ecstasy	0-8217-5447-5	$5.99US/$6.99CAN
__Follow the Wind	0-8217-5449-1	$5.99US/$6.99CAN
__Wild Winds	0-8217-6026-2	$6.99US/$8.50CAN
__Defiant Hearts	0-8217-5563-3	$6.50US/$8.00CAN
__Golden Torment	0-8217-5451-3	$5.99US/$6.99CAN
__Bittersweet Ecstasy	0-8217-5445-9	$5.99US/$6.99CAN
__Taking Chances	0-8217-4259-0	$4.50US/$5.50CAN
__By Candlelight	0-8217-5703-2	$6.99US/$8.50CAN
__Chase the Wind	0-8217-4740-1	$5.99US/$6.99CAN
__Destiny Mine	0-8217-5185-9	$5.99US/$6.99CAN
__Midnight Secrets	0-8217-5280-4	$5.99US/$6.99CAN
__Sweet Savage Heart	0-8217-5276-6	$5.99US/$6.99CAN
__Moonbeams and Magic	0-7860-0184-4	$5.99US/$6.99CAN
__Brazen Ecstasy	0-8217-5446-7	$5.99US/$6.99CAN

Call toll free **1-888-345-BOOK** to order by phone, use this coupon
to order by mail, or order online at **www.kensingtonbooks.com**.
Name _____
Address _____
City _____ State _____ Zip _____
Please send me the books I have checked above.
I am enclosing $_____
Plus postage and handling $_____
Sales tax (in New York and Tennessee only) $_____
Total amount enclosed $_____
*Add $2.50 for the first book and $.50 for each additional book.
Send check or money order (no cash or CODs) to:
Kensington Publishing Corp., Dept. C.O., 850 Third Avenue, New York, NY 1002
Prices and numbers subject to change without notice.
All orders subject to availability.
Visit our website at **www.kensingtonbooks.com**

Simply the Best . . .
Katherine Stone

_**Bel Air** 0-8217-5201-4	$6.99US/$7.99CAN
_**The Carlton Club** 0-8217-5204-9	$6.99US/$7.99CAN
_**Happy Endings** 0-8217-5250-2	$6.99US/$7.99CAN
_**Illusions** 0-8217-5247-2	$6.99US/$7.99CAN
_**Love Songs** 0-8217-5205-7	$6.99US/$7.99CAN
_**Promises** 0-8217-5248-0	$6.99US/$7.99CAN
_**Rainbows** 0-8217-5249-9	$6.99US/$7.99CAN

all toll free **1-888-345-BOOK** to order by phone, use this coupon
order by mail, or order online at **www.kensingtonbooks.com**.

ame _____

ddress _____

ity _____ State _____ Zip _____

lease send me the books I have checked above.

am enclosing	$_____
lus postage and handling*	$_____
ales tax (in New York and Tennessee only)	$_____
otal amount enclosed	$_____

Add $2.50 for the first book and $.50 for each additional book.
end check or money order (no cash or CODs) to:
ensington Publishing Corp., Dept C.O., 850 Third Avenue, 16th Floor,
ew York, NY 10022

ices and numbers subject to change without notice.

l orders subject to availability.

sit our website at **www.kensingtonbooks.com**.

Enjoy *Savage Destiny*
A Romantic Series from
Rosanne Bittner

__#1: **Sweet Prairie Passion** $5.99US/$6.99CAN
    0-8217-5342-8

__#2: **Ride the Free Wind Passion** $5.99US/$6.99CAN
    0-8217-5343-6

__#3: **River of Love** $5.99US/$6.99CAN
    0-8217-5344-4

__#4: **Embrace the Wild Land** $5.99US/$7.50CAN
    0-8217-5413-0

__#7: **Eagle's Song** $5.99US/$6.99CAN
    0-8217-5326-6

Call toll free **1-888-345-BOOK** to order by phone or use thi
coupon to order by mail.

Name _____

Address _____

City _____ State _____ Zip _____

Please send me the books I have checked above.

I am enclosing $_____

Plus postage and handling* $_____

Sales tax (in New York and Tennessee) $_____

Total amount enclosed $_____

*Add $2.50 for the first book and $.50 for each additional book.

Send check or money order (no cash or CODs) to:

Kensington Publishing Corp., 850 Third Avenue, New York, NY 1002

Prices and Numbers subject to change without notice.

All orders subject to availability.

Check out our website at **www.kensingtonbooks.com**